**Whirlwind dates and shotgun weddings!**

*But what happens
when convenient romance becomes real?*

Find out in:

**SOS: CONVENIENT HUSBAND REQUIRED**
by Liz Fielding

**WINNING A GROOM IN 10 DATES**
by Cara Colter

Enjoy our new 2-in-1 editions of stories by your
favourite authors—*for double the romance!*

**Dear Reader**

Welcome back to Maybridge, a town I created back in 1994. SOS: CONVENIENT HUSBAND REQUIRED is the sixth of my books to be set there (the full list is on my website), and if it existed it would undoubtedly be one of the most romantic places in Britain.

Along with the nearby city of Melchester, the villages of Little Hinton and Upper Haughton, I have created a world of my own from the places I grew up in. There's the river, the regenerated industrial areas, and the vibrant arts and crafts centre in a huge old coaching inn, with delightful boutiques around the cobbled courtyard.

May Coleridge comes from an old Maybridge family—the ones who lived in 'the big house'—but she fell in love with Adam Wavell, who comes from the other end of the social scale, when they were both in high school. Now the tables are turned. Adam is rich and powerful while May is about to lose everything. Adam can't quite escape his past, his family, or the memory of May's sweet kisses, no matter how hard he tries. Nor can he rid himself of the memory of his humiliation at the hand of May's grandfather. Or her coldness in the years since then.

He's sure that a temporary marriage of convenience will give him closure, but being close to May rekindles feelings he'd thought dead. Can a convenient marriage become something more?

Walk through the park with them and watch them fall in love all over again.

Warmest wishes

*Liz*

# SOS: CONVENIENT HUSBAND REQUIRED

BY
LIZ FIELDING

MILLS & BOON

All the characters in this book have no existence outside the imagination of the author, and have no relation whatsoever to anyone bearing the same name or names. They are not even distantly inspired by any individual known or unknown to the author, and all the incidents are pure invention.

First published in Great Britain 2010
Harlequin Mills & Boon Limited,
Eton House, 18-24 Paradise Road, Richmond, Surrey TW9 1SR

ISBN: 978 0 263 87685 7

Harlequin Mills & Boon policy is to use papers that are natural, renewable and recyclable products and made from wood grown in sustainable forests. The logging and manufacturing process conform to the legal environmental regulations of the country of origin.

Printed and bound in Spain
by Litografia Rosés, S.A., Barcelona

**Liz Fielding** was born with itchy feet. She made it to Zambia before her twenty-first birthday and, gathering her own special hero and a couple of children on the way, lived in Botswana, Kenya and Bahrain—with pauses for sightseeing pretty much everywhere in between. She finally came to a full stop in a tiny Welsh village cradled by misty hills, and these days mostly leaves her pen to do the travelling. When she's not sorting out the lives and loves of her characters she potters in the garden, reads her favourite authors, and spends a lot of time wondering 'What if…?' For news of upcoming books—and to sign up for her occasional newsletter—visit Liz's website at www.lizfielding.com

For my patient, long-suffering husband,
who unfailingly keeps his sense of humour through all
the crises, the rubbish meals when the deadline escapes
me, and makes me believe on those horrible days
when the confidence falters. He is my hero.

# CHAPTER ONE

MAY COLERIDGE stared blankly at the man sitting behind the desk, trying to make sense of what he'd told her.

Her grandfather's will had been simplicity itself. Apart from the bequests to local charities, everything had been left to his only living relative. Her.

Inheritance tax would mop up pretty much everything but the house itself. She'd always known that would happen, but Coleridge House was the only home she'd ever known and now, because of a clause in some centuries old will, she was about to lose that too.

'I don't understand,' she said, finally admitting defeat. 'Why didn't you tell me all this when you read Grandpa's will?'

'As you're no doubt aware,' Freddie Jennings explained with maddening pomposity—as if she hadn't known him since he'd been a kid with a runny nose at kindergarten— 'my great-uncle took care of your grandfather's legal affairs until he retired. He drew up his last will after the death of your mother—'

'That was nearly thirty years ago,' she protested.

He shrugged. 'Believe me, I'm as shocked as you are.'

'I doubt that. Jennings have been the Coleridge family solicitor for generations,' she said. 'How could you not know about this?'

Freddie shifted uncomfortably in his chair. 'Some of the Coleridge archives were damaged during the floods a few years ago. It was only when I applied for probate that this particular condition of inheritance surfaced.'

May felt as if she'd stepped into quicksand and the ground that she was standing on, everything that had been certain, was disintegrating beneath her feet. She had been so sure that this was a mistake, that Freddie has got his knickers in a twist over nothing, but it wasn't nothing. It was everything.

Everything she'd known, everything she'd loved was being taken away from her…

'The last time this clause would have been relevant was when your great-grandfather died in 1944,' he continued, as if that mattered. 'Your grandfather would have been told of the condition then.'

'In 1944 my grandfather was a fourteen-year-old boy who'd just lost his father,' she snapped, momentarily losing her composure at his attempt to justify their incompetence. 'And, since he was married by the time he was twenty-three, it wouldn't have been an issue.' And by the time it had become one, the stroke that had incapacitated him had left huge holes in his memory and he hadn't been able to warn her. She swallowed as an aching lump formed in her throat, but she refused to let the tears fall. To weep. 'People got married so much younger back then,' she added.

'Back then, there wasn't any alternative.'

'No…'

Her mother had been a beneficiary of the feminist movement, one of that newly liberated generation of women who'd abandoned the shackles of a patriarchal society and chosen her own path. *Motherhood without the bother of a man under her feet* was the way she'd put it in one of the many articles she'd written on the subject.

As for her, well, she'd had other priorities.

'You have to admit that it's outrageous, Freddie. Surely I can challenge it?'

'I'd have to take Counsel's opinion and even if you went to court there is a problem.'

'I think we are both agreed that I have a problem.'

He waited, but she shook her head. Snapping at Freddie wasn't going to help. 'Tell me.'

'There can be no doubt that this restriction on inheritance would have been explained to your grandfather on each of the occasions when he rewrote his will. After his marriage, the birth of your mother, the death of your grandmother. He could have taken steps then to have this restriction removed. He chose to let it stand.'

'Why? Why would he do that?'

Freddie shrugged. 'Maybe because it was part of family tradition. Maybe because his father had left it in place. I would have advised removal but my great-uncle, your grandfather came from a different age. They saw things differently.'

'Even so—'

'He had three opportunities to remove the entailment and the Crown would argue that it was clearly his wish to let it stand. Counsel would doubtless counter that if he hadn't had a stroke, had realised the situation you were in, he would have changed it,' Freddie said in an attempt to comfort her.

'If he hadn't had a stroke I would be married to Michael Linton,' she replied. *Safely married.* That was what he used to say. Not like her mother…

'I'm sorry, May. The only guarantee I can give is that whichever way it went the costs would be heavy and, as you are aware, there's no money in the estate to cover them.'

'You're saying that I'd lose the house anyway,' she said dully. 'That whatever I do I lose.'

'The only people who ever win in a situation like this are the lawyers,' he admitted. 'Hopefully, you'll be able to realise enough from the sale of the house contents, once the inheritance tax is paid, to provide funds for a flat or even a small house.'

'They want inheritance tax *and* the house?'

'The two are entirely separate.'

She shook her head, still unable to believe this was happening. 'If it was going to some deserving charity I could live with it, but to have my home sucked into the Government coffers…' Words failed her.

'Your ancestor's will was written at the beginning of the nineteenth century. The country was at war. He was a patriot.'

'Oh, please! It was nothing but an arm twisted up the back of a philandering son.

Settle down and get on with producing the next generation or I'll cut you off without a shilling.'

'Maybe. But it was added as an entailment to the estate and no one has ever challenged it. There's still just time, May. You could get married.'

'Is that an offer?'

'Unfortunately, bigamy would not satisfy the legal requirements.'

Freddie Jennings had a sense of humour? Who knew?

'You're not seeing anyone?' he asked hopefully.

She shook her head. There had only ever been one boy, man, who'd ever lit a fire in her heart, her body…

'Between nursing Grandpa and running my own business, I'm afraid there hasn't been a lot of time to "see" anyone,' she said.

'There's not even a friend who'd be prepared to go through the motions?'

'I'm all out of unattached men at the moment,' she replied. 'Well, there is Jed Atkins who does a bit for me in the garden now and then,' she said, her grip on reality beginning to slip. 'He's in his seventies, but pretty lively and I'd have to fight off the competition.'

'The competition?'

'He's very much in demand with the ladies at the Darby and Joan club, so I'm told.'

'May...' he cautioned as she began to laugh, but the situation was unreal. How could he expect her to take it seriously? 'I think I'd better take you home.'

'I don't suppose you have any clients in urgent need of a marriage of convenience so that they can stay in the country?' she asked as he ushered her from his office, clearly afraid that she was going to become hysterical.

He needn't have worried. She was a Coleridge. Mary Louise Coleridge of Coleridge House. Brought up to serve the community, behave impeccably on all occasions, do the right thing even when your heart was breaking.

She wasn't about to become hysterical just because Freddie Jennings had told her she was about to lose everything.

'But if you are considering something along those lines,' he warned as he held the car door for her, 'please make sure he signs a pre-nuptial agreement or you're going to have to pay dearly to get rid of him.'

'Make that a lose/lose/lose situation,' she said. Then, taking a step back, 'Actually, I'd rather walk home. I need some fresh air.'

He said something but she was already walking away. She needed to be on her own. Needed to think.

Without Coleridge House, she would not only lose her home, but her livelihood. As would Harriet Robson, her grandfather's housekeeper for more than thirty years and the nearest thing to a mother she'd ever known.

She'd have to find a job. Somewhere to live. Or, of course, a husband.

She bought the early edition of the local newspaper from the stand by the park gates to look at the sits vac and property columns. What a joke. There were no jobs for a woman weeks away from her thirtieth birthday who didn't have a degree or even a typing certificate to her name. And the price of property in Maybridge was staggering. The lonely hearts column was a boom area, though, and, with a valuable house as an incentive, a husband might prove the easiest of the three to find. But, with three weeks until her birthday, even that was going to be a tough ask.

Adam Wavell looked from the sleeping infant tucked into the pink nest of her buggy to the note in his hand.

*Sorry, sorry, sorry. I know I should have
told you about Nancie, but you'd have
shouted at me...*

Shouted at her. Shouted at her! Of course he
would have shouted at her, for all the good it
had ever done.

'Problem?'

'You could say that.' For the first time since
he'd employed Jake Edwards as his PA, he regretted not choosing one of the equally qualified women who'd applied for the job, any
one of whom would by now have been
clucking and cooing over the infant. Taking
charge and leaving him to get on with running
his company. 'My sister is having a crisis.'

'I didn't know you had a sister.'

No. He'd worked hard to distance himself
from his family.

'Saffy. She lives in France,' he said.

Maybe. It had taken only one call to discover
that she'd sublet the apartment he'd leased for
her months ago. Presumably she was living
off the proceeds of the rent since she hadn't
asked him for money. Yet.

Presumably she'd moved in with the
baby's father, a relationship that she hadn't
chosen to share with him and had now, presumably, hit the skids.

Her occasional phone calls could have come from anywhere and any suggestion that he was cross-examining her about what she was doing, who she was seeing only resulted in longer gaps between them. It was her life and while she seemed happy he didn't pry. At twenty-nine, she was old enough to have grown out of her wildness and settled down. Clearly, he thought as he reread the letter, he'd been fooling himself.

*I've got myself into some real trouble, Adam...*

Trouble. Nothing new there, then. She'd made a career of it.

*Michel's family set their bloodhounds on me. They've found out all the trouble I was in as a kid, the shoplifting, the drugs and they've used it to turn him against me. He's got a court order to stop me taking Nancie out of France and he's going to take her away from me...*

No. That wasn't right. She'd been clean for years...
Or was he still kidding himself?

*A friend smuggled us out of France but I can't hide with a baby so I'm leaving her with you...*

Smuggled her out of France. Ignored a court order. Deprived a father of access to his child. Just how many felonies did that involve? All of which he was now an accessory to.

Terrific.

One minute he'd been sitting in his board-room, discussing the final touches to the biggest deal in his career, the next he was having his life sabotaged—not for the first time—by his family.

*I'm going to disappear for a while...*

No surprise there. His little sister had made a career of running away and leaving someone else to pick up the pieces. She'd dropped out, run away, used drugs and alcohol in a desper-ate attempt to shut out all the bad stuff. Following the example of their useless parents. Making a bad situation worse.

He'd thought his sister had finally got herself together, was enjoying some small success as a model. Or maybe that was what he'd wanted to believe.

*Don't, whatever you do, call a nanny agency. They'll want all kinds of information and, once it's on record, Nancie's daddy will be able to trace her...*

Good grief, who was the father of this child? Was his sister in danger?

Guilt overwhelmed those first feelings of anger, frustration. He had to find her, somehow make this right, but, as the baby stirred, whimpered, he had a more urgent problem.

Saffy had managed to get her into his office without anyone noticing her—time for a shake-up in security—but that would have to wait. His first priority was to get the baby out of the building before she started screaming and his family history became the subject of the kind of gossip that had made his—and Saffy's—youth a misery.

'Do you want me to call an agency?' Jake asked.

'An agency?'

'For a nanny?'

'Yes... No...'

Even if Saffy's fears were nothing but unfounded neurosis, he didn't have anywhere to put a nanny. He didn't even have a separate bedroom in his apartment, only a sleeping gallery reached by a spiral staircase.

It was no place for a baby, he thought as he stared at the PS Saffy had scribbled at the end of the crumpled and tear-stained note.

*Ask May. She'll help.*

She'd underlined the words twice.
May. May Coleridge.
He crushed the letter in his hand.
He hadn't spoken to May Coleridge since he was eighteen. She and Saffy had been in the same class at school and, while they hadn't been friends—the likes of the Wavells had not been welcome at Coleridge House, as he'd discovered to his cost—at least not in the giggly girls, shopping, clubbing sense of the word, there had been some connection between them that he'd never been able to fathom.

But then that was probably what people had thought about him and May.

But while the thought of the untouchable Miss Coleridge changing the nappy of a Wavell baby might put a shine on his day, the woman had made an art form of treating him as if he were invisible.

Even on those social occasions when they found themselves face to face, there was no eye contact. Only icy civility.

'Is there anything I can do?'

He shook his head. There was nothing anyone could do. His family was, always had been, his problem, but it was a mess he wanted out of his office. Now.

'Follow up on the points raised at the meeting, Jake.' He looked at the crumpled sheet of paper in his hand, then folded it and stuffed it in his shirt pocket. Unhooked his jacket from the back of his chair. 'Keep me posted about any problems. I'm going home.'

It took a kitten to drag May out of her dark thoughts.

Her first reaction to the news that she was about to lose her home had been to rush back to its shabby comfort—no matter how illusory that comfort might be—while she came to terms with the fact that, having lost the last surviving member of her family, she was now going to lose everything else. Her home. Her business. Her future.

Once home, however, there would be no time for such indulgence. She had little enough time to unravel the life she'd made for herself. To wind down a business she'd fallen into almost by accident and, over the last few years, built into something that had given her something of her own, something to live for.

Worst of all, she'd have to tell Robbie.

Give notice to Patsy and the other women who worked for a few hours a week helping with the cleaning, the cooking and who relied on that small amount of money to help them pay their bills.

There'd be no time to spare for the luxury of grieving for the loss of their support, friendship. Her birthday was less than a month away. *The* birthday. The one with a big fat zero on the end.

Yesterday that hadn't bothered her. She'd never understood why anyone would want to stop the clock at 'twenty-nine'.

Today, if some fairy godmother were to appear and offer her three wishes, that would be number one on the list. Well, maybe not number one…

But, while fairy godmothers were pure fantasy, her date of birth was a fact that she could not deny and, by the time she'd reached the last park bench before home, the one overlooking the lake that had once been part of the parkland surrounding Coleridge House, her legs had been shaking so much that she'd been forced to stop.

Once there, she'd been unable to find the will to move again. It was a sheltered spot, a sun trap and, despite the fact that it was the first week in November, pleasantly warm. And while she sat on this park bench she was still Miss Mary Louise Coleridge of Coleridge House. Someone to be respected.

Her place in the town, the invitations to sit on charitable committees were part of her life. Looked at in the cold light of day, it was obvious that it wasn't her they wanted, it was the Coleridge name to lend lustre to their endeavours. And Coleridge House.

No one would come knocking when she didn't have a grand room where they could hold their meetings, with a good lunch thrown in. An elegant, if fading house with a large garden in which to hold their 'events'.

It was the plaintive mewing of a kitten in distress that finally broke through these dark thoughts. It took her a moment to locate the scrap of orange fur clinging to the branch of a huge old beech tree set well back from the path.

'Oh, sweetie, how on earth did you get up there?'

Since the only reply was an even more desperate mew, she got to her feet and went closer.

'Come on. You can do it,' she cooed, standing beneath it, hoping to coax it back down the long sloping branch that came nearly to the ground. It edged further up the branch.

She looked around, hoping for someone tall enough to reach up and grab it but there wasn't a soul in sight. Finally, when it became clear that there wasn't anything else for it, she took off her jacket, kicked off her shoes and, skirting a muddy puddle, she caught hold of the branch, found a firm foothold and pulled herself up.

Bitterly regretting that he'd taken advantage of the unseasonably fine weather to walk in to the office, Adam escaped the building via his private lift to the car park. He'd hoped to pick up a taxi at the rank on the corner but there were none waiting and he crossed the road to the park. It was a slightly longer way home, but there was less chance of being seen by anyone he knew.

Oblivious to the beauty of the autumn morning, he steered the buggy with one hand, using the other to call up anyone who might have a clue where Saffy was heading for.

His first action on finding Nancie had been to try her mother's mobile but, unsurprisingly, it was switched off. He'd left a message on her voicemail, asking her to ring him, but didn't hold out much hope of that.

Ten minutes later, the only thing he knew for certain was that he knew nothing. The new tenants of the apartment, her agent—make that ex-agent—even her old flatmate denied any knowledge of where she was, or of Michel, and he had no idea who her friends were, even supposing they'd tell him anything.

Actually, he thought, looking at the baby, it wasn't true that he knew nothing.

While the movement of the buggy had, for the moment, lulled her back to sleep, he was absolutely sure that very soon she would be demanding to be fed or changed.

*Ask May. She'll help.*

Ahead of him, the tall red-brick barley twist chimneys of Coleridge House stood high above the trees. For years he'd avoided this part of the park, walked double the distance rather than pass the house. Just seeing those chimneys had made him feel inadequate, worthless.

These days, he could buy and sell the Coleridges, and yet it was still there. Their superiority and the taint of who he was.

Asking her for help stuck deep in his craw, but the one thing about May Coleridge was that she wouldn't ask questions. She knew Saffy. Knew him.

He called Enquiries for her number but it

was unlisted. No surprise there, but maybe it was just as well.

It had been a very long time since he'd taken her some broken creature to be nursed back to health, but he knew she'd find it a lot harder to say no face to face. If he put Nancie into her arms.

It is not high, May told herself as she set her foot firmly on the tree. All she had to do was haul herself up onto the branch and crawl along it. No problem…

Easy enough to say when she was safely on the ground.

Standing beneath the branch and looking up, it had seemed no distance at all. The important thing, she reminded herself, was not to look down but keep her eye on the goal.

'What on earth are you doing up there, Mouse?'

Sherbet dabs!

As her knee slipped, tearing her tights, she wondered how much worse this day could get. The advantage that she didn't have to look down to see who was beneath her—only one person had ever called her Mouse—was completely lost on her.

'What do you think I'm doing?' she asked through gritted teeth. 'Checking the view?'

'You should be able to see Melchester Castle from up there,' he replied, as if she'd been serious. 'You'll have to look a little further to your left, though.'

She was in enough trouble simply looking ahead. She'd never been good with heights—something she only ever seemed to remember when she was too far off the ground to change her mind.

'Why don't you come up and point it out to me?' she gasped.

'I would be happy to,' he replied, 'but that branch doesn't look as if it could support both of us.'

He was right. It was creaking ominously as she attempted to edge closer to the kitten which, despite her best efforts not to frighten it further, was backing off, a spitting, frightened orange ball of fur.

It was far too late to wish she'd stuck to looking helpless at ground level. She'd realised at a very early age that the pathetic, *Where's a big strong man to help me?* routine was never going to work for her—she wasn't blonde enough, thin enough, pretty enough—and had learned to get on and do it herself.

It was plunging in without a thought for the consequences that had earned her the mocking nickname 'Mouse', short for 'Danger Mouse', bestowed on her by Adam Wavell when she was a chubby teen and he was a mocking, nerdy, glasses-wearing sixth-former at the local high school.

Her knee slipped a second time and a gasp from below warned her that Adam wasn't the only one with a worm's eye view of her under-wear. A quick blink confirmed that her antics were beginning to attract an audience of mid-morning dog-walkers, older children on their autumn break and shoppers taking the scenic route into the town centre—just too late to be of help.

Then a click, followed by several more as the idea caught on, warned her that someone had taken a photograph using their mobile phone. Terrific. She was going to be in tomorrow's edition of the *Maybridge Observer* for sure; worse, she'd be on *YouTube* by lunch time.

She had no one to blame but herself, she reminded herself, making a firm resolution that the next time she spotted an animal in distress she'd call the RSPCA and leave it to them. That wasn't going to help her now, though, and the sooner she grabbed the kitten and returned to earth the better.

'Here, puss,' she coaxed desperately, but its

only response was to hiss at her and edge further along the branch. Muttering under her breath, she went after it. The kitten had the advantage. Unlike her, it weighed nothing and, as the branch thinned and began to bend noticeably beneath her, she made a desperate lunge, earning herself a cheer from the crowd as she managed to finally grab it. The kitten ungratefully sank its teeth into her thumb.

'Pass it down,' Adam said, his arms raised to take it from her.

Easier said than done. In its terror, it had dug its needle claws in, clinging to her hand as desperately as it had clung to the branch.

'You'll have to unhook me. Don't let it go!' she warned as she lowered it towards him. She was considerably higher now and she had to lean down a long way so that he could detach the little creature with the minimum of damage to her skin.

It was a mistake.

While she'd been focused on the kitten everything had been all right, but that last desperate lunge had sent everything spinning and, before she could utter so much as a *fudge balls*, she lost her balance and slithered off the branch.

Adam, standing directly beneath her, had no

time to avoid a direct hit. They both went down in a heap, the fall driving the breath from her body, which was probably a good thing since there was no item in her handmade confectionery range that came even close to matching her mortification. But then embarrassment was her default reaction whenever she was within a hundred feet of the man.

'You don't change, Mouse,' he said as she struggled to catch her breath.

Not much chance of that while she was lying on top of him, his breath warm against her cheek, his heart pounding beneath her hand, his arm, flung out in an attempt to catch her—or, more likely, defend himself—tight around her. The stuff of her most private dreams, if she discounted the fact that it had been raining all week and they were sprawled in the muddy puddle she had taken such pains to avoid.

'You always did act first, think later,' he said. 'Rushing to the aid of some poor creature in distress and getting wet, muddy or both for your pains.'

'While you,' she gasped, 'always turned up too late to do anything but stand on the sidelines, laughing at me,' she replied furiously. It was untrue and unfair, but all she wanted right at that moment was to vanish into thin air.

'You have to admit you were always great entertainment value.'

'If you like clowns,' she muttered, remembering all too vividly the occasion when she'd scrambled onto the school roof in a thunderstorm to rescue a bird trapped in the guttering and in danger of drowning, concern driving her chubby arms and legs as she'd shinned up the down pipe.

Up had never been a problem.

He'd stood below her then, the water flattening his thick dark hair, rain pouring down his face, grinning even as he'd taken the bird from her. But then, realising that she was too terrified to move, he'd taken off his glasses and climbed up to rescue her.

Not that she'd thanked him.

She'd been too busy yelling at him for letting the bird go before she could wrap it up and take it home to join the rest of her rescue family.

It was only when she was back on terra firma that her breathing had gone to pot and he'd delivered her to the school nurse, convinced she was having an asthma attack. And she had been too mortified—and breathless—to deny it.

He was right. Nothing had changed. She might be less than a month away from her thirtieth birthday, a woman of substance, respected for her charity work, running her own business, but inside she was still the overweight and socially inept teen being noticed by a boy she had the most painful crush on. Brilliant but geeky with the family from hell. Another outsider.

Well, he wasn't an outsider any more. He'd used his brains to good effect and was now the most successful man not just in Maybridge, but just about anywhere and had exchanged the hideous flat in the concrete acres of a sink estate where he'd been brought up for the luxury of a loft on the quays.

She quickly disentangled herself, clambered to her feet. He followed with far more grace.

'Are you all right?' he asked. 'No bones broken?'

'I'm fine,' she said, ignoring the pain in her elbow where it had hit the ground. 'You?' she asked out of politeness.

She could see for herself that he was absolutely fine. More than fine. The glasses had disappeared years ago, along with the bad hair, bad clothes. He'd never be muscular, but he'd filled out as he'd matured, his shoulders had broadened and these days were clad in the finest bespoke tailoring.

He wasn't just fine, but gorgeous. Mouthwateringly scrumptious, in fact. The chocolate nut fudge of maleness. And these days he had all the female attention he could handle if the gossip magazines were anything to judge by.

'At least you managed to hang onto the kitten,' she added, belatedly clutching the protective cloak of superiority about her.

The one thing she knew would make him keep his distance.

'I take no credit. The kitten is hanging onto me.'

'What?' She saw the blood seeping from the needle wounds in his hand and everything else flew out of the window. 'Oh, good grief, you're bleeding.'

'It's a hazard I expect whenever I'm within striking distance of you. Although on this occasion you haven't escaped unscathed, either,' he said.

She physically jumped as he took her own hand in his, turning it over so that she could see the tiny pinpricks of blood mingling with the mud. And undoing all her efforts to regain control of her breathing. He looked up.

'Where's your bag?' he asked. 'Have you got your inhaler?'

Thankfully, it had never occurred to him that his presence was the major cause of her problems with breathing.

'I'm fine,' she snapped.

For heaven's sake, she was nearly thirty. She should be so over the cringing embarrassment that nearly crippled her whenever Adam Wavell was in the same room.

'Come on,' he said, 'I'll walk you home.'

'There's no need,' she protested.

'There's every need. And this time, instead of getting punished for my good deed, I'm going to claim my reward.'

'Reward?' Her mouth dried. In fairy tales that would be a kiss... 'Superheroes never hang around for a reward,' she said scornfully as she wrapped the struggling kitten in her jacket.

'You're the superhero, Danger Mouse,' he reminded her, a teasing glint in his eyes that brought back the precious time when they'd been friends. 'I'm no more than the trusty sidekick who turns up in the nick of time to get you out of a jam.'

'Just once in a while you could try turning up in time to prevent me from getting into one,' she snapped.

'Now where would be the fun in that?' he asked, and it took all her self-control to keep her face from breaking out into a foolish smile.

'Do you really think I want to be on the front page of the *Maybridge Observer* with my knickers on show?' she enquired sharply. Then, as the teasing sparkle went out of his eyes, 'Don't worry. I'm sure I'll survive the indignity.'

'Having seen your indignity for myself, I can assure you that tomorrow's paper will be a sell-out,' he replied. She was still struggling with a response to that when he added, 'And if they can tear their eyes away from all that lace, the kitten's owners might recognise their stray.'

'One can live in hopes,' she replied stiffly.

She shook her head, then, realising that, no matter how much she wanted to run and hide, she couldn't ignore the fact that because of her he was not only bloody but his hand-stitched suit was covered in mud.

'I suppose you'd better come back to the house and get cleaned up,' she said.

'If that's an offer to hose me down in the yard, I'll pass.'

For a moment their eyes met as they both remembered that hideous moment when he'd come to the house with a bunch of red roses that must have cost him a fortune and her grandfather had turned a garden hose on him, soaking him to the skin.

'Don't be ridiculous,' she said, her insides curling up with embarrassment, killing stone dead the little heart-lift as he'd slipped so easily into teasing her the way he'd done when they were friends.

She picked up her shoes, her bag, reassembling her armour. But she wasn't able to look him in the eye as she added distantly, 'Robbie will take care of you in the kitchen.'

'The kitchen? Well, that will be further than I've ever got before. But actually it was you I was coming to see.'

She balanced her belongings, then, with studied carelessness, as if she had only then registered what he'd said, 'See?' she asked, doing her best to ignore the way her heart rate had suddenly picked up. 'Why on earth would you be coming to see me?'

He didn't answer but instead used his toe to release the brake on a baby buggy that was standing a few feet away on the path. The buggy that she had assumed belonged to a woman, bundled up in a thick coat and head-scarf, who'd been holding onto the handle, crooning to the baby.

# CHAPTER TWO

'ADAM? What are you doing?'

'Interesting question. Mouse, meet Nancie.'

'Nancy?'

'With an i and an e. Spelling never was Saffy's strong point.'

Saffy Wavell's strong points had been so striking she'd never given a fig for spelling or anything much else. Long raven-black hair, a figure that appeared to be both ethereal and sensual, she'd been a boy magnet since she hit puberty. And in trouble ever since. But a baby...

'She's Saffy's baby? That's wonderful news.' She began to smile. 'I'm so happy for her.' The sleeping baby was nestled beneath a pink lace-bedecked comforter. 'She's beautiful.'

'Is she?'

He leaned forward for a closer look, as if it

hadn't occurred to him, but May stopped, struck by what he'd just done.

'You just left her,' she said, a chill rippling through her. 'She's Saffy's precious baby and you just abandoned her on the footpath to come and gawp at me? What on earth were you thinking, Adam?'

He looked back then, frowning; he stopped too, clearly catching from her tone that a grin would be a mistake.

'I was thinking that you were in trouble and needed a hand.'

'Idiot!' For a moment there she'd been swept away by the sight of a powerful man taking care of a tiny infant. 'I'm not a child. I could have managed.'

'Well, thanks—'

'Don't go getting all offended on me, Adam Wavell,' she snapped, cutting him off. 'While you were doing your Galahad act, anyone could have walked off with her.'

'What?' Then, realising what she was saying, he let go of the handle, rubbed his hands over his face, muttered something under his breath. 'You're right. I am an idiot. I didn't think.' Then, looking at the baby, 'I'm way out of my depth here.'

'Really? So let me guess,' May said, less

than amused; he was overdoing it with the 'idiot'. 'Your reason for dropping in for the first time in years wouldn't have anything to do with your sudden need for a babysitter?'

'Thanks, May. Saffy said you'd help.'

'She said that?' She looked at the baby. All pink and cute and helpless. No! She would not be manipulated! She was in no position to take on anyone else's problems right now. She had more than enough of her own. 'I was stating the obvious, not offering my services,' she said as he began to walk on as if it was a done deal. 'Where is Saffy?'

'She's away,' he said. 'Taking a break. She's left Nancie in my care.'

'Good luck with that,' she said. 'But it's no use coming to me for help. I know absolutely nothing about babies.'

'You've already proved you know more than me. Besides, you're a woman.' Clearly he wasn't taking her refusal seriously, which was some nerve considering he hadn't spoken to her unless forced to in the last ten years. 'I thought it came hard-wired with the X chromosome?'

'That is an outrageous thing to say,' she declared, ignoring the way her arms were aching to pick up the baby, hold her, tell her that she wouldn't allow anything bad to happen to her. Ever. Just as she'd once told her mother.

She already had the kitten. In all probability, that was all she'd ever have. Ten years from now, she'd be the desperate woman peering into other people's prams…

'Is it?' he asked, all innocence.

'You know it is.'

'Maybe if you thought of Nancie as one of those helpless creatures you were always taking in when you were a kid it would help?' He touched a finger to the kitten's orange head, suggesting that nothing had changed. 'They always seemed to thrive.'

'Nancie,' she said, ignoring what she assumed he thought was flattery, 'is not an injured bird, stray dog or frightened kitten.'

'The principle is the same. Keep them warm, dry and fed.'

'Well, there you are,' she said. 'You know all the moves. You don't need me.'

'On the contrary. I've got a company to run. I'm flying to South America tomorrow—'

'South America?'

'Venezuela first, then on to Brazil and finally Samindera. Unless you read the financial pages, you would have missed the story. I doubt it made the social pages,' he said.

'Samindera,' she repeated with a little jolt of concern. 'Isn't that the place where they have all the coups?'

'But grow some of the finest coffee in the world.' One corner of his mouth lifted into a sardonic smile that, unlike the rest of him, hadn't changed one bit.

'Well, that's impressive,' she said, trying not to remember how it had felt against her own trembling lips. The heady rush as a repressed desire found an urgent response... 'But you're not the only one with a business to run.' Hers might be little more than a cottage industry, nothing like his international money generator that had turned him from zero to a Maybridge hero, but it meant a great deal to her. Not that she'd have it for much longer.

Forget Adam, his baby niece, she had to get home, tell Robbie the bad news, start making plans. Somehow build a life from nothing.

Just as Adam had done...

'I've got a world of trouble without adding a baby to the mix,' she said, not wanting to think about Adam. Then, before he could ask her what kind of trouble, 'I thought Saffy was living in Paris. Working as a model? The last I heard from her, she was doing really well.'

'She kept in touch with you?' Then, before

she could answer, 'Why are you walking barefoot, May?'

She stared at him, aware that he'd said something he regretted, had deliberately changed the subject, then, as he met her gaze, challenging her to go there, she looked down at her torn tights, mud soaked skirt, dirty legs and feet.

'My feet are muddy. I've already ruined my good black suit…' the one she'd be needing for job interviews, assuming anyone was that interested in someone who hadn't been to university, had no qualifications '…I'm not about to spoil a decent pair of shoes, too.'

As she stepped on a tiny stone and winced, he took her by the arm, easing her off the path and she froze.

'The grass will be softer to walk on,' he said, immediately releasing her, but not before a betraying shiver of gooseflesh raced through her.

Assuming that she was cold, he removed his jacket, placed it around her shoulders. It swallowed her up, wrapping her in the warmth from his body.

'I'm covered in mud,' she protested, using her free hand to try and shake it off. Wincing again as a pain shot through her elbow. 'It'll get all over the lining.'

He stopped her, easing the jacket back onto her shoulder, then holding it in place around her. 'You're cold,' he said, looking down at her, 'and I don't think this suit will be going anywhere until it's been cleaned, do you?'

Avoiding his eyes, she glanced down at his expensively tailored trousers, but it wasn't the mud that made her breath catch in her throat. He'd always been tall but now the rest of him had caught up and those long legs, narrow hips were designed to make a woman swoon.

'No!' she said, making a move so that he was forced to turn away. 'You'd better send me the cleaning bill.'

'It's your time I need, May. Your help. Not your money.'

He needed her. Words which, as a teenager, she'd lived to hear. Words that, when he shouted them for all the world to hear, had broken her heart.

'It's impossible right now.'

'I heard about your grandfather,' he said, apparently assuming it was grief that made her so disobliging.

'Really?' she said.

'It said in the *Post* that the funeral was private.'

'It was.' She couldn't have borne the great

and good making a show of it. And why would Adam have come to pray over the remains of a man who'd treated him like something unpleasant he'd stepped in? 'But there's going to be a memorial service. He was generous with his legacies and I imagine the charities he supported are hoping that a showy civic send-off will encourage new donors to open their wallets. I'm sure you'll get an invitation to that.' Before he could answer, she shook her head. 'I'm sorry. That was a horrible thing to say.'

But few had done more than pay duty visits after a massive stroke had left her grandpa partially paralysed, confused, with great holes in his memory. Not that he would have wanted them to see him that way.

'He hated being helpless, Adam. Not being able to remember.'

'He was a formidable man. You must miss him.'

'I lost him a long time ago.' Long before his memory had gone.

'So, what happens now?' Adam asked, after a moment of silence during which they'd both remembered the man they knew. 'Will you sell the house? It needs work, I imagine, but the location would make it ideal for company offices.'

'No!' Her response was instinctive. She knew it was too close to the town, didn't have enough land these days to attract a private buyer with that kind of money to spend, but the thought of her home being turned into some company's fancy corporate headquarters—or, more likely, government offices—was too much to bear.

'Maybe a hotel or a nursing home,' he said, apparently understanding her reaction and attempting to soften the blow. 'You'd get a good price for it.'

'No doubt, but I won't be selling.'

'No? Are you booked solid into the foreseeable future with your painters, garden designers and flower arrangers?'

She glanced at him, surprised that he knew about the one-day and residential special interest courses she ran in the converted stable block.

'Your programme flyer is on the staff noticeboard at the office.'

'Oh.' She'd walked around the town one Sunday stuffing them through letterboxes. She'd hesitated about leaving one in his letterbox, but had decided that the likelihood of the Chairman being bothered with such ephemera was nil. 'Thanks.'

'Nothing to do with me,' he said. 'That's the office manager's responsibility. But one of the receptionists was raving about a garden design course she'd been on.'

'Well, great.' There it was, that problem with her breathing again. 'It is very popular, although they're all pretty solidly booked. I've got a full house at the moment for a two-day Christmas workshop.'

Best to put off telling Robbie the bad news until after tea, when they'd all gone home, she thought. They wouldn't be able to talk until then, anyway.

'You don't sound particularly happy about that,' Adam said. 'Being booked solid.'

'No.' She shrugged. Then, aware that he was looking at her, waiting for an explanation, 'I'm going to have to spend the entire weekend on the telephone cancelling next year's pro-gramme.'

Letting down all those wonderful lecturers who ran the classes, many of whom had become close friends. Letting down the people who'd booked, many of them regulars who looked forward to a little break away from home in the company of like-minded people.

And then there were the standing orders for her own little 'Coleridge House' cottage industry. The homemade fudge and toffee. The honey.

'Cancel the courses?' Adam was frowning. 'Are you saying that your grandfather didn't leave you the house?'

The breeze was much colder coming off the lake and May really was shivering now.

'Yes. I mean, no…He left it to me, but there are conditions involved.'

Conditions her grandfather had known about but had never thought worth mentioning before the stroke had robbed him of so much of his memory.

But why would he? There had been plenty of time back then. And he'd done a major matchmaking job with Michael Linton, a little older, steady as a rock and looking for a well brought up, old-fashioned girl to run his house, provide him with an heir and a spare or two. The kind of man her mother had been supposed to marry.

'What kind of conditions?' Adam asked.

'Ones that I don't meet,' she said abruptly, as keen to change the subject as he had been a few moments earlier.

The morning had been shocking enough without sharing the humiliating entailment that Freddie Jennings had missed when he'd read her grandfather's very straightforward will after the funeral. The one Grandpa had made after her mother died which, after generous bequests to his favourite charities, bequeathed everything else he owned to his only living relative, his then infant granddaughter, Mary Louise Coleridge.

Thankfully, they'd reached the small gate that led directly from the garden of her family home into the park and May was able to avoid explanations as, hanging onto the kitten, she fumbled awkwardly in her handbag for her key.

But her hands were shaking as the shock of the morning swept over her and she dropped it. Without a word, Adam picked it up, unlocked the gate, then, taking her arm to steady her, he pushed the buggy up through the garden towards the rear of the house.

She stopped in the mud room and filled a saucer with milk from the fridge kept for animal food. The kitten trampled in it, lapping greedily, while she lined a cardboard box with an old fleece she used for gardening.

Only when she'd tucked it up safely in the warm was she able to focus on her own mess.

Her jacket had an ominous wet patch and her skirt was plastered with mud. It was her best black suit and maybe the dry cleaners could do something with it, although right at the moment she didn't want to see it ever again.

As she unzipped the skirt, let it drop to the floor and kicked it in the corner, Adam cleared his throat, reminding her that he was there. As if every cell in her body wasn't vibrating with the knowledge.

'Robbie will kill me if I track dirt through the house,' she said, peeling off the shredded tights and running a towel under the tap to rub the mud off her feet. Then, as he kicked off his mud spattered shoes and slipped the buckle on his belt, 'What are you doing?'

'I've been on the wrong side of Hatty Robson,' he replied. 'If she's coming at me with antiseptic, I want her in a good mood.'

May swallowed hard and, keeping her eyes firmly focused on Nancie, followed him into the warmth of the kitchen with the buggy, leaving him to hang his folded trousers over the Aga, only looking up at a burst of laughter from the garden.

It was the Christmas Workshop crossing the courtyard, heading towards the house for their mid-morning break.

'Flapjacks!'

'What?'

She turned and blinked at the sight of Adam in his shirt tails and socks. 'We're about to have company,' she said, unscrambling her brain and, grabbing the first aid box from beneath the sink, she said, 'Come on!' She didn't stop to see if he was following, but beat a hasty retreat through the inner hall and up the back stairs. 'Bring Nancie!'

Adam, who had picked up the buggy, baby, bag and all to follow, found he had to take a moment to catch his breath when he reached the top.

'Are you all right?' she asked.

'The buggy is heavier than it looks. Do you want to tell me what that was all about?'

'While the appearance of Adam Wavell, minus trousers, in my kitchen would undoubtedly have been the highlight of the week for my Christmas Workshop ladies…' and done her reputation a power of good '…I could not absolutely guarantee their discretion.'

'The highlight?' he asked, kinking up his eyebrow in a well-remembered arc.

'The most excitement I can usually offer is a new cookie recipe. While it's unlikely any of them will call the news desk at *Celebrity*, you can be sure they'd tell all their friends,' she said, 'and sooner or later someone would be bound to realise that you plus a baby makes it a story with the potential to earn them a bob or two.' Which wiped the suspicion of a grin from his face.

'So what do we do now?' he asked. 'Hide at the top of the stairs until they've gone?'

'No need for that,' she said, opening a door that revealed a wide L-shaped landing. 'Come on, I'll clean up your hand while you pray to high heaven that Nancie doesn't wake up and cry.'

Nancie, right on cue, opened incredibly dark eyes and, even before she gave a little whimper, was immediately the centre of attention.

May shoved the first aid box into Adam's hand.

'Shh-sh-shush, little one,' she said as she lifted her out of the buggy, leaving Adam to follow her to the room that had once been her nursery.

When she'd got too old for a nanny, she'd moved into the empty nanny's suite, which had its own bathroom and tiny kitchenette, and had turned the nursery into what she'd been careful to describe as a sitting room rather than a study, using a table rather than a desk for her school projects.

Her grandfather had discouraged her from thinking about university—going off and 'getting her head filled with a lot of nonsense' was what he'd actually said. Not that it had been a possibility once she'd dropped out of school even if she'd wanted to. She hadn't been blessed with her mother's brain and school had been bad enough. Why would anyone voluntarily lengthen the misery?

When she'd begun to take over the running of the house, she'd used her grandmother's elegant little desk in her sitting room, but her business needed a proper office and she'd since converted one of the old pantries, keeping this room as a place of refuge for when the house was filled with guests. When she needed to be on her own.

'Shut the door,' she said as Adam followed her in with the buggy. 'Once they're in the conservatory talking ten to the dozen over a cup of coffee, they won't hear Nancie even if she screams her head off.'

For the moment the baby was nuzzling contently at her shoulder, although, even with her minimal experience, she suspected that wasn't a situation that would last for long.

'The bathroom's through there. Wash off the mud and I'll do the necessary with the antiseptic wipes so that you can get on your way.'

'What about you?'

'I can wait.'

'No, you can't. Heaven knows what's lurking in that mud,' he replied as, without so much as a by-your-leave, he took her free hand, led her through her bedroom and, after a glance around to gain his bearings, into the bathroom beyond. 'Are your tetanus shots up to date?' he asked, quashing any thought that his mind was on anything other than the practical.

'Yes.' She was the most organised woman in the entire world when it came to the details. It was a family trait. One more reason to believe that her grandfather hadn't simply let things slide. That he'd made a deliberate choice to keep things as they were.

Had her mother known about the will? she wondered.

Been threatened with it?

'Are yours?' she asked.

'I imagine so. I pay good money for a PA to deal with stuff like that,' he said, running the taps, testing the water beneath his fingers.

'Efficient, is she?' May asked, imagining a tall, glamorous female in a designer suit and four-inch heels.

'He. Is that too hot?'

She tested it with her fingertips. 'No, it's

fine,' she said, reaching for the soap. 'Is that common? A male PA?'

'I run an equal opportunities company. Jake was the best applicant for the job and yes, he is frighteningly efficient. I'm going to have to promote him to executive assistant if I want to keep him. Hold on,' he said. 'You can't do that one-handed.'

She had anticipated him taking Nancie from her, but instead he unfastened his cuffs, rolled back his sleeves and, while she was still transfixed by his powerful wrists, he took the soap from her.

'No!' she said as she realised what he was about to do. He'd already worked the soap into a lather, however, and, hampered by the baby, she could do nothing as he stood behind her with his arms around her, took her scratched hand in his and began to wash it with extreme thoroughness. Finger by finger. Working his thumb gently across her palm where she'd grazed it when she'd fallen. Over her knuckles. Circling her wrist.

'The last time anyone did this, I was no more than six years old,' she protested in an attempt to keep herself from being seduced by the sensuous touch of long fingers, silky lather. The warmth of his body as he leaned into her back, his chin against her shoulder. His cheek against hers. The sensation of being not quite in control of any part of her body whenever he was within touching distance, her heartbeat amplified so that he, and everyone within twenty yards, must surely hear.

'Six?' he repeated, apparently oblivious to her confusion. 'What happened? Did you fall off your pony?'

'My bike. I never had a pony.' She'd scraped her knee and had her face pressed against Robbie's apron. She'd been baking and the kitchen had been filled with the scent of cinnamon, apples, pastry cooking as she'd cleaned her up, comforted her.

Today, it was the cool, slightly rough touch of Adam's chin against her cheek but there was nothing safe or comforting about him. She associated him with leather, rain, her heartbeat raised with fear, excitement, a pitiful joy followed by excruciating embarrassment. Despair at the hopelessness of her dreams.

There had been no rain today, there was no leather, but the mingled scents of clean skin, warm linen, shampoo were uncompromisingly male and the intimacy of his touch was sending tiny shock waves through her body, disturbing her in ways unknown to that green and heart-broken teen.

Oblivious to the effect he was having on her, he took an antiseptic wipe from the first aid box and finished the job.

'That's better. Now let's take a look at your arm.'

'My arm?'

'There's blood on your sleeve.'

'Is there?' While she was craning to see the mingled mud and watery red mess that was never going to wash out whatever the detergent ads said, he had her shirt undone. No shaky-fingered fumbling with buttons this time. She was still trying to get her tongue, lips, teeth into line to protest when he eased it off her shoulder and down her arm with what could only be described as practised ease.

'Ouch. That looks painful.'

She was standing in nothing but her bra and pants and he was looking at her elbow? Okay, her underwear might be lacy but it was at the practical, hold 'em up, rather than push 'em up end of the market. But, even if she wasn't wearing the black lace, scarlet woman underwear, the kind of bra that stopped traffic and would make Adam Wavell's firm jaw drop, he could at least *notice* that she was practically naked.

In her dreams… Her nightmares…

His jaw was totally under control as he gave his full attention to her elbow.

'This might sting a bit...'

It should have stung, maybe it did, but she was feeling no pain as his thick dark hair slid over his forehead, every perfectly cut strand moving in sleek formation as he bent to work. Only a heat that began low her belly and spread like a slow fuse along her thighs, filling her breasts, her womb with an aching, painful need that brought a tiny moan to her lips.

'Does that hurt?' he asked, looking up, grey eyes creased in concern. 'Maybe you should go to Casualty, have an X-ray just to be on the safe side.'

'No,' she said quickly. 'It's fine. Really.'

It was a lie. It wasn't fine; it was humiliating, appalling to respond so mindlessly to a man who, when he saw you in public, put the maximum possible distance between you. To want him to stop looking at her scabby elbow and look at her. See her. Want her.

As if.

These days he was never short of some totally gorgeous girl to keep him warm at night. The kind who wore 'result' shoes and bad girl underwear.

She was more your wellington boots kind of

woman. Good skin and teeth, reasonable if boringly brown eyes, but that was it. There was nothing about her that would catch the eye of a man who, these days, had everything.

'You're going to have a whopping bruise,' he said, looking up, catching her staring at him.

'I'll live.'

'This time. But maybe you should consider giving up climbing trees,' he said, pulling a towel down from the pile on the rack, taking her hand in his and patting it dry before working his way up her arm.

'I keep telling myself that,' she said. 'But you know how it is. There's some poor creature in trouble and you're the only one around. What can you do?'

'I'll give you my cell number...' He tore open another antiseptic wipe and took it over the graze on her elbow. Used a second one on his own hand. 'Next time,' he said, looking up with a smile that was like a blow in the solar plexus, 'call me.'

Oh, sure...

'I thought you said you were going to South America.'

'No problem. That's what I have a personal assistant for. You call me, I'll call Jake and he'll ride to your rescue.'

In exactly the same way that he was using her to take care of Nancie, she thought.

'Wouldn't it be easier to give me his number? Cut out the middle sidekick.'

'And miss out on having you shout at me?'

First the blow to the solar plexus, then a jab behind the knees and she was going down...

'That's all part of the fun,' he added.

Fun. Oh, right. She was forgetting. She was the clown...

'My legs are muddy. I really need to take a shower,' she added before he took it upon himself to wash them, too. More specifically, she needed to get some clothes on and get a grip. 'There's a kettle in the kitchenette if you want to make yourself a drink before you go.'

She didn't give him a chance to argue, but dumped Nancie in his arms and, closing her ears to the baby's outraged complaint, shut the door on him.

She couldn't lock it. The lock had broken years ago and she hadn't bothered to get it fixed. Why would she when she shared the house with her invalid grandfather and Robbie, neither of whom were ever going to surprise her in the shower?

Nor was Adam, she told herself as, discarding what little remained of her modesty, she dumped her filthy shirt in the wash basket, peeled off her underwear and stepped under the spray.

It should have been a cold shower, something to quench the fizz of heat bubbling through her veins.

Since it was obvious that even when she was ninety Adam Wavell would have the same effect on her, with or without his trousers, she decided to forgo the pain and turned up the temperature.

# CHAPTER THREE

ADAM took a long, slow breath as the bathroom door closed behind him.

The rage hadn't dimmed with time, but neither had the desire. Maybe it was all part of the same thing. He hadn't been good enough for her then and, despite his success, she'd never missed an opportunity to make it clear that he never would be.

But she wasn't immune. And, since a broken engagement, there had never been anyone else in her life. She hadn't gone to university, never had a job, missing out on the irresponsible years when most of their contemporaries were obsessed with clothes, clubbing, falling in and out of love.

Instead, she'd stayed at home to run Coleridge House, exactly like some Edwardian miss, marking time until she was plucked off the shelf, at which point she would do pretty much the same thing for her husband. And, exactly like a good Edwardian girl, she'd abandoned a perfect-fit marriage without hesitation to take on the job of caring for her grandfather after his stroke. Old-fashioned. A century out of her time.

According to the receptionist who'd been raving about the garden design course, what May Coleridge needed was someone to take her in hand, help her lose a bit of weight and get a life before she spread into a prematurely middle-aged spinsterhood, with only her strays to keep her warm at night.

Clearly his receptionist had never seen her strip off her skirt and tights or she'd have realised that there was nothing middle-aged about her thighs, shapely calves or a pair of the prettiest ankles he'd ever had the pleasure of following up a flight of stairs.

But then he already knew all that.

Had been the first boy to ever see those lush curves, the kind that had gone out of fashion half a century ago, back before the days of Twiggy and the Swinging Sixties.

But when he'd unbuttoned her shirt—the alternative had been relieving her of Nancie and he wasn't about to do that; he'd wanted her to feel the baby clinging to her, needing her—

he'd discovered that his memory had served him poorly as he was confronted with a cleavage that required no assistance from either silicon or a well engineered bra. It was the real thing. Full, firm, ripe, the genuine peaches and cream experience—the kind of peaches that would fill a man's hand, skin as smooth and white as double cream—and his only thought had been how wrong his receptionist was about May.

She didn't need to lose weight.

Not one gram.

May would happily have stayed under the shower until the warm water had washed away the entire ghastly morning. Since that was beyond the power of mere water, she contented herself with a squirt of lemon-scented shower gel and a quick sluice down to remove all traces of mud before wrapping herself in a towel.

But while, on the surface, her skin might be warmer, she was still shivering.

Shock would do that, even without the added problem of the Adam Wavell effect.

Breathlessness. A touch of dizziness whenever she saw him. Something she should have grown out of with her puppy fat. But the puppy fat had proved as stubbornly resistant as her pathetic crush on a boy who'd been so far out of her reach that he might as well have been in outer space. To be needed by him had once been the most secret desire shared only with her diary.

Be careful what you wish for, had been one of Robbie's warnings from the time she was a little girl and she'd been right in that, as in everything.

Adam needed her now. 'But only to take care of Saffy's baby,' she muttered, ramming home the point as she towelled herself dry before wrapping herself from head to toe in a towelling robe. She'd exposed enough flesh for one day.

She needn't have worried. Adam had taken Nancie through to the sitting room and closed the door behind him. Clearly he'd seen more than enough of her flesh for one day.

Ignoring the lustrous dark autumn gold cord skirt she'd bought ages ago in a sale and never worn, she pulled on the scruffiest pair of jogging pants and sweatshirt that she owned. There was no point in trying to compete with the girls he dated these days. Lean, glossy thoroughbreds.

She had more in common with a Shetland

pony. Small, overweight, a shaggy-maned clown.

What was truly pathetic was that, despite knowing all that, if circumstances had permitted, May knew she would have still succumbed to his smile. Taken care of Saffy's adorable baby, grateful to have the chance to be that close to him, if only for a week or two while her mother was doing what came naturally. Being bad by most people's standards, but actually having a life.

Nancie began to grizzle into his shoulder and Adam instinctively began to move, shushing her as he walked around May's private sitting room, scarcely able to believe it had been so easy to breach the citadel.

He examined the pictures on her walls. Her books. Picked up a small leather-bound volume lying on a small table, as if she liked to keep it close to hand.

Shakespeare's *Sonnets*. As he replaced it, something fluttered from between the pages. A rose petal that had been pressed between them. As he bent to pick it up, it crumbled to red dust between his fingers and for a moment he remembered a bunch of red roses that, in the middle of winter, had cost him a fortune. Every penny of which had to be earned labouring in the market before school.

He moved on to a group of silver-framed photographs. Her grandparents were there. Her mother on the day she'd graduated. He picked up one of May, five or six years old, holding a litter of kittens and, despite the nightmare morning he was having, the memories that being here had brought back into the sharpest focus, he found himself smiling.

She might have turned icy on him but she was still prepared to risk her neck for a kitten. And any pathetic creature in trouble would have got the same response, whether it was a drowning bird on the school roof—and they'd both been given the maximum punishment short of suspension for that little escapade—or a kitten up a tree.

Not that she was such an unlikely champion of the pitiful.

She'd been one of those short, overweight kids who were never going to be one of the cool group in her year at school. And the rest of them had been too afraid of being seen to be sucking up to the girl from the big house to make friends with her.

She really should have been at some expensive private school with her peers instead of being tossed into the melting pot of the local comprehensive. One of those schools where they wore expensive uniforms as if they were designer clothes. Spoke like princesses.

It wasn't as if her family couldn't afford it. But poor little May Coleridge's brilliant mother—having had the benefit of everything her birth could bestow—had turned her back on her class and become a feminist firebrand who'd publicly deplored all such elitism and died of a fever after giving birth in some desperately inadequate hospital in the Third World with no father in evidence.

If her mother had lived, he thought, May might well have launched a counter-rebellion, demanding her right to a privileged education if only to declare her own independence of spirit; but how could she rebel against someone who'd died giving her life?

Like her mother, though, she'd held on to who she was, refusing to give an inch to peer pressure to slur the perfect vowels, drop the crisp consonants, hitch up her skirt and use her school tie as a belt. To seek anonymity in the conformity of the group. Because that would have been a betrayal, too. Of who she was.

It was what had first drawn him to her. His

response to being different had been to keep his head down, hoping to avoid trouble and he'd admired, envied her quiet, obstinate courage. Her act first, think later response to any situation.

Pretty much what had got them into so much trouble in the first place.

Nancie, deciding that she required something a little more tangible than a 'sh-shush' and a jiggle, opened her tiny mouth to let out an amazingly loud wail. He replaced the photograph. Called May.

The water had stopped running a while ago and, when there was no reply, he tapped on the bedroom door.

'Help!'

There was no response.

'May?' He opened the door a crack and then, since there wasn't a howl of outrage, he pushed it wide.

The room, a snowy indulgence of pure femininity, had been something of a shock. For some reason he'd imagined that the walls of her bedroom would be plastered in posters of endangered animals. But the only picture was a watercolour of Coleridge House painted when it was still surrounded by acres of parkland. A reminder of who she was?

There should have been a sense of triumph at having made it this far into her inner sanctum. But looking at that picture made him feel like a trespasser.

May pushed open the door to her grandfather's room.

She still thought of it as his room even though he'd long ago moved downstairs to the room she'd converted for him, determined that he should be as comfortable as possible. Die with dignity in his own home.

'May?'

She jumped at the sound of Adam's voice.

'Sorry, I didn't mean to startle you, but Nancie is getting fractious.'

'Maybe she needs changing. Or feeding.' His only response was a helpless shrug. 'Both happen on a regular basis, I understand,' she said, turning to the wardrobe, hunting down one of her grandfather's silk dressing gowns, holding it out to him. 'You'd better put this on before you go and fetch your trousers.' Then, as he took it from her, she realised her mistake. He couldn't put it on while he was holding the baby.

Nancie came into her arms like a perfect fit. A soft, warm, gorgeous bundle of cuddle nestling against her shoulder. A slightly damp bundle of cuddle.

'Changing,' she said.

'Yes,' he said, tying the belt around his waist and looking more gorgeous than any man wearing a dressing gown that was too narrow across the shoulders, too big around the waist and too short by a country mile had any right to look.

'You knew!'

'It isn't rocket science,' he said, looking around him. 'This was your grandfather's room.'

It wasn't a question and she didn't bother to answer. She could have, probably should have, used the master bedroom to increase the numbers for the arts and crafts weekends she hosted, but hadn't been able to bring herself to do that. While he was alive, it was his room and it still looked as if he'd just left it to go for a stroll in the park before dropping in at the Crown for lunch with old friends.

The centuries-old furniture gleamed. There were fresh sheets on the bed, his favourite Welsh quilt turned back as if ready for him. And a late rose that Robbie had placed on the dressing table glowed in the thin sunshine.

'Impressive.'

'As you said, Adam, he was an impressive man,' she said, turning abruptly and, leaving him to follow or not as he chose, returned to her room.

He followed.

'You're going to have to learn how to do this,' she warned as she fetched a clean towel from her bathroom and handed it to him.

He opened it without a word, lay it over the bed cover and May placed Nancie on it. She immediately began to whimper.

'Watch her,' she said, struggling against the instinct to pick her up again, comfort her. 'I'll get her bag.'

Ignoring his, 'Yes, ma'am,' which was on a par with the ironic 'Mouse', she unhooked Nancie's bag from the buggy, opened it, found a little pink drawstring bag that contained a supply of disposable nappies and held one out to him.

'Me?' He looked at the nappy, the baby and then at her. 'You're not kidding, are you?' She continued to hold out the nappy and he took it without further comment. 'Okay. Talk me through it.'

'What makes you think I know anything about changing a baby? And if you say that I'm a woman, you are on your own.'

Adam, on the point of saying exactly that, reconsidered. He'd thought that getting through the door would be the problem but that had been the easy part. Obviously, he was asking a lot but, considering Saffy's confidence and her own inability to resist something helpless, he was meeting a lot more resistance from May than he'd anticipated.

'You really know nothing about babies?'

'Look around you, Adam. The last baby to occupy this nursery was me.'

'This was your nursery?' he said, taking in the lace-draped bed, the pale blue carpet, the lace and velvet draped window where she'd stood and watched his humiliation at the hands of her 'impressive' grandfather.

'Actually, this was the nanny's room,' she said. 'The nursery was out there.'

'Lucky nanny.' The room, with its bathroom, was almost as big as the flat he'd grown up in.

May saw the casual contempt with which he surveyed the room but didn't bother to explain that her grandfather had had it decorated for her when she was fifteen. That it reflected the romantic teenager she'd been rather than the down-to-earth woman she'd become.

'As I was saying,' she said, doing her best to hold onto reality, ignore the fact that Adam

Wavell was standing in her bedroom, 'the last baby to occupy this nursery was me and only children of only children don't have nieces and nephews to practise on.' Then, having given him a moment for the reality of her ignorance to sink in, she said, 'I believe you have to start with the poppers of her sleep suit.'

'Right,' he said, looking at the nappy, then at the infant and she could almost see the cogs in his brain turning as he decided on a change of plan. That his best move would be to demonstrate his incompetence and wait for her to take over.

He set about unfastening the poppers but Nancie, thinking it was a game, kicked and wriggled and flung her legs up in the air. Maybe she'd maligned him. Instead of getting flustered, he laughed, as if suddenly realising that she wasn't just an annoying encumbrance but a tiny person.

'Come on, Nancie,' he begged. 'I'm a man. This is new to me. Give me a break.'

Maybe it was the sound of his voice, but she lay still, watching him with her big dark eyes, her little forehead furrowed in concentration as if she was trying to work out who he was.

And, while his hands seemed far too big for the delicate task of removing the little pink sleep suit, if it had been his intention to look clumsy and incompetent, he was failing miserably.

The poppers were dealt with, the nappy removed in moments and his reward was a great big smile.

'Thanks, gorgeous,' he said softly. And then leaned down and kissed her dark curls.

The baby grabbed a handful of his hair and, as she watched the two of them looking at one another, May saw the exact moment when Adam Wavell fell in love with his baby niece. Saw how he'd be with his own child.

Swallowing down a lump the size of her fist, she said, 'I'll take that, shall I?' And, relieving him of the nappy, she used it as an excuse to retreat to the bathroom to dispose of it in the pedal bin. Taking her time over washing her hands.

'Do I need to use cream or powder or something?' he called after her.

'I've no idea,' she said, gripping the edge of the basin.

'Babies should come with a handbook. Have you got a computer up here?'

'A what?'

'I could look it up on the web.'

'Oh, for goodness' sake!' She abandoned

the safety of the bathroom and joined him beside the bed. 'She's perfectly dry,' she said, after running her palm over the softest little bottom imaginable. 'Just put on the nappy and...and get yourself a nanny, Adam.'

'Easier said than done.'

'It's not difficult. I can give you the number of a reliable agency.'

'Really? And why would you have their number?'

'The Garland Agency provide domestic and nursing staff, too. I needed help. The last few months...'

'I'm sorry. I didn't think.' He turned away, opened the nappy, examined it to see how it worked. 'However, there are a couple of problems with the nanny scenario. My apartment is an open-plan loft. There's nowhere to put either a baby or a nanny.'

'What's the other problem?' He was concentrating on fastening the nappy and didn't answer. 'You said there were a couple of things.' He shook his head and, suddenly suspicious, she said, 'When was the last time you actually saw Saffy?'

'I've been busy,' he said, finally straightening. 'And she's been evasive,' he added. 'I bought a lease on a flat for her in Paris, but

I've just learned that she's moved out, presumably to move in with Nancie's father.
She's sublet it and has been pocketing the rent
for months.'

'You're not a regular visitor, then?'

'You know what she's like, May. I didn't
even know she was pregnant.'

'And the baby's father? Who is he?'

'His name is Michel. That's all I know.'

'Poor Saffy,' she said. And there was no
doubt that she was pitying her her family.

'She could have come to me,' he protested.
'Picked up the phone.'

'And you'd have done what? Sent her a
cheque?'

'It's what she usually wants. You don't think
she ever calls to find out how I am, do you?'

'You are strong. She isn't. How was she
when she left the baby with you?'

'I'd better wash my hands,' he said.

Without thinking, she put out her hand and
grabbed his arm to stop him. 'What aren't you
telling me, Adam?'

He didn't answer, but took a folded sheet of
paper from his shirt pocket and gave it to her
before retreating to the bathroom.

It looked as if it had been screwed up and
tossed into a bin, then rescued as an afterthought.

She smoothed it out. Read it.

'Saffy's on the run from her baby's father?' she asked, looking up as he returned. 'Where did she leave the baby?'

'In my office. I found her there when I left a meeting to fetch some papers. Saffy had managed to slip in and out without anyone seeing her. She hasn't lost the skills she learned as a juvenile shoplifter.'

'She must have been absolutely desperate.'

'Maybe she is,' he said. 'But not nearly as desperate as I am right at this minute. I know you haven't got the time of day for me, but she said you'd help her.'

'I would,' she protested. 'Of course I would…'

'But?'

'Where's your mother?' she asked.

'She relocated to Spain after my father died.'

'Moving everyone out of town, Adam? Out of sight, out of mind?'

A tightening around his mouth suggested that her barb had found its mark. And it was unfair. He'd turned his life around, risen above the nightmare of his family. Saffy hadn't had his strength, but she still deserved better from him than a remittance life in a foreign country. All the bad things she'd done had been a cry for the attention, love she craved.

'She won't have gone far.'

'That's not the impression she gives in her note.'

'She'll want to know the baby is safe.' Then, turning on him, 'What about you?'

'Me?'

'Who else?' she demanded fiercely because Adam was too close, because her arms were aching to pick up his precious niece. She busied herself instead, fastening Nancie into her suit. 'Can't you take paternity leave or something?'

'I'm not the baby's father.'

'Time off, then. You do take holidays?'

'When I can't avoid it.' He shook his head. 'I told you. I'm leaving for South America tomorrow.'

'Can't you put it off?'

'It's not just a commercial trip, May. There are politics involved. Government agencies. I'm signing fair trade contracts with cooperatives. I've got a meeting with the President of Samindera that it's taken months to set up.'

'So the answer is no.'

'The answer is no. It's you,' he said, 'or I'm in trouble.'

'In that case you're in trouble.' She picked up the baby and handed her to him, as clear a statement as she could make. 'I'd help Saffy in a heartbeat if I could but—'

'But you wouldn't cross the road to help me.'

'No!'

'Just cross the road to avoid speaking to me. Would I have got anywhere at all if you hadn't been stuck up a tree? Unable to escape?'

That was so unfair! He had no idea. No clue about all the things she'd done for him and it was on the tip of her tongue to say so.

'I'm sorry. You must think I've got some kind of nerve even asking you.'

'No... Of course I'd help you if I could. But I've got a few problems of my own.'

'Tell me,' he said, lifting his spare hand to wipe away the stupid tear that had leaked despite her determination not to break down, not to cry, his fingers cool against her hot cheek. 'Tell me about the world of trouble you're in.'

'I didn't think you'd heard.'

'I heard but you asked where Saffy was...' He shook his head. 'I'm sorry, May, I've been banging on about my own problems instead of listening to yours.' His hand opened to curve gently around her cheek. 'It was something about the house. Tell me. Maybe I can help.'

She shook her head, struggling with the temptation to lean into his touch, to throw herself into his arms, spill out the whole sorry story. But there was no easy comfort.

All she had left was her dignity and she tore herself away, took a step back, then turned away to look out of the window.

'Not this time, Adam,' she said, her voice as crisp as new snow. 'This isn't anything as simple as getting stuck up a tree. The workshop ladies have returned to the stables. It's safe for you to leave now.'

She'd been sure that would be enough to drive him away, but he'd followed her. She could feel the warmth of his body at her shoulder.

'I'm pretty good at complicated, too,' he said, his voice as gentle as the caress of his breath against her hair.

'From what I've read, you've had a lot of practice,' she said, digging her nails into her hands. 'I'm sure you mean well, Adam, but there's nothing you can do.'

'Try me,' he challenged.

'Okay.' She swung around to face him. 'If you've got a job going for someone who can provide food and accommodation for a dozen or so people on a regular basis, run a production line for homemade toffee, is a dab hand with hospital corners, can milk a goat, keep bees and knows how to tame a temperamental lawnmower, that would be a start,' she said in a rush.

'You need a job?' Adam replied, brows kinked up in a confident smile. As if he could make the world right for her by lunch time and still have time to add another company or two to his portfolio. 'Nothing could be simpler. I need a baby minder. I'll pay top rates if you can start right now.'

'The one job for which I have no experience, no qualifications,' she replied. 'And, more to the point, no licence.'

'Licence?'

'I'm not related to Nancie. Without a child-minding licence, it would be illegal.'

'Who would know?' he asked, without missing a beat.

'You're suggesting I don't declare the income to the taxman? Or that the presence of a baby would go unnoticed?' She shook her head. 'People are in and out of here all the time and it would be around the coffee morning circuit faster than greased lightning. Someone from Social Services would be on the doorstep before I could say "knife".' She shrugged. 'Of course, most of the old tabbies would assume Nancie was mine. "*Just* like her mother…"' she said, using the disapproving tone she'd heard a hundred times. Although, until now, not in reference to her own behaviour.

'You're right,' he said, conceding without another word. 'Obviously your reputation is far too precious a commodity to be put at risk.'

'I didn't say that,' she protested.

'Forget it, May. I should have known better.' He shrugged. 'Actually, I did know better but I thought you and Saffy had some kind of a bond. But it doesn't matter. I'll call the authorities. I have no doubt that Nancie's father has reported her missing by now and it's probably for the best to leave it to the court to—'

'You can't do that!' she protested. 'Saffy is relying on you to get her out of this mess.'

'Is she? Read her letter again, May.'

# CHAPTER FOUR

THERE was the longest pause while he allowed that to sink in. Then he said, 'Is there any chance of that coffee you promised me?'

May started. 'What? Oh, yes, I'm sorry. It's instant; will that do?'

'Anything.'

The tiny kitchenette was in little more than a cupboard, but she had everything to hand and in a few minutes she returned with a couple of mugs.

'I'll get a blanket and you can put Nancie on the floor.'

'Can you do that?'

She didn't answer, just fetched a blanket from the linen cupboard, pausing on the landing to listen. The silence confirmed that the workshop coffee break was over but the thought of going downstairs, facing Robbie with her unlikely visitor, was too daunting.

Back in her sitting room, she laid the folded blanket on the floor, took Nancie from Adam and put her down on it. Then she went and fetched the teddy she'd spotted in her bag. Putting off for as long as possible the moment when she would have to tell Adam the truth.

'I know you just think I'm trying to get you to take this on, dig me out of a hole,' Adam said when she finally returned. Picking up her coffee, clutching it in front of her like a shield, she sat beside him on the sofa. 'But you really are a natural.'

'I think you're just trying to avoid putting off telling me the whole truth.'

'All I know is what's in Saffy's letter.' He dragged long fingers through his dark hair, looking for once less than the assured man, but more like the boy she remembered. 'I've called some of her friends but if she's confided in them, then aren't telling.'

'What about her agent?' she prompted.

'It seems that they parted company months ago. Her modelling career was yet another fantasy, it seems.'

May picked up the letter and read it again. 'She doesn't sound exactly rational. She could be suffering from post-natal depression. Or maybe having Nancie has triggered a bipolar episode. She always did swing between highs and lows.'

'And if she was? Would you help then?' He shook his head before she could answer. 'I'm sorry. That was unfair, but what I need right now, May, is someone I can trust. Someone who knows her. Who won't judge. Or run to the press with this.'

'The press?'

'Something like this would damage me.'

'You! Is that all you're worried about?' she demanded, absolutely furious with him. 'Yourself. Not Saffy? Not Nancie?'

Nancie, startled, threw out a hand, lost her teddy and began to cry. Glad of the chance to put some distance between them, May scrambled to her knees to rescue the toy, give it back to the baby. Stayed with her on the floor to play with her.

'The Garland Agency has a branch in Melchester,' she said. 'I suggest you call them. They've a world class reputation and I have no doubt that discretion comes with the price tag.'

'As I said. There are a number of problems with that scenario. Apart from the fact that my apartment is completely unsuitable. You've read Saffy's letter. They'll want details. They'll want to know where her mother is.

Who she is. What right I have to make child-care arrangements. Saffy is on the run, May. There's a court order in place.'

'You must have some idea where she'd go? Isn't there a friend?'

'If anyone else had asked me that I'd have said that if she was in trouble, she'd come to you.' He stared into the cup he was holding. 'I did ring her a few months ago when there was a rumour in one of the gossip mags about her health. Probably someone heard her throwing up and was quick to suggest an eating disorder. But she was bright, bubbly, rushing off to a shoot. At least that's what she said.' He shrugged. 'She was too eager to get me off the phone. And maybe I was too eager to be reassured. I should have known better.'

'She sounds almost frightened.'

'I know. I'm making discreet enquiries, but until I know who this man is I'm not going to hand over my niece. And I'm doing my best to find Saffy, too. But the last thing we need is a hue and cry.'

He put down the mug, knelt beside her.

'This time I'm the one up the drainpipe, Mouse, and it's raining a monsoon. Won't you climb up and rescue me?'

'I wish I could help—'

'There is no one else,' he said, cutting her off.

The unspoken, *And you owe me...* lay unsaid between them. But she knew that, like her, he was remembering the hideous scene when he'd come to the back door, white-faced, clutching his roses. It had remained closed to his knock but he hadn't gone away. He'd stayed there, mulishly stubborn, for so long that her grandfather had chased him away with the hose.

It had been the week before Christmas and the water was freezing but, while he'd been driven from the doorstep, he'd stayed in the garden defiantly, silently staring up at her room, visibly shivering, until it was quite dark.

She'd stood in this window and watched him, unable to do or say anything without making it much, much worse. Torn between her grandfather and the boy she loved. She would have defied her grandpa, just as her mother had defied him, but there had been Saffy. And Adam. And she'd kept the promise that had been wrung from her even though her heart was breaking.

She didn't owe him a thing. She'd paid and paid and paid...

'I can't,' she said, getting up, putting distance between them. 'I told you, I know no more than you do about looking after a baby.'

'I think we both know that your experience as a rescuer of lame ducks puts you streets ahead of me.'

'Nancie is not a duck,' she said a touch desperately. Why wouldn't he just take no for an answer? There must a dozen women who'd fall over themselves to help him out. Why pick on her? 'And, even if she were,' she added, 'I still couldn't help.'

She couldn't help anyone. That was another problem she was going to have to face. Finding homes for her family of strays.

There wasn't much call for a three-legged cat or a blind duck. And then there were the chickens, Jack and Dolly, the bees. She very much doubted if the Crown would consider a donkey and a superannuated nanny goat an asset to the nation's coffers.

'Why not, May?' he insisted. He got to his feet too, but he'd kept his distance. She didn't have to turn to know that his brows would be drawn down in that slightly perplexed look that was so familiar. 'Tell me. Maybe I can help.'

'Trust me,' she said. Nancie had caught hold of her finger and she lifted the little hand to her lips, kissed it. 'You can't help me. No one can.'

Then, since it was obvious that, unless she

explained the situation, Adam wasn't going to give up, she told him why.

Why she couldn't help him or Saffy.

Why he couldn't help her.

For a moment he didn't say anything and she knew he would be repeating her words over in his head, exactly as she had done this morning when Freddie had apologetically explained the situation in words of one syllable.

Adam had assumed financial worries to be the problem. Inheritance tax. Despite the downturn in the market, the house was worth a great deal of money and it was going to take a lot of cash to keep the Inland Revenue happy.

'You have to be married by the end of the month or you'll lose the house?' he repeated, just to be certain that he'd understood.

She swallowed, nodded.

She would never have told him if he hadn't been so persistent, he realised. She'd told him that she couldn't help but, instead of asking her why, something he would have done if it had been a work-related problem, he'd been so tied up with his immediate problem that he hadn't been listening.

He was listening now. And there was only one thought in his head. That fate had dropped her into his lap. That the boy who hadn't been good enough to touch Coleridge flesh, who'd shivered as he'd waited for her to defy her grandfather, prove that her hot kisses had been true, now held her future in the palm of his hand.

That he would crack the ice in May Coleridge's body between the fine linen sheets of her grandfather's four-poster bed and listen to the old man spin in his grave as did it.

'What's so important about the end of the month?' he asked. Quietly, calmly. He'd learned not to show his thoughts, or his feelings.

'My birthday. It's on the second of December.'

She'd kept her back to him while she'd told him her problems, but now she turned and looked up at him. She'd looked up at him before, her huge amber eyes making him burn, her soft lips quivering with uncertainty. The taste of them still haunted him.

He'd liked her. Really liked her. She had guts, grit and, despite the wide gulf in their lives, they had a lot in common. And he'd loved being in the quiet, ordered peace of the lovely gardens of Coleridge House, the stables where she'd kept her animals. Everything so clean and well organised.

He'd loved the fact that she had her own

kettle to make coffee. That there was always homemade cake in a tin. The shared secrecy. That no one but she knew he was there. Not her grandfather, not his family. It had all been so different from the nightmare of his home life.

But taking her injured animals, helping her look after them was one thing. She wasn't the kind of girl any guy—even one with no pretensions to street cred—wanted to be seen with at the school disco.

But their meetings weren't as secret as he'd thought. His sister had got curious, followed him and blackmailed him into asking May to go as his date to the school disco.

It had been as bad as he could have imagined. While all the other girls had been wearing boob tubes and skirts that barely covered their backsides, she'd been wearing something embarrassingly sedate, scarcely any make-up. He was embarrassed to be seen with her and, ashamed of his embarrassment, had asked her to dance.

That was bad, too. She didn't have a clue and he'd caught hold of her and held her and that had been better. Up close, her hair had smelled like flowers after rain. She felt wonderful, her softness against his thin, hard body had roused him, brought to the surface all those feelings that he'd kept battened down. This was why he'd gone back time after time to the stables. Risked being caught by the gardener. Or, worse, the housekeeper.

Her skin was so beautiful that he'd wanted to touch it, touch her, kiss her. And her eyes, liquid black in the dim lights of the school gym, had told him that she wanted it too. But not there. Not where anyone could see them, hoot with derision...

They had run home through the park. She'd unlocked the gate, they'd scrambled up to the stables loft and it was hard to say which of them had been trembling the most when he'd kissed her, neither of them doubting what they wanted.

That it was her first kiss was without doubt. It was very nearly his, too. His first real kiss. The taste of her lips, the sweetness, her uncertainty as she'd opened up to him had made him feel like a giant. All powerful. Invincible. And the memory of her melting softness in the darkness jolted through him like an electric charge...

'You need a husband by the end of the month?' he said, dragging himself back from the hot, dark thoughts that were raging through him.

'There's an entailment on Coleridge House,' she said. 'The legatee has to be married by the time he or she is thirty or the house goes to the Crown.'

'He's controlling you, even from the grave,' he said.

She flushed angrily. 'No one knew,' she said. 'No one?'

'My grandfather lost great chunks of his memory when he had the stroke. And papers were lost when Jennings' offices were flooded a few years ago…'

'You're saying you had no warning?'

She shook her head. 'My mother was dead long before she was thirty, but she thought marriage was an outdated patriarchal institution…' The words caught in her throat and she turned abruptly away again so that he shouldn't see the tears turning her caramel-coloured eyes to liquid gold, just as they had that night when her grandfather had dragged her away from him, his coat thrown around her. 'She'd have told them all to go to hell rather than compromise her principles.'

He tried to drown out the crowing triumph. That this girl, this woman, who from that day to this had crossed the road rather than pass him in the street, was about to lose everything.

That her grandfather, that 'impressive' man who thought he was not fit to breathe the same air as his precious granddaughter, had left her at his mercy.

'But before the stroke? He could have told you then.'

'Why would he? I was engaged to Michael, the wedding date was set.'

'Michael Linton.' He didn't need to search his memory. He'd seen the announcement and Saffy had been full of it, torn between envy and disgust.

Envy that May would be Lady Linton with some vast country estate and a house in London. Disgust that she was marrying a man nearly old enough to be her father. 'Her grandfather's arranged it all, of course,' she'd insisted. 'He's desperate to marry her off to someone safe before she turns into her mother and runs off with some nobody who gets her up the duff.' She'd been about to say more but had, for once, thought better of it.

Not that he'd had any argument with her conclusion. But then her grandfather had suffered a massive stroke and the wedding had at first been put off. Then Michael Linton had married someone else.

'What happened? Why didn't you marry him?'

'Michael insisted that Grandpa would be better off in a nursing home. I said no, but he kept bringing me brochures, dragging me off to look at places. He wouldn't listen, wouldn't hear what I was saying, so in the end I gave him his ring back.'

'And he took it?'

'He wanted a wife, a hostess, someone who would fit into his life, run his home. He didn't want to be burdened with an invalid.'

'If he'd taken any notice of your lame duck zoo, he'd have known he was on a hiding to nothing.'

She shook her head and when she looked back over her shoulder at him her eyes were sparkling, her cheeks wet, but her lips were twisted into a smile.

'Michael didn't climb over the park gate when the gardener was looking the other way, Adam. He was a front door visitor.'

'You mean you didn't make him help you muck out the animals?' he asked and was rewarded with a blush.

'I didn't believe he'd appreciate the honour. He'd have been horrified if he'd seen me shin up a tree to save a kitten. Luckily, the situation never arose when he was around.' A tiny shuddering breath escaped her. 'You don't notice creatures in distress from the back seat of a Rolls-Royce.'

'His loss,' he said, his own throat thick as the memories of stolen hours rushed back at him.

'And mine, it would seem.'

'You'd have been utterly miserable married to him.'

She shook her head.

'You aren't going to take this lying down, are you?' he asked. 'I can't believe it would stand up in a court of law and the tabloids would have a field day if the government took your home.'

'A lot of people are much worse off than me, Adam. I'm not sure that a campaign to save a fifteen-room house for one spoilt woman and her housekeeper would be a popular cause.'

She had a point. She'd been born to privilege and her plight was not going to garner mass sympathy.

'Is that what Freddie Jennings told you?' he asked. 'I assume you have taken legal advice?'

'Freddie offered to take Counsel's opinion but, since Grandpa had several opportunities to remove the Codicil but chose not to, I don't have much of a case.' She lifted her shoulders in a gesture of utter helplessness. 'It makes no difference. The truth is that there's no cash to spare for legal fees. As it is, I'm going to have to sell a load of stuff to meet the inheritance tax bill. Even if I won, the costs would be so high that I'd have to sell the house to pay them. And if I lost…'

If she lost it would mean financial ruin.

Well, that would offer a certain amount of satisfaction. But nowhere near as much as the alternative that gave him everything he wanted.

'So you're telling me that the only reason you can't take care of Nancie is because you're about to lose the house? If you were married, there would be no problem,' he said. He didn't wait for her answer—it hadn't been a question. 'And your birthday is on the second of December. Well, it's tight, but it's do-able.'

'Do-able?' she repeated, her forehead buckled in a frown. 'What are you talking about?'

'A quick trip to the register office, a simple "I do", you get to keep your house and I'll have somewhere safe for Nancie. As her aunt-in-law, I don't imagine there would be any objection to you taking care of her?'

And he would be able to finally scratch the itch that was May Coleridge while dancing on the grave of the man who'd shamed and humiliated him.

But if he'd imagined that she'd fling her arms around him, proclaim him her saviour, well, nothing had changed there, either.

Her eyes went from blank to blazing, like lightning out of a clear blue sky.

'That's not even remotely funny, Adam. Now, if you don't mind, I've got a house full of guests who'll be expecting lunch in a couple of hours.'

She was wearing shabby sweats but swept by him, head high, shoulders back. Despite her lack of inches, the fact that her puppy fat hadn't melted away but had instead evolved into soft curves, she was every inch the lady.

'Mouse...' he protested, shaken out of his triumph by the fact that, even in extremis, she'd turn him down flat. As if he was still a nobody from the wrong side of the tracks. 'May!'

She was at the door before she stopped, looked back at him.

'I'm serious,' he said, a touch more sharply than he'd intended.

She shook her head. 'It's impossible.'

In other words, he might wear hand stitched suits these days instead of the cheapest market jeans, live in an apartment that had cost telephone numbers, be able to buy and sell the Coleridge estate ten times over, but he could never wash off the stink of where he'd come from. That his sister had been a druggie, his mother was no better than she ought to be and his father had a record as long as his arm.

But times had changed. He wasn't that kid any more. What he wanted, he took. And he wanted this.

'It would be a purely temporary arrangement,' he said. 'A marriage of convenience.'

'Are you saying that you wouldn't expect...?'

She swallowed, colour flooding into her cheeks, and it occurred to him that if Michael Linton's courtship had been choreographed by her grandfather it would have been a formal affair rather than a lust-fuelled romance. The thought sent the blood rushing to a very different part of his anatomy and he was grateful for the full stiff folds of the dressing gown he was wearing.

She cleared her throat. 'Are you saying that you wouldn't expect the full range of wifely duties?'

Not the full range. He wouldn't expect her to cook or clean or keep house for him.

'Just a twenty-four seven nanny,' she continued, regaining her composure, assuming his silence was assent. 'Only with more paperwork, a longer notice period and a serious crimp in your social life?'

'I don't have much time for a social life these days,' he assured her before she could gather herself. 'But there are formal business occasions where I would normally take a guest. Civic functions. But you usually attend those, anyway.'

Nancie, as if aware of the sudden tension, let out a wail and, using the distraction to escape the unexpected heat of May's eyes, he picked her up, put her against his shoulder, turned to look at her.

'Well? What do you say?'

She shook her head, clearly speechless, and the band holding her hair slipped, allowing wisps to escape.

Backlit by the sun, they shone around her face like a butterscotch halo.

'What have you got to lose?' he persisted, determined to impose his will on her. Overwrite the Coleridge name with his own.

'Marriage is a lot easier to get into than it is to get out of,' she protested. Still, despite every advantage, resisting him. 'There has to be an easier solution to baby care than marrying the first woman to cross your path.'

'Not the first,' he replied. 'I passed several

women in the park and I can assure you that it never crossed my mind to marry any of them.'

'No?'

He'd managed to coax the suggestion of a smile from her.

'Divorce is easy enough if both parties are in agreement,' he assured her. 'You'll be giving up a year of your freedom in return for your ancestral home. It looks like a good deal to me.'

The smile did not materialise. 'I can see the advantage from my point of view,' she said. 'But what's in it for you? You can't really be that desperate to offload Nancie.'

'Who said anything about "offloading" Nancie?' He allowed himself to sound just a little bit offended by her suggestion that he was doing that. 'On the contrary, I'm doing my best to do what her mother asked. It's not as if I intend to leave you to manage entirely on your own. I have to go away tomorrow, but I'll pull my weight until then.'

'Oh, right. And how do you intend to do that?'

'I'll take the night watch. The master bedroom is made up. I'll pack a bag and move in there today.'

# CHAPTER FIVE

'WHAT?'

The word was shocked from her.

May swallowed again, tucked a loose strand of hair behind her ear in a nervous gesture that drew attention to her neck. It was long and smooth. She had the clearest ivory skin coloured only by the fading blush…

'If we get married, people will expect us to live together,' he pointed out. 'You wouldn't want the Crown Commissioners getting the impression that it was just a piece of paper, would you? That you were cheating.'

'But—'

Before she could put her real objection into words, Nancie, bless her heart, began to grizzle.

'What do I do now?' he asked, looking at her helplessly. That, at least, wasn't an act.

'I think the fact that she's chewing your neck is the clue,' she said distractedly.

'She's hungry?'

'Feeding her, like changing her nappy, is something that has to happen at regular intervals. No doubt there's a bottle and some formula in that bag.'

She didn't wait for him to check, but went into her bedroom, fetched the bag and emptied it on the table.

'There's just one carton. I wonder what that means.'

'That we'll probably need more very soon,' he replied, picking up on her unspoken thought that it might offer a clue about how long Saffy intended to stay out of sight. Always assuming she was thinking that rationally.

'Adam!' she protested as she turned the carton over, searching for instructions.

'I'm sorry. I can plan a takeover bid to the last millisecond, but I'm out of my depth here.'

'Then get help.'

'I'm doing my best,' he replied. 'If you'd just cooperate we could both get on with our lives.'

May was struggling to keep up a calm, distant front. She'd been struggling ever since he'd stood beneath the tree in the park. Used that ridiculous name.

Inside, everything was in turmoil. Her heart, her pulse were racing.

'Please, Adam…' Her voice caught in her throat. He couldn't mean it. He was just torturing her… 'Don't…'

He lifted his hand, cradling her cheek to still her protest. His touch was gentle. A warm soothing balm that swept through her, taking the tension out of her joints so that her body swayed towards him.

'It wouldn't be that bad, would it, Mouse?'

Bad? How much worse could it get?

'It seems a little…extreme,' she said, resisting with all her will the yearning need to lean into his palm. Surrender everything, including her honour.

'Losing your home, your business, is extreme,' he insisted. 'Getting married is just a piece of paper.'

*Not for her…*

'A mutually beneficial contract to be cancelled at the convenience of both parties,' he added. 'Think of Robbie, May. Where will she go if you lose the house?'

'She's got a pension. A sister…'

'Your business,' he persisted.

The bank loan…

'And what about your animals? Who else will take them in? You know that most of them will have to be put down.'

'Don't!' she said, her throat so tight that the words were barely audible.

'Hey,' he said, pulling her into her arms so that the three of them were locked together. 'I'm your trusty sidekick, remember? As always, late on the scene but ready to leap into action when you need a helping hand.'

'This is a bit more than a helping hand.'

'Hand, foot and pretty much everything in between,' he agreed. 'Take your pick.'

He was doing his best to make her laugh, she realised, or maybe cry.

Either would be appropriate under the circumstances. What would her mother have done? Spit in the devil's eye? Or screw the patriarchal system, using it against itself to keep both her house and her freedom?

Stupid question. Heaven knew that she was not her mother. If she'd had her courage she'd be long gone. But all she had was her home. Robbie. The creatures that relied on her. The life she'd managed to make for herself.

As for breaking the promise to her grandfather, her punishment for that was built into the bargain of a barren marriage with a self-destruct date.

'May?' he prompted.

Decision time.

What decision…? There was only ever going to be one answer and, taking a deep breath, her heart beating ten times faster than when she'd climbed that tree, her voice not quite steady, she said, 'You're absolutely sure about this? Last chance.'

'Quite sure,' he replied, his own voice as steady as a rock. No hint of doubt, no suggestion of intestinal collywobbles on his part. 'It's a no-brainer.'

'No…' she said, wondering why, even now, she was hesitating.

'No?'

'I mean yes. You're right. It's a no-brainer.'

'Shall we aim for something a little more decisive?' he suggested. 'Just so that we know exactly where we stand?'

'You're not planning on going down on one knee?' she demanded, appalled.

'Heaven forbid. Just something to seal the bargain,' he said, taking his hand from her back and offering it to her.

'A handshake?' she said, suddenly overcome with the urgent need to laugh as she lifted her own to clasp it. 'Well, why not? Everything else appears to be shaking.'

As his hand tightened around hers, everything stilled. Even Nancie stopped nuzzling and grumbling. All she could hear was her pulse pounding through her ears. All she could see were his eyes. Not the bright silver of the boy she'd known but leaden almost unreadable. A shiver ran through her as he closed the gap between them, kissed her, but then she closed her eyes and all sense of danger evaporated in the heat of his mouth, the taste of him and the cherished bittersweet memory flooded back.

It was different. He was different.

The kiss was assured, certain and yet, beneath it all, she recognised the boy who'd lain with her in the stable loft and kissed her, undressed her, touched her. And for a moment she was no longer the woman who'd subjugated her yearning for love, for a family of her own into caring for her grandfather, creating a business, building some kind of life for herself.

As Adam's lips touched hers, she was that girl again and an aching need opened up before her, a dizzying void that tempted her to plunge headlong into danger, to throw caution to the winds and boldly kiss him back.

'Oh...'

At the sound of Robbie's shocked little exclamation, May stumbled back, heat rushing to her face.

That girl reliving the moment of guilt, embarrassment, pain when they'd been discovered...

'Robbie...'

'I thought I heard you come in earlier,' she said.

'I had a fall. In the park. Adam came to my rescue.'

'That would account for the kitten, then,' she said stiffly. 'And the trousers hanging over the Aga.'

'We both got rather muddy,' Adam said.

'I'm sure it's nothing to do with me what you were doing in the park,' Robbie said, ignoring him. 'But Jeremy is here.'

'Jeremy?' she repeated, struggling to gather her wits.

'He's brought the designs for the honey labels.'

'Has he? Oh, right...' Expanding honey production had been part of the future she'd planned and Jeremy Davidson had volunteered to design the labels for her.

'He's doing you a favour, May. You won't want to keep him waiting,' she said primly before turning to leave.

'Robbie, wait!' she began, then glanced at Adam, suddenly unsure of herself. She wanted to tell Robbie that the kiss had meant nothing. That it was no more than a handshake on a deal. Except when Robbie paused, her shoulders stiff with disapproval, the words wouldn't come.

'Go and see the man about your labels,' Adam urged, then nodded, as if to reassure her that she could go ahead with her plans. That she had a future. 'Leave this to me.'

'But Nancie…' She looked at the baby. It was easier than meeting his eyes, looking at Robbie.

'I'll bring her down in a moment.'

Adam watched as she stumbled from the room in her haste to escape her embarrassment and he could have kicked himself.

Most women in her situation would have leapt at the deal he'd offered, no questions asked, but her first response had been flat refusal, anger at his presumption, and that had caught him on the raw.

His kiss had been intended as a marker. A promise to himself that she would pay for every slight, every insult but, instead of the anticipated resistance, she had responded with a heat that had robbed him of any sense of victory. Only left him wanting more.

He did not want her.

He could have any woman he wanted. Beautiful women. The kind who turned heads in the street.

All he wanted from May Coleridge was her pride at his feet. And he would have it.

She had been his last mistake. His only weakness. Since the day he'd walked away from this house, his clothes freezing on his back, he'd never let anything, any emotion, stand in his way.

With his degree in his pocket, a mountain of debt to pay off, his mother incapable of looking after either herself or Saffy, the only job he had been able to get in his home town was in an old import company that had been chugging along happily since the days when the clipper ships brought tea from China. It wasn't what he'd dreamed of, but within five years he'd been running the company. Now he was the chairman of an international company trading commodities from across the globe.

His success didn't appear to impress May's disapproving housekeeper.

'It's been a while, Mrs Robson.'

'It has. But nothing appears to have changed, Mr Wavell,' she returned, ice-cool.

'On the contrary. I'd like you to be the first to know that May and I are going to be married.'

'Married!' And, just like that, all the starch went out of her. 'When...?'

'Before the end of the month.'

'I meant...' She shook her head. 'What's the hurry? What are you after? If you think May's been left well off—'

'I don't need her money. But May needs me. She's just been told that if she isn't married by her birthday, she's going to lose her home.'

'But that's less than four weeks...' She rallied. 'Is that what Freddie Jennings called about in such a flap this morning?'

'I imagine so. Apparently, some ancient entailment turned up when he took James Coleridge's will to probate.'

The colour left her face but she didn't back down. 'Why would you step in to help, Adam Wavell? What do you get out of it?' She didn't give him a chance to answer. 'And that little girl's mother? What will she have to say about it?'

'Nancie,' he said, discovering that a baby made a very useful prop, 'meet Hatty Robson. Mrs Robson, meet my niece.'

'She's Saffy's daughter?' She came closer, the rigid lines of her face softening and she touched the baby's curled up fist. 'She's a pretty thing.' Then, 'So where is your sister? In rehab? In jail?'

'Neither,' he said, hanging onto his temper by a thread. 'But we are having a bit of a family crisis.'

'Nothing new there, then.'

'No,' he admitted. A little humility wouldn't hurt. 'Saffy was sure that May would help.'

'Again? Hasn't she suffered enough for your family?'

Suffered?

'I met her in the park. She was up a tree,' he added. 'Rescuing a kitten.'

She rolled her eyes. An improvement.

'The only reason she told me her troubles was to explain why she couldn't look after Nancie.'

'And you leapt in with an immediate marriage proposal. Saving not one, but two women with a single bound?' Her tone, deeply ironic, suggested that, unlike May, she wasn't convinced that it was an act of selfless altruism.

'Make that three,' he replied, raising her irony and calling her. 'I imagine one of May's concerns was you, Mrs Robson. This is your home, too.'

If it hadn't been so unlikely, he would have sworn she blushed. 'Did she say that?' she demanded, instantly on the defensive. 'I don't matter.'

'You know that's not true,' he said, pushing his advantage. 'You and this house are all she has.'

And this time the blush was unmistakable. 'That's true. Poor child. Well, I'm sure that's very generous of you, Mr Wavell. Just tell me one thing. Why didn't your sister, or you, just pick up the phone and call one of those agencies which supplies temporary nannies? I understand you can afford it these days.'

He'd already explained his reasons to May and he wasn't about to go through them again. 'Just be glad for May's sake,' he replied, 'that I didn't.'

She wasn't happy, clearly didn't trust his motives, but after a moment she nodded just once. 'Very well. But bear this in mind. If you hurt her, you'll have to answer to me. And I won't stop at a hosing down.'

'Hurt her? Why would I hurt her?'

'You've done it before,' she said. 'It's in your nature. I've seen the string of women you've paraded through the pages of the gossip magazines. How many of them have been left with a bruised heart?' She didn't wait for an answer. 'May has spent the last ten years nursing her grandpa. She's grieving for him, vulnerable.'

'And without my help she'll lose her home,

her business and the animals she loves,' he reminded her.

She gave him a long look, then said, 'That child is hungry. You'd better give her to me before she chews a hole in your neck. What did you say her name was?'

'Nancie, Mrs Robson. With an i and an e.'

'Well, that's a sweet old-fashioned name,' she said, taking the baby. 'Hello, Nancie.' Then, looking from the baby to him, 'I suppose you'd better call me Robbie.'

'Thank you. Is there anything I can do, Robbie?'

'Go and book a date with the Registrar?' she suggested. 'Although you might want to put your trousers on first.'

The kitchen was empty, apart from a couple of cats curled up on an old armchair and an old mongrel dog who was sharing his basket with a duck and a chicken.

None of them took any notice of him as he unhooked his trousers from the rail above the Aga and carried them through to the mud room, where the kitten had curled up in the fleece and gone to sleep. He hoped Nancie, jerked out of familiar surroundings, her routine, would settle as easily.

Having brushed off the mud as best he could and made himself fit to be seen in polite society, he hunted down May. He found her in a tiny office converted from one of the pantries, shoulder to shoulder with a tall, thin man who was, presumably, Jeremy, as they leaned over her desk examining some artwork.

'May?'

She turned, peering at him over a pair of narrow tortoiseshell spectacles that were perched on the end of her nose. They gave her a cute, kittenish look, he thought. And imagined himself reaching for them, taking them off and kissing her.

'I've talked to Robbie,' he said, catching himself. 'Put her in the picture.'

That blush coloured her cheeks again, but she was back in control of her voice, her breathing as she said, 'You've explained everything?'

'The why, the what and the when,' he assured her. 'I'll give you a call as soon as I've sorted out the details. You'll be in all afternoon?'

'You're going to do it today?' she squeaked. Not that in control…

'It's today, or it's too late.'

'Yes…' Clearly, it was taking some time for

the reality of her situation to sink in. 'Will you need me? For the paperwork?'

'I'll find out what the form is and call you. I'll need your number,' he prompted when she didn't respond. 'It's unlisted.'

Flustered, May plucked a leaflet from a shelf above her desk and handed it to him. 'My number is on there.'

For a moment they just looked at one another and he wondered what she was thinking about. The afternoons they'd spent together in the stables with him ducking out of sight whenever anyone had come near? The night when they had been too absorbed in each other to listen? Or the years that had followed...?

'What are you doing?' he asked, turning to look at the artwork laid out on the table.

'What?' He looked up and saw that she was still staring at him and her poise deserted her as, flustered, she said, 'I'm ch-choosing a label for Coleridge House honey. Do you know Jeremy Davidson? He's head of the art department at the High School.' Then, as if she felt she had to explain how she knew him, 'I'm a governor.'

'You're a school governor?' He didn't bother to suppress a grin, and yet why should he be surprised? She'd been born to sit on charitable committees, school boards. In the fullness of time she'd no doubt become a magistrate, like her grandfather. 'I hope you've done something about those overflowing gutters.'

'It was my first concern.' For a moment there was the hint of a smile, the connection of a shared memory, before she turned to Jeremy Davidson. 'Adam and I were at the High School at the same time, Jeremy. He was two years above me.'

'I'm aware that Mr Wavell is one of our more successful ex-pupils,' he said rather stiffly. 'I'm delighted to meet you.'

He was another of those old school tie types. Elegant, educated. A front door visitor who would have met with James Coleridge's approval. His manners were impeccable, even if his smile didn't quite reach his eyes.

'I have an Emma Davidson on my staff,' he said. 'I believe her husband is an art teacher. Is that simply a coincidence or is she your wife?'

'She's my wife,' he admitted.

'I thought she must be. You're on half term break, I imagine. While she's at work catching up with Saminderan employment law, you're here, playing with honey pot labels—'

'*Was* my wife. We're separated.' His glance

at May betrayed him. 'Our divorce will be finalised in January.'

'Well, that's regrettable,' he said. 'Emma is a valued member of my organisation.'

'These things happen.'

So they did. But not fast enough to save May, he thought. Were they having an affair? he wondered. Or was she saving herself for the big wedding? Or was he waiting to declare himself until he was free?

Best put him out of his misery. 'Has May told you our good news?' he asked.

'Adam...'

She knew.

'We're getting married later this month,' he continued, as if he hadn't heard her.

Jeremy's shocked expression told its own story and, before he could find the appropriate words, May swiftly intervened.

'I can't decide which design I like best, Adam. What do you think?'

He waited pointedly until Davidson moved out of his way, then put his hand on the desk and leaned forward, blocking him out with his shoulder.

They were pretty enough floral designs with 'Coleridge House Honey' in some fancy script. About right for a stall at a bazaar.

'You produce handmade sweets too, don't you?' he asked her, looking at the shelf and picking up a fairly basic price list that, like the brochure, had obviously been printed on her computer. 'Is this all the literature that you have?'

She nodded as he laid it, with the brochure, beside the labels.

'There's no consistency in design,' he said. 'Not in the colours, or even the fonts you've used. Nothing to make it leap out from the shelf. Coleridge House is a brand, May. You should get some professional help to develop that.'

'Jeremy—'

'There's a rather good watercolour of the house in your bedroom. The country house, nostalgia thing would be a strong image and work well across the board. On labels, price lists and on the front of your workshop brochure.'

She looked up at him, a tiny frown creasing the space between her eyes.

'Just a thought.' With a touch to her shoulder, a curt nod to Davidson, he said, 'I'll call you later.'

He found Robbie in the kitchen preparing a feed for Nancie, who was beginning to sound very cross indeed. Resisting the urge to take the child from her—the whole point of the exercise was to leave Nancie in May's capable hands and not get involved in baby care, or her cottage industry, for that matter—he took a card from his wallet and placed it on the table.

'This is my mobile number should you need to get hold of me urgently.'

'Stick it on the cork board, will you?'

He found a drawing pin and stuck it amongst a load of letters, appointment cards and post-cards. The kind of domestic clutter so notably absent from the slate and steel kitchen in his apartment.

'Is this bag all you have?' she asked.

'I'm afraid so. You'll be needing rather more than that, I imagine?'

'You imagine right.'

'Well, just get whatever you want. Better still, make a list and I'll have it delivered. May can give it to me when I ring her about the wedding arrangements.'

Robbie said nothing when May returned to the kitchen after seeing Jeremy Davidson out, just handed her the baby and the feeder and left her to get on with it, while she set about cleaning salad vegetables at the old butler's sink.

'Any hints about how to do this?' she asked, using her toe to hook out a chair so that she could sit down.

'You'll learn the way I did when your grandfather brought you home, no more than a month old,' she said abruptly.

'Robbie…'

'You'll find that if you put it to the little one's mouth she'll do the rest.' She ripped up a head of lettuce. 'Just keep the end of the bottle up so that she's not sucking air.'

May settled the baby in the crook of her arm and, as she offered Nancie the bottle, she latched onto it, sucking greedily. She watched her for a while, then, when Robbie's silence became oppressive, she looked up and said, 'Are you angry with me, Robbie?'

'Angry with you! Why would I be angry with you?'

'You're angry with someone.'

'I'm angry with your grandfather. That foolish, pig-headed old man. Just because your mother wouldn't listen to him. Wouldn't live her life the way he wanted…'

'You're talking about the will?'

'Of course I'm talking about the will. How could he put you in such a position?'

She breathed out a sigh of relief.

She'd been anticipating a tirade about promises made and broken. About marriage being for love, not convenience. She wouldn't take a schoolgirl crush into account.

'The will wasn't about my mother, Robbie,' May said. 'It was about history. Tradition.'

'Tradition, my foot! I can't believe he'd do this to you.'

'He didn't. Not deliberately. He thought I was going to marry Michael. If he'd known…'

'Who knows anything?' she demanded. 'If I'd known my husband was going to drop dead of a heart problem when he was twenty-six I wouldn't have insisted on waiting to have a baby until we had a house, until everything was just as I wanted it…' Without warning, her eyes were full of tears. 'Life is never just as you want it, May. There are no certainties. How could he look after me and not take care of you? It's so cruel,' she said, dashing them away with the back of her hand. 'After the way you cared for him all those years when you could have been married, with a family of your own…'

'Hush, Robbie, it's all right. It's going to be all right,' she repeated, wanting to go to her, comfort her but hampered by Nancie, who had snuggled into her shoulder as if she belonged there.

'Only because Adam Wavell happened by when you needed him.'

'He didn't just happen by. He was on his way to ask for my help. This is a mutual aid package.'

'And if he hadn't needed you? What would you have done then?'

'Well,' she said, 'I was going to sit down and make a list of all the unmarried men I know. Jed Atkins was favourite.'

'Jed!' Robbie snorted. 'Well, he'd be a safer bet than Adam Wavell. And no baby.'

'But hundreds of relations who'd all expect to be invited for Christmas. Would there be a turkey big enough?'

Robbie groaned and they both laughed, but then her smile faded and she said, 'Don't fall for him, May. It's just a piece of paper.'

'I know.'

'Do you?' Robbie asked, her look searching, anxious. 'That kiss…'

'He kissed me to seal the bargain we'd made. It was nothing.'

'Nothing to him.'

'And nothing to me,' she said, pressing her lips tightly together in an attempt to stop them tingling at the memory. Forget the desperate need that his touch had awakened.

Trying not to read too much into his edgy reaction to Jeremy Davidson. The poor man had fallen apart when his wife left him and she'd offered him a distraction with her labels, something to keep his mind occupied. Something to make him feel needed. But the way Adam had made it so obvious that he'd been in her bedroom... If he'd been a dog, she'd have said he was marking his territory.

Which was ridiculous.

Adam only wanted her as a nanny.

'Absolutely nothing,' she said with emphasis. It was only in her head that she'd kissed him back, seduced him with her mouth and then her body...

Robbie made the 'humphing' noise she used when she was unconvinced.

'What did you expect us to do? Shake hands?' she asked, ignoring the fact that it had started out that way.

'Why not? If it's just a business arrangement.'

'We've known one another for a very long time. I see him all the time at civic functions. He's saving my home, for heaven's sake.'

'And you're saving him a world of trouble,' she replied. 'Just remember that as soon as this "family crisis" of his is resolved—'

'He'll be gone.'

'Let's just hope it isn't before he's put the ring on your finger. Signed the register.'

# CHAPTER SIX

'HE WOULDN'T…'

'Lead you on, then back out at the last minute? He has no reason to love this family. Be kind to you.'

No reason that he knew.

'He needs my help,' she said. Then, as the baby paused to draw breath, 'Do you think you can manage lunch on your own? I'll have to wash the cot down.'

'Chance would be a fine thing,' she replied, letting it go.

'Sorry?'

'You gave it to the vicar last year. For that family whose house burned down.'

'Oh, fudge! I'd forgotten.'

'Adam said to make a list of anything you need,' Robbie said, resuming her attack on the vegetables.

'Right. I'll do that,' she said, then was distracted by Nancie, who was opening her mouth like a little fish, waving her sweet, plump arms to demand her attention. May was familiar with the powerful instinct to survive in small mammals blindly seeking out their mother's milk, but this urgency in a small helpless baby went straight to her heart.

'An extra pair of hands wouldn't go amiss, either,' Robbie said. 'You've got that order for toffee to deliver by the end of the week.'

'No problem. Adam wants to help. I'll have to clear a wardrobe in Grandpa's room for him.'

'He's moving in? To your grandfather's room?'

'It's ready. And there's nowhere else until the guests have gone.' Her only response was the lift of an eyebrow. 'It's not like that, Robbie.'

She shook her head. 'Leave your grandpa's room to me. I'll see to it.'

'Thank you.' Then, as Nancie pulled away from the bottle, wrinkled up her little nose, distancing herself from it, 'Have you had enough of that, sweetheart?'

She set the bottle on the table and just looked at her. She was so beautiful. Just like her mother.

'You'll need to wind her,' Robbie said. 'Put her on your shoulder and rub her back gently.'

'Oh, right.'

She lifted her, set her against her shoulder. Nancie didn't wait for the rub but obligingly burped. Before she could congratulate herself, she realised that her shoulder was wet and something warm was trickling down her back.

'Eeugh! Has she brought it all back up?'

'Just a mouthful. A little milk goes a very long way,' Robbie said, grinning as she handed her a paper towel. 'You used to do that all the time.'

'Did I?' No one had ever talked to her about what she was like as a baby. 'What did you do?'

'Changed my clothes a lot until I had the sense to put a folded towel over my shoulder before I burped you.'

'Well, thanks so much for the warning,' she said, using the towel to mop up the worst. 'What else did I do?'

'You cried a lot. You were missing your mother.'

Right on cue, Nancie began to grizzle and May stood up, gently rubbing her back as she walked around the kitchen.

'Poor baby. Poor Saffy.'

'So what did he tell you? What is this family crisis? Where is she?'

'Adam doesn't know. She dropped the baby off at his office and ran. He showed me the note she left with the baby, but she didn't sound quite in control, to be honest. It seems that Nancie's father has found out about her problems and he's trying to get custody.'

'In other words, he's pitched you into the middle of his family's messy life.'

'Saffy told him I would help.' Then, as she saw the question forming on Robbie's lips, 'He was desperate, Robbie.'

'Clearly, if he's prepared to marry you to get a babysitter.'

'My good luck.'

'Maybe. Do you remember that young jackdaw with the broken wing that he left on the doorstep?'

He'd left all kinds of creatures until Robbie had caught him and sent him packing. After that, he'd come over the park gate, dodging the gardener, keeping clear of the house, coming to look for her in the stables. She'd made him instant coffee while he'd emptied her biscuit tin, stayed to help her clean out the cages. It had been a secret. No one at home, no one at school had known about it. Only Saffy.

'I remember,' she said. 'What about it?'

'You cried for a week when it flew away.'

She swallowed. 'Is that a warning not to get too attached to Nancie?'

'Or her uncle.' She didn't wait for denial but, tapping the tip of her knife thoughtfully against the board, said, 'There's that old wooden cradle upstairs in one of the box rooms. You could use that for now. In fact, it might be a good idea to get Nancie out of here before the Christmas lot break for lunch.'

'Can you and Patsy manage?'

'Everything's done but the salad.' She jerked her head. 'Off you go.'

Well aware that Robbie could handle lunch with one hand tied behind her back, May returned to the peace of her sitting room, fastened Nancie into her buggy and went to find the old cradle.

When it was ready, she put it at the foot of her bed. 'Here you go, sweetie,' she said, putting down Nancie, then rocking her gently, humming the tune to an old lullaby to which she'd long since forgotten the words.

'Very pretty.'

She started, looked up.

Adam was leaning, legs crossed, arms folded, against the architrave of the door between her sitting room and bedroom. He'd abandoned the muddy pinstripes for what looked like an identical suit, a fresh white shirt. Only the tie was different. It had a fine silver stripe that echoed the bright molten flecks that lifted his eyes above the ordinary grey.

'How long have you been standing there?' she demanded, hot with embarrassment.

'Long enough. Robbie directed me to the morning room to wait for the lady of the house but, since I brought my bag with me, I decided to bring it up. Put it in my bedroom. I used the back stairs.'

'Don't be so touchy. She probably thought you'd blunder in and wake Nancie.'

'She's never seen me slip over the back gate and dodge the gardener.'

'No.' She looked away. It was the first time he'd alluded to the past. The golden days before she'd lied to her grandfather, lied to Robbie and gone to the school disco with him.

'How many generations of Coleridge babies have been rocked to sleep in that cradle?' he asked, pushing himself off from the door frame, folding himself up beside her.

'Generations,' she admitted. Probably even the children of the man whose unwillingness to settle down was causing her so much grief.

'Everything in this house looks as if it's been here for ever.'

'Most of it has. Unfortunately, there's one thing missing,' she said, scrambling to her feet, needing to put a little distance between them so that she could concentrate on what was important.

Kneeling shoulder to shoulder with him by the cradle she was far too conscious of the contrast between his immaculate, pressed appearance and her own.

He'd showered and smelled of fresh rain on grass, newly laundered linen. Everything clean, expensive.

She smelled of disinfectant, polish and the sicky milk that had dried on her shoulder. The band holding her hair back had collapsed so that it drooped around her face and she didn't need to check the mirror to know what that looked like. A mess.

'Nancie really should have a proper cot. Unfortunately I gave ours away. I'm going to have to run over to the baby store in the retail park after lunch and buy a few things. I can pick one up then.'

'We can get do that while we're out.'

'Out?'

'That's why I'm here. I've spoken to the Registrar. He can fit us in on the twenty-ninth.'

May opened her mouth. Closed it again. Then said, 'The twenty ninth?'

'Apparently, there have to be sixteen clear

days from notice. That's the first day after that. He's free at ten o'clock. If that's convenient? It's a Monday. You haven't got anything planned for that day that you can't put off?'

She shook her head. 'We have mid-week courses and weekend courses, but Monday is always a clear day. What about you?' she asked.

'Nothing that won't keep for ten minutes,' he assured her. 'I assume you just want the basics?'

She hadn't given the ceremony any thought at all. Not since she was an infatuated teen, anyway, when she'd had it planned out to the last detail. But this wasn't an occasion for the local church scented with roses, choristers singing like angels and the pews packed with envious class mates as she swept up the aisle in a size 0 designer gown.

'The basics.' She nodded. 'Absolutely.'

'We'll need a couple of witnesses. Robbie, obviously. I thought we might ask Freddie Jennings to be the other one.'

'Good idea,' she said.

'I'm full of them today. All we need to do now is go to the office with our birth certificates and sign a few papers.'

'Now? But I can't leave Nancie.'

'Then you'll have to bring her along.'

'Yes. Of course,' she said, looking at Nancie. Looked at the buggy. Trying to imagine herself wheeling it through town with everyone thinking it was her and Adam's baby. 'I'd... um...better get changed.'

She grabbed the nearest things from her wardrobe. The discarded gold cord skirt and a soft V-necked black sweater, a fresh pair of tights from a drawer and backed into her bathroom. Where she splashed her face with cold water. Got a grip.

Because she was going to arrange her wedding and the Registrar would expect her to have made an effort, she put on some make-up, twisted her hair up into a knot, then stared at her reflection. Was that too much? Would Adam think she was making an effort to impress him?

Oh, for heaven's sake. As if Adam Wavell would care what she was wearing. And yet there was something so unsettling about the fact that he was in her home, sitting in her most private space, waiting for her.

It was too intimate. Too...

Nothing!

Absolutely nothing.

She wrenched open the door and he looked up, startled by the ferocity of her entrance.

Calm, Mary Louise. Calm…

'Okay?' he said.

'Fine. I just need my boots.' She took them from the closet, pulled them on, doing her best not to think about Adam standing at her bedroom window, Nancie against his shoulder.

'I'll just get my birth certificate and then we can go. I'll take Nancie if you'll bring the buggy.'

'Well, that was painless,' Adam said as they emerged from the register office.

May nodded, but she was very pale. And, while it might have been painless for him, everyone who worked in the Town Hall, the Registrar's Office, had known her. They'd been eager to congratulate her and cooed over the baby, assuming it was hers.

'Why did you let everyone think Nancie was your baby?' he said.

'I thought that it would be safer.'

'Safer?' He frowned.

'For Saffy.'

He was momentarily lost for words. While everyone knew her, she was an intensely private person and inside she must have been dying of embarrassment at being the centre of attention, but she'd smiled and smiled and let everyone think whatever they wanted in order to protect his wayward sister.

'I don't know about you, but I've missed lunch…' he said. 'Let's grab a sandwich.'

'I thought we were going to the business park. Nancie will need feeding again soon.'

'You won't be any use to her if you collapse from hunger,' he said, taking her arm, steering her across the road to the thriving craft centre that had once been a big coaching inn in the centre of the town.

It was lit up for the holiday season and packed with shoppers, but the lunch time rush was over in the courtyard café and they took a table near the window where there was room for the buggy.

'A BLT for me, I think. You?'

She nodded.

He ordered, adding a pot of tea without asking. 'You've had a shocking morning—we both have. Hot, sweet tea is what the doctor orders,' he said when the waitress had gone.

'The reality is just beginning to sink in.'

'It was a terrible thing to do to you,' he said.

'What? Oh.' She shook her head. 'His memory had gone. He didn't know.'

He'd assumed that she'd been talking about the loss of her home, but it seemed that marrying him was the shocker.

Well, if she'd been looking forward to an artistic partnership with the well-bred, public school educated but presumably penniless Jeremy Davidson—divorce would strip him of a large part of his assets—she had every reason to be in shock.

But, like her ancestor before her, she was prepared to do whatever it took to hold onto the family estate. Not so much a fate worse than death as a fate worse than being a nobody, living in an ordinary little house, the wife of a man who no one had ever heard of.

'Did you sort out your honey labels?' he asked.

She stared at him, then, as their food arrived, 'Oh, the labels. I took your advice and gave Jeremy the watercolour. He's going to scan it into his computer, see what he can do with it.'

Adam discovered he wasn't anywhere near as happy about that as he should have been, considering it had been his idea, but what could he say? That he didn't want the man in her bedroom, getting hot and sweaty at the thought of her peaches and cream body nestled in all that white linen and lace.

'My advice was to use a professional.'

'How much honey do you think I produce?' she asked. 'I can't justify the kind of fees a professional designer would charge. Jeremy's doing it as a favour.'

'He's going to a lot of trouble to keep in with the school governor,' he said, pouring the tea. Loading it with sugar before handing her a cup. 'Is there a promotion in the offing?'

'Not that I know of.' She took a sip of the tea, pulled a face.

'Not sweet enough?' he asked and was rewarded with a wry smile that tugged at something deeper than the bitter memories.

'You are so funny,' she said, taking a dummy from the baby's carrier, unwrapping it and handing it to Nancie to suck.

'May…' His phone began to ring but he ignored it. Her relationship with Davidson was more important than whatever Jake wanted. If she thought that she could carry on—

May glanced up when Adam ignored his phone. 'Aren't you going to get that? It could be Saffy.'

'What?' He took the phone from his pocket, snapped, 'Yes,' so sharply that if she'd been Saffy she'd have hung up. Clearly it wasn't because, after a moment, he said, 'Fifteen minutes.' Then, responding to her expectant look, 'My office. I'm afraid I'll have to give the business park a miss. Can I have this to go, please?' he said, holding out his plate to the waitress before turning back to her. 'Let me have a list of what you need and I'll sort something out.'

'Get Jake to sort something out, don't you mean?' she said, edgy, although she couldn't have said why. Just something about the way he'd looked at her, the way he'd said her name before his phone rang.

Was he having second thoughts?

'It's the same thing. He'll have to know where Nancie is in case Saffy turns up while I'm away next week. And you'll need someone to call on in the event of an emergency. He'll sort out a credit card for you as well.'

'I don't need your money, Adam.'

'Maybe not, but I understand from colleagues that babies are expensive and I don't expect you to subsidise my sister. With a card you can get whatever she needs.'

'She needs love, Adam, not a piece of plastic.'

'If you give her half as much as you lavished on your broken animals then she's in good hands,' he said. 'But it's not just Nancie. You'll need a wardrobe upgrade.' Before she could respond, he said, 'The sweats are practical, and the little black dress you've been wearing to every civic reception for the last five years is a classic, but when I present you to the world as my wife I will be looking for something a little more in keeping with my status.'

Presenting her...

His status...

Which answered any question about whether he'd changed his mind. He was going to marry her, but didn't want to be seen out with her until she'd had a makeover.

'Maybe you should consider an upgrade in your wife,' she snapped. 'Get one of those skinny blondes you're so fond of to take care of Nancie,' she continued, getting up so quickly that her chair scraped against the floor, causing heads to turn.

'Now who is there in the county who could outclass Miss May Coleridge?' he enquired, catching her hand. The shock of the contact, the squeeze of his fingers around hers, warning her that she was in danger of making a scene, took the stuffing out of her knees and she fell back into her seat.

An unreadable smile briefly crossed Adam's face and it was there again. The feeling that she'd had just before he'd kissed her. Nothing that she could pin down. Just the realisation that this Adam Wavell was not the boy who'd trembled as he kissed her. He was a man who'd been thrown the smallest lifeline and within a decade had ousted the dead wood from an old family firm, seized control and built himself an empire. That took more than hard work, brains. It required ruthlessness.

She would have felt guilty about her part in flinging him the rope secretly begging an old family friend to give him a job, but for the fact that the family had come out of it with more money that they'd ever seen in their lives before.

'I was simply suggesting, with my usual lack of finesse,' he said when she didn't respond, 'that you might want to indulge yourself in some clothes for the Christmas party season.' He was still holding her hand just firmly enough to stop her from pulling away.

He'd always had big hands, all out of proportion to his skinny wrists, but they'd been gentle with animals. Gentle with her. The kind of hands you'd want to find if you reached out, afraid, in the dark.

He'd grown into them now. But were they safe?

'I'll ask Jake to give you a call next week so that he can go through the diary with you,' he said, with just enough edge to warn her that it was not up for discussion.

'Christmas parties should be the least of your worries,' she replied, refusing to submit. 'My only concern is Nancie. And Saffy. Have you done anything about finding her?'

He released her hand, took out his wallet and exchanged a bank note for the paper bag that the waitress offered him, telling her to keep the change.

'I've called a friend who runs a security company. Even as we speak, he's doing everything he can to trace her. And he's discreetly checking out what's happening in France, too.'

Oh, damn! Of course he was looking for her… 'I'm sorry,' she said, realising that she'd allowed her pride to override common sense. 'I didn't mean to snap at you.'

His hand rested on her arm for a moment in a gesture of reassurance. 'Forget it. Neither of us are having a good day.'

'Are you going to tell Jake everything?' she asked. 'I mean that you…me…we…' She couldn't say it.

'That you…me…we are going to get married?' he asked, smiling, but not unkindly, at her inability to say the words.

She nodded.

'It's a matter of necessity, May. I'm going to have to leave him to make all the arrangements.'

'Arrangements? What arrangements are involved in a ten-minute ceremony?'

He shrugged. 'Does it have to be ten minutes? I thought we might manage something a little more exciting than the Register Office.'

'Exciting? You think I need excitement?'

'Elegant, then. Somewhere where we can have lunch, or dinner afterwards so that I can introduce you to my directors and their wives.'

She opened her mouth. Closed it again.

'He'll sort out flowers, cars, photographs, press announcements. Arrange an evening reception for my staff.'

'You've given it quite a bit of thought.'

'I haven't had a baby to take care of.'

'No. It's just that I assumed… I thought…'

Adam had forgotten the way that he could read exactly what May was thinking. It had hit him with a rush when she'd lost it in the park, yelling at him for leaving Nancie, with everything she was feeling right there on her face. Nothing held back. All those years when she'd locked him out, avoided him had disappeared in the heat of it. The truth of it.

He could read her now as she tried to come to terms not with being married to him, but everyone knowing that she was his wife. Having to act out the role in public.

'You thought that no one need know?' he prompted, calling on years of hiding what he was thinking to disguise how that made him feel.

'I… Yes…' she admitted. 'It's a paper formality, after all. I didn't expect so much fuss. Show.'

'But that's the whole point of it, May,' he said gently. 'The show.' He'd got everything he wanted after all. And so had she. But both of them were going to have to pay. In his case, it would simply be money. In hers, pride. A fair exchange…'You wouldn't want the Crown Commissioners suspecting that you were just going through the motions to deny them Coleridge House, would you?'

'I thought asking Freddie Jennings to be a witness took care of that,' she said, her face unreadable. 'I'm sure it will make his day and once he gets home and tells his wife you needn't bother with a newspaper announcement. The news will be all around the town by nightfall.'

He didn't doubt it but the formality of an an-

nouncement in *The Times* was not something
he intended to omit.

'I have to go. If you want a lift—'

'No. Thank you. I'll walk home. Introduce
Nancie to the ducks.'

'Right. Well, I'll see you later. I don't know
what time.'

She looked up at him, taking his breath away
with an unexpected smile. 'If you're late, I'll do
the wifely thing and put your dinner in the
oven.'

Dinner? He'd never, in all his life, gone home
to a cooked dinner. His mother's best effort was
a pizza. Then it had been university and living on
his own. Since his success, he was expected to
be the provider of dinner in return for breakfast.
At whatever restaurant was the place to be seen.

'What time do you eat?' he asked.

'It's a moveable feast. Seven?'

'I should be done by then.'

'Well, in case you're held up…' she opened
the soft leather bag she carried over her
shoulder, found a key fob '…you'd better have
a key.' She sorted through a heavy bunch and,
after hesitating over which one to give him, she
unhooked a businesslike job and handed it to
him. 'That's for the front door. I'll sort you out
a full set before tomorrow.'

# CHAPTER SEVEN

JAKE, being the perfect PA, didn't raise an eyebrow when Adam informed him that he was about to get married.

He simply listened, made a few notes and an hour later returned with a list of available wedding venues for May to choose from, a guest list for lunch and the reception and a draft of the announcement to go into *The Times*.

He scanned it, nodded. 'I mean to warn you that May will be calling with a list of things she needs for Nancie.'

'I've already spoken to Miss Coleridge. I needed her full name for the announcement in *The Times* and, since you were on a conference call—'

'Yes, yes,' Adam said with an unexpected jab of irritation as he realised, looking at the draft, that he hadn't known that her name was not May but Mary. Pretty obvious now that he thought about it. It was a month name and her birthday was in December…

'Show me the list.'

'It's a bit basic,' he said. 'I suggested a few things, but she insisted that was all she needed.'

She probably had most things, he realised. Like the antique cradle. When a family lived in the same house for generations nothing got thrown away. But she would have nothing new. Bright. Modern.

He'd made a mess of the clothes thing, but she wouldn't be able to refuse his insistence that she indulge Nancie. He wanted her to enjoy spending his money.

He wanted to make his mark on the house. Leave his imprint. Become part of the fabric of the house. Part of Coleridge history.

'Forget this, Jake,' he said. 'Call that big baby store on the business park and invite the manager to fulfil any new mother's wildest fantasies. Clothes, toys, nursery furniture. Just be sure that it's all delivered to Coleridge House before five o'clock today.'

Jake glanced at his watch. 'It's going to be tight.'

'I'm sure they'll find a way.'

'No doubt. I've ordered a credit card for May. It will be here on Monday. I'll deliver it myself.'

'A first class stamp will be quite sufficient,' he said. 'She isn't desperate.' Persuading her to use it would be the problem.

'It's no trouble. I have to pass Coleridge House on my way home and I can make sure that she's got everything she needs at the same time. I received the distinct impression, when I spoke to her, that Miss Coleridge isn't the kind of woman who would find it easy to pick up a phone to ask.'

'You're right. In fact, you might do worse than touch base with her housekeeper, Mrs Robson.'

When he'd gone, Adam sat back in his chair and turned to look out across the park to where the chimneys of Coleridge House were visible above the bare branches of the trees.

One phone call and Jake had got May's character down perfectly. She had never asked for anything. Never would. If Saffy hadn't sent him, reluctantly, in her direction today the first he—anyone—would have known about her loss would have been the 'For Sale' boards going up at the house.

Not that it would have been a totally lost opportunity. He could have bought it, moved his company in. Paved over the site of his humiliation and used it as a car park.

But that would not have been nearly as satisfying as the thought that tonight he'd sleep in James Coleridge's four-poster bed. And that in less than three weeks his granddaughter would become Mrs Mary Louise Wavell.

It took May a few moments to find her phone in the muddle of bags and boxes that had been piled up in her sitting room.

'Yes?' she snapped.

'You sound a little breathless, Mouse.'

'Adam…' She hadn't expected him to ring and if she hadn't been breathless from unpacking the cot, the sound of his voice would have been enough.

'I hope you're not overdoing it.'

'Overdoing it?' she repeated, propping the end of the cot with one hand, blowing hair out of her face. 'Of course I'm overdoing it. What on earth were you *thinking*?'

'I have no idea. Why don't you help me out?'

'I asked for a cot. One cot, a changing mat, a few extra clothes and some nappies. What I've got is an entire suite of nursery furniture. Cupboards, shelves, a changing trolley with drawers that does everything but actually change the baby for you and enough nappies, clothes, toys for an entire…' he waited while she hunted for the word '…*cuddle* of babies!'

'A cuddle?' he repeated, clearly struggling not to laugh out loud. 'Is that really the collective noun for babies?'

'Cuddle, bawl, puke, poo. Take your pick.'

'Whoa! Too much information,' he said, not bothering to hide his amusement.

'I hate to be ungracious, Adam, but, as you can probably tell, I'm a bit busy.'

'You can leave the furniture moving until I get there.'

'Moving?' She looked around at the mess of packaging and furniture parts. 'This isn't just moving furniture, this is a construction project!'

'Are you telling me that it arrived flat-pack?'

'Apparently everything does these days.' She looked helplessly at the pile of shiny chrome bits that had come with the cot. 'And I have to tell you that I can't tell a flange bracket from a woggle nut.'

'Tricky things, woggle nuts,' he agreed.

'It's not funny,' she declared, but in her mind she saw that rare smile, the whole knee-wobbling, breath-stealing package… 'Is Jake there? He sounds a handy sort of man. Tell him if he can put this cot together I'll lavish him with Robbie's spiced beef casserole, lemon drizzle cake and throw in a slab of treacle toffee for good measure.'

'Jake is busy. I'm afraid you're going to have to manage with me.'

'You?'

'Do try to curb your enthusiasm, May.'

'No… It's just… I'm sorry, I didn't mean to sound ungrateful but I thought the whole point of this exercise was that you were *busy*. Up to your eyes in work. You couldn't even spare half an hour for lunch. Why are you calling, anyway?'

'I was going through the to-do list that Jake compiled for me and had just got to the rings.'

She lost control of the foot board of the cot, which she had been holding when the phone rang, and it fell against the arm of the sofa.

'May?' His voice was urgent in her ear.

'It's okay. Just a little flange bracket trouble.'

'Is there such a thing as a *little* flange bracket trouble?' he said, and she laughed.

Laughed!

How long was it since she'd done that?

'You've done this before,' she said.

'Once or twice,' he admitted. 'Actually, I called about the rings.'

'Rings?' The word brought her up with a jolt. 'No. I've got nuts, bolts, brackets,' she said, doing her best to turn it into a joke. Keep laughing. 'I can't see—'

'The wedding rings. I thought you'd want to choose your own.'

'No,' she said quickly.

'You're sure?'

'I meant no, you don't have to worry about it. I'll wear my grandmother's wedding ring.'

It was the ring she'd been going to wear when she married Michael Linton and took her place in society as a modern version of her grandmother. The perfect wife, hostess and, in the fullness of time, mother.

'I doubt your grandfather would be happy with the thought of me putting a ring he bought on your finger.'

'Probably not.' But it had to be better than picking out something that was supposed to be bought with love, 'forever' in your heart and pretending it was for real, she thought, the laughter leaking out of her like water from a broken pipe. 'But it's what I want.'

'Well, if you're sure.'

She was sure. Besides, if he bought her some fancy ring, she'd have to give it back but she could wear her grandmother's ring for ever.

'I am. Is that it?'

'No. There's a whole list of things you have to decide on, but they can wait until I've sorted out your flange thingies from your whatnots. Give me half an hour and I'll be with you.'

'It has to go there,' May declared, jabbing at the diagram with a neat unpolished nail.

They were kneeling on the floor of May's small sitting room, bickering over the diagram of a cupboard that did not in any way appear to match the pieces that had come out of the box.

He'd never noticed how small her hands were until he'd held them in his, soaping away the dirt of the park, applying antiseptic to her scratches. In the last couple of hours, as she'd held the pieces in place while he'd screwed the nursery furniture together—in between keeping Nancie happy—he'd found it increasingly difficult to concentrate on anything else.

'There is nowhere else,' she insisted.

Small, soft, pretty little hands that had been made to wear beautiful rings.

'I'd agree with you, except that you're looking at the diagram the wrong way up.'

'Am I? Oh, Lord, I do believe you're

right.' She pulled off her glasses and sat back on her heels. 'That's it, then. I'm all out of ideas. Maybe it's time to admit defeat and call Jake.'

He looked up, about to declare that there wasn't anything that Jake could do that he couldn't do better, but the words died on his lips.

May had taken out her frustration on her hair and she looked as if she'd been dragged back, front and sideways through a very dense hedge. She was flushed with the effort of wrestling together the cot, then the changing trolley with its nest of drawers. None of which, despite the photographs of a smiling woman doing it single-handed on the instructions, she could ever have managed on her own.

But her butterscotch eyes were sparkling, lighting up her face and it was plain that, despite the frustration, the effort involved, she was actually enjoying herself.

And discovered, rather to his surprise, that he was too. Which, since it couldn't possibly have anything to do with constructing flat-pack furniture, had to be all about who he was constructing it with.

'You think I'm going to allow myself to be defeated by a pile of timber?' he declared.

'What an incredibly male response,' May said with a giggle that sucked the years away.

In all the frozen years he'd never forgotten that sound. Her smile. How it could warm you, lift your heart, make everything bad go away. No other woman had ever been able to do that to him. Maybe that was why he'd never been able to forgive her, move on. As far as the world was concerned, he'd made it; inside, he was still the kid who wasn't good enough...

'Anyone would think I was questioning your masculinity.'

'Aren't you?' He'd meant it as a joke but the words came out more fiercely than he'd intended, provoking a flicker of something darker in May's eyes that sent a finger of heat driving through his body and, without thinking, he captured her head and brought his mouth down on hers in a crushing kiss. No finesse, no teasing sweetness, no seduction. It was all about possession, marking her, making her pay for all the years when he couldn't get the touch of her hands on him, her mouth, out of his head.

He wanted her now, here, on the floor.

It was only Nancie's increasingly loud cries that brought him to his senses and, as he let her go, May stumbled to her feet, picked the baby up, laid her against her shoulder, shushing her gently to soothe her, or maybe soothe herself.

'I have to feed her,' she said, not looking at him as she made her escape.

Every cell in his body was urging him to go after her, tell her how he felt, what she did to him, but if he'd learned anything it was control and he stayed where he was until he was breathing normally.

Then he turned back to the cupboard, reread the instructions. Without the distraction of her hair, her hands, her soft and very kissable mouth just inches from his own, everything suddenly became much clearer.

May leaned against the landing wall, her legs too weak to carry her down the stairs, her hand pressed over her mouth. Whether to cool it or hold in the scalding heat of Adam's mouth on hers she could not have said.

It had been nothing like the kiss they'd shared that morning. That had been warm, tender, stirring up sweet desires.

This had been something else. Darker, taking not giving, and the shock of it had gone through her like lightning. She'd been unable to think, unable to move, knowing only that as his tongue had taken possession of her mouth she wanted more, wanted everything he had to give her. The roughness of his cheek, not just against her face, but against her breast. Wanted things from him that she had never even thought about doing with the man she had been engaged to.

She had been so aware of him all afternoon.

Adam had arrived, taken off his jacket and tie, rolled up his sleeves and her concentration had gone west as they'd worked together to construct the nursery furniture.

All she could think about was the way his dark hair slid across his forehead as he leaned into a screwdriver he'd had the foresight to bring with him.

The shiver of pleasure that rippled through her when his arm brushed against hers.

A ridiculous, melting softness as he'd looked up and smiled at her when something slotted together with a satisfying clunk.

When he'd grabbed her hand as she wobbled on her knees, held her until she'd regained her balance.

She'd just about managed to hold it together while they'd put together the cot. The changing trolley had been more of a challenge.

There were more pieces, drawers, and they'd had to work more closely together, touching close, hand-to-hand close. She'd had the dizzying sensation that if she turned to look at him he would kiss her, would do more than kiss her. Would make all her dreams come true.

By the time they'd got to the cupboard her concentration had gone to pieces and she was more hindrance than help. She had been looking at the plan, but her entire focus had been on Adam. His powerful forearms. His chin, darkened with a five o'clock shadow. The hollows in his neck.

She'd felt as if she was losing her mind. That if she didn't escape, she'd do something really stupid. Instead, she'd said something really stupid and her dreams had evaporated in the heat of a kiss that had nothing to do with the boy she'd loved, everything to do with the man he'd become.

Adam was tightening the last screw when, Nancie fed and in need of changing, she could not put off returning to the nursery a moment longer.

'You did it!' she exclaimed brightly, forcing herself to smile. The reverse of the last years when she'd had to force herself not to smile every time she saw Adam.

'Once I'd got the woggle nuts lined up in a

row,' he assured her as he tested the doors to make sure they were hanging properly, 'it was a piece of cake.'

'Would that be a hint?'

'Not for cake but something smells good,' he said, positioning a mini camera on top of the cupboard, angling it down onto the changing mat, where Nancie was wriggling like a little fish as she tried to undress her. 'This really is the business.'

'Amazing.' She leaned across to look at the monitor at the same time as Adam. Pulled away quickly as her shoulder brushed against his arm. 'She's amazing.'

They were both amazing, Adam thought.

Throughout the afternoon he'd seen a different side to the shy, clumsy girl he'd known, the dull woman she'd become. He'd struggled to see her running a business that involved opening her home to strangers, putting them at their ease, feeding them.

'You'd be better off on your own,' she'd said, and he was about to agree when he'd realised that her hand, closed tightly over a runaway nut, was shaking.

He'd wrapped his hand over hers, intending only to hold it still while he recovered the nut, but her tremor transferred itself to him, rippling through him like a tiny shock wave, throwing him off balance, and he'd said, 'Stay.'

He'd been off balance ever since.

Totally lost it with a kiss that he could still see on her bee stung lips.

'What shall I do with all this packaging?'

'There's a store room in the stables,' she said as she eased Nancie out of her pink tights. 'Look, gorgeous, you're on television.'

Then, as she realised what she'd said, she glanced up at him and he saw her throat move as she swallowed, an almost pleading look in her eyes. Pleading for what? Forgiveness? Obliteration of memory?

'It's where we hold the craft classes,' she said quickly. 'They're always desperate for cardboard.'

Nancie made a grab for her hair and May, laughing, caught her tiny hand and kissed the fingers. As Adam watched her, the memories bubbled up. He'd kissed May's fingers just that way. Kissed her lovely neck, the soft mound of her young breast.

A guttural sound escaped him and she turned, tucking the loose strand of hair behind her ear.

'Saffy is so lucky,' she said.

'Lucky?'

'To have Nancie…'

And as he looked into her eyes, he realised that the smile that came so easily to her lips was tinged with sadness.

Nearly thirty, she had no husband, no children, no life. Not his fault, he told himself. He'd come for her but she wanted this more than him. Well, he would give it to her. And she would finish what she'd started. Maybe in the hayloft…

'Is there any news of her? Saffy?' she prompted.

'Not yet,' he said abruptly, gathering a pile of flattened boxes and carrying them down into the yard, glad of the chill night air to clear his head.

It was pitch dark but the path and stable yard were well lit. There had been no horses here in a generation, no carriage for more than a century, but nothing much, on the outside, had changed.

The stable and carriage house doors shone with glossy black paint, wooden tubs containing winter heathers and pansies gave the area a rustic charm. A black and white cat mewed, rubbed against his legs.

There was even the smell of animals and a snort from the low range of buildings on the far side of the yard had him swinging round to where a donkey had pushed his head through the half door. A goat, standing on her hind legs, joined him.

The class had finished a while back. He'd heard cars starting up, cheerful voices shouting their goodbyes to one another as he'd finished the cupboard. But the lights were on and a girl, busy sweeping the floor, looked up as he entered and came to an abrupt halt.

'Miss Coleridge is in the house,' she said.

'I know. She asked me to bring this out here.'

'Oh, right. You want the storeroom. It's down at the bottom. The door on the left.'

He'd expected to find the interior much as it had always been, still stables but cleaned up, with just enough done to provide usable work space.

He couldn't have been more wrong.

Serious money had been spent gutting the building, leaving a large, impressively light and airy workspace.

The loft had gone, skylights installed and the wooden rafters now carried state-of-the-art spotlights that lit every corner.

A solid wooden floor had been laid, there were deep butler's sinks along one wall, with wooden drainers and stacking work tables and chairs made the space infinitely adaptable. And, at the far end, the old tack room where they'd made coffee, eaten cake and shortbread, had been converted into bathroom facilities with disabled access. Everything had been finished to the highest standard.

Fooled by those useless labels, he'd assumed this was just a cosy little business that she'd stumbled into, but it was obvious that she'd been thinking ahead. Understood that there would be a time when Coleridge House would have to support itself, support her, if she was going to keep it.

He thought he knew her, understood her. That he was in control.

Wrong, wrong, wrong…

May settled Nancie, not looking up when Adam returned to collect the remainder of the packaging. Then, having angled the monitor camera on to Nancie in the cot, she went downstairs and checked the kitten, who she'd introduced to the kitchen cats, a couple of old sweethearts who were well used to stray babies—rabbits, puppies, even chicks, keeping them all clean and warm.

They'd washed him, enveloped him in their warmth and, as she stroked them, they licked at her, too. As if she was just another stray.

There was a draught as the back door opened and she turned as Adam came in.

'All done? Did you manage to cram everything in?'

'No problem. That's an impressive set-up you've got out there.'

She quirked an eyebrow at him. 'Did you imagine we just flung down some hay to cover the cobbles?'

'I didn't think about it at all,' he lied, looking around the kitchen rather than meet her eyes. Looking at the animals curled up in the basket by the Aga. The cats in the armchair, licking at the kitten. 'But now I'm wondering about the other side of your business. How you cater for your guests. Make your sweets. This is a very picturesque country kitchen, but I can't see it getting through a rigorous trading standards inspection for a licence to feed the paying public.'

'Oh? And what do you know about catering standards?'

'Amongst other things, my company imports the finest coffee from across the globe. It wouldn't look good if the staff had to go to a chain to buy their morning latte.'

'I suppose not.'

May knew, on one level, that Adam was

hugely successful, but it was difficult to equate the boy who'd nicknamed her Danger Mouse, who'd always been around when she'd got into trouble, who'd stood outside this house, soaked and freezing, as he'd defied her grandfather, shouting out for her to go with him, as a serious, responsible business-man with the livelihood of hundreds, maybe thousands of people in his hands.

'How do you do it?' he asked, opening the fridge.

'Well, I had two choices,' she said, dragging herself out of the past. It was now that mattered. Today. 'What are you looking for?'

'A beer.' He pulled a face. 'My mistake.'

'You'll find beer in the pantry.' And, enjoying his surprise, 'Not all our workshops are women only affairs.'

'I'll replace it.'

'There's no need.'

'I'm not a guest.' And, before she could con-tradict him, he said, 'Can I get you anything?'

She shook her head. 'I'm babysitting.'

'Right.' He fetched a can from the pantry, popped it open and leaned back against the sink, watching as she donned oven gloves and took the casserole out of the oven. 'Two choices?'

'I could have torn this kitchen out, replaced

it with something space age in stainless steel and abolished the furred and feathered brigade to the mud room, but that would have felt like ripping the heart out of the house.'

'Not an option.'

'No,' she said and, glad that he understood, she managed a smile. 'It was actually cheaper to install a second kitchen in the butler's parlour.'

Adam choked as his beer went down the wrong way. 'The butler's parlour?'

'Don't worry. It's been a long time since Coleridge House has warranted a butler,' she said and the tension, drum tight since he'd kissed her, dissipated as the smile she'd been straining for finally broke through.

'Well, that's a relief. It must still have been a major expense. Is it justified?'

'The bank seemed to think so.'

'The bank? You borrowed from the bank?'

May heard the disbelief in his voice.

'I suppose I could have borrowed from Grandpa,' she said. She'd had an enduring power of attorney. Paid the bills. Kept the accounts. Kept the house together. No one could have, would have stopped her. On the contrary. Grandpa's accountant had warned her that big old houses like this were a money sink and she needed to think about the future. Clearly, he hadn't known about the inheritance clause, either.

'Why didn't you?'

'It was my business. My responsibility.' Hers… Then, as she saw his horrified expression, 'You don't have to worry, Adam. I don't make a fortune, but I have enough bookings to meet my obligations. You won't have to bail me out.'

'What? No… I was just realising how much trouble you would have been in if I hadn't come along this morning. If I hadn't needed you so badly that I badgered you until you were forced to explain. You would have lost the lot.'

He wasn't thinking about himself? The realisation that, as her husband, he'd be responsible for her debts.

He was just thinking about her.

'It wouldn't have been the end of the world,' she said, putting the casserole on the table, the dish of potatoes baked in their jackets. Almost, but not quite. 'Once the contents of the house were sold, I'd have been able to pay them back.'

He caught her wrist. 'Promise me one thing, May,' he said fiercely. 'That, the minute you're married, you instruct Jennings to do whatever if takes to break that entailment.'

'It's number one on my list,' she assured him.

Not that there seemed much likelihood of her ever having a child of her own to put in this position. She hadn't thought much about that particular emptiness in her life until today when Nancie had clung to her, smiled at her.

'I'll have to make a new will, anyway. Not that there's anyone to leave the house to. I'm the last of the Coleridges.'

'No cousins?'

'Only three or four times removed.'

'They're still family and there's nothing like the scent of an inheritance to bring long lost relatives out of the woodwork.'

'Not to any purpose, in this case. I'll leave it to a charity. At least that way I won't feel as if I've cheated.'

'Cheated?'

'By marrying you just to keep the house.'

'You're not cheating anyone, May. If your grandfather hadn't had a stroke you would have been married to Michael Linton.'

'Maybe.' She'd been so very young and he'd been so assured, so charming. So *safe*.

That was the one thing she could never say

about Adam. Whether he was rescuing her from disaster, mucking out a rabbit cage or cleaning her wounds, as he had today, apparently oblivious to the fact that she was half naked, she had never felt safe with him.

Whenever she was near him she seemed to lose control of not just her breathing, but her ability to hold anything fragile, the carefully built protective barrier she'd erected around herself at school. One look and it crumbled.

She didn't feel safe, but she did feel fizzingly alive and, while he might not have noticed the effect he had on her, his sister hadn't missed it.

'You had doubts?' Adam asked, picking up on her lack of certainty.

'Not then.' At the time, marriage to Michael Linton had offered an escape. From her grandfather. From Maybridge. From the possibility of meeting Adam Wavell.

'And now?'

'Looking back, the whole thing seems like something out of a Jane Austen novel.'

'While your grandfather's will is more like something out of one of the more depressing novels of George Eliot.'

'Yes, well, whatever happens to the house in the future, it won't happen by default because

I did nothing,' she assured him as she gestured for him to sit down. 'Actually, I'm sure the infallible Jake has it on his list but, just in case he'd missed it, you'll have to make a new will, too.'

'This is cheery.'

'But essential,' she said as she ladled meat onto a plate. 'Marriage nullifies all previous wills, which means that, should you fall under a bus—'

'Have you ever heard of someone falling under a bus?' he asked.

'Should you fall under a bus, the major part of your assets will come to me by default,' she persisted, determined to make her point. 'Not that I'd keep it,' she assured him. 'Obviously.'

'Why obviously?'

'You have a family.'

'There's always a downside,' he said, taking the plate. 'You'd get the assets, but you also get the bad debts.'

'Adam!'

'Would you entrust an international company to either my sister or my mother?' he demanded.

'Well, obviously—'

'They'd sell out to the first person who offered them hard cash, whereas you, with your highly developed sense of duty and the Coleridge imperative to hold tight to what they have, would be a worthy steward of my estate.'

She assumed he was teasing—although that remark about the Coleridges' firm grasp on their property had been barbed—but, as she offered him the dish of potatoes, his gaze was intent, his purpose serious.

'You'll get married, have children of your own,' she protested.

'I'm marrying you, Mary Louise. For better or worse.'

'That's a two-way promise,' May said, equally intent.

Adam held the look for long seconds, as if testing her sincerity, before he nodded and took the dish.

'Where's Robbie?' he asked, changing the subject. 'Isn't she eating with us?'

'It's quiz night at the pub,' she said, serving herself. Not that she had much appetite. 'She offered to give it a miss, but it's semi-final night and her team are red-hot.'

'She didn't trust me alone with you? What is she going to do? Sleep across your door?'

'Does she need to?' she asked flippantly, but as she looked up their eyes met across the table and the air hummed once more with a tension that stretched back through the years.

All the pain, the shame she'd masked from him each time, despite every attempt to avoid one another, they'd found themselves face to face in public. Both of them achingly polite, while he'd looked at her as if breathing the same air hurt him.

# CHAPTER EIGHT

ADAM'S hand was shaking slightly as he picked up his fork. Robbie was no fool, he thought. She didn't trust him further than she could throw him and with good reason.

'Help yourself to another beer,' May prompted. 'Whatever you want.'

'I'm good, thanks,' he said, then, spearing a piece of carrot, 'I took a couple of carrots from the sack in the mud room and gave them to the donkey and his mate, by the way,' he said in a desperate attempt to bring things back to the mundane. 'I hope I didn't mess up their diet.'

'Everyone gets mugged by Jack and Dolly,' she said, clearly glad to follow his lead away from dangerous territory. 'They're a double act. Inseparable, couldn't be parted. And you're looking at the original mug. The one who took them both in.'

'I'll bet they didn't have to work anywhere

near as hard as I did,' he said. 'One pitiful bleat from Dolly and I'll bet you were putty in their hooves.'

'Under normal circumstances I'd have been putty in yours,' she replied. And then she blushed. 'At least Jack keeps the paddock grazed.'

'Not Dolly?'

'She prefers bramble shoots, with a side snack of roses when no one's looking.' Maybe it was the mention of roses, but she leapt up. 'Nancie's awake,' she said, pushing back her chair, grabbing the monitor from the table. 'Help yourself,' she said, waving at the table. 'I've had enough.'

'Enough' had been little more than a mouthful, but she dashed from the room and he didn't try to stop her. Not because he believed the baby needed instant attention, but because suddenly every word seemed loaded.

He finished eating, cleared both their plates and stacked them in the dishwasher. Covered the food. Filled the coffee maker and set it to drip. Then, when May still hadn't appeared, he went upstairs to find her.

She was sitting in the dark, watching Nancie as she slept. The light from the landing touched her cheeks, made a halo of her hair.

'May?' he said softly.

She looked up. 'Adam. I'm sorry. I'm neglecting you,' she said, getting up and, after a last look at Nancie, joining him. 'There's leftover crème brulée in the fridge…'

'What happened to the lemon drizzle cake?'

'The Christmas course ladies finished it when they had tea. I'm sorry. It was always your favourite.'

'Was it? I don't remember,' he lied. 'I'm making coffee.'

'Well, good. You must make yourself at home. Have whatever you want. You'll find the drinks cupboard in the library.'

'Library?' He managed a teasing note. 'First a butler, now a library.'

'It's not a very big library. Do you want a tour of the house? I should probably introduce you to the ancestors.'

'If you're sure they won't all turn in their graves.'

She looked up at him and for a moment he thought she was going to say something. But after a pause she turned and led the way down a fine staircase lined with portraits, naming each of them as she passed without looking. But then, near the bottom, she stopped by a fine portrait of a young woman.

'This is a Romney portrait of Jane Coleridge,' she said. 'She's the woman who Henry Coleridge had his arm twisted to marry. The cause of all the bother.'

'You have the look of her,' he said. The same colouring, the same soft curves, striking amber eyes.

'Well, that would explain it,' she said, moving on, showing him the rest of the house. The grand drawing and dining rooms, filled with the kind of furniture and paintings that would have the experts on one of those antiques television programmes drooling. There was a small sitting room, a room for a lady. And then there was the library with its vast desk, worn leather armchairs.

She crossed to the desk and opened a drawer.

'These were Grandpa's,' she said, handing a large bunch of keys to him.

'What are they all?' he asked.

She took them from him and ran through them. 'Front, back, cellar—although we don't keep it locked these days. The gate to the park.' There were half a dozen more before she said, 'This one's for the safe.'

'The safe?'

She opened a false panel in one of the bookshelves to display a very old safe.

'Family documents, my grandmother's jew-ellery. Not much of that. She left it to my mother, and she sold most of it to fund Third World health care.'

Which was ironic, he thought, considering how she'd died. 'Her wedding ring? Can I see it?'

She shrugged. 'Of course.' She took the keys from him, opened the safe, handed him a small velvet pouch.

He wasn't sure what he'd expected. From her insistence that she wear it, he'd imagined some-thing special, something worthy of a Coleridge, but what he tipped into his palm was a simple old-fashioned band of gold without so much as a date or initials inscribed on the inside.

It was a ring made to take the knocks of a lifetime. In the days when this had been forged, people didn't run to the divorce courts at the first hint of trouble but stuck to the vows they'd sworn over it.

'It's not fancy,' she said, as if she felt the need to apologise.

'It's your choice, May,' he said, wishing he'd insisted on buying a ring of his own. But he'd obliterate its plainness with the flash of the ring he'd buy to lie alongside it. He kept that to himself, however, afraid she'd insist on wearing her grandmother's engagement ring, too. Always assuming her mother hadn't sold that. He didn't ask, just removed the key to the back door and the park gate and added them to his own key ring, returning the rest to the drawer. 'Can I borrow it? So that I make sure my own ring matches it.'

There was just the barest hesitation before she said, 'Of course.'

'I'll take good care of it,' he assured her. 'Shall we have that coffee now? We have to make a decision on where we're going to hold the wedding.'

'There's a fire in the morning room. I'll bring it through.'

May took a moment as she laid the tray with cups, shortbread, half a dozen of the fudge balls she'd created for the Christmas market. Anything to delay the moment when she had to join him.

While she was with Adam, she was constantly distracted by memories, tripped up by innocent words that ripped through her.

Roses…

She'd never been able to see red roses without remembering Adam standing back from the door, shouting her name up at her window, oblivious to the approaching danger.

The bunch of red roses in his fist had

exploded as her grandfather had turned the hose on him, hitting him in the chest and, for a terrible moment, she had thought it was his blood.

She'd tried to scream but the sound would not come through the thick, throat-closing fear that he was dead. It was only later, much later, when it was dark and everyone was asleep, that she'd crept outside to gather up the petals by the light of her torch.

Adam stretched out in front of the fire. His apartment was the height of luxury, everything simple, clean, uncluttered. It had been a dream back in the days when he'd been living in a cramped flat with his mother and his sister, the complete antithesis of this room, with its furniture in what could only be described as 'country house' condition. In other words, worn by centuries of use.

But the room had a relaxed, confident air. It invited you to sit, make yourself comfortable because, after all, if you'd made it this far into the inner sanctum, you were a welcome visitor.

He leapt up as May appeared with a tray, but she shook her head and said, 'I can manage,' as she put it on the sofa table. 'Is it still black, no sugar?'

'Yes...' She remembered?

'Would you like a piece of Robbie's short-bread?' She placed the cup beside him. Offered him the plate. 'Or a piece of fudge?'

'These are the sweets you make?'

'This is a seasonal special. Christmas Snowball Surprise. White chocolate and cranberry fudge rolled in flaked coconut.'

He took one, bit into it and his mouth filled with an explosion of flavour, heat. 'You forgot to mention the rum.'

'That's the surprise,' she said, but her smile was weary and he saw, with something of a shock, that there were dark smudges beneath her eyes.

'Are you all right, May?' he asked when she didn't move, didn't pour herself a cup.

She eased her shoulder. 'I'm a bit tired. I think the fall has finally caught up with me.'

'Are you in pain?' he asked, crossing to her, running his hands lightly over her shoulder and she winced. 'You should have gone to Casualty. Had an X-ray.'

'It's just a strain,' she assured him. 'I'll be fine after a soak.' Then, before he could protest, 'I'm afraid the television is rather old, but it works well enough. And don't worry about security. Robbie will check the locks, set the alarm when she comes in.'

'Where is her room?' he asked.

That, at least, raised a smile from May. 'Don't worry. You won't run into her in her curlers. She's got her own self-contained apartment on the ground floor.' She hesitated. 'You've got everything you need?'

He nodded, touched her cheek. 'Give me the monitor. I'll take care of Nancie if she wakes.'

'No. You've got a long flight tomorrow. You'll be in enough trouble with jet lag without having a sleepless night.'

'That's why I'm here,' he said.

'Is it?' She pushed a hand distractedly through her hair, as if she'd forgotten his promise to take the night shift. 'There's no need for that. You've done your hero stint with the furniture. What time are you leaving?'

'The car will pick me up at nine.'

'I hadn't realised you were leaving so early.' She looked at the coffee on the tray in front of her. 'Another half an hour—'

'There'll be plenty of time to sort out the wedding details over breakfast. Go and soak your aches.'


Adam couldn't sleep. He'd hung his suit in the great oak wardrobe made from trees that had been growing in the seventeenth century.

Tossed his dirty linen in the basket. Soaked a few aches of his own away in the huge roll-top Victorian bath, no doubt the latest thing when it had been installed. Having a fully grown woman fall on you left its mark and he'd found a bruise that mirrored May's aches on his own shoulder.

Then he'd stretched his naked limbs between the fine linen sheets on the four-poster bed, lay there, waiting for the sense of triumph to kick in. But, instead, all he could think about was May.

May not making a fuss, even though she'd clearly been in pain.

May trembling when he touched her. The hot, dark centre of her eyes in the moment before he'd kissed her. Wishing he was lying with his arms around her amongst the lace and frills, instead of the icy splendour of James Coleridge's bed.

The phone startled May out of sleep and she practically fell out of bed, grabbing for it before it woke Nancie.

'Hello?'

'May...'

'Saffy! Where are you? Are you safe?'

'I'm okay. Is Nancie all right?'

'She's fine. Gorgeous, but what about you? Where are you? Why didn't you come straight to me? You know I'd have helped you.'

'I wasn't sure. It's been a long time…'

'Come now. Adam's desperate with worry. Let me get him—'

'He's there?'

'He's staying with Nancie,' she said, keeping it simple. Explanations could wait. 'Saffy? Saffy, I've got plenty of room. You should be with Nancie,' she said quickly. But, before she'd finished, she was talking to herself.

She dialled one four seven one, to find out what number had called but the number had been withheld.

'There was no point in disturbing you,' May protested in response to his fury that she hadn't bothered to come and tell him that his sister had called in the night. 'There was nothing you could do.'

In contrast to the quiet of his own apartment first thing, the kitchen was bedlam. Nancie grizzling on May's shoulder, the chicken was squawking at the cats, the dog was barking and there was some schmaltzy Christmas song on the radio. He reached out and switched it off.

'That's not the point.'

He'd spent most of the night lying awake, then when he had fallen asleep, he'd been plagued by dreams he couldn't remember, overslept. He felt like a bear with a sore head and apparently it showed because she stuck a glass of orange juice in his hand.

'Here. Drink that.'

He swallowed it down and took a breath. The last thing he was going to tell her was that she wouldn't have been disturbing him. If she knew that he'd been lying awake, had heard the phone, she'd want to know why he hadn't come to check for himself.

He could hardly tell her that he'd lain in James Coleridge's hard bed imagining some private middle of the night exchange between her and Jeremy Davidson.

Imagining her reassuring him that her marriage would only be a paper thing. That in a year she'd be free. That if they were discreet…

Because that was what lovers did. Called one another in the small hours when they couldn't sleep.

It hadn't crossed his mind that it would be Saffy. He hadn't been thinking about her at all, he realised. Or his baby niece, crying for her mother.

May had accused him of thinking only about himself and she was right.

'Here, give her to me,' he said, taking the baby, holding her at arm's length. Shocked out of her misery, she stared back him, her cheeks flushed, her black curls in disarray, a beauty in the making. His sister's child.

There and then he made her a silent promise that, whatever happened, he would ensure that her life was very different from that of her mother. That she would always know she was cherished, loved.

She gave a little shudder.

'Don't fret, sweetheart,' he said, putting her against his shoulder. 'We'll find your mother, but in the meantime May is doing her best so you must be good for her while I'm away.' He looked down at her. 'Do we have a deal?'

'She'll dribble on your shirt,' May warned as she clutched at him, warm and trusting.

'It'll sponge off.' Then he frowned. 'How did Saffy get your number? It's unlisted.'

'I gave it to her once. I'm sorry. If she calls again…' She stopped as she caught sight of his grip, his laptop bag. 'Maybe it's as well that you won't be here. She hung up when I said I'd get you.'

It sounded like a reproach. And, if it was, he

deserved it. He'd worked so hard to distance himself from his family that now his sister was frightened to come to him.

'If she rings again, I'll do my best to persuade her to come here,' she said, then, as the doorbell rang, she glanced at the clock. 'Oh, Lord, that's your car and you haven't had any breakfast. I'm not usually this disorganised.'

'You don't usually have a baby to look after. Don't worry; I'll get something at the airport. If you need anything, you've got Jake's number. He'll know how to get in touch.' He kissed Nancie, surrendered her to May. 'We never did get around to deciding where to hold the wedding.'

'Does it matter?' she asked. Then, maybe realising that was less than gracious. 'Why don't we leave it to Jake? Let him surprise us.'

'If that's what you want.' He picked up his bags and she made to follow him, but he said, 'Don't come to the door. Stay in the warm.'

'You will be careful, Adam?'

'I'll watch out for low flying buses,' he said flippantly.

After he'd gone everything went quiet. The chicken, stupid thing, stopped tormenting the cats who, embarrassed, settled down to give each other and the kitten a thorough wash. The dog dropped his head back on his paws. Nancie sighed into her shoulder.

It was quiet, peaceful and if all the tension had gone out of the room, out of the house with Adam, he'd taken all the life with him, too.

Abandoning any thought of breakfast, she took Nancie upstairs. 'Okay, little one. This is going to be an adventure for both of us,' she said as she filled the baby bath, checked the temperature. 'Now, promise you'll be gentle with me.'

Ten minutes later, and considerably damper, she wrestled the baby into a pair of the sweetest pink velvet dungarees, then put her down in the cot and turned on the musical mobile.

She'd just finished mopping up the bathroom and changed into dry clothes when Robbie put her head around the door.

'Is the coast clear?'

'Sorry?'

'Has he gone?'

'Adam? Yes. Half an hour ago. And where were you hiding when I needed you? I've never bathed a baby in my life.'

'Then it's time you learned how. I was

feeding the livestock and just look what I found sharing Jack and Dolly's bed of hay.'

She opened the door wider to reveal a shivering and sorry looking woman, bundled up in a thick coat, headscarf and peering at her through heavy-framed glasses.

She looked vaguely familiar… The woman in the park yesterday. She took off the glasses and pushed the scarf back to reveal glossy black hair and said, 'Hello, May.'

'Saffy!'

'I'll go and make some tea,' Robbie said, leaving them to it.

'I saw you. Yesterday.'

'I didn't mean to stay. I was going back to France, to confront Michel. I just wanted to be sure that he was bringing Nancie to you but the idiot left her on the path where anyone could have taken her…'

'That's what I said. I shouted at him.'

'Did you?' That made her smile. 'You were always shouting at him. That's how I knew you liked him,' she said. 'It's why I twisted his arm, forced him to ask you to the disco that night. You'd been so kind…' Then, 'I just wanted you to have a good time.'

'I know. Nothing that happened was your fault.' It had been hers. If she'd been braver, instead of hiding her friendship with Adam, if her grandfather had been given a chance to get to know him… 'Have you been out there all this time?'

Saffy nodded and May frowned. 'But I don't understand. If you were going to see Michel…'

'I lost my nerve. I thought I might be arrested. That the police might be watching for me at Adam's office. In the end I wandered around for a bit. Bought some food. I stayed in the library for a long time. It was late night closing. I spent as long as I could eating a burger to stay in the warm.'

'Why on earth didn't you come to me?'

'Because I'm wanted by the authorities. I didn't want to get you into trouble.'

'Oh, for goodness' sake, come here,' she said, holding out her arms and gathered her in, holding her tight.

'I tried to sleep in the park, but it was so cold and I when I tried your gate it was unlocked and I thought, maybe you wouldn't mind but when you said Adam was here… He's going to be so angry with me…'

'Not half as angry as I'm going to be with him,' she said.

Then, standing back, 'Saffy Wavell, you stink of goat. Out of those things and into the bath with you before you go anywhere near your gorgeous little girl.'

Adam had just reached the airport when his phone rang. It was number withheld. 'Saffy?'

'Adam—'

'May…' He'd been trying to block out the scene in her kitchen. Noisy, alive, full of warmth and life, a total contrast to his own sterile existence.

He hadn't lacked for female company, but he dated women who were more interested in being seen in the gossip magazines than in anything more domestic than opening a bottle of champagne. The kind of women that his sister had always wanted to be. Tall, beautiful but, despite May's accusation, not always blonde. The colour of their hair hadn't mattered. The only unchangeable requirement was that they didn't remind him of her.

But the unexpected sound of her voice against his ear brought her so close that he felt as if she were touching him.

Just one day in her company and he was in danger of falling under the spell she'd cast on him when he was too young to protect himself from the kind of pain that brought. Forgetting what this was about.

'Is there a problem?' he asked, keeping his voice cool.

'No. I only wanted to let you know that Saffy's here with me. That she's safe.'

Relief flooded through him. Gratitude. He held it in. 'You were right, then. She wasn't far away. Can I talk to her? Or is she determined to avoid me?'

'She's in the bath right now and then I'm going to feed her and put her to bed.'

'I'll take that as a yes.' Well, what did he expect? He'd kept her at arm's length for years. She knew he didn't want her around, reminding people who he was. Where he came from. 'I'll see what I can do about damage limitation,' he said. 'I'll get Jake to organise a family lawyer.' He could do that for her. 'Try and sort out the mess.'

'It's the weekend. Nothing is going to get done until Monday. Let me talk to her, Adam. Find out what's happened. If it can't be straightened out, I'll call Jake myself.'

'Damn it—'

'Your priority is your trip, Adam. And there's no harm in trying honey before we go for the sting.'

'You should know.' But she was undoubtedly right. In cases like this, soft words might well prove more effective than going in heavy-footed. Something that he wouldn't have had to be told if this was a business negotiation. But his family had never been exactly good when it came to relationships. 'Try it your way first, but tell Saffy she has to stay with you until I get back.'

'Oh, that will work.'

'May! I'm concerned about her. Please ask her to stay with you until I get back.'

'Better.'

'What is this, family relationship counselling?' She didn't answer. 'Tell her that I'm not angry, okay. That I'm glad she's safe.'

'Wow.'

'Sarcasm does not become you, Miss Coleridge.'

'Forget she's your sister, Adam. Think of her as some frightened creature that you've found,' she said, using his own words to her when he'd been trying to persuade her to take Nancie. 'It's in pain and you've picked it up and brought it to me.'

'Damn it!' Was she mocking him? 'Do whatever you want,' he said and hung up.

Around him, the terminal buzzed with people wheeling heavy suitcases as they searched for their check-in desks. They were harassed but excited, looking forward to going on holiday or to stay with family.

He had a sister and a mother who he kept at arm's length. Out of sight, out of mind. He had no one. No one except May. He looked at the phone in his hand, scrolled down to her number.

'Adam?'

From the way she said his name, he suspected that she hadn't moved, but had been waiting for him to call back. And he couldn't make up his mind whether the feeling that ripped through him was anger that she could read him that well or an ache for something precious that had been trampled on, destroyed and was lost for ever.

'You can tell my sister,' he said, 'that, whatever happens, she can count on me. That I won't let her down. That I won't let anyone take Nancie away from her.'

'And that you won't shout at her?' she insisted, but now there was a smile in her voice.

'You're one tough negotiator, Danger Mouse. I don't suppose you'd reconsider that job offer?'

'As a nanny? I'm already redundant.'

'If you think that, you're in for a rude awakening. You now have two babies to take care of.' She didn't say a word and, after a moment, he laughed.

'Okay. I'll do my best, but you'll have to stand very close so that you can jab me with your elbow if I forget.'

'My elbow? My pleasure,' she said, but she was laughing too and he was glad he'd called.

'I have to go.'

'Yes. Please be careful, Adam.'

'May…'

'Yes?'

There was a long pause while a hundred possibilities rushed into his head.

'I'll call you in the morning. Maybe you'll have got some sense out of Saffy by then.'

# CHAPTER NINE

MAY surrendered her room to Saffy so that she was next to the nursery, loaning her a night-dress since she didn't seem to have any luggage. Sorting her out some clothes.

She slept most of the day, waking only when Nancie cried to be fed, the pair of them curled up in bed together.

She and Robbie worked quietly, stripping the bedrooms, getting them ready for the next group of guests who would be arriving the following Friday for a three-day garden design course. Then she took Nancie for a walk, sticking up posters with a picture of the kitten to the lamp posts in the park on her way in to Maybridge to pick up some underwear for Saffy who, despite having given birth recently, was still at least two sizes smaller than her.

Keeping herself busy, counting off the long hours until Adam's flight landed.

By the evening, Saffy had recovered. Robbie announced she was going to the cinema with a friend, leaving them to spend the evening catching up.

'I really love Michel,' she said after she'd given chapter and verse on how they'd met. How handsome he was. How romantic. 'It's his mother. She never liked me. She is such a snob. She's done everything she can to split us up and when that didn't work she dug up all that stuff from when I was a kid. Telling Michel that I was a danger to Nancie. That I couldn't be trusted.'

'Did he ask you about it?'

'Of course and I told him everything. Not that I nearly went to jail. That you saved me. But everything else,' she said.

'You can't hide, Saffy. Michel has rights, too. And you've put yourself in the wrong. He must be frantic with worry. Not just for the baby,' she added.

'I was frightened.'

'Of course you were. Do you think it would help if I spoke to him? Explained?'

It took a while to persuade her but, an hour later, a sobbing Saffy was talking to Michel, declaring how much she loved him.

\* \* \*

Adam finally rang at ten the following morning.

May, in an unfamiliar bed, had scarcely slept and jumped every time a phone rang. Once it had been Jake, to let her know that Adam had arrived safely just after ten the previous evening and to ask if she needed anything.

Mostly it was Michel calling Saffy to mutter sweet nothings. Clearly the thought of losing her had brought him to his senses.

'I tried earlier, but the line was engaged.'

'It's the French lover.'

'They're talking?'

'Endlessly. I've suggested he comes to stay but, from his reluctance, I suspect he hasn't told his parents that they're reunited. *Maman* sounds like a dragon.'

'There are worse things than an over-protective mother.'

'True.'

'I'm sorry, May. At least I had one.'

'Forget it. How was the flight?'

'Long. Boring. I'd seen the film. The food was terrible. Pretty much what you'd expect.'

'Well, you've got that Presidential dinner to look forward to.'

'Not until the end of the week.' He told her his itinerary; she gave him her mobile number.

'I have to go, May. I'll call you later. Take care.'

'Take care,' she repeated softly when he'd hung up, holding the phone to her breast.

He called every morning on the landline and talked, not just to her, but Saffy. Called every evening on her mobile when she was in bed. She updated him on the saga of the French lover and his mother. He told her what he'd been doing. Nothing of any importance. The words weren't important. It was hearing his voice.

May, up to her eyes preparing for the arrival of a houseful of guests as well as preparing a rush order of fudge, snatched the phone off the hook.

It was the tenth time it had rung that morning. The announcement of their forthcoming wedding had appeared in *The Times* that morning and she'd been inundated with calls. Only Adam hadn't rung.

'Yes!' She snapped as snatched up the phone.

'Whoa. Bad morning?' Adam said, making the whole hideous morning disappear with a word.

'You could say that.' But not now… 'I'm

just busy. Michel and his parents are arriving this afternoon.'

'His parents?'

'It was my idea to invite them. He's finally owned up to his *maman* that the relationship is back on and he wants to marry the mother of his child.'

'Not before time.'

'His mother still thinks that Saffy is a scheming little nobody with a bad history who's not fit to clean her boy's boots, let alone raise her grandchild. I'm going to change her mind. Prove to her that the Wavells have connections. Robbie and Saffy are polishing the family silver even as we speak.'

'You're giving them the full country house experience?'

'Absolutely. The best crystal, the Royal Doulton, Patsy in a white apron waiting table. I'm even going to wear my grandmother's engagement ring. Just to emphasize that Saffy is about to become my sister-in-law.'

There was a silence, a hum on the line and for a moment she thought she'd lost the connection.

'Your mother didn't sell that?'

'It's been in the family for ever. Jane Coleridge is wearing it in the Romney portrait, something I'll point out when I introduce them to the ancestors. Knock them out with centuries of tradition.'

'Just as long as they don't think that I'm too cheap to buy you one of your own.'

'Adam…'

'You've clearly got everything under control, there. I'll call later and see if you've managed to cement the entente cordiale.'

He rang off. May replaced the receiver rather more slowly. Clearly he'd been annoyed about the ring but there was no point in worrying about it.

If she was going to hit them with afternoon tea in the drawing room, install Michel's parents in state in the master bedroom and then serve the kind of traditional British food at dinner that would make a Frenchman weep with envy, she didn't have a minute to spare.

'Did I wake you?'

'No.' May had snatched up the phone at the first hint of a ring, on tenterhooks, not sure that he'd ring. 'I've just this minute fallen into bed. I wanted to lay up for breakfast in the conservatory before I turned in.'

'How did it go?'

'My face is aching from smiling,' she admitted. In truth, every muscle was throb-

bing, more from the tension than the effort.
Catering for charity lunches, receptions, had
been part of her life for as long as she could
remember but so much had been riding on this.
'But in a good cause. I think Michel's *maman*
is finally convinced that Saffy's youthful indis-
cretions were no more than high jinks.'

'If she believes that, you must have done
some fast talking.'

'The fact that Grandpa was a magistrate was
the final clincher, I think. And maybe the four-
poster bed.'

'You put them in *my* bed?'

'In the state bedroom,' she said, chuckling.
'I dug out a signed picture that the Prince of
Wales gave my great-grandfather in 1935 and
put it on the dressing table.'

'Nice touch.'

'And then, of course, we wheeled out the
family star.'

'Nancie?'

'Well, she played her part. But I was actually
talking about you. *Maman* had no idea that
Saffy's brother was the billionaire Chairman of
the company whose coffee she cannot, she
swears, live without.'

'Oh.'

'A double whammy. Class and cash. How

could she resist? Whether you'll thank me when you've got them as in-laws is another matter. Michel and his father are both gorgeous to look at, but totally under the matriarchal thumb.'

'Why, May?'

She'd been snuggling down under the duvet, warm, sleepy and this morning's misunderstanding forgotten, loving the chance to tell him about her triumph on his behalf.

'Why what?' she asked.

'Why would you go to so much trouble for Saffy?'

'I wasn't…' She wasn't doing it for Saffy; she was doing it for him.

'Don't be coy. You've pulled out all the stops for her. What is it between you two?'

'She never told you?'

'My little sister lived for secrets. It gave her a sense of power.'

'I was being bullied. When I first went to the High School. A gang of girls was taking my lunch money every day. They cornered me, took my bag and ripped pages out of my books until I gave them everything I had.'

'Why on earth didn't you tell someone? Your year head?'

'The poor little rich girl running to teacher? That would have made me popular.'

'Your grandfather, then?'

'His response would have been to say "I told you so" and take me away. He'd always wanted to send me to some fancy boarding school.'

'Maybe you should have gone. I never got the impression you enjoyed school much.'

'I didn't. But I couldn't bear to be sent away. I didn't have a mother or a father, Adam. All I had was my home. The animals.'

Coleridge House. And a cold man who probably hated having a love-child for a granddaughter.

'What made you go to Saffy?' he asked.

'I didn't. I don't know how she found out. But one day she was at the school gate waiting for me. Didn't say a word, just hooked her arm through mine as if she was my best friend. To be honest, I was terrified. I knew they'd all gone to the same primary school.'

'It was pretty rough,' he admitted.

'Well, I thought it was some new torture, but she appointed herself my minder. Walked me in and out of school, stayed with me at lunch and break times until they got the message. I was protected. Not to be touched.'

'That's why she knew you'd take Nancie? Because you owed her.'

'No. I paid my debts in full a long time ago...' She stopped, realising that, tired, she'd let slip more than she'd intended. 'Ancient history,' she said dismissively. 'Tell me about your day, mixing with the great and good. There was something about Samindera on the news this evening, but it was a bit of a madhouse and I didn't catch it.'

'Well, obviously the fact that I had dinner with the President would make the national news,' he said.

'There's nothing wrong?' she persisted.

She'd meant to check but, by the time she'd finished, she was fit for nothing but a warm bath and bed.

'His Excellency's hand was steady enough on his glass,' he assured her.

'Oh, well, what can possibly be wrong? Tell me what you ate,' she asked, then lay back as he told her about the formal dinner, the endless speeches, apparently knowing exactly what would make her laugh. Then, as her responses became slower, he said, 'Go to sleep, Mouse. Tell Saffy that I'll call her in the morning. And that I'll want to talk to Michel when I get home.'

'How long? Three days?' It had been nearly two weeks since she'd seen him, but it felt like a lifetime. 'Are you going to play the big brother and ask him his intentions?'

'I think he's already demonstrated his intentions beyond question. I just want to be sure that this is settled and it's not going to end in some painful tug of love scenario. Saffy might be an idiot, but she's my sister and no one is going to take her baby from her.'

'Actually, she was talking about going back with them tomorrow.'

'Show her my credit card. Ask her to go shopping with you. That should do it.'

'Too late. She's dragged me out shopping half a dozen times, although I'm not sure if it's my trousseau she's interested in or her own.'

'I hope you've been indulging yourself rather than her.'

'She's a very bad influence.' she admitted.

'That sounds promising.'

She'd been led utterly astray by his sister, and now possessed her own sexy 'result' shoes with ridiculously high heels. And had rather lost her head in an underwear shop. Not that she anticipated a result. Adam had been very quick to make it clear that this was a marriage in name only, but at least she'd *feel* sexy. And taller.

'Just make sure she knows that I want to see

her. And my mother. That I want to make things right.'

'No problem. I've invited them all to the wedding.'

There was a pause. Then he said, 'Let's elope.'

Adam sat on the edge of the bed, her giggle a warm memory as he imagined her slipping into the warm white nest of her bed, already more asleep than awake.

She wouldn't have let it slip that she'd already paid her debt to his sister if she'd been fully awake. Even then, she'd done her best to cover it, move on before he pressed her to tell him what she'd done. But he hadn't needed to. He knew.

Saffy had been caught with several tabs of E in her bag when the police had raided a club a few days before his and May's big night out had been brought to an abrupt end in the hayloft.

It wasn't the first time his sister had been in trouble. She'd been caught shoplifting as a minor, drinking underage, all the classic symptoms of attention seeking. But this had been serious.

She'd sworn she'd got the tabs for friends

who'd given her the money, but technically it was dealing and she was older. Culpable. But she'd shrugged when he'd found out, gone ballistic at her stupidity. Said it was sorted. And then, two weeks later, when she'd been summoned to the police station, she'd got away with no more than a formal caution. It would be on her record, but that was it.

That was what May had done. She'd talked to her grandfather, pleaded Saffy's case. And left them both wide open to the retribution of a hard old man.

What had he threatened?

What had she surrendered?

School. She'd never come back. The rumour was that she'd gone off to some posh boarding school and he'd allowed himself to believe it, hope that was what had happened, why she hadn't called him, written. Until he'd seen a photograph of her in the local newspaper, all dressed up at some charity do with her grandfather. Surrounded by Hooray Henrys in their DJs.

And him, he thought. She'd given up him to save Saffy from the minimum of three months in prison she'd have got at the Magistrates' Court. Much more if the Bench had decided the case was too serious for them and sent it up to the Crown Court. Which he didn't doubt would have happened.

No. That was wrong.

He dragged his hands through his hair. He was only seeing it from his point of view. How it had affected him.

Narrow, selfish…

May had surrendered herself. Given up every vestige of freedom for his sister. And maybe for him, too. He hadn't broken any laws, couldn't be got at that way. But he'd had an offer from Melchester University. He'd been encouraged to apply to Oxford, but he needed to be near enough to take care of his mother and sister. He had no doubt James Coleridge could have taken that from him.

Was that what May had been trying to tell him as she'd stood at her window shaking her head as he'd called her name?

Watching while the hose had been turned on him, smashing the roses he'd bought her in an explosion of red petals…

He groaned, slid from the bed to the floor as he remembered picking up the book of *Sonnets*. That was what had fallen from it. The petal from a red rose. He'd recognised it for what it was and brushed it off his fingers as if tainted…

Stupid, stupid…

If, that first time when their paths had crossed at some civic or charity reception, he'd forgotten his pride and, ignoring the frost, reached out and taken her hand, how long would she have held out?

He'd assumed that he'd caught her offside up that tree, but maybe that was all it would have taken. A smile, a, *Hello, Danger Mouse*, a touch to melt the icy mask.

But pride was all he'd had and he'd clung to it like ivy to a blasted oak.

He had to talk to her. Now. Tell her that he was sorry…

The phone dragged May back from the brink of sleep. She fumbled for it, picked it up. Couldn't see the number without her glasses. 'Hello?'

'May…'

'Adam? Is something wrong?'

'No… Yes…'

She heard a noise in the background. 'What was that? I heard something…'

'Thunder, lightning. Storms are ten a penny here. Are you awake?'

'Yes,' she said, pushing herself up. 'What is it? What's wrong?'

'Everything… Damn it, the lights have gone out.'

'Adam? Are you okay?'

'Yes. That happens, too. It doesn't matter…' He broke off and she could hear shouting, banging in the background.

'Adam!'

'Hold on, there's some idiot hammering on the door. Don't go away. This is important—'

Whatever else he was going to say was drowned out by the sound of an explosion. And then there was nothing.

---

Robbie found her sitting, white-faced, frozen in front of the television, watching rolling news of the attempted coup in Samindera. Pictures of the Presidential Palace, hotels blackened by fire, shattered by shells.

Reports of unknown casualties, missing foreigners. The fierce fighting that was making communication difficult.

She fetched a quilt to wrap around her, lit the fire, made tea. Didn't bother to say anything. She knew there was nothing she could say that would mean a thing.

Jake called on his way into the office, where the directors had called a crisis meeting, promising to let her know the minute he heard anything.

The French contingent finally emerged,

then, when they heard the news, they hugged both her and Saffy a lot, talking too fast for May's schoolgirl French but clearly intent on reassuring her that they were all family now.

Michel sat holding Saffy's hand, their baby on his lap, watching the news with her. And that made her feel even more alone.

She leapt up when the phone rang, but it was Freddie. He'd seen the forthcoming wedding announcement in *The Times*.

'There isn't going to be a wedding,' she said and hung up.

'May!' Saffy looked stricken. 'Don't say that. Adam's going to be all right.'

'No. He isn't.' She wrapped her arms around herself, staring at the same loop of film that was being rerun on the television screen, rocking herself the way she'd done as a child when her dog had died. 'He phoned last night. I was talking to him when…' She couldn't say it. Couldn't say the words. 'I heard an explosion. Right there, where he was. He's dead. I know he's dead and now he'll never know. I should have told him, Saffy.'

'What? But you said you were marrying him to save the house? That it was just a paper arrangement.' Then, as reality dawned, she said, 'Oh, drat. You're in love with him.'

May didn't answer, but collapsed against her and, as she opened her arms and gathered her in, shushed her, rubbing her back as if she were a baby.

When Adam regained consciousness he was lying face down in the dark. His ears were ringing, the air was thick with choking dust.

As he pushed himself up, leaning back against something he couldn't see, a nearby explosion briefly lit up the wreckage of his room and the only familiar thing was the cellphone he was clutching in his hand.

He'd been talking to May. He'd had something important to tell her but someone had been hammering on the door...

He put the phone to his ear. 'May?' He began to choke as the dust hit the back of his throat. 'May, are you still there?' No answer. He pressed the redial button with his thumb and the screen lit up, 'No signal'.

He swore. He had to find a phone that worked. He had to talk to May. Tell her that he was a fool. That he was sorry. That he loved her... Always had. Always would. And he began to crawl forward, using the light from his phone to find his way.

\* \* \*

May turned off the television. Pulled the plug out of the wall. It was the same thing over and over. Regional experts, former ambassadors, political pundits all saying nothing. Filling the airways of the twenty-four hour news channels day after day with the same lack of news told a thousand different ways.

That the fighting was fierce, that communications were limited to propaganda from government and rebel spokesmen. That casualties were high and that billionaire Adam Wavell, in Samindera to negotiate a major contract, was among those unaccounted for.

'Go out, Saffy,' she said. 'Take Nancie for a walk. Better still, go back to Paris and get on with your life. There's nothing either you or Michel can do here.'

She saw Robbie and Saffy exchange a look. 'May…'

'What?' she demanded. 'It's just another day.'

Not her wedding day. There was never going to be a wedding day.

That wasn't important.

She'd have surrendered the house, her business, everything she had just to know that Adam was safe.

She jumped as the phone rang but she didn't

214 SOS: CONVENIENT HUSBAND REQUIRED

run to pick it up. She'd stopped doing that after the first few days, when she'd still hoped against hope that she was wrong. That he had somehow survived.

Now, each time she heard it, she knew it was going to be the news that she dreaded. That they'd found his body amongst the wreckage of one of those fancy hotels in the archive footage they kept showing.

Robbie picked it up. 'Coleridge House.'

She frowned, straining to hear, and then, without a word, she put the phone into her hand.

'May…'

The line was crackling, breaking up, but it sounded like…

'May!'

'Adam…' She felt faint, dizzy and Robbie caught her, eased her back into the chair. 'Are you hurt? Where are you?'

'God knows. The hotel…rebels…city. I'm sorry…wedding…'

She could barely follow what he said, the line was so bad, but it didn't matter. Just hearing his voice was enough. He was alive!

'Forget the wedding. It doesn't matter. All that matters is that you're safe. Adam? Can you hear me? Adam?' She looked up. 'The line's gone dead,' she said. Then burst into tears.

# CHAPTER TEN

ADAM cursed the phone. He'd crawled through the blasted hotel liked the Pied Piper, using his phone to light the way, gathering the dazed and wounded, leaving them in the safety of the basement while he went to find water. First aid. Anything.

All he'd found were a group of rebels, who'd taken him with them as they'd retreated. He'd had visions of being held hostage for months, years, but as the government forces had closed in they'd abandoned him and melted away into the jungle.

He returned the useless cellphone to the commander of the government forces who'd finally caught up with them that morning.

'There's no signal.'

The man shrugged.

'How long before we get back to the capital?'

Another shrug. 'Tomorrow, maybe.'

'That will be too late.'

'There's no hurry. The airport is closed. The runway was shelled. There are no planes.'

'There must be some way out of here.'

The man raised an eyebrow and Adam took off his heavy stainless steel Rolex, placed it beside him on the seat of the truck. Added his own top of the range cellphone, the battery long since flat. Then he took out his wallet to reveal dollars, sterling currency and tossed that on the pile. The man said nothing and he emptied his pockets to show that it was all he had.

'What is that?' the man asked, nodding at the tiny velvet drawstring pouch containing May's wedding ring. He opened it, took out the ring and held it up.

'If I'm not there,' he said, 'you might as well shoot me now.'

The silence after hearing from Adam was almost unbearable. To know that he was alive, but have no idea where he was, whether he was hurt…

May called Jake, called the Foreign Office, called everyone she could think of but, while the government was back in control, the country was still in chaos.

'Come on. It's your birthday tomorrow. I'm

going to make a chocolate cake,' Saffy declared after breakfast.

'Can you cook?' She'd seen no evidence of it in the week since she'd arrived.

'Don't be silly. You're the domestic goddess. You'll have to show me how.'

Obviously it was in the nature of a distraction, but Saffy must be climbing the wall too, she realised.

They had just put it in the oven when the back door opened and Jake, not bothering to knock, tumbled through.

'Get your passport,' he said.

'Sorry?'

'Adam called. He's been driving through the jungle for the last couple of days. He's in the back of beyond somewhere and it's going to take him at least three flights to get to the US. There's no way he can get home in time to beat the deadline, so you're going to have to go to him. I've booked you on a flight to Las Vegas—'

'Las Vegas?'

'You're getting married there, today.'

'But…' she glanced at the clock '…I can't possibly get there in time.'

'You're flying east. You'll arrive a few hours after you leave.'

'Yes!' Saffy said, jumping up and punching the air, grinning broadly.

'But…' She looked at Jake. Looked at Robbie, who was grinning broadly. 'I never bought a dress.'

'Forget the dress,' Jake said. 'You haven't got time to pack. We've barely got time to get to the airport.'

'What's the purpose of your visit to the United States, Mr Wavell?'

'I'm getting married today,' he replied.

The man looked him up and down. He'd been wearing his dinner jacket when the rebels had opened fire on his hotel. It was filthy, torn and there was blood on his shirt. It was scarcely surprising that he'd been pulled over at Immigration for a closer look.

'Good luck with that, sir,' he said, grinning as he returned his passport.

There was a driver waiting for him in the arrival hall.

'Miss Coleridge's flight is due in ten minutes, Mr Wavell,' he said, handing him an envelope containing a replacement cellphone and a long message from Jake detailing all the arrangements he'd made.

\* \* \*

May paused as she entered the arrivals hall. Jake had told her she'd be met but she couldn't see her name on any of the cards. And then, with a little heart leap, she saw Adam and she let out a little cry of anguish. His clothes were filthy and torn, the remains of his shirt spattered with blood. He looked as if he hadn't slept for a week and he'd lost weight.

And his cheek… She put out her hand to touch a vivid bruise but he caught her hand. 'It's nothing. No luggage?' he asked.

'I didn't have time to pack. I didn't even have time to change,' she said, looking down at the smear of chocolate on her T-shirt. 'The wedding pictures should be interesting.' Then, keeping it light because it was all she could do not to weep all over him, 'But you know if you didn't want your mother to come to the wedding you only had to say. You didn't have to go to all this trouble.'

'I called her,' he said a little gruffly. 'Called Saffy. When I got to Dallas.' He cleared his throat. 'Dust,' he explained. 'From the explosion.'

'Adam…'

'Let's go. Apparently we have to get a licence at the courthouse before we go to the wedding chapel.'

* * *

'Well, that was easy,' May said as they walked out of the courthouse half an hour later with their licence. 'I hope, for your sake, that the divorce will be as simple.'

'Don't!' Then, seeing her startled look, realising that he had been abrupt, Adam shook his head.

He might have been seized by the sudden conviction that May was everything he'd ever wanted in a woman but she was doing this for only one reason.

To keep her home.

Crawling through the wreckage of the hotel, it had been the thought of May that had kept him going. The need to talk to her, tell her how sorry he was, what a fool he'd been. The hope that maybe they might, somehow, be able to begin again.

But, as the days had passed, all that had been swept away in the need to keep his promise to her. Because words meant nothing. No amount of sorry was worth a damn unless he backed it up with action.

Then, seeing the tiny frown buckling the space between her eyes, a frown that he wanted to kiss away, 'I'm sorry. I've had the worst week of my life and I vote that today we forget about everything, everyone else and just have some fun.'

'Fun?'

That was what he'd told Jake when he'd finally got to a phone that worked. To forget all the pompous nonsense he'd planned. He had, apparently, taken his brief very seriously. Instead of a simple limo, they'd been picked up at the airport in a white vintage open-topped Rolls, the kind that had great sweeping mud-guards, a wide running board, the glamour of another age.

Or maybe that *was* simple in Las Vegas.

'Any objections to that?' he asked, taking her hand as she stepped up into the car. Kept hold of it as he joined her.

'None.' May laughed out loud. 'I can't believe this. It seems unreal.'

'It is. Totally unreal,' he said, content to be sitting next to a woman wearing the biggest smile he'd ever seen. 'You've been given a magic day, stolen from the time gods by travel-ling east.'

'It doesn't work like that,' she said, leaning back against the soft leather, her hair unravell-ing, a smear of chocolate across her T-shirt. She looked exactly like the girl he'd fallen in love with, he thought, allowing himself to remember the heart-pounding edge as he'd climbed over the gate from the park. The heart lift as she'd looked up and smiled at him. He'd loved her before he knew the meaning of the word. And when he'd learned it was too late.

'I'll have to give it back when we fly home. You can't mess with time.'

'We give back the hours, but not anything that happens during them. You'll still be married. Your house will be safe. What we do, the memories we make. They are pure gain. That's why it's magic.'

She turned and looked at him. 'They should only be good memories, then.'

'They will be.'

'Seeing you in one piece is as good as it gets,' she said. 'I thought…'

May swallowed, turned away, tears clinging to her lashes. She'd promised herself she would not cry, but the shock of seeing him had been intense. She could not imagine what he'd been through while she was sitting in front of the television thinking that she was suffering.

She'd been so sure that the first thing she would do was tell him that she loved him. Worked out exactly what she was going to say on the long hours as she flew across the Atlantic, across America. But the moment she set eyes on him she knew that it was an emotional burden he didn't need. That she was doing what she'd accused him of. Thinking of herself. What she was feeling.

'Saffy was in bits,' she said when she could trust herself to speak.

'More than I deserve.'

Before she could protest, the car turned into a tropical garden and her jaw dropped as they swept up to the entrance to their hotel.

'Wow!' she said. Then, again, as they walked through the entrance lobby, 'Wow! This is utterly amazing.'

She was in Las Vegas and had expected their hotel to be large, opulent, over the top glitzy. But this was elegant. Stunningly beautiful.

'Good morning, Miss Coleridge, Mr Wavell. I hope you had a good flight?'

The duty manager smiled as he invited them to sit at the ornate Buhl desk, completely ignoring Adam's appearance. Her own.

'Just a few formalities. Miss Coleridge, you have an appointment at the beauty salon in half an hour,' he said, handing her an appointment card. 'We were warned that you would have no luggage and you'll find a selection of clothes in your size as well as your usual toiletries in your suite, as will you, Mr Wavell.'

She shook her head. 'Jake is great on the details,' she said. 'He thinks of everything.'

'You do have some messages, Mr Wavell. You can pick them up on voicemail from your room.' He looked from Adam to her and back again. 'Is there anything else I can do for you?'

'Just one thing,' Adam said. 'We're getting married this afternoon. Miss Coleridge will need something very special to wear.'

'That's not a problem. We have a number of designer boutiques within the hotel and our personal shopper is at your disposal, Miss Coleridge. I'll ask her to call you.'

And Adam looked across at her with a mesmerising smile.

'Nearly everything,' he said.

The suite was beyond luxurious. A huge sitting room with wide curved windows that opened onto a private roof garden with a pool, a tiny waterfall, tropical flowers, a hot tub. There was an office, a bar, two bedrooms, each with its own bathroom.

There was also Julia, who introduced herself as their personal butler. While Adam picked up his messages, she had ordered a late breakfast for them, drawn them each a bath, and then unwrapped and put away their new clothes.

This is magic, May thought, sinking into the

warm, scented water. She'd just closed her eyes when a phone, conveniently placed within reach so that she didn't have to move, rang once, twice. Was it for Adam? It rang again and she chided herself. This was the sort of hotel where if the phone rang in the bathroom it was for the person lying in the bath.

'Hello?'

'Good morning, Miss Coleridge. I'm Suzanne Harper, your personal shopper. I understand that you're getting married today and need something special to wear. Just a few questions and I'll get started.'

The few questions involved her colouring, style. Whether she preferred Armani, Chanel or Dior.

Dior! She couldn't afford that.

About to declare that she really didn't need anything, she thought of the way that Adam had looked at her as he'd said 'nearly everything'. He'd thought of this, arranged this. It was part of the magic and if she had to sell a picture to pay for it, it would be worth it.

'I don't have a particular preference for a designer. I'd just like something simple.'

That only left the embarrassing disclosure of her measurements.

'I'll go and see what I find,' she said thoughtfully. 'You'll be going down to the salon shortly?'

'My appointment's at twelve.'

'I'll bring a few ideas along for you to look at and we can take it from there.'

'Right.' Then, since she had the phone in her hand, she called home to let Robbie know that she'd arrived safely. Reassure Saffy that her brother was in one piece.

Adam looked up as May appeared wrapped in a heavy towelling robe, the partner of the one he was wearing, and smelling like heaven. 'Hi.'

'Hi,' she said, perching on the side of the desk. 'Everything under control?'

'Pretty much. How about you?'

'Well, I've just been through the mind-curdling embarrassment of giving every single one of my measurements to a woman I've never met.'

'Did she faint with shock?' he asked.

'She might have. There was a very long silence.'

'She was probably struggling to hold back a sob of envy that you have the confidence not to starve yourself to skin and bones.'

'I make sweets and cakes, Adam. I have to taste them to make sure I've got them right.'

'Your sacrifice is appreciated,' he said, holding out his hand to her and, when she took it, he pulled her down onto his lap, put his arms around her, and she let her head fall against his shoulder.

She'd pinned her hair up to get into the bath but damp tendrils had escaped, curling around her face. One of them tickled his chin and he smoothed it back, kissed it where it lay against her head. Saw a tear trickling down her cheek.

'Hey… What's the matter?'

'I thought you were dead.'

'I might as well have been if I'd let you down.'

'Idiot!' she said, throwing a playful punch at his arm.

'Ouch,' he said, covering his wince with a smile. 'Is that any way to speak to a man who's offering to show you a good time?'

She opened her mouth, closed it again. 'I'm so sorry, Adam. I thought this was going to be so simple.'

'It is, sweetheart. It is. But it's time you were moving,' he said before she became aware just how simple it was. Not even the thickness of the towelling robe could for long disguise just how basic his response to holding her like this had been. 'You'll be late for your appointment.'

She gave a little yelp, rushed off to the bedroom, returning a few minutes later in linen trousers the colour of bitter chocolate, a bronze silk shirt that brought out the colour of her eyes, her thick, wayward hair curling about her shoulders. The kind of hair that could give a man ideas. If he hadn't already got them.

'I'll meet you in the lobby at half past three.'

'In the lobby? But…'

'I'll finish up here, get ready and go out for a stroll in the garden.' He needed to put some distance between himself and temptation. 'You won't want me under your feet while you're getting ready.'

'Won't I?'

Without warning, her eyes hazed, darkened, an instinctive, atavistic response to what she must see in his; the kind of hot, ungovernable desire for a woman that he hadn't felt in longer than he could remember. The kind that set his senses ablaze, threatened to overwhelm him.

'Suppose I need a hand with a zip?'

'I only know how to undo them,' he said. A warning. As much to himself as to her. May trusted him. Believed his motives to be pure.

Not that she'd blame him. Knowing May, she'd almost certainly blame herself, apologise for taking advantage of him. He wasn't sure whether the thought of that made him want to smile, or to weep for her. A little of both, perhaps, and he wanted to hold her, tell her that she was amazing, sexy, beautiful and that any man would be lucky to have her.

She didn't move. Continued to stare at him, eyes dark, lips slightly parted, her cheeks flushed.

'May!'

She started. 'I'm gone.'

May wasn't sure what had just happened.

No. She wasn't that naïve. She knew. She just didn't know *how* it had happened.

How a jokey comment fired by nervous tension had created a primitive pulse that made every cell in her body sing out to Adam, made every cell in his body respond to her so that the air shimmered like a heat haze around them. So that the rest of the room seemed to disappear, leaving him in the sharpest, clearest focus. His dark, expressive brows. The copper glints heating up his grey eyes. His mouth, lips that had kissed her to seal their bargain, kissed her again for no reason at all in a way that made her own burn just to think of them.

For a moment she leaned back against the suite door, weak to the knees with hot raw need, knowing that if he'd lifted a hand, touched her, she would have fallen apart.

And he'd known it, too.

He'd warned her. *'I only know how to undo them.'*

And, remembering just how adept he'd been with her shirt buttons, she didn't doubt it.

Even then she hadn't moved. Hadn't wanted to move.

All she'd wanted was him. To hold him in her arms. Know that he was safe. To show him with her body all the things that she couldn't say.

Adam could not remember the last time he'd felt the need for a cold shower.

He had fudged his promise when she'd asked if he intended a paper marriage. Lied with his heart, if not his tongue, planning an ice-cold seduction, determined that she should beg for him to take her.

But he knew that she had done nothing to hurt him. She had given him her heart, her soul, would have given him her body too, if they had not been discovered before his virgin fumblings had found the mark.

It had not taken a close call with death to teach him that there was no joy in revenge, only in life. He would marry May, then, as his captive partner for a year or so, living in the same house, he would woo her. Wait for her. Propose a real marriage when the false one was at an end.

But, while he could control his own desires, if May lit up like that again he wasn't sure he could fight them both.

May spent what seemed like an age in the salon. When she finally emerged, her unmanageable mess of mousy hair had been washed, trimmed and transformed. It was still mousy, but she was a very sleek, pampered mouse and her hair had gone up into a smooth twist, the only escaping tendrils those that had been teased out and twisted into well behaved curls.

The facial had toned and smoothed her skin to satin. The manicurist had taken one horrified look at her hard-working nails and transformed them with the application of acrylics. And someone she never actually got to see performed 'pedicure' on her feet, giving her toenails a French polish so exquisite that when she was ready to leave the salon, she felt guilty for putting her shoes back on.

And, all the while this had been happening, Suzanne had whisked outfits by her to gauge her reaction to style, colour, fabric.

Everyone had had an opinion and between them they'd whittled it down to four.

'That's the one,' Suzanne said when, back in their suite, she'd tried on an exquisite silk two-piece the warm, toasted colour of fine brandy. 'I knew it as soon as I saw your shirt. It's the perfect colour for you.'

'I do always feel good in it,' she admitted. 'Is it vulgar to ask the price?'

'I understood that Mr Wavell…'

'Mr Wavell is not paying for this.'

He'd already paid for a first class air fare, first class travel, the hotel, but that was all.

When Suzanne still hesitated—clearly the suit cost a small fortune—she said, 'Unless you tell me, Suzanne, you're going to have to take it back and I'll wear these trousers.'

She told her.

May did her best not to gulp, at least not noticeably. She wasn't going to have to part with some small picture by a minor artist, something she wouldn't miss. She was going to have to sell something special to pay for this. But she'd never look this good again and, whatever the sacrifice, it would be worth it, she decided, as she handed over her credit card.

'All of it, Suzanne. Shoes, bag, underwear, everything.'

'He's a lucky man.'

'I'm the lucky one,' she said, but more to herself than Suzanne and when, half an hour later, professionally made-up, dressed and ready to go, May regarded her reflection she couldn't stop smiling.

The skirt was a little shorter than she'd normally choose and straight, a style she usually avoided like the plague but it was so beautifully cut that it skimmed her thighs in a way that made them look sexy rather than a pair of hams. But it was the jacket that had sold her.

The heavy silk had been woven into wide strips to create a fabric that reflected the light to add depth to the colour. It had exquisite stand-away revers that crossed low over her breast. And, aided and abetted by the underwear that Suzanne had chosen, the shape emphasized rather than disguised her figure.

The final touch, the shoes, dark brown suede with cutaway sides, peep toes, a saucy bow and stratospherically high heels, would have made Cinderella weep.

'You look gorgeous, May. Go break his heart.'

# CHAPTER ELEVEN

ADAM caught sight of himself in one of the mirrored columns and straightened the new silk tie he'd spotted in one of the boutiques.

Right now he knew exactly how a groom must feel as the minutes ticked by while he waited at the altar for a bride who wanted to give him a moment of doubt. A moment to face the possibility of life without her.

Doing his best to ignore the indulgent smiles of passing matrons who saw the spray of tiny orchids he was holding, the single matching orchid in his buttonhole and drew their own conclusions, he checked his new wristwatch.

And then, as he looked up, she was there.

Hair messed up in a band incapable of holding it, wearing baggy sweats, spectacles propped on the end of her nose, May had managed to steal his heart.

Now, as their eyes met across the vast

distance of the lobby, she stole his ability to breathe, to move, his heart to beat.

May was the first to move, lifting her feet with care in her high heels, moving like a catwalk model in the unfamiliar clothes. Displaying her show-stopping ankles.

Heads turned. Men and women stopped to watch her. And then he was walking towards her, flying towards her, standing in front of her and, another first for him, he felt like a tongue-tied teenager.

'Nice flowers,' she said, looking at the spray of bronze-splashed cream orchids he was clutching. 'They really go with your tie.'

About to tell her that he'd chosen the tie, the flowers because they matched her eyes, he got a grip. 'Fortunately, they also match your suit,' he said, offering them to her.

'They're beautiful. Thank you,' she said, brushing a finger lightly over a petal, then lifting her fingers to the one in his buttonhole. 'You thought of everything.'

Nearly everything.

When he'd been clutching at straws, the last thought in his head was that he would fall in love with May Coleridge. He couldn't even say when it had happened. He'd spent the last hour wandering along the hotel's shopping mall, buying the tie, choosing flowers, looking at the yellow diamonds in Tiffany's window, trying to decide which shade would match her grandmother's engagement ring.

He took her hand, looked at it. 'I was going to buy you a ring.'

'I didn't mean...' She looked up. 'I was wearing it when Jake came for me.'

He shook his head. 'I don't think there's another ring in the world that would suit you more, so I bought this instead.' He took a small turquoise pouch from his pocket, tipped out a yellow diamond pendant. 'I think it matches.'

'Adam...' She put her hands to her cheeks as she blushed. 'I don't know what to say.'

'You don't say anything. You just turn around and let me fasten it for you.'

She might blush like a girl, he thought, as she did as she was told and he fastened the clasp at the nape of her lovely neck. But she lived her life as a mature, thoughtful, *real* woman.

One who'd worked at making a life, a future for herself, who might need a hand down once in a while when she'd climbed above her comfort level, but never looked to anyone else to prop her up.

He felt as if he'd been sleepwalking

through his life. Putting all his energy, all his heart into building up his business empire, ignoring what was real, what was important.

He was awake now, he thought as he looked at May. Wide awake and tingling with the same anticipation, excitement as any of the other men who'd been queuing up for their wedding licences this morning.

'You look amazing.' Then, because he was in danger of making a fool of himself, 'I didn't mean for you to pay for it. The suit.'

'I know, Adam. But my grandmother once told me that when a man buys a woman clothes he expects to be able to take them off her.'

That had come out so pat that he knew she must have been rehearsing it for just this moment. A reminder…

'Your grandma was a very smart woman,' he said. 'I wish she was here to see what a lovely granddaughter she has.'

'Me too.' Then, with a sudden brightening of her eyes, 'Shall we go?'

He offered her his arm and, as they walked towards the door, there was a smattering of applause. The doorman whisked the car door open for them, raised his hat and then they drove out into the soft afternoon sunshine.

* * *

On the surface, May was calm, collected, knees braced, breath under control. It was the shoes that did it. Wearing heels that high required total concentration and while she was walking in them she didn't have a brain cell to spare for anything else.

The minute she slipped her hand under Adam's arm and she knew that if she tripped he'd catch her, everything just went to pot. He'd been in danger, hurt, tired, but he'd done this for her and, while the legs kept moving, everything else was just jelly.

'Are you okay?' he asked.

She nodded, not trusting herself to speak and then, just when she was absolutely sure she was going to hyperventilate, the car slowed and she saw the big sign and let out a little gasp.

'A Drive-thru Wedding?'

'You did say to let Jake surprise us,' Adam reminded her. Then he groaned. 'You hate it. I'm so sorry, May. This is all wrong. You look so elegant, so beautiful. Maybe it's not too late—'

'You deserve something more than this, May. Something special. The hotel have a wedding chapel. Maybe they can fit us in—'

'No!' He looked so desolate that she took his

hand in hers, all the shakes forgotten in her determination to convince him. 'This is absolutely perfect,' she assured him. 'I love it.'

And it was true; she did. It was sweet. It was also as far from anything she could ever have imagined as possible. A wedding to make her laugh rather than cry. Nothing solemn about it. Nothing to break her heart.

'I love it,' she repeated.

*I love you...*

The minister, dressed in a white suit, was waiting at the window. 'Miss Coleridge? Mr Wavell?'

'Er, yes...'

'Welcome to the Drive Thru Wedding Chapel. Do you have your licence?' he asked.

Adam took it from his jacket pocket, handed it over for him to check it.

'Are you both ready to take the solemn vows of matrimony?'

He looked at her.

'Absolutely,' she said quickly.

He turned to Adam, who said, 'Positively.'

They said their vows without a hitch. Adam slipped her grandmother's ring onto her finger. Opened his palm for her to take the second plain gold band, exactly like hers, only much larger.

It was as if the whole world was holding its

breath as she reached for it, picked it up, slipped it onto his finger.

'I now pronounce you man and wife. You may kiss the bride.'

'May I kiss the bride, Mrs Wavell?' he asked.

She managed to make some kind of sound that he took for yes and, taking her in his arms, he touched his lips to hers in what began as a barely-there kiss but deepened into something that melted her insides and might have lasted for ever but for the command from the photographer to hold that for one more.'

They collected the pictures, along with the souvenir certificate of their wedding vows at the next window.

'Photographic evidence,' he said, glancing through them, offering her a picture of them kissing with the Drive Thru Wedding sign behind them. 'Maybe we should send it to *Celebrity*?'

'Set a new trend in must-have weddings, you think?'

'Maybe not. But it should keep Freddie happy until Jake has organised all the legal registrations.'

She nodded, then said, 'There's just one more thing.' He waited. 'Where are the burger and fries?'

'I'm sorry?'

'A drive thru wedding should have a drive thru wedding breakfast.'

'You're hungry?' he asked.

'Hollow.'

She'd been so wrapped up in taking care of her grandfather, the house, keeping her mind occupied with the workshops. Never giving herself a moment to think. She was, she'd discovered, starving, but not for food.

The emptiness went far deeper than that.

She was hungry for Adam to look at her as he had in their suite. To touch her. To touch him. To kiss him, be his lover as well as his friend. Yearned for his child to hold. To be, if only for a magic afternoon, his wife in every sense of the word.

'I don't know whether it's lunch time, dinner time or breakfast time,' she said a touch lightheadedly, but I haven't eaten since I left the plane and you should know that I'm not a woman who's accustomed to subsisting on a lettuce leaf.' She turned as they passed a familiar logo. 'There! We could drive in there and pick up a cheeseburger and some fries.'

He grinned. 'You are such a cheap date, May.'

'Hardly. You've already paid for a first class air fare, a hotel suite fit for a prince and a diamond pendant.' She touched the diamond where it lay in the hollow of her throat. 'It's clear that you need a wife to curb your extravagance. But I will want a strawberry milkshake.'

They were laughing over their impromptu picnic as they arrived back in their suite.

Julia, undoubtedly warned of their return by the front desk, was waiting for them with champagne on ice, a tray of exotic canapés, chocolates, a cake. And a basket of red roses so large that it seemed to dominate the huge room.

May went white when she saw them.

'Could you take those away, Julia?' she managed. 'I'm allergic to roses.'

'Of course, Mrs Wavell. Congratulations to you both.'

'Thank you.'

That was Adam. She couldn't speak. Couldn't look at him. Didn't move until she felt his hand on her shoulder.

'It's okay, May. I know.'

'Know?' She looked up at him. 'What do you know?'

'About the rose petals.'

She stared at him, scarcely daring to breathe.

'What do you know?' she whispered.

'I know that you gathered them up and pressed them between the pages of a poetry book.'

Gathered them up. That made it sound like something pretty. But it hadn't been pretty, any of it. She'd crawled around on her hands and knees in the dark, slipping where the water had frozen, refusing to give up until she had them all. She couldn't pick them up in gloves and her hands had been so cold that she hadn't felt the scrapes, the knocks.

'How? No one knew…'

'I picked it up when I was waiting for you in your sitting room. A petal fell out. I didn't realise the significance until later, when I understood what you'd done for Saffy. That was why I called you the second time. You saved my life. If I'd been in bed instead of sitting on the floor talking to you…'

'He gave me a choice,' May said quickly, not wanting to hear how close she'd come to losing him. Not when he was here, safe. 'Swear that I would never speak to you, contact you, ever again. Or Saffy would go to jail.'

'But once she'd been cautioned…'

'I gave my word. He kept his.' She lifted her hands to his face, cupping it gently. Kissed the bruise that darkened his cheekbone. 'Forget it, Adam. It's over.'

'How can it ever be over?' he said. 'It was your face that kept me going when I was crawling through that hotel. The thought of you…'

She stopped his words with a kiss, then slowly began to unfasten her jacket.

'What are you doing?'

'Making up for lost time,' she said, letting it drop. 'Taking back what was stolen from us.' She unhooked her skirt, hesitated, looked up and her eyes, liquid bronze beneath long dark lashes, sent a charge of heat through him that wiped everything from his brain. 'Any chance of some help with the zip?'

Never taking his eyes from her face, he lowered the zip and then, as the skirt slithered to the floor, he left his hand on the warm curve of her hip as he lowered his lips to hers.

It was as if they were eighteen again. Teenagers, touching each other, awed by the importance of it, realising that this was a once and forever moment that would change them both.

This was how she'd been then. Lit up. Telegraphing what she wanted with eyes like lamps. She'd been both shy and eager. Naïve and bold. Innocent as a baby and yet knowing more than he did. Knowing what she wanted. What he wanted. Slowing everything down, making him wait, making him feel like a god...

She was doing it now. Unfastening the buttons of his shirt as she backed him towards the bedroom, pushing it off his shoulders. Kissing each bruise she uncovered with a little groan until he bent and caught her behind the knees.

Lost in the heat of her kisses, the pleasure of her touch he felt reborn, made over until, her tiny cries obliterating everything but one final need, he was poised above her to make her, finally, his.

'Please, Adam,' she begged as he made her wait. 'Please...'

And in those three words his world shattered.

He rolled away from her, practically throwing him from the bed in his shame, his desperation to escape what he'd so nearly done.

It took May a moment to gather herself, but then, concerned that after his ordeal he was sick, hurt, she grabbed a robe, found him slumped in a chair, his head in his hands.

'What is it? Darling, please.' She knelt at his feet. 'Are you hurt? Sick?'

'No.'

She sat back on her heels. 'Tell me.'

'I was going to make you beg.'

She frowned, took his hand, but he pulled it away.

'I was going to make you beg. Take you in your grandfather's bed.' He looked up. 'When you told me you were going to lose your house, do you think I was touched with concern? I was cheering. I had you. I was going to wipe out the Coleridge name with my own. Parade you as Mrs Adam Wavell, the wife of the kid from the sink estate. Take you in your grandfather's bed and make you beg.'

'So, what are you saying? That I didn't beg hard enough?' she asked. 'Or do you want to wait until we get home? Do it there?'

His head came up.

'No! No…' He shook his head. 'I was wrong. I don't deserve you, but I thought if I waited, wooed you, showed you that I was worthy of you, maybe, at the end of the year, when you could be free if you wanted to be, I could ask you then to marry me properly.'

'A year?'

'As long as it takes. I love you, May. I've never wanted another woman the way I wanted you. Want you.'

'No.' She shook her head. Stood up. Took a step back.

'I spent a week of agony thinking you were dead. Regretting that I hadn't told you how much I love you when I had the chance. And then, idiot that I was, I decided not to burden you with my emotional needs. Well, here it is. I understand why you felt the way you did, but I've waited more than ten years for you to finish what you started, Adam Wavell.' She untied the belt of the robe she'd thrown about her. Let it drop to the ground. 'I'm not prepared to waste another year. How about you?'

She held out her hand, held her breath for what seemed like forever before he reached out, took it, then pulled her to him.

The bell-ringers were waiting to give it everything they had. The choir was packed with angel-voiced trebles and, behind May, the church was crowded with everyone she knew. And lots of people she didn't but planned to in the future. Freddie was there. Adam's mother. Saffy with Michel and his parents, Nancie decked out in pink frills as an honorary bridesmaid. Robbie, standing as her matron of honour.

It was exactly as she'd imagined it all those years ago. Every pew end decorated with a knot of roses, myrtle and ivy. The bouquet of bronze David Austin roses she was carrying, one taken for Adam's buttonhole.

Nearly as she'd imagined. Not even the celebrated local designer, Geena Wagner, could squeeze her into a dress her usual size. The truth was that one of her seamstresses had been working on her gown as late as last night— letting it out half an inch around the waist to accommodate the new life she and Adam had created on their impromptu honeymoon.

Exactly as she'd imagined and totally different. What she hadn't known as a teenager was how she would feel.

That dream had been the yearning for triumph of an unhappy girl. Make-believe. Window-dressing.

Today it was real and as she and Adam stood before the altar and the vicar began to speak... 'Dearly beloved, we are gathered here today to bless the marriage of May and Adam Wavell...' the overwhelming emotion was that of joy, celebration of a blessed union, of love given and received.

# WINNING A GROOM
# IN 10 DATES

BY
**CARA COLTER**

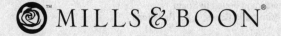

All the characters in this book have no existence outside the imagination
of the author, and have no relation whatsoever to anyone bearing the
same name or names. They are not even distantly inspired by any
individual known or unknown to the author, and all the incidents are
pure invention.

First published in Great Britain 2010
Harlequin Mills & Boon Limited,
Eton House, 18-24 Paradise Road, Richmond, Surrey TW9 1SR

© Cara Colter 2010

ISBN: 978 0 263 87685 7

Harlequin Mills & Boon policy is to use papers that are natural,
renewable and recyclable products and made from wood grown in
sustainable forests. The logging and manufacturing process conform
to the legal environmental regulations of the country of origin.

Printed and bound in Spain
by Litografia Rosés, S.A., Barcelona

**Dear Reader**

I always use humour in my writing, because I think laughter is one of the best parts of all relationships. We've been together twenty years and my guy, Rob, still makes me laugh out loud. So I was thrilled to be asked to write a romantic comedy for Mills & Boon® Romance.

What I didn't expect was that I would be facing a tragedy as I wrote.

As you will see from my dedication, my friend Judy died while I was working on this story. I had the great privilege of being able to spend time with her every day for the last weeks of her life. When I delivered her eulogy I said I felt I had experienced love at its truest and deepest and most breathtaking in those final days with Judy.

I came away with a sense of having been inspired by Judy's courage, humility and grace. Her final gifts to me were these: spirit is in life *and* death, in joy *and* sorrow; it is profoundly present in every single sacred breath. Laughter is a light that can pierce the deepest dark. And finally: love is an energy so powerful it cannot be destroyed. Love truly is for ever.

My greatest wish is that this book honours Judy by bringing you, the reader, moments where you experience each of those three elements.

I am yours in spirit, in laughter, and in love.

*Cara*

In Loving Memory
Judy Michelle Moon
1949–2009

# PROLOGUE

"I SEE you've lost the hippie hair and the face stubble and the earring, Sheridan."

"Yes, sir." Brand had been so deep under-cover for so long, answering to his own name was difficult.

"You don't even look like him anymore," his boss said approvingly. "Brian Lancaster is dead. We made it look as if his private plane went down over the Mediterranean under suspicious circumstances. No one in what's left of the Looey's operation will be questioning why Mr. Lancaster wasn't one of the twenty-three arrests made across seven different countries.

"Amazing work, Sheridan. None of us could have predicted this when you answered that ad on the Internet. You took FREES in a new direction."

FREES, First Response Emergency Eradication Squad, was an antiterrorism unit made up of tough, highly disciplined men with specialty training. Brand, recruited right after his first tour of active duty with the marines, had physical prowess and a fearlessness that had made him a top vertical-rescue specialist. But it was that gift, along with his knowledge of languages, that had earmarked him for FREES.

Answering an Internet ad out of Europe that offered to buy highly restricted weapons had changed everything. Brand had found himself moving away from his specialty, immersed in a murky world where he was part cop, part soldier, part agent, part operative.

But it had taken its toll. The truth was, Brand preferred hard assignments as opposed to soft ones—assignments where training and physical strength came together in a rush of activity, in and out, and over. It didn't mess with your head as much as the past four years had. He longed for the relative simplicity of being an expert at something as technical as rope rescue.

"Look, even though it looks like Lancaster bit the dust, we've got a bit of mop-up to do. Bit players, loose ends. You need to lie low for a while. Really low. As if you really did disappear off the face of the earth. Know any place to do that?"

Brand Sheridan knew *exactly* where he could do that. The kind of place where no one would ever look for the likes of Brian Lancaster. A place of tree-lined, shady streets, where no one locked their doors, and the scent of petunias cascading out of window boxes perfumed the night air. It was a place where the big excitement on Friday night was the Little League game in Harrison Park.

It was the place that had piqued his fascination with all things that took a man high off the ground, but it had also been the place his younger self couldn't wait to get away from.

And the truth was, he dreaded going back there now. But he had to.

"I've got some leave coming, sir." That was an understatement. Brand Sheridan had been undercover for four years. The deeper in he got, the less the assignment had lent itself to taking holidays.

He'd been so good at what he did, had achieved the results he had, because of his ability to immerse himself in that world, to play that role as if his life depended on it.

Which it had.

His boss was looking askance at him.

"I need to go home."

The word *home* felt as foreign to him as answering to his own name had done.

"It'll be safe there?"

"If you were looking for a hidey-hole, the place where someone like Brian Lancaster would be least likely to be found? Sugar Maple Grove would be it."

"One-horse town?"

"Without the horse," he said wryly. "On the edge of the Green Mountains, Vermont. As far as I know, they still have a soda fountain and the kids ride their bikes to school. The big deal is the annual yard tour and rose show."

He hesitated. "My sister has been in touch. She's afraid my dad's not coping very well with the death of my mother. I need to go see if he's okay."

Not that his father would appreciate it. At all.

"Your mother died while you were out, didn't she?"

*Her pride and joy the fact her yard had been on that annual tour of spectacular gardens, that her roses had been prize-winners.* "Yes, sir."

"I'm sorry. I know we weren't able to bring you in when it happened."

"That's the nature of the job, sir." And only people who did that job, like the man sitting across from him, could fully get that.

His father, the small-town doctor? Not so much.

"Good work on Operation Chop-Looey," his boss said. "Exceptional. Your name has been put in for a commendation."

Brand said nothing. He'd lived in a shadowy world where you were rewarded for your ability to pretend, your ability to betray the people you befriended and led to trust you. Getting a commendation for that? At this point he had mixed feelings about what he had done and about himself. One of those feelings definitely wasn't pride.

He didn't really want to go back to Sugar Maple Grove. His father was angry, and rightfully so. His sister had given him an unsavory assignment.

So, at the same time Brand Sheridan dreaded going back there, he was aware something called him that he could not run from any-more...

"I should be able to wrap up what I need to do in Sugar Maple in a week, two tops." Brand asked.

"Let's give it a month. That will give us time to put some protective measures in place for you."

*A month in Sugar Maple Grove?* He hadn't expected to stay that long. What on earth was he going to find to do there for a month?

But Brand Sheridan didn't have the kind of job where you argued with the boss.

"Yes, sir," he said, and to himself he thought, *maybe I'll catch up on my sleep.*

# CHAPTER ONE

STARS studded an inky summer sky. Bright sparks drifted upward to dance briefly with fireflies before disappearing forever. It was the perfect night to say good-bye.

"Good-bye," Sophie Holtzheim said out loud. "Good-bye foolish romantic notions and dreams."

Her voice sounded small and lonely against the stillness of the night, the voice of a woman who was saying farewell to the future she had planned out so carefully for herself.

Sophie was in her aging neighbor's backyard. She was taking advantage of the fact he was away for the night to utilize his fire pit, though the absolute privacy of his huge yard and mature landscaping had irresistible appeal, too.

Sophie's own house, in this 1930s neighborhood of Craftsman-style homes, was next to this one, on a Sugar Maple Grove corner lot. Despite a barrier of thick dogwood hedges surrounding her property, she did not want to risk a late-night dog-walker catching a glimpse of a fire burning…or of a woman in a white dress muttering to herself.

Let's face it: when a woman was wearing her wedding dress, alone, at midnight on a Saturday, she wanted guaranteed privacy. And reprieve from the small-town rumor mill.

Sophie Holtzheim had fueled that quite enough over the past six months!

Taking a deep breath, Sophie smoothed a hand over the white silk of her wedding gown. She had loved it instantly, with its simple spaghetti straps, non-dramatic V-neck, fabric floating in a subtle A-line to the ground.

"I am never going to walk down the aisle in this dress." She hoped to sound firm, resolved, *accepting*. She hoped saying it out loud would help, somehow, but it didn't.

Sighing, Sophie opened the lid of the box beside her, and contemplated its contents.

"Good-bye," she whispered.

It was a wedding-in-a-box. Inside were printer's samples of invitations and name plates, patterns for bridesmaids' dresses, magazine cuttings of flower arrangements and table settings, brochures for dream honeymoon destinations.

Sophie forced herself to pick up the invitation sample that sat on the very top of the bulging box.

"Don't read it," she ordered herself. "Just throw it in the fire."

Naturally, she did no such thing. In the flickering light of the bonfire she had roaring in Dr. Sheridan's stone-lined pit, she ran her hand over the raised cream-colored lettering of the printer's sample. It was the invitation she had selected for her wedding.

"This day," she read, "two become one. Mr. and Mrs. Harrison Hamilton invite you to join them in a celebration of love as their son, Gregg, joins his life to that of Miss Sophie Holtzheim…."

With a choking sob, Sophie tossed the invitation into the fire, watched its ivory edges turn brown and curl before it burst into flame.

Gregg was not joining his life to Miss Sophie Holtzheim. He was joining his life to Antoinette Roberts.

For the past few months Sophie had held out hope that this was all going to get better, that Gregg would come to his senses.

But that hope had been dashed this afternoon when she had been handed a brand-new invitation, with Antoinette Roberts's name on it. *Instead of hers.*

It wasn't a wedding invitation, but an invitation to an engagement celebration at Gregg's parents' posh estate on the outskirts of Sugar Maple Grove.

"Gregg and I were engaged. We never had an engagement party." Sophie felt ridiculously slighted that all stops were being pulled out for the *new* fiancée.

It was the final straw and set the tears that had been building all afternoon flowing freely. She was glad she hadn't applied any makeup for her good-bye-hopes-and-dreams ceremony!

How could Claudia Hamilton, Gregg's mother, do this to her? Sophie was the one who was supposed to be marrying Gregg. It was too cruel to invite her to the engagement party where all of Sugar Maple Grove would be introduced to the woman Gregg had replaced Sophie with!

But his mother, who had once pored over the bridal magazines with Sophie, had made her motivations very clear.

"It can't look like we're snubbing you, dear. The whole town is going to be there. And you *must* come. For your own good. Your split was months ago. You don't want to start looking pathetic. Try not to come alone. Try to look as if you're getting on with your life."

Meaning, of course, it was way too obvious that she wasn't.

"We can't have the whole town talking *forever* about Gregg breaking the heart of the town sweetheart. It will be bad for his and Toni's new law practice. It's really not fair that he's looking like the villain in all this, is it, Sophie?"

No, it wasn't. This whole catastrophe was of Sophie's own making.

"If only I could take it back," she whispered, as she rubbed a fresh cascade of tears from her cheeks. If only she could take back the words she had spoken.

She relived them now, adding fuel to the fire in front of her in the form of a picture of a wedding cake, three tiers, yellow roses trailing down the sides.

"Gregg," she'd said, as he was heading back to South Royalton to complete law school, and pressing her to set a date for their wedding, "I need some time to think."

Now she had her whole life to *think,* to mull over the fact she had thrown everything away over a case of cold feet.

The truth was Sophie had thought she'd

known Gregg as well as she knew herself. But she could never have predicted how Gregg would react. She had pictured him being gently understanding. But in actual fact, Gregg had been furious. How dare *she* need time to think about *him?* And who could blame him really?

The Hamiltons were Sugar Maple Grove royalty.

And Sophie Holtzheim was just the sweet geek whom the whole town had come to know and love for putting Sugar Maple Grove on the map a decade ago as a finalist in the National Speech Contest with, "What Makes a Small Town Tick."

Even years after she'd shed the braces and glasses, Sophie had never quite shed her geeky image.

So, naturally, she'd been bowled over when Gregg Hamilton had noticed *her.*

If he seemed a little preoccupied with how things looked to others, and if he had always been more pragmatic than romantic, those could hardly be considered flaws.

Especially in retrospect!

But it hadn't been those things that bothered her. It had been something else, something she couldn't name, just below the surface where she couldn't see it, identify it. It had niggled, and then wiggled, and then huffed, and then puffed and then, finally, it had blown her whole world apart.

Because when she couldn't ignore it for one more second, when her stomach hurt all the time, and she couldn't sleep, she had told Gregg, hesitantly, apologetically, *I can't put my finger on it. Something's wrong. Something's missing.* And she'd slid the huge solitaire diamond off her finger and given it back to him.

But nothing could have prepared Sophie for the startling swiftness of Gregg's reaction. He had replaced her. Rumors that Gregg had been dating a new girl around the campus had found their way home within weeks of her returning his ring.

Sophie had thought he was just trying to make her jealous. Surely what they'd had was not so superficial that Gregg could replace her within weeks?

But today, hand-delivered confirmation had come that, no, he wasn't trying to make her jealous. She *really* had been replaced. It was no joke. He was not on the rebound. He was not going to realize that Antoinette, beautiful and brilliant as she might be, was no replacement for Sophie. Gregg was not going to come back to her. Ever. An invitation to an engagement party could not be rationalized away.

It was final. It was over. *Over.*

Claudia had instructed her not to become pathetic. Was it too late? Was she already pathetic? Was that how everyone saw her?

If Claudia Hamilton could see Sophie now, conducting her druidlike ceremony, hunched over her box of dreams in a dress she would never wear again, it would no doubt confirm the diagnosis.

Pathetic. Burning up her box of dreams, reliving those fateful words and wondering what would have happened if she had never spoken them…

"I am not going to that party," she said, out loud, her voice strong and sure for the first time. "Never. Wild horses could not drag me there. I don't care how it *looks* to the Hamiltons."

There. She relished her moment of absolute strength and certainty for the millisecond that it lasted.

And then she crumpled.

"What have I done?" she wailed.

What had she done?

"I wanted to feel on fire," she said mournfully. "I threw it all away for that." She sat in the silence of the night contemplating her rashness.

Suddenly the hair on the back of her neck rose. She *sensed* him before she saw him. A scent on the wind? An almost electrical change in the velvety texture of the summer night?

Someone had come into the yard. She knew it. Had come in silently, and was watching her. How long had he been there? Who was it? She could feel something hotter than the fire burning the back of her neck.

She turned her head, carefully. For a moment, she saw nothing. And then she saw the outline of a man, blacker than the night shadows.

He was standing silently just inside the gate, so still he didn't even seem to be breathing. He was over six feet of pure physical presence, his stance both alert and calm, like a predatory cat, a cougar.

Sophie's heart began to hammer. But not with fear. With recognition.

Even though the darkness shrouded his features, even though it had been eight years since he had stood in this yard, even though his body had matured into its full power, Sophie *knew* exactly who he was.

The man who had wrecked her life.

And it wasn't the same man whose name was beside hers on a mock-up wedding invitation, either.

It was the one she had thought of when she'd made that fateful statement that she needed some time to think. That *something* was missing.

Oh, she hadn't named him, not even in her own mind. But she had *felt* a longing for something only he, Brand Sheridan, wayward doctor's son, wanderer of the world, had ever made her feel.

She knew it was ridiculous to toss her whole life away on something that had begun whispering to her when she was a preteen, and had become all-consuming by the time she was fifteen years old.

But there was no substitute for that feeling. It was like the swoosh in the pit of your stomach when you jumped off the cliff at Blue Rock. There was a thrilling suspended moment after the decision to go and before you hit the ice-cold pool of water, where you felt it. Intensely alive. Invigorated. As if that one glorious moment was all that mattered.

Brand had made her feel that. *Always*. She'd been twelve when her family had moved in next door to his, he'd been seventeen.

Just setting eyes on him had been enough to make her whole day go as topsy-turvy as her insides. Filled with a kind of wonder, and an impossible hope.

Sophie had loved the man who stood behind her in the darkness as desperately as only a young teen could love. She had loved him unrealistically, furiously, unrequitedly.

The fact that she had been only the teeniest glitch on Brand Sheridan's radar had intensified her feelings instead of reducing them.

She felt the familiar shiver in her belly—the damn *something missing*—when he spoke, his voice rough around the edges, sexy as a touch.

"What the hell?"

She knew his eyes to be a shade of blue that was deeper than sapphire. But in the shadows where he stood, they looked black, sultrier than the summer night, smoky with new and unreadable mysteries.

For a moment she was absolutely paralyzed by his puzzled gaze on her. But then she came to her senses and lurched to her feet.

This was not how Brand Sheridan was going to see her after an eight-year absence! *Pathetic.*

Sophie scrambled toward the safety of the little hole in the hedge that she could squeeze through, and that she hoped he couldn't—or wouldn't. She would have made it, too, if she hadn't remembered the damned box.

She wasn't leaving it there for him to find, a box full of her romantic notions, as ridiculously unrealistic as a princess leaving a glass slipper for her prince to find.

The rest of the town might know she was pathetic, still think of her affectionately as their sweet geek—a romantic catastrophe now adding to her reputation—but she could keep it a secret from him.

She turned back, grabbed the box and then, disaster. She tripped over the hem of a dress she had left too long in the hope it would make her look taller and more graceful as she glided down the aisle.

Sophie crashed to the ground, face-first, and the box sailed from her hands and spilled its contents to the wind. Papers and pictures scattered.

He moved toward her before she could find her breath or her feet.

And then his hand was on her naked shoulder, and he turned her over. And she gazed up into his face and felt the sizzle of his hand on the tender flesh of her shoulder, whatever had been missing between her and

Gregg bubbled up so sweetly in her it felt as if she had drunk a bottle of champagne.

He stared down at her, his brow furrowed, his expression formidable and almost frightening. *This was Brand?*

And then the hard lines of his face softened marginally. Puzzlement knitted the line of dark brows. "Sweet Pea?"

She drank in his face. Still a face that could stop the sun, but a new dimension to it, the lines cast in steel, his eyes colder, she thought, dazed. *Something in his expression that had never been there. Haunted.*

His hand moved from her shoulder, he brushed a smudge of something from her cheek.

It would be way too easy to mistake the leashed strength in those hands for all kinds of things that it wasn't.

Just taking care of his awkward-situation-prone little neighbor, as always. Picking her up and dusting her off after yet another catastrophe. Her love for him giving her an absolute gift for clumsiness, for downright dumbness, for attracting mishap and mayhem.

She closed her eyes against the humiliation of it. The truth was, in those tender adolescent years after he had gone away and joined the military, she had imagined his return a million times. Maybe a zillion. The day he would come home and *discover* her. Not a gawky teenager with not a single curve, unless you counted the metallic one of the braces on her teeth.

But a woman.

She had imagined his voice going husky with surprise. Delight. *Sophie, you've become so beautiful.*

But of course, *nothing* ever went as she imagined it.

"Sweet Pea, is that you?"

She allowed herself just to look up at him, to drink in his scent and his presence and his mystery.

Brand Sheridan had always been crazy sexy. It wasn't just that he was breathtakingly good-looking, because many men were breathtakingly good-looking. It wasn't just that he was built beautifully, broad and strong, at ease with himself and his body, because many men had that quality, too.

No, there was something else, unnamable, just below the surface, primal as a drumbeat, that made something in Sophie Holtzheim go still.

If he had ever gone through an awkward

teenage stage, she had been blind to it. Since
the day she had moved in next door, Sophie
had worshipped her five-years-older neighbor.

Laughter-filled, devil-may-care Brand
Sheridan had always been too *everything* for
sleepy Sugar Maple Grove. He'd been too
restless, too driven, too adventure-seeking, too
energetic, too fast, too impatient.

His father, the town doctor, had been con-
ventional, Brand had defied convention. And
his father's vision for him.

To Dr. Sheridan's horror, Brand had defied
the white-collar traditions of his family, quit
college and joined the military. He had left this
town behind without so much as a glance back.

Sophie had rejoiced with his parents when
he had returned safely to the United States
after a tour of duty abroad.

When had that that been? Five years ago?
No, a little longer, because he had been
overseas when her parents had died. But, in
truth, Brand had never really returned.

He had not come home, and to his mother's
horror, before they had really even finished
celebrating his safe return from the clutches of
danger, he had been recruited into an elitist
international team of warriors known as
FREES. For the most part, he lived and trained

overseas or on the west coast. He worked in the thrum of constant threat, in the shadows of secrecy.

In those years away, Sophie was aware he had met his parents in California, in London, in Paris. She knew he occasionally showed up for family gatherings at his sister, Marcie's, house in New York.

It had, over the years, become more than evident Brand Sheridan had left Sugar Maple Grove behind him, and that he was never coming back. He'd been unconvinced of the joys of small-town life that Sophie had once outlined in her national-speech-competition talk, "What Makes a Small Town Tick."

Still, the whole town had felt the shock of it when Brand had not even returned home for his mother's funeral. The framed picture of him staring out sternly from under the cap of a United States Marine uniform had disappeared from Dr. Sheridan's mantel.

"Brandon," Sophie said, suddenly flustered, aware she had studied him *way* too long. She used his full name to let him know she was prepared to see him as an adult and that they could leave the endearment, *Sweet Pea,* behind them.

"I wasn't expecting you." As soon as the

words were out of her mouth, she regretted them. She *always* had a gift for saying exactly the wrong thing around him, as awkward as the Sweet Pea she was anxious to leave behind her.

Of course she wasn't expecting him! She was in a wedding dress at midnight! If she'd been expecting him, what would she be wearing?

*Well, a wedding dress would be nice,* a part of her, the hopelessly romantic part of her she'd set out to kill tonight, said dreamily.

She shivered at the thought of Brand Sheridan as a groom. Glanced into the hard planes of that face and tried to imagine them softening with tenderness.

The tenderness she'd heard in his voice when he'd called her after the death of her parents. *Aww, Sweet Pea...*

That had been sympathy, Sophie reminded herself sternly. It was not to be mistaken for that stupid *something* she had tossed her life away for!

"Expecting someone else, if not me?" he asked.

He held out his hand to her, and she took it, trying to ignore another jolt of shimmering, stomach-dropping awareness as her hand met the unyielding hardness of his.

He pulled her to her feet with effortless strength, stood there regarding her.

"No, no," she said. "Just, uh, burning some urgent rubbish."

"Urgent rubbish," he said, and a hint of a smile tickled across the hard line of his lips.

She was suddenly aware that she truly, at this moment, was living up to Mrs. Hamilton's assessment of her as pathetic. A simple touch, her hand enfolded in his, not even a romantic gesture, made her feel things she had not felt through her entire engagement.

And that was before she added in the fact she had not had a decent haircut in months. Or put on a lick of makeup. Of all the people to catch her in her wedding dress, conducting ritualistic ceremonies at midnight, did it have to be him?

Did it have to be Brand Sheridan?

He let go of her hand as soon as she was steady on her feet, and turned away from her. He began to pick up the scattered wedding-dream debris, and shoved stuff back in the box, Sophie saw thankfully, without showing the least bit of interest in what that stuff was.

Sophie could have made her getaway through the hedge, but she found herself unwilling to abandon the box, and even though

CARA COLTER 29

she knew better, unwilling to walk away. She
felt as if she had not had a drink for days and
he was clear water.

Days? No, longer. Months. Years.

And so she drank him in, thirstily. Part of
her parched with a sense that only he could
quench it, even though she despised herself
for thinking that.

He was more solid than he had been before,
boyish sleekness had given way to the devilishly attractive maturity of a man: broadness
of shoulder, deepness of chest. And that was
not all that had changed.

His dark hair was very short, his face clean-
shaven. His dress was disappointingly conser-
vative, even if the short-sleeved golf shirt did
show off the breathtaking muscles of his biceps
and forearms.

She felt a sharp sense of missing the boy
who had walked away from here and not
looked back. That boy of her memory had been
a renegade. Back then, he had gone for black
leather jackets and motorcycles.

To his mother's consternation, he had
favored jeans with rips in them—sometimes in
places that had made Sophie's adolescent heart
beat in double time. His dark hair had been too
long, and he'd always let a shadow of stubble

darken the impossibly handsome planes of his face.

Now his hair was short, his face completely clean-shaven. There was the hard-edged discipline of a soldier in the way he held himself—an economy of movement that was mouth-dryingly masculine, graceful and powerful.

But, then her eyes had caught on the tiny hole in his ear.

Whoo, boy. Really too easy to imagine him as a pirate, legs braced against a tossing sea, powerful arms folded over the broadness of his chest—naked, she hoped—his head thrown back, welcoming the storms that others cringed from—

*Stop,* she pleaded with herself. God, she had been a reasonable person for years now! Years. She had almost married the world's most reasonable man, hadn't she?

And here he was, Brand Sheridan, wrecking it all. Wrecking her illusions, making her see she was not a reasonable person at all.

And probably never had been.

# CHAPTER TWO

"Do you have a pieced ear?" Sophie gasped, despite the fact she had *ordered* herself not to ask. More of her gift for getting it *so* wrong. It would have been so much better if she hadn't noticed, or at least pretended not to have noticed!

Brand frowned, apparently not pleased that she had noticed, either. "I did," he said, touched the lobe of that ear, let his hand fall away. But his voice invited no more questions, even while his ears invited nibbling....

Ever since she'd been voted "girl least likely to nibble earlobes" in her high-school annual, she'd thought about what it would be like to do just that. Not that she had ever let those raucous boys who had voted for her know that.

Let them think she was prim and stiffly uptight. They would have teased her even more unmercifully if they'd guessed at her secret romantic side.

She'd never had any urges to nibble Gregg's ears. She'd been pleased that he had brought out her *reasonable* side. But of course, the *something missing* had reared its ugly head, and it probably had something to do with the forbidden temptations of earlobe-nibbling.

*Especially ones that bore the mark of a piercing!*

Sophie reminded herself she did not even know this man who shared the shadows with her at the moment.

He was not the same man who had called her all those years ago, on the worst night of her life, his voice alone penetrating the darkness, husky with pain. *Aww Sweet Pea*...she needed to remember that.

Brand Sheridan was not the same man who had left here. Really, he'd only been a boy when he left. And she'd been a girl, a carefree one, her biggest trouble trying to leave her nerdy reputation behind her. She'd been blissfully unaware of the tragedies that awaited her, both her parents killed in a terrible accident when she was eighteen.

Brand, apparently oblivious to her fascination with his earlobes, picked up another paper, stuffed it in the box, scanned the yard and then turned back to her.

Now, she could see it was the look in his eyes, not his earlobes, that was the most changed. Sapphire-dark, the firelight winked off that impossible shade of blue, deep and mysterious as the ocean.

Back then, she remembered, there was an ever-present sparkle of mischief in them, laughter never far away, a devil-may-care grin always tickling around the edges of that too-sexy mouth.

Now his eyes were wary. And weary. A shield was up in them that Sophie somehow doubted he ever let down.

And his mouth had a stern line etched around it, as if he no longer smiled, as if the mischievous boy who had caught the neighbor's snotty Siamese cat and tied a baby bonnet on it before releasing it was banished from him somehow. In the place of that boy was a warrior, *ready* for things that were foreign to the citizens of this tiny town.

She wanted to touch the firm line of that mouth, as if she would be able to feel the smile that had once been there. She wanted to say, *Brand, what's happened to you?*

Thankfully, sensible Sophie took charge before she made a complete fool of herself.

"Thank you, Brandon," she said, and

wrested the box from him. Realizing she sounded stiffly formal, she added, "I'll remember you in my will."

*Stop it,* she pleaded with her inner geek. *Please just stop!*

But the tiniest of smiles teased the hard line around his mouth, and she found herself surprised and pleased that he remembered the line she always thanked him with when he had come to her defense.

"That's a line from my past," he said wryly.

"I did have a gift for getting into scrapes," she admitted reluctantly.

"I remember. What was the name of that kid who chased you home after the game at Harrison Park?"

"I don't remember," she said stiffly, though of course she remembered perfectly.

"Ned?"

"Nelbert," she offered reluctantly, even though it was an admission she might remember after all.

"Why was he chasing you?"

"I don't remember."

"Just a sec. I do!"

*Please, no.*

"You told him he was more stupid than a dog who chased skunks," Brand recalled, "Right?"

"I thought because I'd learned to say it in Japanese I could get away with it. As it turned out, tone was everything."

And just when she had thought she was dead, because she had made it all the way home and no one had been there, Nelbert practically breathing down her neck, Brand had stepped out of the shadows off his porch. He had folded his arms across his chest, planted his legs and smiled, only it hadn't really been a smile.

He hadn't done anything else, nor had to. Nelbert had stopped dead, and skulked off, not even daring to glare at her. Nelbert had never tried to even the score again, either.

"Japanese," Brand said, and gave a rueful little shake of his head. "You were always a character."

*A character. Thanks. I'm hoping for my own comic-book series.*

"So, what are you doing in my dad's yard in your—" He studied her intently for a minute. "—is that a nightgown?"

"Oh, you know, just doing what comes naturally. Being a character."

See? Just when she thought she had nothing to be grateful for, Sophie had been saved from getting married in front of the whole town in a dress that people would say looked like a night-gown, her gift for getting things exactly wrong not as far in her past as she might have hoped.

She continued brightly, "I was just doing a little burning. Some rubbish." She began to edge her way toward the hole in the hedge. Men like Brand Sheridan were like drugs. He could make her forget what she'd come out here to do—say good-bye to romantic notions.

Not to start believing in them all over again. A man like him could make a woman like her—determined to face the world, strong, realistic, independent—capitulate to a weaker side. A side that leaned toward the fantastic—pirates, earlobe nibbling, or the worst fantasy of all: *forever*.

"You're burning rubbish at—" He glanced at his watch, frowned. "—midnight?" He frowned and shot a glance at the house. "Does my dad know you're out here?"

"He's away." She edged closer to the hedge. "Didn't he know you were coming?"

Dr. Sheridan was busy wooing Sophie's grandmother, who had come from Germany after Sophie's parents had died, reading between the lines of Sophie's proclamations she was just fine, *knowing,* as only a grandmother knew, that she wasn't *fine,* trying to fix it with schnitzel and *kaese spechle*.

Magic foods that had helped, if not healed. Helped not just her, but Dr. Sheridan after Mrs. Sheridan had died so suddenly.

This weekend her grandmother and Brand's father were taking in Shakespeare at the Park in Waterville, the next town over. They were staying the night.

Sophie had not enquired about whether their accommodations were single or double. She didn't want to know, and they were always so sweetly discreet. But it certainly didn't feel like her place to update Brand on his father's love life.

"I thought I'd surprise him," Brand said.

There was something in the way he said that, with a certain flat grimness in his tone, that made her think Brand probably knew his picture had been taken off the family mantel.

She should remember that when his scent was acting like a drug on her resolutions. He was a man who couldn't even come home for his own mother's funeral. His father had not said *couldn't,* but *wouldn't.*

"Your dad will be home tomorrow." She remembered the lateness of the hour. "Or is that today? I guess it is today, now. Sunday. Yes."

He'd always had this effect on her. Smart, articulate woman manages to make a fool out of herself every time she opens her mouth.

*I'm not fifteen,* her inner voice shouted. Out loud, she said pleasantly, "And I'm sure he will be surprised. Well, good—"

The wind picked that moment to sail a wayward wedding picture cartwheeling across the ground in front of him. He stooped, snagged it, straightened and studied it.

Handed it to her silently.

It was a picture of the inside of a stone chapel, with a bride kneeling at the altar alone, her dress spilling down stone stairs.

A bride alone. At the time the picture had seemed blissfully romantic, with a serenity to it, a sacredness. In light of her new circumstances, the bride looked abandoned. She should have been more careful about the pictures she cut out.

Sophie crumpled it and threw it in the box.

"Rubbish," she reiterated proudly.

He studied her for a long, stripping moment. It occurred to her he might be able to tell she'd been crying. She hoped not!

"That's not a nightgown, is it, Sweet Pea?" His voice was suddenly soft, impossibly gentle for a man with such hard lines in his face and such a cynical light in his eyes.

Just like that, he was the man who had called her the night her parents had been killed, getting her through the hours that followed, *awww, Sweet Pea.*

She steeled herself against his pirate charm.

"No," she said and tilted her chin proudly, "It's not a nightgown."

"Are you going to up and get married?" he asked, and his tone had that familiar teasing note in it, a note that did not match the new lines in his face.

Had Brand and his father become that estranged? That Dr. Sheridan didn't even share the town news with him? The gossip, everyone knowing everyone else's business, who was having babies and who was getting married— and who was splitting up—was part of what made a small town tick!

Still, there was something refreshing, freeing, about being with the only person in her world who didn't know her history. Who wasn't sending her sideways looks, loaded with sympathy now that Gregg had chosen another.

"I'm marrying the mystery of the night," she told him solemnly. "It's an ancient ceremony that dates back to the worship of goddesses."

He contemplated her for a moment, and she had that feeling again. Why did she always feel *driven* to say foolish things around him?

But then he rewarded her with a smile that, ever so briefly, chased the dark shadow from his eyes.

"Sweet Pea, you were always an original."

"Yes, I know, an original *character*."

"Do you know how rare that is in the world?" The sadness in his eyes had returned.

She didn't. She wanted to invite him to the fire so he could tell her what a good thing it was. Wanted to chase the shadows from his eyes and make him laugh. And feel his touch again.

He was a weakness in a life she was determined to make about strength and independence. If she really practiced ancient ceremonies, which she didn't, Brand Sheridan's sudden arrival would surely be interpreted as a test of her commitment.

"Good night," she said firmly, and pushed her way, finally, through the gap in the prickly hedge. She felt sick when the dress caught, somewhere high up the back of her rib cage, the snagging sound loud against the quiet of the night.

She froze, then pulled tentatively, but she was caught, and even though she reminded herself she didn't need this dress anymore, she couldn't bring herself to risk wrecking it by yanking free.

Now what? Set down the box to free up her hands so she could untangle the dress? Even bending to set down the box was probably going to damage the dress further.

She cast a look over her shoulder, hoping Brand had departed at her firm good-night. But, oh no, he stood there, arms folded over the solidness of his chest, watching her, amusement playing with the stern cast of his features.

Around him, everything always went wrong. Would a dignified departure have been too much to ask for?

Sophie backed up a half step hoping that would release the twig caught in her dress. Instead she heard a brand-new snagging sound at her waist.

How was it she had managed to get through the hedge the first time without incident?

Now she was afraid to move at all in case she tangled the dress further in the twigs. She could throw down the box, but what if its contents scattered *again?*

It seemed like an hour had passed as she contemplated her options. A gentleman would have figured out she needed help.

But Brand, black sheep of his family, was no gentleman. That was evident when she slid him another look.

He was *enjoying* her situation. His shoulders were actually shaking with mirth, though he was trying to keep his expression inscrutable.

"Could you give me a hand?" she snapped.

She would have been better off, she realized, too late, to rip the dress or throw down the box. Because she had invited him in way too close.

He shoved through the hedge, oblivious to the prickles and the fact the gap was way too small to accommodate him. He stood at her shoulder, pressed close. For the second time, the scent of him, warmly, seductively masculine, filled her nostrils. Now, she could also feel the warmth of his breath tickling the nape of her neck, touching the delicate lobe of her ear.

She was instantly covered in goose bumps.

Naturally, he noticed!

"Are you cold, Sophie?" he asked, his voice a rough whisper that intensified the goose bumps.

"Frozen," she managed to mumble, "it's chilly at this time of night."

That declaration gave her an excuse to shiver when his hand touched her arm, heated, Brand branding her.

He laughed softly, not fooled, all too certain

of his charm around women. And she was absurdly, jealously aware this was not the first time he had handled the intricacies of women's clothing.

He might have been touching a wounded, frightened bird, his fingers on her tangled gown were so exquisitely gentle.

*Experienced,* she told herself. Brand Sheridan had been out of her league before he had made a career of being an adventurer. Now, every exotic world he had visited was in his touch.

"There," he said.

She gritted her teeth. "I think I'm caught in one more place. Left side. Waist."

His breath moved away from her ear, she felt his hand trace the line of her waist in the darkness.

With a quick flick of his wrist that came both too soon and not nearly soon enough, she felt him free her. She dashed away without saying thank you and without looking back.

But his chuckle followed her. "By the way, Sweet Pea, you can't marry the night. You promised you were going to wait for me."

Yes, she had. In one of those rash moments of late-night letter writing shortly after he'd left, full of the drama and angst and emotion a girl feels at fifteen and really never again, Sophie had promised she would love him forever. And had she done that? Thrown away the bird in hand for a complete fantasy she had sold herself when she was a young teen?

"Brand Sheridan," she called back, grateful for the distance and the darkness that protected her from his all-seeing gaze, "don't you embarrass me by reminding me of my fifteen-year-old self!"

"I loved your fifteen-year-old self."

A test. A black, star-filled night, a fire roaring in the background, her in a wedding dress, and Brand Sheridan *loving* her, even if it was who she used to be. Not that she should kid herself he'd had an inkling who she was, then or now. Or that what he so casually called love should in any way be mistaken for the real thing.

"You did not," Sophie told him sternly. "You found me aggravating. And annoying. Exceedingly."

His laughter nearly called her back to the other side of the hedge, but no, she was making her escape. She was not going to be charmed by him.

Time to get over it! Maybe it was a good thing Brand Sheridan had finally come home.

Maybe a person had to close the door on the past completely before they could have a hope for the future.

Maybe that's why things had not worked out between her and Gregg.

Ignoring the rich invitation of his laughter, and her desire to see if it could possibly erase whatever haunted his eyes, Sophie scuttled across her own backyard, and through the door of her house, letting it slam behind her.

Brand was aware, as he walked through the darkness back to the front of his father's home, that he felt something he had not felt in a long, long time.

It took him a moment to identify it.

And then he realized that his heart felt light. Sophie Holtzheim, Sweet Pea, was as funny as ever. The fact that it was largely unintentional only made it funnier.

"The goddess in the garden burning *urgent* rubbish *and* marrying the night," he muttered to himself, with a rueful shake of his head.

Still, there was a part that wasn't funny, Brand thought, searching over the casing of the front door for his father's hidden house key. Sweet Pea now looked like the goddess she had alluded to.

He wasn't even quite sure how he'd known it was her, she was so changed. He remembered a freckled face, a shock of reddish hair, always messy, constantly sunburnt and scraped. He remembered glasses, knobby elbows and knees, her hand coming up to cover a wide mouth glittering with silvery braces.

He remembered earnestness, a worried brow, a depth that sometimes took him by surprise and made him feel like the uneasy, superficial boy that he had been.

And no doubt still was.

He also remembered, with a rueful smile, she had been correct. He'd found her intensely irritating.

From the lofty heights of a five-year age difference he had protected his funny little neighbor from bullies, rescued her from scrapes and tolerated, just barely, her crush on him.

For his first year in the military, her letters, the envelopes distinctive in her girlish hand and different colored inks, had followed him. At first just casual, tidbits of town news, a bit of gossip, updates on people they both knew, but eventually she'd been emboldened by the distance, admitting love, promising to wait, pleading for pictures.

He'd felt the kindest thing—and happily also the most convenient—had been to ignore her completely.

He'd been in touch with her only once, in the eight years since he had left here, a call when her parents had been killed in that terrible accident at the train crossing on Miller Street. She'd only been eighteen and he remembered wishing he could be there for her, poor kid.

Sophie had been part of the fabric of his life, someone he had taken for granted, but been fiercely protective of at the same time. He'd always had a thing about protecting Sophie Holtzheim.

He'd been overseas, at a base with one bank of telephones, when his mother had e-mailed him the news within minutes of it happening. He'd waited in line for hours to use one of those phones, needing to say *something* to Sophie. And instead of wise and comforting words coming out of his mouth, he'd held the phone and heard himself say, across the thousands of miles that separated them, *aww, Sweet Pea.*

How much he cared about his aggravating, funny nuisance of a neighbor had taken him by surprise, because if asked he probably would have claimed he was indifferent to her. That was certainly how he had acted the majority of the time. But on the phone that night, his heart felt as if it was breaking in two as he helplessly listened to her sob on the other end of the line. Brand felt as if he'd failed her by being a million miles away, instead of there.

Maybe it was always her eyes that had made him feel so attached to his young neighbor, despite the manly pretense of complete indifference.

Her eyes had a worried look that often creased her brow; they were hazel and huge. Even behind those glasses, they had been gorgeous way before the rest of her was. There had been something in them that was faintly unsettling and certainly older than she was: calm, as if she looked at a person and *knew* secrets about them they had not yet told themselves.

Seeing her tonight, *touching* her, he realized Sophie had grown into the promise of those eyes. And then some.

Her hair had lost the red and deepened to a shade of auburn that the firelight had licked at the edges of, making a man itch to touch it to see if it was fire or silk or a seductive combination of both.

He was not sure where freckles went when

they went away, but there was no hint she had ever been a freckle-face. Her complexion now was creamy and perfect. Not that he had thought about it, but if he had, he would not have envisioned a grown-up Sweet Pea being quite so lovely.

Seeing her as a woman had been slightly unsettling. She had filled out that gown pretty nicely. If he hadn't realized just in time that it was Sweet Pea, he might have let his eyes drift to where the fabric clung to breasts that had been unfettered with anything as sinful as a bra.

But he was still the guy who had stood between her and her tormentors, and there had been as many who tormented her about her success with "What Makes a Small Town Tick" as there had been those who were happy for her.

She'd never known when to back down, either. That girl had a gift for saying the wrong thing at the wrong time.

He'd even vetted her rare suitors, doing his best to scare them off, and given her unsolicited advice.

*Sweet Pea, all men are swine.*

*Including you?*

*Especially me.*

Brand had been the older brother she didn't have but badly needed.

Sweet Pea still lived next door. Didn't anything in Sugar Maple Grove ever change?

Yes, it did. Because she was not the same Sweet Pea he remembered. And he was not the same guy she thought she knew, either. He didn't feel like her older brother anymore.

He had not set foot in this town for eight years. Family occasions had long since moved to his sister's in New York, and his parents had visited him in California.

Brand suddenly remembered his mother's childlike enjoyment of Disneyland, how she would get off the Pirates of the Caribbean ride, and then get right back in line to go again.

*Mom.*

The light heartedness left him, and another feeling hit. Hard. On this porch where his mother had rocked and waited for him to come home, hours after the curfews he had always chaffed against, careless of her feelings.

He was aware he had managed to outrun his grief and his sense of failure toward his family until the exact moment he drove back into town, under that canopy of huge maples that lined the Main Street, past the tidy redbrick-fronted businesses, their bright awnings rolled up for the night.

The residential streets had been so quiet

tonight, the sidewalks between the tree-lined boulevards and large grassy yards with their whitewashed picket fences completely empty.

He could sense people sleeping peacefully under those moss-covered roofs, curtains fluttering out of open, unlocked windows.

It was postcard-pretty small-town America. The place he had sworn his life to protect, and that, ironically, when he was young, he could not wait to get away from.

Now, standing on the porch of the house he had grown up in, searching for a key he knew would still be hidden in the same place, his mother's sweetness gathered around him.

He could practically taste her strawberry lemonade.

His father had made it clear he would never forgive him for not being at her funeral.

The words *deep cover* meant nothing to Dr. Sheridan, who did not consider a career chasing the world's bad guys to be in any way honorable.

There had been no explaining to his father that years of carefully laid work could have been lost if Brand had come home. Lives could have been endangered by breaking the cover.

"I don't want to hear your *excuses*," Dr. Sheridan had said the last time Brand had called.

"He's mad at you, anyway," his sister had told him, always pragmatic, when she had enlisted Brand to make this journey to their childhood home. "There's no sense his being mad at both of us, is there?"

Marcie had told Brand there had been an *incident*. A fire in the kitchen. An unattended frying pan.

His sister had some legitimate concerns and questions about whether their dad, seventy-four on his next birthday, who had never cooked for himself or looked after a house, should be starting now.

*Brand, what if he's losing it? Then what?*

That's what Brand was here to find out.

To do the job nobody else had the stomach for. Didn't that have a familiar ring to it? His whole adult life had been spent stepping up to the plates that wiser men stepped away from.

Finding the key, he went in. Without turning on lights, Brand went up the stairs and into a room with a steeply sloped roof that had once been his.

An open box inside the door was crammed full of Brand's football trophies and school photos—his grad picture was on the top—the one that had once been on the mantel.

He kicked off his shoes, flopped down,

coughing slightly at the cloud of dust that rose out of the unused bedding. He closed his eyes. The whole house had a scorched smell to it that made him miserably aware of his mission.

He opened his eyes again, contemplated the flicker of light on the ceiling and realized the fire was still burning in the yard. He tried to reclaim the lightness he had felt earlier by thinking of his encounter with Sophie.

A thought blasted through his brain, unwelcome and uninvited.

*Had Sweet Pea been crying?*

He got it suddenly. Ah. She wasn't marrying the night. She'd just tried to distract him from the real story with her legendary cleverness. She was in his father's backyard at midnight burning wedding pictures in a wedding dress because somebody had broken her heart.

And it was only a sign of how tired he was, how the world he'd left behind was colliding with the one he'd made for himself, that instead of feeling sad for her, he felt oddly glad.

He didn't want Sweet Pea marrying anyone without his approval. It was as if eight years of separation didn't exist at all, and he was stepping back into the role he'd always assumed around her.

Big brother. Protector.

Only now, he thought, thinking of her huge eyes and the swell of her naked breast beneath the film of that sheer dress, he didn't exactly feel like a big brother. In fact, he could probably add himself to whomever or whatever he was protecting her from.

# CHAPTER THREE

"I THINK I'll call the police," his father said, eyeing him from the bedroom door. "Break and enter is still against the law."

Brand turned over, winced at the light pouring into the room, eyed his father and then the clock. From his sister's reports he had expected his father to look older, frazzled, his white hair sticking up à la Albert Einstein.

Dr. Sheridan, in fact, had already combed his rather luxurious steel-gray hair, and looked quite dapper in dark pants, a crisp white shirt, a suit vest that matched the pants.

"It's not break and enter if you have a key," Brand said mildly. "Hi, Dad." It was nearly noon. Brand had slept for close to twelve hours.

"Humph. I guess you're the expert on all things criminal. If I called the cops, you'd probably flash your badge at them, wouldn't

you? You'd probably have *me* arrested.
Shipped off to an old folks' home. That's why
you're here, isn't it?"

Whoo boy. Everything was going to be a
fight—if he let it. Brand wasn't going to let it.
There was absolutely no point telling his father
he wasn't a cop, and he didn't have a badge.
He was an *operative*. But he wasn't a doctor,
and that's all his father really cared about.

"How are you, Dad?"

"That fire could have happened to anyone,"
his father said, defensively. "Your sister sent
you here, didn't she?"

Brand felt relieved that his dad was obviously mentally agile enough to figure that out.

"Any chance of getting a cup of coffee?"

"Get your own damn coffee," his father
snorted, "I'm having coffee next door."

"At Sophie's?" Brand asked, intrigued.

But his father didn't answer, gave him a dark
look that let him know he was not included in
coffee plans, and slammed the bedroom door.

*That went well,* Brand thought. On the bright
side, Dr. Sheridan hadn't ordered Brand to get
out of his house and never come back. Maybe
there was something here they could salvage.

Unless his sister was right. If his dad was
losing it, not capable of living on his own

anymore, and if Brand was the one who had gathered the evidence, there would be nothing left to salvage.

"How did I get myself into this?"

He'd known he'd have to come home sooner or later, and, as it happened, he needed a place to be safe. God, if Sugar Maple Grove didn't qualify in spades. As if to confirm that, a church bell pealed in the distance.

Brand got up, stretched mightily, aware of how deeply rested he felt.

In four years deep undercover, assuming an identity, moving in a glitzy world of wealth and crime, a man lost something of himself. And he never quite slept. One eye open, part of him ever alert, part of him *hating* the life he lived, making people he would betray like him and trust him.

Well, not him. The role he played—Brian Lancaster—though who he was and who he pretended to be had begun to fuse together in ways he had not expected.

Now, having slept well, Brand felt more himself than he had felt for a long time. Or was it because he had seen the reflection of himself as he used to be, in Sophie's huge hazel eyes?

A funny irony that the place he couldn't wait to get away from might have something to give him back now, all these years later.

"Who could have predicted I would become a man who would treasure a good night's sleep more than most men would treasure gold?" he muttered ruefully to himself.

Brand showered and dressed, then moved downstairs, guiltily aware he was looking for evidence his father might be slipping.

Everything seemed to be in need of repairs, but Dr. Sheridan had never been gifted at things like that, faintly flabbergasted when Brand had shown an early knack with something so primitive as a hammer.

Brand's sister, Marcie, had said, vaguely: *if there's something wrong, you'll know. Mittens in the fridge, that kind of thing.*

"No mittens in the fridge," Brand said, opening the fridge door and peering inside. "No food, either." Did he report that to Marcie?

He went out the front door to his car—a little sports number he'd purchased before his Brian Lancaster assignment. Now, it seemed too much like a car Lancaster would have chosen, and he was aware of wanting to get rid of it.

Brand needed coffee. Did everyone still go for coffee at Maynard's, morning coffee house, afternoon soda fountain and evening ice-cream parlor?

Brand was aware of a reluctance to see *everyone,* the chasms that separated his life from the life in this small town probably too deep to cross.

He never made it to the car.

"Young man. You! Come!"

An old woman, dapper in a red hat, was waving at him from Sophie's porch. He saw his dad and Sophie out there, too, and remembered Sunday brunch on the porch was always something of a pre-church tradition in Sugar Maple Grove.

He could smell the coffee from here and it smelled rich and good and added to that sense of coming home to small-town America.

He hesitated only for a moment, was drawn by curiosity to see Sophie in the light of day, and went through the gap in the hedge that separated the front lawns. The path between the houses was worn.

He registered, peripherally, a man trained to notice everything, that there was a lot of going back and forth between these two houses.

When his dad wasn't around, he would have to thank Sophie for looking in on him.

Sophie's porch was out of the American dream: deep shadows, dark wicker furniture with bright-yellow striped cushions, a gray-painted wood floor, purple-and-white petunias spilling color and scent out of window boxes.

And she was part of the same dream. Despite the fact his father and the old woman were there, Brand could see only Sophie. Somehow, in the years between them, she had gone from being a delightful little nerd to the all-American girl.

"Good morning, Sweet Pea," he said, taking the empty seat beside her.

"Don't call me that." Then, with ill grace, remembering her manners, "Brandon, this is my grandmother, Hilde Holtzheim."

"The pleasure is mine, but my granddaughter, she is not a sweet pee in the morning," the old woman said in heavily accented English, "More like a sour poop."

He could tell from the accent that Sophie's grandmother was German, and he almost greeted her in that language, one of three he spoke fluently thanks to countless hours in language school getting ready for overseas undercover assignments.

But before he could speak, Sophie did.

"Grandma! He doesn't mean that kind of pee! He's talking about a flower." Sophie was blushing. Brand could already feel that heavy place in him lightening.

"Oh." Sophie's grandmother's eyes widened. "He compares you with flowers?" she asked in German. "That's romantic!"

Maybe, he decided, it would be way more fun not to let on he spoke German. His father, colossally indifferent to any career choice outside of medicine, did not know his only son spoke any language other than English.

His decision paid off immediately when Hilde turned to Sophie and said in rapid German, "Ach. Gorgeous. You and him. Beautiful babies."

Sophie shot him a glance, and Brand kept his expression carefully bland, congratulated himself because it was obviously going to be so entertaining *not* to let on he spoke German.

"What did she say?" he asked Sophie innocently.

Today, Sophie wore a white T-shirt and shorts. Her hair, that amazing shade of mink browns and coppers mixed, was thick and sleep-rumpled. It was half caught up, half falling out of a rubber band. She didn't have a lick of makeup on.

She looked all of sixteen, but he knew she hadn't looked like this at sixteen because he had been the recipient of a picture taken at her sixteenth birthday party and she'd still been awkward then, duckling, pre-swan.

Now, it occurred to Brand that Sophie was going to be one of those women who came more and more into herself as she got older, but who would somehow look young and fresh when she was fifty.

"She said you don't look like the kind of man who would be interested in flowers." She shot Hilde a warning look.

"What kind of man do I look like?" he asked Hilde.

He was aware of liking sitting beside Sophie. She smelled of soap, nothing else, and he was surprised by how much he had missed something as simple and as real as a girl sitting on her front porch with no makeup and no perfume and her hair not styled.

She tried to hide her naked legs under the tablecloth, but before they disappeared, he noticed her toenails were painted candy-floss pink.

And he was struck again with a sense of having missed such innocence. In the world of Brian Lancaster, there had been no modesty. The types of women who were attracted to the wealth and power of the types of men he had been dedicated to putting in jail all aspired to be swimsuit models or actresses.

They were tanned, fit, artificially enhanced

and wore lots of makeup and very little clothing. He did not think he had seen a natural hair color in four years. They had also been slickly superficial, materialistic and manipulative. For four years he had been surrounded by the new and international version of the old-fashioned mafia moll. His colleagues envied him the lifestyle he pretended at, but he had felt something souring in his own soul.

Brand had not even allowed himself to think of this world back here, of women who didn't care about flashy rings, designer clothes, parties, lifestyles so decadent it would have put the Romans to shame.

It occurred to him that he might have died of loneliness if he had allowed his thoughts to drift to someone like Sophie as he immersed himself deeper and deeper into a superficial world where people were willing to do anything—absolutely anything—to insure their place in it.

"You look like a man," Hilde said, starting in English and switching to German, "who would have a kiss that could change lead into gold."

"She says you look like a man with a good appetite," Sophie said, without missing a beat. "She wants you to eat something."

The table was loaded with croissants and muffins and homemade jams, fresh fruit, frosty glasses oi juice—the simple meal seemed so good and so real after the world he had come from.

His stomach rumbled as the old lady in the red hat glared at her granddaughter, smiled approvingly at him, poured him a juice and then coffee.

"Eat," she insisted, and then in German, "A man like you needs his strength."

Sophie's German was halting. "Stop," she warned her grandmother, "be good."

"I'm supposed to be the old lady, not you," Hilde muttered, unrepentant. In German. "Look at his lips."

He was aware that Sophie looked, then looked away.

"Enough to make any woman," Hilde searched for the word in German, blurted out in English, "swine."

"Swoon," Sophie corrected her automatically, and then turned beet-red. "She says to tell you the raspberry jam is to swoon for. She means to die for."

The old woman was staring at his lips. "Yes, to die for."

He laughed. "That's mighty good jam."

Brand was aware his father had his arms folded stubbornly over his chest, not finding the hilarity all that hilarious. Brand dutifully looked at his father for any signs of malnourishment, given the condition of his fridge, but the elder Sheridan actually looked fleshier than Brand could ever remember in the past.

He turned his attention back to Sophie, who was still blushing. In the light of day, he was aware again how pretty she had become in a wholesome way, and how watching a girl like her blush was an underrated pleasure.

After the life he had lived undercover—infiltrating a gang of exceedingly wealthy and sophisticated weapons smugglers and currency counterfeiters—there was something about her wholesomeness—her ability to blush—that appealed to him, shocked him by making him yearn for a road not taken.

It occurred to him that maybe people should listen to the adage "you can't go home again" and not even try.

Because he could never be this innocent again. But maybe he could just enjoy this moment for what it was: simple, enjoyable, companionable.

He was aware, again, that that was the first

time in years he had felt relaxed in a social situation.

*Safe,* he thought in a way only someone who lived with constant danger could appreciate. Once, he had hated how this place never changed.

Now, he thought, maybe a month here wouldn't be so bad after all.

He could see Hilde eyeing him with unremitting interest, despite Sophie elbowing her in the ribs and warning her in soft German to quit staring.

"Your father tells me you're a secret agent," Hilde said, pushing Sophie's elbow away.

"No," he said firmly, though it surprised him his father had said anything about him, since he was persona non grata. "I belong to a military branch that was developed as an antiterrorism squad. I'm just a soldier."

"Very exciting," Hilde declared.

"Not really. Ninety-nine percent pure tedium, one percent all hell breaking loose."

"But you were under the covers?"

He saw Sophie, who was just beginning to recover from her last blush, turning a lovely shade of pink all over again beside him. In the world he had just come from, women didn't blush. And they said things a whole lot more suggestive than *you were under the covers*. Sophie's blush was so refreshing.

"I was. It's not as exciting as it sounds, believe me." The grandmother didn't look like she believed him, so he headed her off at the pass. "Sophie, I didn't have a chance to catch up with you last night. It's been what? Eight years? What do you do now?"

"Last night?" his father sputtered.

Brand could tell by Sophie's sudden slathering of marmalade on a croissant that what she had been doing last night was private to her. That instinct to protect her rose to the surface instantly.

"We ran into each other briefly when I arrived." He watched her out of the corner of his eye, saw her catch a breath of relief that the details of her secret ceremony by the fire were safe with him.

Still, if he remembered correctly, Sophie didn't even like marmalade.

"Oh," his father said, his tone crotchety.

Her grandmother looked disappointed, Sophie looked relieved. She took a bite of her croissant, and her eyes nearly crossed. She glared at the marmalade.

"I'll take that one," he said smoothly and passed her his own croissant and the jar of raspberry jam. "As I recall, your grandmother says this is the one to swine for."

He smiled at her to let her know he'd noticed she was rattled. And he raised an eyebrow evilly that asked if it was him that was rattling her.

But when she took a little nibble of the new croissant, ignoring the jam, and a crumb stuck at the corner of her mouth, he wondered just who was rattling whom.

"I work for the Historical Society," Sophie said, but reluctantly. "I'm sure you would find what I do exceedingly boring."

"It's not," his father rushed to her defense. "Sophie is our only paid employee at the Society. She's a whiz at organization. A whiz! She's going to write a book."

"Well, not exactly," she said swiftly, blushing sweetly *again*. "I'm going to gather material for a book. A collection of remembrances of Sugar Maple Grove during the Second World War. I won't really be writing it so much as selecting and editing."

It occurred to Brand that once upon a time he *would* have found Sophie's choice of work exceedingly boring. But having just spent four years around women who were ditzy, who thought it was cute to be dumb, he found himself intrigued by Sophie's career choice.

His father began to talk about the book with great relish—and considerable savvy.

Brand allowed himself to hope his sister was wrong, and to sink deeper into the feeling of being somewhere good. And decent.

Then the mood suddenly changed. A bright-red sports car was slowing in front of the house, then, apparently having spotted the people on the porch, it pulled in.

Sophie had been starting to relax as Dr. Sheridan had waxed lyrical about Sugar Maple Grove's contribution to the war.

Now Brand was aware of her freezing, like a deer caught in headlights. Unless he was mistaken, she was getting ready to bolt.

"The nerve," her grandmother said, and then in German, "I'd like to cover him in honey and stake him out over an ant hill. Naked."

Brand, practiced at deception, never let on with so much as a flicker of a smile that he understood her perfectly. He watched, as did they all, as the man got out of his car.

If there was one thing Brand had gotten very good at spotting—and not being the least impressed by—it was wealth and all its trappings, the car, the designer sweater, the knife-pressed pants, the flash of a solid-gold pinkie ring.

"Mama's boy," his father hissed with disdain,

and then shot Brand a look and muttered sulkily, "not that that's *always* such a bad thing."

But as he was reading the shift of mood at the table, it was Sophie that Brand was most aware of.

She had gone white as a sheet, and he could see tension in the curve of her neck, in the sudden locking of her fingers. She had hunched over as if she was trying to make herself smaller.

He had a memory from a long time ago. He and some friends shooting baskets at the riverside park where Main Street ended. Sophie had been walking home from school. She'd been thirteen, it had been after her speech in that national competition.

"Hey, metal mouth," some Main Street big shot had yelled at her. "What makes a small-town *hick?* You!"

Brand's eyes had flown to Sophie. He had seen her hunch over those books, trying hard to make herself invisible.

Brand had come out of that group shooting baskets and been across the street in a breath. He'd picked up that loser by his T-shirt collar, shoved him against the wall and held him there.

"Don't you ever pick on that girl again,"

he'd said, his quietness not beginning to hide his rage. "Or I'll make you into a small-town brick, pound you down to dust, make you into a little square and stick you on this wall forever. *Comprende?*"

Even then he'd had a certain warped gift for tackling things in a way that had made him a prime find, first for the United States Marine Corps and then for the unit he now served.

Through those organizations, Brand had become much more disciplined in his use of force, at channeling righteous fury to better purpose, at choosing when aggression was the appropriate response.

A frightened nod, and Brand had let the creep go, caught up to Sophie and slipped the books away from her.

"Put your head up," he'd told her. "Don't you ever let a dork like that control you, Sweet Pea."

No gratitude, of course.

She'd given him her snotty look, and said, "Brand Sheridan, don't even pretend you know what a dork is."

"It's a guy like that."

"It's a whale penis," she told him. And then she blushed as if she had said or done something *really* bad, and surprisingly, he had blushed, too.

Now, sitting here beside her, he tried to think if he had blushed like that since then. Or at all. He doubted it.

But she still blushed.

Suddenly, Brand was aware she had flexed the muscles in her legs, just enough to push back slightly from the table, and he just knew she was going to bolt.

And that for some reason he couldn't let her. It was a variation of holding her head up high. He laid a hand on her arm, not holding her down, just resting his fingers lightly on her skin, his own hand completely still, willing his own stillness into her.

He felt her eyes on his face, but he didn't look at her, didn't take his eyes off the man who had made her shrink as if she was still the town brainiac carrying her books down Main Street, a target for every smart aleck with an opinion.

Brand was aware, even as he made himself go still, even as he let her see and feel only his stillness, that something in him coiled, *ready,* ready to protect her with his life if need be.

He didn't know exactly what was going on. But Brand knew whatever it was she couldn't run from this. Whoever Slick was coming up her front walk, Sophie shouldn't let him know he had that much power over her.

*Why did he?*

Slick came up the steps, sockless in designer sandals, and flashed them a smile made astoundingly white by perfect porcelain veneers.

"Dr. Sheridan. The *misses* Holtzheim."

He seemed unaware that no one looked happy to see him, that he would have to search long and hard to find a more unwelcoming group in Sugar Maple Grove.

He raised spa-shaped eyebrows at Brand, and put out his hand.

Brand half rose, took it, felt the softness, and squeezed just a little harder than might be considered strictly polite.

He did not return the smile, intensely aware of how stiff Sophie had become, her face rigid with pride, even as her hands gripped the table-cloth just out of view, white-knuckled.

"Brand Sheridan," he introduced himself.

"Oh, our war vet! What an honor, the hero returning to Sugar Maple Grove." His tone was *aw, shucks,* but Brand did not miss something faintly condescending in it. "I'm Gregg Hamilton."

Ah, the Hamiltons. Strictly white-collar. Old money. That explained the underlying disdain for the public servant.

"I think you might have gone to school with my brother, Clarence."

*I think I might have taken a round out of him behind the school for having exactly the same snotty look on his face that you do.*

Somewhere along the line the military had managed to channel all that aggression he'd visited on others. His father might not be willing to admit what a good thing that was, but Brand knew he was a better man for it.

Brand shrugged, letting nothing of his own growing disdain show in his face. This was what he was good at, after all, never letting on what he was really feeling.

"Sophie, Mama told me she dropped by yesterday. I just wanted to echo her invitation to come to Toni's and my engagement party. It would be so good if you came. I think you'll adore Antoinette. I'm hoping you'll be friends."

Hilde Holtzheim muttered something in German that was the equivalent of *go screw yourself, worm face.*

Suddenly Brand put together Sophie sitting in front of that fire last night in her wedding dress, burning all manner of wedding paraphernalia with her tension at the unexpected arrival of Slick Hamilton.

Surely, Sophie hadn't been going to marry this guy? Worm face?

But a quick glance at Sophie, trying so hard to retain her pride, a plastic smile glued across her face, confirmed it.

Not only had she been going to, it looked like she regretted the fact she wasn't! The little ceremony he'd interrupted at the fire pit last night was all beginning to make an ugly kind of sense now.

Well, that's what happened when you left a lovely hometown girl, innocent to the ways of the world, to her own devices for too many years. She had all kinds of room to screw up.

"Um," Sophie stalled, "I haven't checked the calendar yet. What day was it?"

Brand hated seeing her squirm, and he hated it that she was so transparent. The little worm could see just how badly he'd managed to hurt her—which was exactly the kind of thing that made little worms like him feel gleeful with power.

Gregg actually looked as if he was enjoying himself enough to pull up a chair and have a croissant with them!

Brand slid Sophie a look. Slick Hamilton wasn't the kind of threat you had to keep a hand free to get at your hidden holster for.

The look on her face reminded him of another time when he'd found her on this porch, alone, on the swing over there, listening to music drifting up from the high school. It had probably been sometime in that year before he left.

He'd been rushing somewhere, though it was funny how that somewhere had seemed so important at the time, but he couldn't remember it now.

But he could remember the look on her face as clearly as if it had happened yesterday.

"What's up?" he'd asked her.

"Nothing."

"Come on. You can't lie to me, Sweet Pea. How come you aren't at the school dance?"

"It's the Sweetheart Prom," she said and then her face had crumpled even as her chin had tilted proudly. "Nobody asked me to go."

At nineteen what did a guy know about tears except that he didn't want to be anywhere around them? A better person than nineteen-year-old him had been might have dropped his other plans, changed clothes, taken her to the prom.

But he hadn't. He had chucked her on the chin, told her proms rated pretty high on the stupid scale and gotten on with his own life.

Brand thought suddenly of all those cute letters she had sent him when he'd joined up, when he'd been posted overseas. His one-gal fan club. The envelopes always decorated with stickers and different colored inks, the contents unintentionally hilarious enough that he had read every word.

Never answered any, though. Not even once.

Had her younger self waited by the mailbox, hoping?

So, maybe it was because he regretted doing the right thing by her only when it was convenient for him back then that he made a decision now. He owed her something. A smidgen of decency, compassion in a hard world.

Being undercover had taught him to read situations, and this one was obviously going as badly for her as it was going well for Gregg.

It felt like the most natural thing in the world to rescue Sophie.

"I think Sophie's going to have to say no," Brand said smoothly. "I'm only here for a little while. We don't want to waste any of our time together, do we, honey?"

He turned to look at her. She was no actress. If Slick Hamilton saw her mouth hanging open in shock, he'd know the truth.

And Brand didn't want him to know the truth. That she still loved Gregg Slick Hamilton. Or thought she did.

There was one way they both could find out.

He caught her cute little puffy bottom lip with his. Touched it, ran his tongue along it, made her world only about him.

It was probably a sin how much he liked it, but Brand was pretty sure his place was reserved in hell, anyway.

And the kiss accomplished exactly what he wanted.

Sophie was staring at him with wide-eyed awareness as if Gregg had vaporized into a speck in front of them. She licked her lip and her eyes had gone all smoky with longing.

Nope.

No matter what she might have convinced herself, she didn't love Gregg Hamilton and never had.

Not that Brand considered himself any kind of an expert on love.

Lips, though, that was quite another thing.

And he liked hers. A whole lot more than he'd expected to. His sense of having sinned deeply grew more acute.

"Well, Sophie," the swagger was completely gone out of Gregg's voice, "You know you're welcome to come. Bring your new friend with you."

The invitation was issued now with the patent insincerity of a man who saw something he'd been using to puff himself up disappearing before his eyes.

"We might just do that," Brand said easily.

Gregg got in his car and roared away, spitting stones as if they proved his testosterone levels were substantially higher than those of the next guy.

Brand committed to getting rid of his own sports car sooner rather than later.

"Were they to swine for?" Hilde demanded, mixing German and English.

"What?" Sophie asked, dazed.

"His lips!"

"No. Yes." She closed her eyes, gathered herself and then looked sternly at her grandmother. "Stop."

And then she turned to Brand. The dazed expression was completely gone from her face.

"What did you do that for?" she demanded.

He tried not to smile. The girl was transparent! It was written all over her that she was torn between yes and no, stop and go, hitting him or thanking him.

And it was written all over her that that kiss had rocked her tidy world in a way she would never want him to know. But then again, he didn't really want her to suspect it had rocked his, too.

"Your ex was just gloating over your discomfort at his arrival a little too much," he said quietly. "It bugged me."

"How did you know he was my ex?" she asked, aghast.

"I'm good at reading people," he said. He didn't add that it was a survival mechanism, that over the past few years his life had depended on that skill. "I'm glad about the ex part, Sophie. I didn't care for him much."

Her grandmother snickered with approval and Sophie shot her a quelling look.

"You only saw him for thirty seconds!"

"Like I said," he lifted a shoulder elaborately, "I have a gift for reading people."

"He looked like a good kisser," her grandmother insisted in German.

"Stop it!" Sophie said in English.

"Stop what?" Brand asked innocently.

She looked him straight in the face. "Stop rescuing me, Brand. I'm not fifteen anymore. I don't need your help with my personal affairs."

She blushed when she said *affairs* in just about the way she had when she'd said *dork* all those years ago, as if she was fifteen and had just used a risqué word. It was very sweet. *She* was very sweet. The kind of girl he knew nothing about.

She was right. He needed to stop rescuing her.

"It was just an impulse," he said. "It won't happen again."

She struggled to look composed. Instead she looked crushed.

"Unless you want it to," he couldn't resist tossing out silkily.

"I want it to," Hilde said, all in English. She reached across the table, touched Brand's hand. The mischief was gone from her eyes. "The whole town is whispering about my Sophie and *him*. I'd much rather they whispered about my Sophie and you."

# CHAPTER FOUR

SOPHIE was still stuck on the *unless you want it to* part. Good God, she thought, she might be super-nerd of national-speech-contest fame, but of course she wanted it to. Happen again.

Sophie's lips were tingling from being kissed. She felt exactly like a princess who had been sleeping, the touch of those lips bringing her fully to life. She was aware some part of her had waited, longed for, wanted what had just happened since she was a scrawny flat-chested teen in braces and glasses.

His lips had tasted of passion and promises and of worlds she had never been to. Had not even known existed. Places she wanted desperately, suddenly, now that she did know of their existence, to visit.

Who wouldn't want more of that?

But, unless she was mistaken, Brand was

enjoying her discomfort as much as he had just accused Gregg of doing.

Men!

Not that any man could hold a candle to her grandmother, who apparently felt driven to share with Brand Sophie's closely guarded secret, that she was somehow becoming pathetic.

Sophie struggled through her embarrassment to remember her mission last night. To be free of all her romantic notions and nonsense.

She wasn't letting Mr. Brand Sheridan think she was still the starry-eyed fifteen-year-old she had once been.

She wasn't letting him know that one tiny ultra-casual brushing of lips had her ready to pack her bags and travel to unknown territory.

No! Sophie Holtzheim was taking back control and she was doing it right now. If Brand thought she was weak and pathetic and in need of his big, strong, arrogant self to rescue her, he'd better think again!

But Brand was looking at her grandmother, and suddenly he didn't look as if he was enjoying her discomfort over that kiss.

"It's a bad thing to lose face in a small town," he said quietly.

"Yes!" her grandmother crowed, delighted that he had understood her so completely.

"It would be good for Sophie to have a romance so heated it would make the whole town forget she ever knew him," Brand said thoughtfully

"Yes!" Her grandmother was beaming at his astuteness.

"Okay, I'll do it," Brand said, casually, as if he had agreed to his good deed for the day.

"Do what?" Sophie demanded.

"Romance you."

"You will not!"

"It will convince Gregg and the whole town that you're over him," Brand said with aggravating confidence, as if it was already decided.

"It's deceptive," Sophie said, and then realized that wasn't the out-and-out no that such an outlandish suggestion deserved.

"It could be fun," Brand said.

"I doubt that."

He raised an eyebrow at her in clear challenge. And then said, softly, "What are you afraid of?"

Now the only way she was going to show him she wasn't the least bit afraid of what had just happened between them was if she said yes. If she protested this idea too strenuously, he might know the truth: she *was* terrified of him and his ability to tear her safe little world so far apart she might never succeed in putting it back together.

But she had to admit there was something wonderfully seductive about saving face. It really was horrible to be branded as pathetic in a small town.

"Well, Brand," she said slowly, thoughtfully, "maybe we could have a little fake fling, under carefully orchestrated circumstances, of course."

"And let me guess," he said wryly, "you will be in charge of orchestrating the circumstances?"

If she was going to do this, and she had a sinking feeling that she was, she had to maintain absolute control over the situation.

He watched her, some challenge lighting the sapphire depths of his eyes until they sparkled like falling stars in a night sky. It was a look that could take away a woman's courage. It could intimidate. It could shake her belief that she could be in control of everything. Or anything.

If she allowed it to, that was, if she hadn't just vowed in front of her own burning dreams she was going to be a different kind of woman from now on.

The take-charge kind.

"How long are you going to be here,

Brand?" she asked, keeping her voice all business.

"Maybe a month. I've got a lot of leave built up."

"A month?" his father sputtered, and then sent Hilde an aggrieved look that Sophie easily interpreted as his son's presence in his life cramping his romantic ambitions.

Brand's eyes narrowed on his father for a moment, then he glanced at Hilde.

Hilde, naturally, looked unabashedly delighted at Brand's announcement of a long-term stay in Sugar Maple Grove. It was written all over her face that she was already planning Brand and Sophie's wedding.

And an adorable little house filled with babies. She hoped Hilde wouldn't say it, not even in German. Because her grandmother was known to say anything, commenting on Brand's kissing abilities being a case in point. What kind of grandmother did that?

Sophie slid Brand a look. The full force of his attention was back on her. Well, there was no denying he was a good kisser and would produce perfect babies. But if she wanted to stay in control of the perilous situation she was moving herself toward, she'd better not go there!

"What are you going to do here for a month?" Dr. Sheridan asked sulkily. "You'll be bored in three days. Ha. Maybe in three hours."

Once, Sophie knew, Brand would have risen to the bait, argued whether what his father said was true or not, and it probably was. He had been hotheaded, impulsive, impatient.

Now, there was something new in him, something coolly disciplined that made him both harder to read and more intriguing.

Brand just shrugged and said, "It'll probably take me a month to fix everything in your house that is broken."

She looked between the two men, and saw it wasn't just the house that needed fixing.

Sophie could feel her head starting to ache. Those Sheridan men were probably going to need her help to navigate the minefield between them.

Great. She was going to have to do that while never letting Brand know how that kiss had rattled her world. How him sitting beside her on a sleepy Sunday morning made her feel aware and alive.

But, she reminded herself, this was exactly what she needed. To prove to herself she wasn't fifteen anymore, the mere whiff of him enough to make her waste her life dreaming of happily-ever-afters. No, she was all grown up now and immune to his charm, considerable as that was.

Once she did that, longing for things that didn't exist wouldn't have the power to ruin her life anymore.

She could be a realist, dismiss that longing for *something*. It wouldn't be there, like a villain waiting in the wings, ready to rain disaster on her well-planned future and life.

But she knew she was playing with fire. Because that *something* was exactly what she had tasted on his lips.

*Walk into it, girl,* she ordered herself. *If you want to play with fire, walk straight into the flame.* There would be nothing like a dose of reality to kill her fantasies forever.

"Well, Brand," she said, taking that mental leap off Blue Rock, "since you're going to be here, you might as well help me out. It's true, this whole town thinks I'm pining away for my ex-fiancé, Gregg, who is about to become officially engaged to someone else."

"Are you?" he asked softly.

"Of course not!" But she could feel a blush rising up her neck as she said it, and she could see she had not convinced him.

She took a deep breath, walked straight into

the fire. "So, I'll accept your offer. Yes, you can pretend to be my beau."

It was like falling straight off a cliff. And no one hated heights more than she did!

"Beau?" he said, and then laughed. "Who uses a word like that in this day and age? I think you've been spending just a little too much time at the Historical Society, Sweet Pea."

"You are every bit as annoying as I remember!" she said, exasperated. It was hard enough for her to keep her dignity while accepting his offer.

"You *never* thought I was annoying," he said with the silky and aggravating confidence of a man who, unfortunately, women did not find annoying. Ever.

"Remember the time you said you were going to the library and I gave you my books to return and you didn't?"

"I wasn't really going to the library," he said.

"Whatever. Annoying. Six dollars in fines."

"Your only brush with the law?"

She ignored him. "And how about the time you showed up at my door with a kitten two minutes before I was supposed to be leaving for band camp?"

"You *loved* that kitten," he said, with a grin.

She had. The gift had *melted* her.

"That's not the point. The point is that I was late for band camp, and so I didn't get the instrument I wanted, and I had to play the tuba for a whole week and it was your fault."

"Band camp is for nerds."

"My point exactly," she said, triumphantly. "You are annoying! Supremely! You will have to try and keep that in check as we conduct our—" She couldn't bring herself to say romance. "—arrangement."

"Do you still play the tuba?" he asked sweetly. "Didn't you send me a recording? When I was in basic?"

Sophie could feel her face getting very hot. "I didn't!"

"Uh-huh. A tuba solo. A love song."

"It wasn't a tuba," she said petulantly. "Clarinet. My instrument of choice."

He raised a wicked, wicked eyebrow at her.

How could he do this? *Instrument* was not a dirty word!

"Never mind," Sophie said. "I just realized how rash it was to agree to this. I'm not sure I'm desperate enough to have you for my beau, even temporarily."

"Aw, shucks," he said. "Just when I was starting to think it might be fun. Like porcupine-wrestling in my birthday suit."

He had inserted that reference deliberately to see if he could make her blush again.

And damn him, he could.

"Are you backing out?" she demanded.

"No, I think you are."

"I'm not!"

"Ha," Dr. Sheridan muttered, "I'd be interested to see if the all-important Brand Sheridan, secret agent, would do anything as selfless as help an old neighbor so she could hold her head up high again. Trust me, Sophie, it's not in my son's nature to do the decent thing."

Sophie felt shocked at the doctor's bitter tone, and she saw Brand flinch as if he'd been struck.

She had found the bantering back and forth between her and Brand edgy, but playful, dangerously invigorating.

Now the tension that leapt in the air between him and his father was painful and tangible.

But again, the young man who would have risen to the bait, defended himself or argued, was not part of who Brand was now. Instead he replied, disciplined patience in his voice, "I'm just a soldier. I do what I'm told, when I'm told. I was on an undercover assignment. I was told I wouldn't be granted leave. Period."

"Whatever," his father said.

"If I could have been here, I would have."

"Whatever," his father said again.

"And if Sophie agrees, we'll do this thing."

She felt the flutter of her heart. It wasn't a good idea. To play a charade for the whole town was a stupid, impulsive idea that fell solidly into the category of really dumb things that she always did around him.

But could she walk away from giving Brand a perfect opportunity to redeem himself a tiny bit in his father's eyes while he was here?

It would help her, it would help him.

Even now, he and his father were eyeing each other balefully.

And she felt compelled to insert herself between them, to ease the tension.

"I'll do it," she announced decisively.

"Oh, goody," her grandmother said.

"Oh, brother," his father said.

"Oh," Brand said, then, "great." Spoken with the macho bravado of a man who had been chosen from many to diffuse a bomb.

"Let's talk romance," Sophie suggested brightly. "I'll come up with a plan. A few highly visible activities: ice cream at Maynard's, maybe a bike ride or two, an appearance at Blue Rock and then—ta-da—you and I at the engagement party."

Brand watched her talk, ruefully aware she was trying to ease the tension between him and his father. She'd been like that as a kid, too. Always wanting everything to look like a Norman Rockwell painting.

Sugar Maple Grove lent itself to that.

But now Sophie was not a kid. Not if those lips had spoken the truth about her, and he was pretty sure they had.

He was also ruefully aware that, despite her engagement and the promise of those lips, Sophie still seemed to be a sweet geek in the romance department. A plan? What kind of romance had a plan?

*A fake one,* he reminded himself sternly.

Brand was struck by a tingling awareness along the back of his neck. It was his sharply honed instinct. It always warned him when danger was near.

He had done many, many dangerous things.

But he doubted any of them were going to hold a candle to pretending to be Miss Sophie Holtzheim's *beau.*

Why had he agreed to this?

Partly because he couldn't resist protecting

Sophie. It seemed that's what he had been born to do, protect.

It was going to be a long, hot month in Sugar Maple Grove, and a man couldn't be faulted for finding a way to entertain himself.

His father, with one last look at him, not friendly, shoved back his chair. "I'm going to be late for church."

"Oh, that time already?" Hilde said in English, and in German, "We'll leave you two alone, Sophie. Do something romantic, for God's sake."

In a flurry of activity his dad and Hilde left and it was suddenly so quiet he could hear birds singing and bees buzzing.

He waited to see if Sophie would do something romantic. Sophie, predictably, did nothing of the sort.

"Don't you have a girlfriend who's going to object to this?" she asked. It sounded like an effort—albeit a weak one—to find a way out.

"I don't have a girlfriend," he said. "This job busts people up. It's too hard on the ones left behind. I was undercover for four years. Can you imagine what that would do to a woman?"

"The right one would be okay with it," she said with an edge of stubbornness. "It's not just what you do. It's who you are."

"Well, who I am can't just drop everything for the birthday or wedding anniversary. You get in too deep to be pulled out. Sometimes you have to pretend to have a wife or a girl-friend. Another agent plays the role. How does the woman waiting at home handle that?"

"Badly," she guessed.

"Exactly."

"I guess that overcomes the girlfriend thing."

"I guess it does."

"If we do this right," she said, "maybe your father won't be quite so antagonistic toward you."

On the other hand, Brand thought, if he did more damage than good, he would confirm his father's worst thoughts about him.

"I don't understand why he's not proud of you," Sophie said.

He didn't like it that she cut so quickly to his own feelings. Why was it a man never quite got over that longing to be something good in the eyes of his father? To make his family proud?

"There was only one way to make my father proud of me," he said, "and I didn't do it. I didn't go to medical school and become a doctor willing to take over the Sugar Maple Grove General Practice one day."

"I still remember how shocked your parents

were when you quit college and joined the military."

"My dad can trace eight generations of Sheridans. The men are doctors, professors, writers. And then along came me. I couldn't fit the mold he made for me."

"But the marines?"

"A recruiter at college found me on a climbing wall and asked if I'd ever considered making a living doing something like that. He made the whole thing sound irresistibly exciting."

"And has it been?"

Brand was aware it was so easy to talk to Sophie. "It's been pretty much what I told your grandmother. Ninety-nine percent tedium, one percent all hell breaking loose."

Sophie smiled. "And you live for that one percent. Adrenaline junkie."

"You know, that's the part my mom and dad never understood. The military is a good place for an adrenaline junkie. I've always been attracted to adventure. I've always needed the adrenaline rush. Left to my own devices, especially in my younger years, that could have gotten me in a lot of trouble. I needed to balance my love of height and speed with discipline and skill.

"But my dad can't forgive me my career choice. We were a long way down the road of not seeing eye to eye even before I missed my mom's funeral."

"Was there really no way for you to come home, Brand? None?"

He shook his head. "You have to understand how deeply I was in and how long it took me to get there. Word of my mom's death reached me via a quick and risky meeting with my handler—that's your contact with the real world. The less you see anybody from that world, the better.

"At that point in the operation, I had to assume everything was suspect, everything was listened to, everything was watched. One wrong step, one wrong breath could have gotten people killed, could have blown nearly four years of work.

"What I said to my dad was true. I'm basically a soldier. I take orders. Even if it had been my call, which it wasn't, I wouldn't have jeopardized the team. Couldn't.

"And I'll tell you what else I couldn't have done—risked someone following me back here, knowing anything about this place or the people in it, retribution for what I was about to do raining down on the innocent."

Her eyes were wide. "Did you ever tell that to your father?"

"He doesn't listen long enough." Brand was surprised by just how much he'd told Sophie. He usually didn't talk about work. He usually carried his burdens alone.

"Are you in danger now?" she asked, always intuitive.

But he'd said enough, there was no sense scaring her. He sidestepped the question. "My identity will be protected, even in the coming court cases. I'll be kept pretty low-profile for a long time."

His father didn't know about that kind of world, and neither did Sophie Holtzheim. If he told them all the details, if they fully understood the danger, they might feel the kind of helpless fear that tore apart the ones who stayed at home.

Better his father be angry than that.

And her? He could never subject someone as sweet and sensitive as Sophie to what he did for a living. Was this brief tangling of their lives—him entertaining himself at her expense—going to hurt her?

It was going to be just like being undercover. Get the job done, no emotional attachment, keep mental distance. *Pretend.*

He looked at Sophie, so adorable in her earnestness. Pretense around someone so transparent, so genuine, seemed wrong. Still, it bugged him that she wasn't able to hold her head high, so he listened without comment as she outlined her plans for a romance.

Ice cream. A bike ride or two. Blue Rock.

Again, he was struck by the innocence of it all. He felt a flicker of trepidation about his ability to play the role she was outlining. But he didn't let on.

"Sure," he agreed to all her plans when she finally stopped and looked at him with wide-eyed expectation. He took a big bite of his marmalade-covered croissant. "That should be fun."

He remembered, too late, he too hated marmalade.

But just for practice at concealing how he really felt, he chewed thoughtfully and proclaimed it delicious.

Sophie was looking at him as if she didn't believe him. What if she proved to be the person who could see right through all the masks he'd become so adept at wearing?

For some reason that thought was scarier than the four years he had just spent in a den full of rattlesnakes.

Because it threatened him as he had never once allowed himself to be threatened.

It went to the core he'd kept hidden.

What if Sophie Holtzheim could see his heart?

*No worries,* he tried to tell himself. He thought of the work he'd done. Four years building friendships. Building trust. He'd worked with those people, partied with them, attended the baptisms of their children and the marriages of the their daughters.

His work had culminated in twenty-three arrests in four different countries. Bad guys, yes, but also people he had come to know on a different level: sons, husbands, fathers.

His own father probably knew the truth about him after all—Brand Sheridan's heart was as black as the ace of spades.

Early the next morning, Brand was working in his father's backyard, trying to clear the shambles his mother's rosebeds had become.

Nobody had to know that this is how he would honor her. Bring back something she had loved that now looked sorry and neglected. Who knew? Maybe with enough work it could be ready for next year's garden tour.

He was just blotting an angry, bleeding welt

from a thorn when he got that hair-rising-on-the-back-of-his-neck feeling.

He turned slightly. The red hat was highly visible through the hedge. He smiled to himself. He was being watched.

"You must come see," Hilde called in German. "He's taken off his shirt."

He had taken off his shirt, even though the morning was cool, because the thorns were ripping it to tatters.

"Grandma!"

But out of the corner of his eye, he could see Sophie could not resist the temptation and had joined her grandmother at the hedge

He flexed a muscle for them, tried not to smile at the grandma's gasp of appreciation, pretended he had no idea they were there.

"He's bleeding," Hilde whispered, still in German. "You should bring him a Band-Aid."

"Stop it," Sophie said.

"Go over there," her grandma hissed.

"No."

"Ach. You have no idea how to conduct a romance."

"I do so. I was nearly married."

"Ha. Being flattered that someone pays attention to you is not the same as being romanced."

Brand knew it. Sophie hadn't been in love. She hadn't even been infatuated. She'd been *flattered*.

He picked up his shirt, wiped the sweat off with it, wandered over to the hedge, peered through it as if he was surprised to see them there.

"Hey, ladies, nice morning."

"Oh, Brand," Sophie said, and squeezed through the little gap in the hedge where she had made her escape the other night.

Or, from the annoyed glance back at the bobbing red hat, maybe she'd been pushed through it.

She was dressed for work. She looked as if she worked at a library, but he thought it was probably safe to assume the Historical Society would provide the same dusty-tomes atmosphere.

Her remarkable auburn hair had been pinned up, she was wearing a white shirt with a fine navy pinstripe, a stern, straight-line navy blue skirt and flat shoes.

She had her glasses on, making her reminiscent of the national-speech-contest girl she had once been.

Only now there was a twist.

Sophie was all grown up, and he was

stunned to discover he harbored a librarian fantasy. It made his mouth go dry thinking of slipping those glasses off her face, pulling the pins from her hair, flicking open the top button of that primly fastened-to-the-throat blouse.

She intensified his commitment to the fantasy when she stared at him as if she was a sheltered little librarian, who had never seen a half-naked man before. She gulped, looked wildly back at the little hole in the hedge.

She brought out the sinner in him, because he was wickedly delighted in her discomfort. He folded his arms over his chest.

"You're bleeding," her grandmother coached, through the hedge, in German.

"You're, uh, very tanned," Sophie blurted out uncomfortably.

"I lived on a yacht in Spain."

"That was your undercover job?"

"Yes."

So many things she could have said: Was it glamorous? What's Spain like? Why a yacht? What was it like to live there? Were you pretending to be rich and famous? What did you do every day? Who were you trying to catch?

But she asked none of those.

She said, her eyes suddenly quiet on his face, "Were you afraid?"

Until this very moment, he hadn't thought so. But now, standing here in the quiet of the garden with her, the birds singing riotously in the trees, the odd bee buzzing by, he felt the complete absence of fear. And he felt a different kind of tension from the kind he had learned to live with, day in and day out, for four long years.

A delightful tension. A man aware of a woman. A woman aware of a man.

"I guess I was afraid," he admitted slowly. He wondered if he had ever said those words to another human being. It felt as though a vital piece of his armor fell away from him.

Not *It must have been exciting.* "It must have been unbelievably difficult."

He scrambled for the piece of fallen armor, grinned at her, flexed a muscle and was satisfied when her little tongue flicked out and gave the corner of her lip a nervous lick.

"Nah," he said, "just a job."

But despite the distraction, her eyes on his face were still quiet, *knowing.*

He hated that. "What happened to your engagement?" he asked, moving her away from the topic of *him.*

He hoped she wasn't going to tell him something that would make him have to hunt down her ex and have a little talk with him.

Sophie looked wildly uncomfortable.

"I should know," he encouraged her. "As your new beau, I should know why the last guy was dumb enough to ditch you."

"He didn't ditch me," she squeaked. "I told him I needed some time to think. While I was thinking, he was hunting. For my replacement."

Something in Brand whispered softly and entirely against his will, *as if you could replace a girl like her!* "What did you need to think about?"

Her eyes fastened on his naked bicep, he flexed it for her. She licked her lips.

"I don't know, exactly. *Something* was missing."

"Well, then you're a smart girl for calling it off."

"Do you really think so?"

"Really." Even he was surprised by how much he meant that. "You know, your parents were good, good people. They really loved each other, Sophie. Maybe you felt desperate to have what you had lost."

She looked stunned. He was a little shocked himself. Where had that observation come from?

"Ah, well," she said, looking away, finally,

"I'm just on my way to work, but I thought I should let you know I've formalized the plan."

She looked faintly relieved that there were actually neat papers in her hand, an escape from the intensity of the moment and the understanding that had just passed between them.

"I was just going to drop them in the mailbox, but since you're here—

Deliciously flustered, she thrust several sheets of neatly folded paper at him and ducked back through the hedge.

"You didn't say he was bleeding," her grandmother scolded in German. "A little first aid!"

"It wasn't life-threatening," Sophie said. "I'm late for work."

"I fear you are hopeless," her grandmother muttered.

He unfolded the sheets Sophie had handed him and sighed. He feared her grandmother might be right.

Under the boldface heading, **Courtship Itinerary**, Sophie had typed a neat schedule for their romance. It was obviously an effort to keep their arrangement all business, which a part of him applauded, though a different part became fiendishly more committed to shaking her safe librarian/historian world.

Tuesday: 7:00 p.m., bike to Maynard's, ice cream.

Friday: 7:30 p.m., movie at the old Tivoli.

Sunday: 3:00 p.m., swim at Blue Rock, weather permitting.

For a man who had taken weekend trips to Monte Carlo to gamble, attended yacht parties on unbelievably outfitted luxury craft, who had been wined and dined in some of the most famous restaurants in the world, her plan should have been laughable. This is what she had come up with for excitement?

This was the courtship of Miss Sophie?

But oddly, Brand didn't feel like laughing. He felt as if he was choking on something. The choices not made, a sweet way of life left behind.

He shuffled papers. The second sheet, also neatly typed and double-spaced, had the boldface title, **Courtship Guidelines**. As he scanned it, he realized it really meant Sophie's rules, starting with no public demonstrations of affection and ending with the request that he not call her Sweet Pea.

"Oh, lady," he said, crumpling up the rules, needing to regain his equilibrium, "you have so much to learn."

Or maybe he did. Maybe he was being given

a chance to experience a choice not made a long time ago. Maybe it would be kind of fun to pretend to have the life he had walked away from.

Whistling, aware he felt inordinately happy despite the fact he was dancing with danger of a new kind—ah, well, danger had always held an irresistible pull for him—Brand worked a bit longer in the roses and then took the rose clippers to where the sweet peas were running riot along his father's back fence.

Though his mother had loved roses, Brand had always considered the sweet pea the loveliest flower she grew, in all its abundant and delicate pastel shades, the fragrance coming off those cheery blossoms like a little piece of heaven.

An overlooked flower, he thought, scorned by the serious gardeners who babied their roses and clipped their rhododendron bushes and pulled their dahlias in the fall.

Just like Sophie Holtzheim.

An overlooked flower.

When he'd clipped more sweet peas than he could hold in his arms, he went and filled the kitchen sink with water and dropped them in.

"What are you doing with my flowers?" his father asked grumpily, glancing up from his paper. His father apparently hadn't noticed there was nothing for breakfast in the house.

"I'm going to start a rumor," Brand said pleasantly. "And then I'm going to get some groceries. You want to come?"

"To start the rumor?" his father said hopefully.

"No, for the groceries. How come you don't have any food?"

"Why? You writing a report for your sister?"

"She's worried about you, Dad. You don't have to see her as the enemy. That fire rattled her."

"Rattled *her!* What do you think it did to me? Oh well, I didn't like cooking here anyway. Or eating here," Dr. Sheridan said, proud, reluctant. "It makes me miss your mother."

"I miss her, too, Dad. I come in this kitchen and think of strawberry lemonade and cookies warm from the oven, the chocolate chips dripping."

Something in his father's face softened, and, briefly, it almost felt that they might have a moment, share some fond memories. But his father rattled the paper and dove behind it.

Brand headed for the shower.

Later he went out to the bike shed, and found

his mother's bike, complete with the basket which he filled with sweet peas until it overflowed. Then he rode right down Main Street, enjoying the pretense of being a small-town guy who had never, for the good of his country, done things that ate at his soul.

The thing that astonished him was how easy it was to slip from who he knew himself to be—a hardened warrior, heart of ice—into this role of a young man going to woo his girl.

Had he gotten that adept at playing roles?

At least this one had no grim, dark overtones. It just felt *fun*. It would be entertaining, fill up some of his time here, to play this game with Sophie. To break her rules, too.

Maybe, if nothing else, before he left here, he could teach Sophie to be spontaneous, though he doubted if he had enough time to tackle that particular challenge.

He parked the bicycle in front of the old two-story redbrick Edwardian building that housed the Historical Society, gathered the sweet peas in his arms, took the steps two at a time and stopped in front of the stern-faced woman at the reception desk in the outer office.

"I'm looking for my sweet pea," he announced, "Miss Sophie."

That would show Sophie Holtzheim just

how sick and tired he was of other people making the rules that governed his life. He was on leave from his military duties. He wasn't taking orders from a little scrap of a girl!

Not unless they were the delicious kind. The librarian pulling her glasses off, chewing thoughtfully on the arm, watching him with heat in her eyes.

*Brand Sheridan,* he berated himself, *there is a special place in hell for guys like you.*

On second thought, he was already there.

The idea that this was going to be some kind of fun fled from him. He couldn't be sworn to help and protect Sophie and have these kinds of thoughts at the same time.

He needed to be a better man.

The courtship of Sophie was probably going to be the hardest assignment of his life.

# CHAPTER FIVE

"You have a gentleman caller," Bitsy Martin whispered in the door of Sophie's office. "With flowers."

Sophie felt a blush rise up her cheeks. Of course, given how recently she had drawn up her rules of courtship engagement, her gentleman caller could be only one person!

And of all the words she had ever used to describe Brand, and there had been many of them, most recently *pirate,* the word *gentleman* had never been on the list.

She didn't know which was more annoying: the fact that Brand had dispensed with her schedule, or the fact that Bitsy looked so amazed that a man would show up with flowers for her.

She didn't feel ready to deal with him. She still felt the stunning truth Brand Sheridan had so casually unearthed this morning.

She had been going to marry Gregg Hamilton because she missed her parents, had missed being part of that unit called a family.

Thank God he had not uncovered the whole truth. She was only just working toward that herself, and it was painful.

"I thought he was in the wrong place. He's what we would have called a rake back in the day," Bitsy confided. "Devilishly charming."

Again, there was something mildly insulting about Bitsy's disbelief that such a man would show up looking for *her.*

Sophie took a deep breath, got up and went down the hall. She tried to steel herself, but, of course, it was impossible.

The sweet-pea bouquet, abandoned on the counter, had already filled the entire office with its delicate fragrance. Brand had his back to her, restless, pacing, pretending to be interested in the old photos of Sugar Maple Grove that graced the walls.

Sophie fought the desire just to stop and drink in the sweeping masculine lines of that broad back, especially since Bitsy was watching.

*Wait. That's the whole idea. To convince people we're actually interested in each other.* Sophie could study the enticing lines of his back as long as she wanted. It was a heady freedom, as intoxicating as champagne, so she only allowed herself the tiniest sip before she cleared her throat.

"Brand," she said, her brightness forced, "An unexpected pleasure. What brings you here?"

She realized Bitsy was hovering with avid interest, and that for a girl who was supposed to be being romanced she sounded ridiculously formal. Her eyes skittered to the sweet peas. "My darling," she added as an afterthought. It sounded as if she had read a line from a script, badly.

He turned from the pictures on the wall and gazed at her, long and slow. He was going to be good at this! Way too good. Despite the fact that he said he had no girlfriends, she now suspected something else—dozens, *hundreds* of women wooed by the man with the perfect excuse to never commit!

He came back to the counter, leaned across it and planted a rather noisy—and distinctly demonstrative—kiss on her cheek.

*"Ma chérie,"* he greeted her, his voice as liquid and sweet as warmed wild honey. It was as if he'd poured that honey over her naked body when he said something else in French, that she didn't understand but that was undoubtedly wicked.

"You don't speak French," she protested weakly to him.

"Actually, I do."

"I didn't know that." A French-speaking pirate. Whatever forces she had called down upon herself to test her sworn-off-love vow by burning pictures at midnight were extraordinarily powerful ones!

"There is quite a bit about me you don't know." How could he do that? That phrase was not *dirty*.

That was true. The boy next door had always been safe. Even in the darkest throes of her crush on him, there had never been the remotest chance of her love being requited. That had made it so safe somehow. Now, everything seemed different.

Especially him, something the same and something different meeting somewhere where she could not clearly see the lines, could not clearly discern the dangers.

"What did you say in French?"

"Just that I saw these flowers and they reminded me of you."

"Oh." Her cheek could not possibly be tingling! Sophie had to resist an impulse to reach up and touch her cheek where his lips had been.

"You want to go for lunch?"

"No!" Her voice sounded strangled.

He raised a wicked eyebrow at her, enjoying her discomfort, a pirate enjoying the game, enjoying his pretense of being a perfect gentleman.

"Of course you want to come for lunch with me," he coached her in a whisper, "you can't get enough of me."

Unfortunately, true.

"It's not lunchtime."

"That would not stop two people who were falling in love."

His eyes twinkled, a little grin tickled the sensuous curve of lips that had just touched her cheek. That she had tasted yesterday. That she wanted to taste again, with the desperate hunger of a woman who was falling hard and fast.

She'd always been way too susceptible to him. Always. It was time to claim her life back. Really. Past time.

*Pull it together, girl,* Sophie ordered herself. "Even if it is lunchtime, I couldn't possibly. Too busy." She heard Bitsy's muffled gasp of dismay, remembered they had a witness and that was what this was really all about.

It could only mean trouble that Sophie was

aware of the growing disappointment that this was all an act, a role she had, very stupidly, encouraged him to play.

"What are you busy doing, Sweet Pea?" he asked, silkily, smooth, his eyes intent on her face, his fingers moving along the countertop, touching hers. He did a funny little thing with his fingertips, dancing them along her knuckles, feather-light, astonishingly intimate.

Instead of being pleased with his performance, Sophie wanted to cry. What had she gotten herself into? What woman wouldn't want a moment like this to be real?

His fingertips tickled her, drummed an intimate little tattoo across the top of her hand, rested on the bone of her wrist.

Sophie's belly did that roller-coaster dive.

Unless she was mistaken, Bitsy gasped again, not with dismay but with recognition of something white-hot streaking through the stale air of the historical office—sexy, seductive.

"A box of memorabilia came in," Sophie stammered, and yanked her hand away. She brushed it across the top of her thigh, to make the tingling *stop*.

Brand's attention was on her hand, a faint smug smile of male knowing on a face that was just a little too sure of his ability to tempt, entice, seduce.

Unfortunately echoing what she had seen in Bitsy's face. Men like him didn't woo girls like her! Or use words like *woo* either, or as old-fashioned, as prissy, as archaic as *beau.*

Sophie had always been out of step. The sweet geek, walking dictionary, history buff, plagued by a certain awkward uncertainty in herself that she had managed to put away for ten minutes once to give a speech, but otherwise had never quite outgrown.

People didn't get why she had trouble getting over Gregg. No man had really ever noticed her before, and she despaired that one ever would again.

Except Brand.

He'd always noticed her. But in that aggravating, chuck-you-on-the-chin, you're-cute-and-funny-like-a-chimpanzee-who-can-ride-a-tricycle kind of way.

And Brand Sheridan? She had always noticed him, too, and not in the chimpanzee-on-a-trike kind of way.

He had always been hot. Not just good-looking, because really, good looks, while rare and certainly enticing, were not a measure of character. It wasn't even the fact that he had carried himself with such confidence, that he had radiated the mysterious male essence that stole breath as surely as bees stole nectar.

No, Brand had had a way of looking at people, and engaging with people that made them feel as if he could show them the secret to being intensely alive. There was something about him that had been bold and breathtaking.

In high school he had gone for the fast girls, Sophie remembered, a little more sadly than she would have liked. There had been a constant parade of them on the backseat of his motorcycle. Girls who were sophisticated and flirty, who knew how to wear makeup and how to dress in ways that men went gaga for.

She remembered she had tried to tell him once he was way too smart for that. That he should find a girl he could talk to.

What she had meant was a girl who was worthy of him. *Such as herself.*

If she recalled, he had thrown back his head and laughed at her advice, chucked her on the chin, said *Why do I need another girl to talk to, when I have you?*

Naturally, naive little fool that she had been, that off-the-cuff remark had sent her into infatuation overdrive.

He still thought she was that girl! And she was not doing one thing to set him straight!

It was stopping now. Sophie was not going to give him the satisfaction of being right! Even if he was!

Sophie pulled her hand away from her thigh and folded both her hands primly on the counter in front of her. She realized the gesture was a little too *old* for her.

It was time for a *new* Sophie to emerge, a woman who was not intimidated by the likes of him—or who could at least pull off the pretense that she wasn't!

She leaned forward and purred, "Beloved, as happy as I am to see you, I must go back to work. I'm swamped. Simply swamped."

Out of all the endearments she could have picked, she kicked herself for choosing that one! Hopelessly dated. And fraught with emotion. *Beloved.*

To lean toward him and mean it. To let it be the last word on her lips at night and the first in the morning, to let it form in her mind when her eyes rested on him, even from a distance…

"Go away," she snapped at him, when he didn't seem to be getting it.

Another gasp from Bitsy. It was like working with her grandmother. Sophie turned and gave her a glare that she hoped would send her scuttling, but Bitsy stood her ground.

Feeling her hand was being forced, she leaned even closer, and tried to take the sting out of the "Go away."

"I'll make it up to you later." She blinked at him in her best version of the type of girl who had graced the back of his motorcycle.

A smile tickled those handsome lips. Unfortunately she couldn't tell if she'd managed to amuse him or intrigue him just the tiniest bit.

"I can help you with your work," he suggested, "and then we can go for lunch. Or we can go some place where you can make it up to me, whichever you prefer."

Done playing, Sophie picked up the sweet peas, opened the gate that separated the inner office from the outer one and let him through. She pointed down the hall and then marched behind him.

"That one," she said tersely.

He went into her open office, and she slid in behind him and then shut the door. With a snap.

She leaned against it trying to marshal herself.

There was no room for them both in her office, he had turned around to face her and was now leaning his rear up against her desk, arms folded over the solidness of his chest, eyes dancing with mischief and merriment.

*At her expense.*

His largeness made the room seem small and cramped. His vibrancy made the space—and her whole life—feel dull and dreary.

Her office was never going to feel the same now. Something of his larger-than-life presence was going to linger here and *ruin* it.

"What are you doing?" Sophie demanded.

He lifted a big shoulder, smiled. "Getting things started."

"We were supposed to start with a bike ride. To Maynard's. For ice cream. Tomorrow."

Every word sounded clipped, a woman in distress, a woman who had had a plan, and that plan included somehow needing a whole day to *prepare* to be with him.

"Ah, Sophie," he suggested, "lighten up. Be spontaneous."

"I don't like being spontaneous!" *Wait! Remember the new Sophie!*

"I seem to remember that," he said sympathetically, "Never too late to learn."

"I don't want to learn!" Which was a lie. The *new* Sophie thought spontaneity could begin with throwing herself at him and tasting his lips again.

That would wipe the smug look off his face!

"That's sad," he said.

"I am not sad! I will not have you see me as pathetic!" The urge to kiss him grew, just to prove something.

But it could backfire. It could prove she was even more pathetic than she thought.

"I don't see you as pathetic, Sophie, just… er…a little too rigid."

Rigid? This was turning into a nightmare. The world's most glorious man saw her as uptight and rigid? The *new* Sophie had to do something!

"Let's have some fun with this," he coaxed.

What could she say to that? She didn't like having fun? Now she felt driven to prove to him that she was not uptight and rigid!

That she could be flexible and fun.

And of course she could be.

Taking a deep breath, Sophie launched herself over the distance that separated them in a fashion that allowed no chickening out. She caught the widening of his eyes, his quick lean backward, but the desk prevented escape. She wrapped her arms around his neck and pulled him close.

She took his lips with hers.

*There,* she thought dreamily. That should

show him. Nothing rigid or predictable about her. She could be spontaneous! She could have as much *fun* as the next person.

For a moment his lips softened under hers, and the word *fun* dissolved. Fun was a Fourth of July picnic or a new puppy or a good game of Scrabble.

This wasn't fun. It was intense. And dangerous. As exciting, as challenging as riding the rapids of an uncharted river or jumping from an airplane with a parachute that might or might not open.

This was part of her absolute gift for doing the wrong thing around him! She had set out to prove he didn't have any power over her anymore.

And proved the exact opposite. *Beloved.*

Not that he had to know. Ever.

That his lips tasted to her of everything she had longed for when she had said yes to the wrong man and bought a wedding dress and collected pictures. Brand Sheridan's lips tasted of honey and dreams, of dewdrops and hope.

She had said to Gregg that she needed time to think, that *something* was missing.

Sophie reeled back from Brand, feeling aquiver with recognition. The rest of the truth she had been trying to hide from herself slammed into her.

The truth was she had nearly married Gregg because she had *never* wanted to feel love as deeply as she had felt it within her family again. She had wanted to have the security of that place called family, without the emotional investment that could devastate so totally. That could shatter a person's heart into a million jagged pieces. That could steal any semblance of remaining faith or hope from their soul.

Ultimately, Gregg had been safe. He would have never required her heart or her soul.

This man in front of her?

He would never be safe. And he would never accept less from the person he called *beloved* than their full heart, their complete soul.

Of course, with her gift for getting everything exactly wrong, here she was falling in love with the man least likely ever to call anyone *beloved*. The man who had made his work his built-in excuse for not loving anyone.

"There," she said, hoping she did not sound as shaken as she felt. "Spontaneity requirement met?"

"Not unless we were talking about spontaneous combustion," he muttered, his eyes as piercing as a pirate's on her face. Still, Sophie could tell she had managed to shock him.

What she couldn't tell was if it was in a good

way. His eyes were unreadable, the mischief had gone from them.

She suddenly just wanted to hide.

If he had just followed the rules! If he had waited until tomorrow to go for ice cream instead of invading her world, he would have seen her at her most flexible. And fun.

She might have even managed flirty.

She might not have launched herself at him in a full-frontal attack! The sweet geek rides again! Gets it exactly wrong every time!

"Back to work," she said firmly. What she meant was back to her hidey-hole: words and dusty archives, glimpses into worlds long past that triggered her imagination, that she could immerse herself in when her own life seemed way too dreary, when the disappointment of the gap between what she desired and what she could have were inescapable.

She was not going to cry. "Nice of you to drop by. This box of stuff just came in," she fluttered a wrist at it, "and I need to go through it. It's time-consuming. All the letters have to be read—"

"This box?" he said, glancing at her, seeing what she did not want him to see if his faintly worried look was any indication.

Brand Sheridan was probably thinking she was more pathetic than he had ever guessed!

Still, intentionally or not—she suspected it was—he gave her a bit of space to compose herself.

He turned from her, opened the lid of the box, peered in. "I can read the letters for you. World War Two, right? I can sort through anything that pertains to that."

She could see him watching her quietly, waiting to see if she could accept his invitation to back up a bit, to get things back to normal.

How could it be normal after she had kissed him like that? With his big assured self taking all the air out of her space? Applying all that confidence and curiosity to her stuff and her world?

*Get him out of here,* the old Sophie ordered her.

The new Sophie asked how could she have a drop of pride left if she let him see how damned rattled she was by the kiss she had instigated?

"Fine," she said, tightly. "We never turn down volunteer help. I understand you've been home in Sugar Maple Grove for nearly forty-eight hours. It's inevitable that the boredom is setting in. Let me set you up in the conference room."

She did. There. Now he could find out what boredom really was!

"Just keep out anything that pertains to the Second World War," she instructed him sweetly. "Bitsy can sort through the rest later."

And she closed the door firmly on him.

Brand found himself in the conference room, alone, the door shut on him. She'd done that deliberately, kissed him in retribution for his messing with her schedule, just to let him know what was going to happen if he messed with her—that she could be wild and unpredictable, too.

She couldn't really. She was as transparent as a sheet of glass. His sweet little next-door neighbor trying to be something she was not, trying to erase her image as a bookworm, wallflower, *librarian*.

She'd be surprised by how much Brand liked that about her. Sophie, with all her awkwardness and intellect, was different in a world where so much was same old, same old— cookie-cutter women who looked the same and talked the same and were the same.

Didn't Sophie know what a treat it was to unearth an original? He smiled. A long time ago, before she was even old enough to know anything about anything, she'd shown disdain for his taste in women.

Still, for all that he knew she was trying to prove something to him that she couldn't, that kiss *had* been startling.

There had been something disturbingly wild and unpredictable in her lips meeting his for the second time.

What had he tasted?

*Hunger.*

More evidence that agreeing to romance Sophie had been about his worst idea ever.

Still, no wonder she'd fallen for the first guy to pay some attention to her. She wasn't just lonely for the family she had lost.

Nope, she was *hungry,* there was a fire in that girl only one thing was going to put out.

And it wasn't the fire that was roaring to life inside him just thinking about it. He hadn't come here planning to burn up with her. No, he'd wanted her to loosen up a little, throw out her rigidly uptight rule book, encourage her to be herself, to have a little unexpected fun.

The girl was like a tightly coiled spring of tension. Even her kiss had said that.

Ah, well, he'd sort through her dusty box for her, then take her out for lunch, coax that funny, lively original side of her to the surface.

With absolutely no kissing. He could be the

better man. He could resist the temptation of Sophie…for her own good, of course.

He'd put out the fire he was feeling by giving his attention to the kind of stuff she did. If she'd been wrong that he was bored in Sugar Maple Grove—and she had been—the truth was that nobody was more surprised than him. He'd been here nearly two whole days and wasn't climbing the walls yet?

But the box she'd given him to sort through promised to change that!

Much as Brand appreciated that she had not been lured by the temptations of a glitzy world, he couldn't help but think, no wonder Sophie was so *ready* for a little excitement.

The box of so-called memorabilia contained things someone thought were important to the history of Sugar Maple Grove.

He forced himself to focus. He began to scan scraps of paper and old photos.

There were newspaper cuttings of the high-school basketball team making the state finals in 1972, faded color photos of the work team from Holy Trinity Church that had built an orphanage in Honduras in the eighties. There was a whitish-gray plaster mold of a hand that said Happy Mother's Day on the front, and on the back, in pen, Terry Wilson. Died Vietnam, 1969.

Brand had been dealing with subtle and not so subtle forms of evil for four years. For some reason, it felt as though this box immersed him in good, in the plain living of people with small-town values and humble ambitions.

To leave the world better.

No wonder Sophie had ended up here, at the Historical Society, documenting what made a small town tick.

There were several random items, including recipes and an old garter, possibly from a wedding.

And then, in the very bottom of the box, he found a packet of letters, tied up with a frayed black velvet ribbon.

Was this the gem of Second World War memorabilia he was supposed to be hunting for? Brand untied the ribbon, and plucked the first fragile letter out of the bundle. The envelope was addressed in a careful masculine hand to Miss Sarah Sorlington, General Delivery, Sugar Maple Grove. The return address was Private Sinclair Horsenell, a censor's heavy black pen blotting out the rest. But the postmark was February of 1942.

*Pay dirt,* he thought. Was this how Sophie got her thrills? It *was* kind of thrilling.

He carefully unfolded the letter from the

young private. The paper was fragile along the fold marks, and the ink had begun to fade in places. Still, Brand was able to discern that Sinclair Horsenell had just disembarked in Ireland, part of the U.S. Army V Corps, the first Americans to deploy overseas.

"My dearest Sarah," he read, "what an extraordinary adventure I find myself on!"

The letter was beautifully descriptive of the lushness of Ireland, describing sights and sounds, camaraderie, funny incidents around the camp.

Despite all the new things I am seeing, and the grave sense of purpose I feel, the rightness of my being here, I miss you so deeply. I think of that last afternoon we spent and the picnic you prepared, the blue of your eyes matching the blue of the sky, and I feel both that I want to be with you, and that I want to be part of protecting the simple pleasures we were able to enjoy that afternoon. My darling, I am prepared to give my life for the protection of all that we hold dear.

I know you wanted to marry before I left, but that is not what I wanted for you. You deserve so much more than a rushed ceremony. I live to see you in a white dress, floating down the aisle toward me, a bouquet of forget-me-nots to match your eyes.

Wait for me, sweet Sarah. Wait.

Yours forever,

Sinclair

The letters had been carefully saved in their chronological order and Brand soon saw that Sinclair wrote faithfully, sometimes just a line or two, sometimes long letters. As the time passed, Brand noticed the excitement waning, giving way to the tedium of military life. Now the letters held occasional complaints about the lack of action, the officers, the terrible food.

The letter made Brand think, sadly, that things didn't change. Young men went away to war, and left sweethearts behind them.

"Did you find something?"

Things didn't change, but people did.

Sophie stood in the doorway, watching him, and he put away the letter he was reading.

Why did he feel reluctant to let her know what he had found? Because those letters were making him feel something. *Uneasy.*

"Just some old letters. They might have

value. I haven't finished reading them yet. Bitsy is probably better qualified than me to decide what has historical value, but I'm willing to go out on a limb and guess these two items don't."

He handed her the recipe for Corn Flakes casserole and the garter.

She laughed, and it was a good sound. Not a girlish giggle, but genuine. He was unaware how he had longed for genuine things until he heard it. It pulled him toward her like a beacon guiding a fisherman lost in a fog.

"Are you ready for lunch?" she asked.

There was something shy in that, his old Sophie, not the girl she had tried to convince him she was when she had kissed him. This Sophie's laughter was so genuine it made him ache.

Brand glanced at his watch, amazed at how much time had gone by. Somehow the genuineness in her, coupled with the genuineness of the emotion in Sinclair's letters made him feel bad about playing with Sophie's world.

He didn't want to have lunch with her and look at her lips and be the kind of guy who plotted another taste of them.

"You know what?" he said. "You were

probably right. Let's follow your schedule. I'll
see you tomorrow night after supper. We'll ride
our bikes down Main Street, go for ice cream.
It will be a highly visible activity that the
whole town can see."

She stared at him. Disappointed? Annoyed?

That was good, he tried to tell himself. If
they were going to carry off this *courtship*
thing with no one getting hurt, it would be for
the best if she found him disappointing and
annoying.

"I'll take these with me," he said, gathering
up the letters. "And get them back to you when
I'm finished going through them."

Why did he feel that he had to protect her
from the letters? They were just sweet letters
a young, heartsick man had written home.

For some reason, Brand wanted to make
sure they had a happy ending.

As though he needed to protect her if they
didn't.

He had a feeling this desire to protect
Sophie was going to do nothing but get him
in trouble. Especially since it was now
evident this was a more complicated mission
than he had first perceived.

He had to protect her from himself and his
reaction to her *hunger*.

"See you tomorrow," he said breezily. "Are you still a purely vanilla girl?"

"You think I'm really boring," she said.

Her lips had already told him there was a secret side to her that was anything but boring, but he was determined he wasn't going there.

He thought of the world he had lived in for four years, where God forbid anybody should ever be bored, and so they had become adept at manufacturing all the excitement money could buy. And become so addicted to it, they were prepared to do anything to keep a lifestyle they had not legitimately earned, were not legitimately entitled to.

He thought of the letters in his hand, letters from a young man who was probably beginning to yearn for all those things he had once called boring.

"Don't," he told Sophie sternly, moving by her, the letters in his hand, "say *boring* as if it's a bad thing."

# CHAPTER SIX

SOPHIE could not resist going to the window and watching Brand get on an old bicycle and peddle away. It was a woman's bike, and ancient. Probably it had belonged to his mother.

And yet, the way he rode it, he could have been a knight and the bike a war horse. With his colossal confidence he could probably stride down Main Street in a pair of canvas pirate's pants, and nothing else without flinching.

Not that she wanted to be thinking about him like that! Why would he flinch? She had seen his considerable assets, seen him without his shirt, the perfection of skin stretched taut over hard muscle marred only by recent thorn scratches. He knew what he had, the devil, and probably knew exactly the effect it had on women!

The man was maddening! He'd tempted her to kiss him! He had *made* her feel driven to show him that just because she was a small-town girl, naive and heartbroken, his big strong self was not going to march into her world and take control of everything!

Ha! She was going to show him. That kiss had just been a start!

Though when she thought of that it occurred to her she wasn't quite ready to mess with a force that had the potential for so much power.

Even thinking about that, her hand moved to her lips, to the puffiness where his lips had touched her lips—collided really—and she felt a shiver, of longing, of awareness, of aliveness.

No, she had better stick to surprising him with small things.

"Vanilla ice cream, indeed. Tiger passion fruit," she told herself. "Or banana fudge chunk."

*That's it, girl,* she added silently, *live dangerously.*

But she already knew that once you had played with the danger of lips like his, the chances of erasing the thrill of that memory were probably slight to nil.

Sophie willed herself to be only annoyed

with Brand for messing with her plans, for tilting her tidy world so off-kilter, for making her want so badly to be seen in ways she had never been seen before.

*And probably never will be,* she thought with a resigned sigh.

He was a force to be reckoned with, fast and furious, like a hurricane sweeping through. Only a fool thought they could play with a hurricane, or tame it or force it onto a path other than the one it had chosen.

But the scent of the sweet peas filled her office, a poignancy in the fragrance that made it hard to be annoyed, and harder still to build her defenses against his particular kind of storm. It reminded her everything was more complicated than that.

He wasn't just a hurricane.

Sometimes, like when he'd leaned across that counter this morning and played with her fingertips, he was so much what she had remembered him being a devil-may-care boy, full of himself and mischief, his charm abundant, his confidence reckless.

But when she had walked into that conference room and he had looked up at her, and refused to go for the lunch he'd invited her on, it had not been that boy.

Or a hurricane, either.

It had not even been the man she had stolen a daring kiss from.

That new veil had been down in Brand's eyes, something remote and untouchable, the fierce discipline of a warrior surrounding him like impenetrable armor.

That had never been in him before. Something hard and cold, a formidable mountain that defied being climbed. It was something lonelier than the wind howling down an empty mountain valley on a stormy winter day.

She shivered thinking about it, and thinking about the kind of bravery it would take to tackle what she had seen in his eyes, to ignore the No Trespassing signs, to try and rescue him from a place he had been and could not leave.

*Sophie,* she scoffed at herself, *you don't know that.*

But the problem was that she did. And now that she knew it, how could she walk away and leave him there?

Even if that's what he thought he wanted?

The next evening Sophie dressed carefully for their outing to the ice-cream parlor. Her war with herself was evident in her choices: her shorts rolled a touch higher up her thigh than they would normally have been, the V in her newly purchased halter top a touch lower.

Just in case that kiss had not done the trick, she was not going to be dismissed as the little sweet geek from next door! She wanted the days of Brand Sheridan feeling like her brotherly protector to be over!

And at the same time, she didn't want him to get the idea she was trying to be sexy *for him,* because she thought probably every girl in the world had tried way too hard around him for way too long.

So she wore no makeup and pulled her hair back into a no-nonsense ponytail.

Her grandmother approved of the outfit, but not ice cream or bike-riding as romantic choices.

"He loves ice cream, Grandma, he always has."

"Ach. Do you have to ride your bike to get it? You'll be all sweaty. And your hair!" She was still squawking away in German when she went to answer the door.

In German: "The hair! It makes you look like a woman I used to buy fish from." In English, "Hello, Brand," in German, "She died lonely."

"It could have been the fish smell," Sophie

said, in English, because it was too complicated to figure out how to say it in German. Did
her hair look that bad? Not just the careless do
of a woman confident in herself?

Brand stepped in, and Sophie was anxious
about who had come: the carefree boy from
next door, or the new Brand, the weary warrior.

It was the warrior, something in him untouchable. The smile that graced his lips did
not even begin to reach his eyes.

Just like that, it wasn't about her. It was not,
she thought, pulling the band from her hair, a
good thing to die lonely.

"Everything okay?" she asked him quietly,
as she gathered her bag and slipped out the
door he held open for her. She glanced at his
face.

He looked startled, as if he had expected the
smile to fool her. "Yeah, fine."

She looked at him, again, longer. It wasn't.
So, she would work from the present, back-
wards until she found out what had put that
look on his face.

*And then what?* she asked herself, and when
no answer came she hoped she would just
know when the time came.

"How are things with your dad?" she asked,
casually, as they went down the steps. She

thought something had happened in the conference room, but the rejection of his father couldn't be helping.

"Why don't you tell me? How are things with my dad? Is he okay in that house by himself?"

She was aware he was trying to divert her, as if he had sensed she was going to try and go places angels feared to tread.

"Your dad is one of the most capable men I know."

"That answers your question then, doesn't it? Things with my dad are fine."

He got astride the old girl's bike, waited for her…she didn't miss the fact that he looked long and hard at her legs and then took a deep breath and looked away.

"Except for the little matter of him catching his house on fire," he muttered, as they began to pedal down the quiet street, side by side. "Why don't you tell me what you know about that?"

Somehow he had turned it around! He was being the inquisitor. And she'd bet he was darn good at it, too, when he put that cold, hard cop look on his face.

"I'm not spying on your dad for you!"

"You know what happened," he said, watching her face way too closely.

Well, yes, she did. But Dr. Sheridan had specifically asked her not to tell Brand that he and her grandmother had been caught in a fairly compromising position as the house burned around them. He had also asked her, last night, just before he had taken Hilde for dinner, not to mention that he and her grandmother were having a *real* romance.

"But don't you think he'll notice?" Sophie had asked, uncomfortable to be put in yet another position of deception.

"I'm counting on you to be a distraction," the doctor had said pleasantly.

"But why don't you just tell him?"

"He'll see it as a betrayal of his mother. Brand is a man who *likes* being lonely."

Now, looking at the coolly removed expression on Brand's face, Sophie could see there was some truth in the doctor's assessment of his son. Brand had developed a gift for distance.

Who was this man? Once he would have tried to argue it out of her, tease it out of her, coax it out of her.

Now he just cast her a look that was coolly assessing, said nothing more about the fire and quickened his pace so that his bike shot ahead of hers.

And, as aggravating as she had found his appearance in her office yesterday, as much as she had felt vulnerable to him, Sophie decided to try another tack to coax that chilly look off his face and bring the boy she had always known back to the surface.

Sophie put on a bit of steam herself, pulled out beside him and then passed him. She took the lead, then turned around, placed her thumb on her nose and waggled her fingers at him.

"Ha, ha," she said, "you have a girl's bike!"

*So much for the new Sophie, all slick sophistication and suave polish.*

Brand had always been competitive, and he read it as the challenge she had intended. Just as she had known, he could not resist. She could hear the whir of his bike spokes, the rubber tires hissing on the pavement. She pedaled harder. She was on an eighteen-speed, he on a three. He was going to have to work very hard to keep up with her.

Apparently he was up to the task. When she heard him coming up on her right-hand side, she swerved in front of him, heard his yelp of surprise as she cut him off and kept the lead.

"Hey," he called, "you're playing dirty!"

Her laugh of fiendish enjoyment was entirely genuine. She rose off the seat, leaned forward, stood up on those pedals and went hard.

Mr. Machalay crept out on the road in front of her, one arm full of groceries, the other clamped down on the leash of his ancient dog, Max. She rang her bell frantically and swerved around them. She glanced over her shoulder. Brand swerved the other way around Mr. Machalay and Max, both of whom now stood frozen to the spot. Mr. Machalay dropped the leash and waved his fist at them.

"Sorry," she called. Still, she was pleased with her lead. It didn't last long.

"You're going to cause an accident," he panted, way too close to her ear.

"Oh, well," she called back, breathless. "Better than dying of boredom."

"I thought I told you that wasn't a bad thing!"

"Coming from the great adventurer, Brand Sheridan, I found that a little hard to buy."

"Watch your tone," he instructed her, exasperated. "You're supposed to adore me!"

She laughed recklessly.

"You needn't make that sound as if it's impossible," he called, and then he pulled his bike up right beside her.

Sophie thought she'd been pedaling with everything she had, but a sudden whoosh of adrenaline filled her and she dug deep and found something extra.

They were racing full-out, and she loved the breathless feeling, loved the wind in her hair, her heart pumping, her muscles straining. She loved knowing he was beside her. She felt as if she had been asleep and suddenly she was gloriously, wonderfully alive.

He reached out over the tiny distance between them, and touched her, a gentle slap on her shoulder, as if they were playing tag, and then he surged ahead, effortlessly, as if he had only been playing with her all along.

Though his bike was older and less sound, his legs were longer and stronger. But it was his heart, the fierce, competitive heart of a warrior, that made this race impossible for her to win.

She cast him a look as he shot by and smiled to herself. She might not win this race, but she had won in another way.

It was there. A light shone in his face, laughter sparked in his eyes, the line of his mouth, though determined, had softened with fun. It took her back over the years and made her think maybe she did not have to go as far as she thought to find him where he was lost.

Now he was way out in front, weaving fearlessly in and out of the growing traffic as they got closer to Main Street and downtown.

He turned, put his thumb to his nose, waggled his fingers at her as she had done to him. "I might have a girl's bike, but I'm no girl!"

"Don't say that as if there's something wrong with being a girl!"

And then they were both laughing, and he deliberately slowed up and let her catch him.

"Nothing at all wrong with being a girl," he told her, sweetly, solemnly.

By the time they arrived at Maynard's they were together, the couple that they hoped to convince everyone they were.

He threw down his bike, and lay on the grassy boulevard, taking deep breaths, looking up through the canopy of leaves to the sky.

She threw down her own bike, and saw he was choking on laughter. It was a good sight and a good sound. She had broken down the barrier around him, and she was satisfied with that.

She lay down on the grass beside him. Who cared who saw them? Wasn't that the point? Thanks to Grandma she kept her arms glued to her sides in case she was sweaty.

"You nearly killed me," he accused her.

"That would be a cruel irony, wouldn't it? With all the things you've seen and done, to die racing your bicycle down the Main Street of Sugar Maple Grove?"

The laughter was gone.

"Yeah," he said, "that would be a cruel irony."

"What have you seen and done?" she whispered, seeing his defenses down, moving in. *Tell me.*

But he got up and held out his hand to her, pulled her to her feet. She hoped any sweat had dried, but if there was any, he didn't notice or didn't care.

He stood staring at her for a long time, debating something.

She held her breath, knowing somehow he needed this.

And yet not at all surprised when he was able to deny his own need.

Instead, he kidded, "What have I seen and done? Ice-cream flavors you wouldn't believe."

"Such as?"

"On the tame side, Philippine mango. On the wild side, ox tongue in Japan."

"Ox-tongue ice cream?" she said skeptically.

"Or oyster, garlic, or whale. Seriously."

"Did you try those?"

"Of course. Who could resist trying them?"

At the risk of confirming she was boring, she stated, "Me!"

"You only live once. Rose petal is a favorite in the Middle East. You might like that."

"You've eaten rose-petal ice cream?"

"Yeah."

"Really?"

"Really."

And the moment when he had almost told her something, revealed a hidden part of himself was gone, but this was something, too, to have him relaxed at her side, remembering exotic flavors of ice cream, and unless she was mistaken, *enjoying* this little slice of small-town life.

"Surprise me," he told her. "Order something other than vanilla."

And then Sophie was duty-bound to order vanilla, since he had suggested something else!

"Not unless they have rose petal," she decided. "Or if they have ox tongue I might try that."

And he laughed, because they both knew she never would, not even if she was starving to death and ox-tongue ice cream was the only food left on the face of the earth.

After they had gotten their ice cream in chocolate-dipped waffle cones, they left their bikes lying on the grassy boulevard, unlocked, and strolled down Main Street. The evening was not cooling, and even as light leached from the sky it was so hot that the ice cream was melting faster than they could eat it.

There was something about this experience: walking down Main Street with him, licking ice cream while the sun went down on a day that had been scorching hot, that was both simple and profound. She didn't know what it said about her life that this felt like one of the best moments ever.

And it didn't hurt that other women were looking at her with unabashed envy, either! Or that he seemed oblivious to the fuss he caused, to the sidelong looks, to the inviting smiles, as if being with her was all that mattered.

Was he really that good an actor? No, he'd always had that gift. No matter who he had been with, it had always felt as if, when he focused on her, she was all that mattered to him.

He stopped in front of an art gallery, closed for the day.

"Like any of them?" he asked her of the paintings in the window. He crunched down the last of his cone, and licked some stray ice cream off the inside of his wrist.

It was so sexy she nearly fainted.

She studied the paintings with more intensity. "I like that one," she decided, finally. It was safe to glance at him. No more ice-cream licking. "The one with the old red boat tied at the end of the dock."

"What do you like about it?"

*It took my mind off what you could do with that tongue if you set your mind to it.* And she bet he had set his mind to it. Lots.

"The promise," she stammered. "Long summer days that just unfold without a plan."

Moments caught in time, she thought, moments like this one that somehow became profound without even trying.

"Somehow I have trouble imaging you without a plan," he said.

"I'm not uptight!" *Though a woman whose mind went in twisted directions over a lick of ice cream was probably, at the very least, repressed.*

"Of course you aren't," he said soothingly, smiling at her in an annoying way, as if he was going to pat her on the head. Then he studied the painting.

"It's been a long time since I spent a day like

that," he said, and something slipped by his guard. Wistfulness?

"You were never the type of guy who did things like that," she reminded him. "A day fishing? Too quiet for you."

"I know, I was the guy roaring down Main Street on my secondhand motorcycle with no muffler. Leaping from the cliff *above* Blue Rock, that outcrop that we called the Widow Maker. Jumping my bicycle over dirt-pile ramps at high speeds."

"Which you have just proven you still are!"

He smiled, but the wistfulness was there. "After I wrecked my third bicycle my dad wouldn't buy me another one. Everything seemed simple back then," he said. With a certain longing?

Could she help him back to that? And also prove she could be spontaneous, not uptight? A girl who could surrender her plan?

"Want to try it?" she asked. "I could find a boat. Your dad has fishing rods. We could dig some worms."

The new Sophie was appalled, of course, and her grandmother would be, too. What kind of romance plan was that? Digging worms? But the truth was she was suddenly way more anxious to see him enjoy himself, truly and deeply, than she was to manipulate his impressions of her.

Except for the impression that she had to have a plan.

"It's not on the courtship list," he teased her.

"I can adjust the list."

He shrugged, amused. "You can?" he asked, with faked incredulousness. "It's your courtship, Sophie. If you want to dig worms and go fishing, I'll go along."

Good. He'd be so much more amenable if he thought this was about her and not him.

"We can go tomorrow after work," she decided. "I'll track down a boat. Can you look after the worms?"

"Sorry, I'm not depriving you of the pure romance of digging worms with me."

And then he was laughing at the look on her face, and that laughter was worth any price. Even digging worms!

Sophie was less certain when she stood beside him the next evening in his mother's rose garden.

"This looks good," she said of the rose garden, amazed at how the weed-choked beds and overgrown roses were beginning to look as good as they once had. "You've done a lot in a little amount of time."

He handed her a jar with some dirt in it. "Enough small talk. Dig. Worms. Big ones. Wriggly ones. Juicy ones. Ones just like this!"

He dangled a worm in front of her face.

She screamed, and he chuckled. "Come on, Sweet Pea, you were never the kind of girl who was scared of creepy-crawly things."

"I was. I just pretended not to be."

"Really? Why?" He took the jar from her, dropped the worm into it without making her touch it.

"If I had let those boys know I had a weak spot, Brand, I would have been finding worms in my lunchbox, worms in my books and worms in my mittens."

"There was a certain group of boys who picked on you," he recalled affectionately. "Especially after 'What Makes a Small Town Tick.'"

"I think they might have made my life unbearable except for the fact they knew my big, tough next-door neighbor had my back. Brand Sheridan. My hero." She slid him a little look. He was on his hands and knees filling the worm jar, not even asking her to help.

"Actually, I think they probably liked you. You know, guys at a certain age give the girl they like a frog, so she won't know, and so they can hear her scream. I probably prevented you from having a boyfriend for a lot of years when you could have. Or should have."

"I felt like you had my back then," she said, her voice soft with memory, "and here we are, eight years later. And you still have my back."

He glanced up at her, smiled, looked back and snagged a wriggler from the freshly turned black soil and put it in his jar. "I'll always have your back, Sophie."

He said that so casually, but even the casualness of the statement resonated deeply with her, and made her heart stand still. The way he said it, it was as if caring about her was part of who he was, came as naturally to him as breathing.

Just as she was relaxing, he turned and tossed a worm at her and then laughed when she shrieked. A good reminder that for all his sterling qualities, Brand Sheridan was no saint!

"Are you trying to tell me you like me?" she demanded.

"Sure. That, and I wanted to hear you scream. Did those boys stop bugging you by high school, Sweet Pea?"

"By then they ignored me completely," she admitted. "I was the invisible girl."

And somehow, even though this fishing trip

was supposed to be all about him, it was so easy to tell him about her. To talk about the lonely little geek she had once been, not with regret, but with affection.

And it became so easy to show him the life he had said such a firm "no" to eight years ago.

They went fishing at Glover's Pond, but before they got there they had to go through the ritual of him chasing her around the garden with his jar of worms. And then they had to go to Bitsy's house and load her long-dead husband's old wooden rowboat onto the roof of Brand's car—a sporty little number which was not made to carry old wooden rowboats.

After much cursing and sweating and laughing and yelling of orders, they finally made it out of Bitsy's driveway.

And when they got to the pond they had to reverse getting that contraption on the roof, to get it back off.

"Get out of the way," Brand panted at her, trying single-handedly to wrestle the rowboat off the roof of his car. "I don't want you squished by a damn boat."

"Shut up. You're such a chauvinist."

"Get out of the way!"

"Okay. Okay."

"Was that sound my paint job getting scratched?" His voice from underneath the rowboat was muffled.

"You wanted to do it by yourself, Mr. Macho! Now you have a scratch. Live with it."

"Mr. Macho. Are you kidding me? Who says things like that?" he muttered, wobbling his way down to the water with the rowboat on top of him. "How bad's the scratch?"

"Small. About the same size as the worm you threw at me. Maybe worms make good Bondo. Have you ever thought of that?"

"Actually, no, I never have. Imagine that."

He flipped the boat off, kicked off his shoes and hauled it into the water without rolling up his pants. The boat didn't start to float until he was in nearly to his thighs.

"That painting, Sweet Pea? A big, fat lie! Don't get wet, for God's sake. One of us getting wet is enough."

He shoved the boat around, waded back in, guiding it with a rope attached to the pointed bow. Then he stooped, moved his shoulder into her stomach, wrapped his arms around her knees and lifted. She found herself being carried like a sack of potatoes out to the boat. He lowered her in.

When the excitement of being manhandled

by him, and having an intimate encounter with his shoulder subsided, she couldn't help but notice her feet were getting wet. Already.

"Brand?"

"What?"

"The boat appears to be leaking."

He peered in over the side. "It's not like a leak. It's a dribble. That's what the coffee can is for."

And then he nearly dumped the boat trying to scramble over the side to get in. Finally in and settled, he attached the oars while she bailed water from around their ankles. No matter how fast she bailed, the water level stayed about the same.

"Are you sure its just a dribble?"

"Hey, I'm a marine. If the boat goes down, I'll save you."

If that was anything like being manhandled by him, she'd better bail harder.

After a while, he set the fishing lines and handed her a pole, while he bailed and rowed. And swatted bugs.

"I've got a nibble," she cried, rising unsteadily to her feet.

"No, you don't. Sweet Pea. Sit down. You can't stand up in boats. Sit down!"

He was quite masterful when he used that tone of voice. She sat down.

"I lost the fish," she told him.

"I'm beginning to think fishing is over-rated, anyway." He rowed them in a big circle around the pond.

It was a ridiculous way to conduct a courtship, Sophie thought. No flowers, no wine, no fancy dinner, no dancing until dawn. But she was the one who never seemed to get anything right.

But if that was true, why did this feel so right? Probably because watching him pit his strength against a water-filled boat that was growing more uncooperative by the second was just about as sexy as watching him lick ice cream off his wrist.

"You know that painting?" he asked her.

"Uh-huh."

"There's a reason no one's in the damn boat."

And then they were laughing, and the sun was going down, and the water sloshing around her ankles felt wonderful, though not as wonderful as watching him pit his pure strength against the oars until it was so dark they could hardly see each other anymore.

As they exited the boat and wrestled it back up the slippery bank toward his vehicle, the evening seemed to be ringed with magic, suffused with a golden light.

"I'm picking the next date," he told her,

swatting at a mosquito. "If this was your idea of romantic, you are in big trouble."

"It may not have been romantic," she said, "but it was fun, and Brand, given a choice, I think I'd choose fun."

He rolled his eyes. "Fun over romance. Good grief, girl, what kind of a dork were you engaged to, anyway?"

"Don't even pretend you know what a dork is," she teased him.

"But I do, Sweet Pea. Because you taught me."

"So, what is your idea of a romantic date?" she asked him.

"Given the limited choices of the town, its probably still the movies on Friday night."

"This week's feature is *Terror in the Tunnel*. Even you can't make that romantic."

"That just goes to show what you know. It's not about the movie. Besides, if we're trying to be highly visible, I don't think Glover's Pond quite does it."

Sophie decided that Brand Sheridan was both the easiest man she had ever spent time with and the hardest. It was so easy to talk to him, to be with him, to laugh with him, and so hard when she remembered the truth: this was all a charade.

* * *

As she was getting ready to go to the movie, it felt *real*. The hammering of her heart, the tingling anticipation she felt waiting for the doorbell to ring, the way her heart swooped when she saw him in the door watching her come toward him. It felt all too real.

Especially the palpable electrical tension between them.

"Showtime," he said, parking as close to the theater as he could and holding open her door for her. "Pretend you love me, Sweet Pea."

He paid for the show, Sophie slipped out her wallet to pay for the popcorn.

He gave her a look. "Not even in a pretend world would I ever let that happen," he growled in her ear.

The theater was packed. Before the movie started, everyone was sending surprised looks their way. Several people were nudged by others, turned in their seats and craned their necks to look at Sophie and her new beau.

"You were right about this date," she whispered to him, "highly visible."

The lights went down. The movie started. With a bang. A terrible explosion filled the screen.

Sophie gasped. She *hated* this kind of movie. And then his hand found hers in the darkness.

"I'm okay," she whispered. "It just startled me." When he didn't let go of her hand, she leaned closer to him, "You don't have to do that. No one can see us."

"When we walk out of here, it will be written all over you that we did this."

"It won't!"

"If it's done right, it will."

"You are just a little too sure of yourself, mister," she hissed.

"I know," he growled in her ear, "but my supreme confidence in myself is not unfounded."

And then he did that thing with his fingertips on her knuckles, even though that was not in the rules, even though no one could possibly see them. Just when she thought maybe, *maybe,* she could get accustomed to the pure masculine possessiveness of his touch without her heart doing double-time, he moved his hand up to her wrist and traced slow, sensuous circles around the delicacy of her bones.

Who knew wrists could be such zones of sensation?

When he had thoroughly debilitated her with the wrist thing, he turned her hand over, and his fingers did the same sensuous exploration on the palm of her hand.

Throughout the movie he toyed with her

fingers. He lifted her hand to his lips and kissed it, he treated her wrist and her palm as if they were parts of the female body that were worshipped in one of those exotic places he had been.

When the final credits rolled, she didn't know what the movie had been about and she could barely get out of her seat. She stumbled so badly in the aisle that he wrapped his arm around her waist and pulled her in close to him.

"I tried to warn you," he whispered.

"Warn me about what?" she said proudly.

"That it would be written all over you."

"It's not."

He gazed at her, smiled wickedly, "Oh, yeah, baby, it is."

"It isn't."

"Okay, smarty, what was the movie about?" Before she could gather her wits to answer, they had passed through the lobby and were on the street.

"Oh, oh," he said, "heads up, Sophie, it's showtime. For real."

What did that mean? What had happened in there wasn't real? Then she saw Gregg coming toward them, Antoinette in tow.

Suddenly she felt glad that all those moves Brand had done with his hands *showed*.

Antoinette, naturally, was gorgeous—tall, raven-haired, blue-eyed. "Sophie," Gregg said. "And it was Brandon, wasn't it? I want you to meet my Toni."

Sophie thought this rated very high on the awkward-moment list, but naturally Toni was way too classy to let that show.

"You're the woman I owe the biggest thank-you to!" she said. "I'd been watching this guy from the back row of a law class for two years. Oh, my God, when I heard he was available, I pounced. Poor guy didn't know what hit him, did you, sweetie?"

Gregg looked flustered, thrilled and in love.

"And how long have you two been seeing each other?" Antoinette asked.

"Forever," Sophie blurted out at the same time as Brand said, "Just a little while."

Sophie laughed nervously. She should have never uttered that word *forever* in reference to him. Not even as part of the charade, because it opened up a yawning hole of yearning in her that nothing was ever going to be able to fill.

Brand tucked her closer into him. "We've known each other forever," he covered for her.

"Oh," Antoinette said, contemplating them with the genuine interest of someone who liked everyone, "Is it serious?"

"No," Sophie said.

"Yes," Brand said.

Antoinette laughed. "Careful, Sophie, he has that look of a man who gets what he wants. Are you two going to Maynard's? Gregg tells me everyone goes after the show. It's so charming and small-town. I can't wait."

"No," Sophie said. "We're not going."

At the very same time, Brand said, "Of course we're going. *Everyone* does."

"See you there, then. Ta-ra." Antoinette wagged her fingers at them, tucked her arm into Gregg's and they disappeared into the thinning after-show crowd.

Sophie was silent as Brand opened the car door for her. She slid in, waited until he started the car.

"I don't want to go to Maynard's."

"Relax. It's a test. You're going to pass."

But the test felt as if it had changed, and she wasn't going to pass if he did that thing to her wrist again!

She let him think she didn't want to go because of Gregg and Antoinette. "She represents an unfair distribution of attributes," she decided sulkily. "She's smart and she's beautiful. Did she have to be nice, too?"

Brand said nothing.

After a while, she asked, "Did *you* think she was beautiful?"

"Sure. And smart. And nice."

"Oh."

"Sophie, her being those things doesn't make you any less than."

"She's the one he threw me over for!"

"Technically, you let him go."

"Well, I was going to take him back, after I did some thinking."

"So, she's smart, she's beautiful, she's nice *and* she prevented you from making the biggest mistake of your life. I'm liking her more by the second."

Suddenly, the situation they were heading into didn't feel awkward. It felt good, as if maybe Sophie could trust things to work out the way they were supposed to, even if it wasn't the way she had envisaged.

"Thanks, Brand," she said.

"Don't thank me too soon," he said. "I'm not done with you yet. By the time we walk out of Maynard's the whole town is going to know you are so over him."

"What are you planning?

"Just a little romance."

"You're scaring me."

"In my world, a little fear is never a bad

thing." He pulled up in front of Maynard's and took her hand as they walked in. As they stepped over the threshold, he pulled her hand up to his lips and lightly kissed where their fingers were intertwined.

After that, she walked to the table in a daze. As they settled into their seats, he let go of her hand, but with seeming reluctance.

"Ever come here with him after the movie?" he asked. The waitress came and offered them menus. Sophie took one, but he shook his head. "I know what I want," he said, not taking his eyes off Sophie.

The waitress stared at him, looked at Sophie and sighed, "You lucky girl."

"That's how you let the whole town know you're so over him," Brand said with satisfaction when the waitress left, promising to come back in a minute for their order.

"You're embarrassing me," Sophie managed to choke.

"Excellent. You blush when you're embarrassed. Naturally, it will be mistaken for the throes of love."

Mistaken? Dear God, this was feeling less like a charade every minute. She was going to be in deep trouble if Brand kept this up.

"So did you come here with the ex?"

Sophie nodded.

"So, what did you do?"

"Ordered hot chocolate. Drank it. Went home."

"What did you do that was *romantic?*"

She was sure she must have done something, but Brand kissing on her fingers, looking at her with such white-hot intensity and saying he *knew* what he wanted, seemed to have addled her mind, because not one thing she had ever done could compare to this.

When she didn't answer, Brand regarded her sympathetically. "What did he do that was romantic?"

She had to think very hard.

"He held out my chair for me."

"Did he hold your hand?"

"We were drinking hot chocolate!"

Brand looked unimpressed. "Gaze into your eyes? Reach across and fiddle with your hair? Play with your feet under the table?"

His foot reached out and caressed her calf. He grinned evilly before he pulled it away. She felt as if her face was on fire.

"Perfect," he purred.

Antoinette and Gregg came in just then, and Brand watched them unabashedly. Gregg pulled out Antoinette's seat, then turned and talked to the people at the table behind him.

"Anything you did with him" Brand said, turning back to her with a shake of his head, "do the opposite with me."

"I don't know what that means." If he reached out and fiddled with her hair, she'd probably faint and slide under the table like someone who had drunk too much champagne. That was the effect he had on her.

"Okay. Just follow my lead."

The waitress came back. "Sophie, you want something off the menu or your usual?"

"My usual. Hot chocolate."

Brand made an exasperated sound deep in his throat. "The opposite," he reminded her in an undertone. When she didn't get it, he sighed.

"Cancel the hot chocolate. We'll have one large fudge sundae. Don't skimp on the whipped cream and don't forget the cherry."

"Two spoons?" the waitress asked.

"Yes," Sophie said, feeling control slipping away from her as quickly as a glass covered in cooking oil.

"No," Brand said, and smiled wickedly at her. "One spoon."

And when their sundae came, and he leaned across the table and fed her the cherry off their one spoon, something fizzed and crackled in the air between them, and she knew it was the very *something* she had always longed for.

Only what she hadn't expected was that it could be so powerful, would resist taming and would leave her heart feeling as if it had received a direct strike from a lightning bolt.

She didn't walk out of Maynard's. She floated out. And she floated through the rest of the weekend: helping him with his mother's roses the next day, talking on her front porch deep into the night.

They talked about small things: memories, shared acquaintances, the news that had made the paper that day. They talked of reclaiming rosebeds and what she was doing at work.

And they talked of bigger things: how his relationship with his father was slowly improving, and how the visit had reassured him his father was still more than capable of living independently.

Sophie loved hearing the gentleness and respect in Brand's voice when he talked about his dad. She felt only a little guilty that he hadn't figured out his father and her grandmother were a little more than friends, but given how the relationship between the two men was improving, she hoped Dr. Sheridan would tell his son soon.

Now it was Sunday afternoon, sizzling hot, a perfect day to get back on her schedule and go to Blue Rock. Only, somehow, for Sophie, everything was getting blurred. Was this still about letting the town know she was so over Gregg Harrison?

Or had it slipped into something completely different and far more exciting? And did Brand feel it, too?

He really seemed not to and appeared to be able to refuse the temptation of her with baffling ease. Publicly, his romantic skills were dazzling. Privately, he assumed more of a big-brother role. Yet, still, Sophie could not remember when conversation, and companionship had been so satisfying, so absolutely fulfilling, like a sense of coming home to the place you belonged after a long time away.

But today, at Blue Rock, she was determined to make him notice her in a way he wasn't going to forget as soon as they were alone together.

Underneath a too-large men's T-shirt, she had on the teeniest bikini the law would allow.

She knew their plan was succeeding. She knew the whole town was talking about them, about Brand Sheridan and Sophie Holtzheim.

Now her goal had altered itself. She just wanted Brand to notice she had grown up. She wanted him to see her as a woman.

She could see he was slowly being charmed by the town he had left behind. But did that slow charming extend to her, too?

He picked her up in a four-wheel drive, a Jeep that looked like army surplus from the Second World War.

"Where's your car?"

"I traded it in. I like this one better. Better for loading boats."

Did that mean he was planning another fishing trip? Was he planning things with her? The way he was looking at her, no wonder the lines were blurring.

"I took a big hit for the boat scratch, though."

She walked around his new vehicle. The paint was nonexistent, the leather seats were cracked. But it had something wonderful about it. "I love it," she decided. "Very Indiana Jones."

He regarded her thoughtfully for a minute, shook his head. "You're serious, aren't you?"

"It just seems more you than the other one."

Blue Rock was a short hike in to a canyon, a back pool off the Blue River where the water was deep and still and a color of green that put emeralds to shame. A rocky beach lined the pool, and Blue Rock was an outcropping on one side, providing a twelve-foot leap into the water. More cliffs loomed above Blue Rock, including the Widow Maker.

Already half the town was here seeking relief from the heat.

Sophie spread their blanket, aware of interest, aware of being watched. The rumors were starting to circulate, she knew.

And she suspected a lot of the talk was incredulous. What was a guy like him doing with a girl like her? Thanks to his father, people insisted on calling him a secret agent, thanks to her job, they insisted on seeing her as a librarian.

It did seem like the world's most unlikely combo!

But Sophie was about to prove she wasn't the girl everyone thought she was! She was about to break out of the mold the town had put her in ever since "What Makes a Small Town Tick."

She took a deep breath and yanked the T-shirt over her head.

And instead of feeling sexy, she instantly felt naked.

In public.

Oh, God. Hadn't she had dreams that went like this?

# CHAPTER SEVEN

INSTEAD of feeling sexy and powerful, Sophie couldn't even look at Brand, who had gone silent as the stones that rose around them.

"Race you," she said in a strangled tone, then ran for the water and dove in. It was a cool release from the heat of the day and the heat in her face.

But the bathing suit? Fragile at best, held together with spiderweb strings, it nearly parted company with her. And when she reached to tug it up into place, the fabric felt oddly mushy in her hand.

Brand had hit the water right behind her, and he came up, shaking droplets of water from the darkness of his hair and looking at her with a light in his eyes she had hoped to see.

But naturally, nothing in her world ever went as planned, especially in the courtship department. She had pictured that light in his eyes, had pictured them chasing each other around this pool like playful dolphins, had pictured him catching her....

She shook the vision away. She had to deal with reality. Treading water delicately, she said, "Brand, I'm in big trouble here."

The look on his face—the one she had dreamed of since she was fifteen—was replaced instantly with concern. He reached for her. "What do you mean, big trouble?"

"Don't touch me."

"Excuse me. I assumed big trouble might mean you were about to drown."

"I think my bathing suit is disintegrating," she hissed at him. "Why is this my life?"

"Your bathing suit is disintegrating?" he asked with far more interest than sympathy.

"Why does everything go so wrong for me?" Even though she was whispering, it sounded like a wail. "Especially around you!"

"Hey, you can't blame me."

"Is it? Disintegrating?"

He was peering beneath the water.

"Don't look!"

"How the hell can I tell if it's disintegrating if I don't look?"

"Shh. I'm going to die of embarrassment."

"Nobody *dies* of embarrassment."

"Unfortunately." She tugged at the fabric.

None of it actually seemed to be disintegrating. "Maybe it's not disintegrating. Melting. Imagine toilet paper getting wet."

"Sweet Pea?"

"What?"

"Sometimes swimsuits that, um, look like that one…"

Well, at least he'd noticed it before disaster struck!

"They aren't actually meant for swimming."

"What are you? The world's foremost expert on swimwear?"

"Unfortunately," he said.

She thought of him living on a yacht off the coast of Spain. What had she been thinking, trying to impress him with skimpiness?

"Were you surrounded by beautiful women all the time?" she asked. She felt absurd, as though she was going to burst into tears. He was out of her league. He'd always been out of her league. She'd spent all this week forgetting that. Believing something else.

Believing the stupid fairy tales she'd sworn to leave behind.

And then, just like that, he made it all right.

He said, quietly and with utter conviction, "Not one of them was as beautiful as you, Sophie Holtzheim."

She trod water and stared at him. He wasn't laughing. He wasn't teasing. She couldn't look at what she saw in his face any longer or she was going to cry.

She glanced down and saw her new, sexy bathing suit, which had been bordering on indecent when dry, had definitely crossed the border now that it was wet. It was as translucent as a sheet of plastic wrap.

Then she did start to cry.

And, without a word, Brand gathered her to him, one arm locked around her, the other moving them toward shore. As soon as he could stand, his feet found the ground, and he wrapped both arms around her.

Under different circumstances she would have mareled at how his wet skin felt against her wet skin.

But under these circumstances, his body felt like a shield as he closed it around her. He lifted her, cradled her into his chest, carried her to their blanket. In one smooth move, he set her feet on the ground, ducked, flicked their blanket up off the rock and tucked it around her.

"I look like the same nerd as always," she said, sniffling.

He smiled. "That's what's beautiful about

you." And then, as if he had said way too much—as if he was the one who had been too revealing and not her—he did that annoying thing where he chucked her on the chin and turned and strode away.

He dove into the pool, crossed it in about four strong strokes and began to climb the rocks on the other side.

At first, Sophie thought it was part of her complete gift for everything going wrong around him. She'd weirded him out with her disintegrating bathing suit and her tears. He hadn't meant it about not one of those women from his other life being as beautiful as her. How could he have meant that?

But suddenly, it became clear to her.

He wasn't trying to escape her or her bathing suit or her tears.

He was doing what he always did. He was somehow making everything right. And he was doing it because he was climbing that cliff for her.

He went by the jut of Blue Rock without even pausing at it, without even acknowledging the teenage boys who were jostling for position there.

He began the more perilous climb, slower now, finding each foothold and each handhold, moving with confidence and purpose. How high above the water was that? Fifty feet?

She felt sick with dread and the absolute thrill of it.

And then, as he stood there on that precipice high above the pool, the one that hardly anyone had ever used before him or would use after him, the one they called the Widow Maker, he paused and looked down, not at the water below him but right at her. And he gave the sweetest little wave.

And that confirmed what he was doing. He was participating in that age-old dance—a man showing a woman that he would be the best, the strongest, the boldest.

He shouted, his voice, deep, sure, echoing off the canyon walls.

"Honor."

Not a person who heard that cry would not have shivers go up and down their spine.

Then he leapt, feet first, hands tucked at his sides, straight as an arrow, plummeting toward the water below him. His act of pure and foolish bravery did to Sophie what such feats of daring had done to women since the beginning of time: it filled her with fear for him, even as it did exactly what it was intended to do. Impressed her. Awed her. Evaporated whatever defenses she had remaining against him.

And it made her very happy she had found the nerve to wear the little white bikini—for her, every bit as bold as his leap from the cliff. Maybe once it was dry and not quite so see-through, she would uncover again. But for now, she was taking advantage of the fact that all eyes were on Brand to slip out from under the blanket and into her T-shirt.

He surfaced, tossed water from his hair, swam lazily across the pool, as if unaware every eye now followed him. He came and lay down on the blanket she had spread, right beside her, not even toweling off.

"Why did you shout 'Honor' before you jumped?" she asked.

"It's a battle cry. It's something worth fighting for. And dying for."

"It's more," she guessed softly. "It's about acknowledging your deepest self, isn't it, Brand? About acknowledging what is at your core, your highest and your best?"

"Ah, you're way too deep for a shallow guy like me, Sweet Pea." His eyes drifted over her lazily, with a possessiveness that made her mouth go dry.

"You know," he said, "we are both covered in

scratches from those rosebushes. It makes it look like we've been up to all kinds of exciting things."

He reached out and traced one of the scratches on her arm.

"Like taming wild kittens?" she teased back, though the touch of his hand made her voice feel squeaky and breathless.

"Oh, yeah, I keep forgetting Sugar Maple Grove has a different standard for excitement than the rest of the world." He, thank God, seemed to lose interest in the scratch.

"In a way," she said, serious again, "for you, doing the dangerous thing, like jumping from that rock, is the safest thing of all, isn't it?"

"Huh?"

He was being deliberately obtuse. But she knew it. He had *felt* something when she had burst into tears. And by climbing up that cliff and throwing himself off that rock, he'd been able to feel something completely different instead.

"You engage yourself at a very physical level to avoid the risks and challenges of emotion."

"If that's a fancy way of saying guys don't like it when girls cry, uh, yeah. You got my number, Dr. Holtzheim. Not that it was that dangerous, even by Sugar Maple Grove standards."

"Apparently the standard is about to change," she said, watching as Martin, one of the more daring of the teenage boys who hung out here, started scrambling up the cliff straight toward the Widow Maker to the cheers of his friends.

He turned his attention from her to watch as the boy finally made it to the edge of the cliff. The boy hesitated and then jumped. His arms and legs windmilled furiously all the way down. He created a big splash, but surfaced, waving his two fingers in the V of victory.

Brand closed his eyes.

Sophie lay on their blanket, drowsing in the sun, staring at the water beading on the golden, perfect skin of the man who shared the blanket with her, his hair crusted with water diamonds, his eyes closed.

He looked so relaxed, and so at ease.

One week.

He'd only been home one week. How could her life feel so totally different? How could she feel so alive, as if energy tingled just below the surface of her skin all the time? And then, seeing him standing on the edge of the rock and seeing the truth about him finding safety in danger. It was as if she had unlocked a little secret about him.

And it probably felt so good because he did not reveal his secrets willingly.

"Mr. Sheridan?"

"Huh?" He rolled over, shielded his eyes from the sun.

"I'm Martin Gilmore."

Brand got to his feet, shook the young man's hand.

"That felt great. Jumping from the cliff." And then in a rush, "I'm thinking of joining the marines."

Without warning, the weariness that Sophie had not seen for days was back in Brand's eyes, the wall was up.

"Son, how old are you?"

"Seventeen."

Brand nodded and said quietly, "You should enjoy what you have here for as long as you can. Sophie, are you ready to go?"

She was surprised by the abruptness of it, but saw something in his face that did not invite argument.

She gathered up their picnic basket and blanket and he carried them to the Jeep, something remote in his face, untouchable.

"What just happened?" she asked him as

they stood together at the open back of his vehicle, loading things in.

"Nothing happened," he said tersely, slamming the trunk shut.

"Yes, it did." She touched his arm, feeling him trying to move away from her. "What happened when Martin asked you about the marines?"

"I've zipped the body bag closed on too many kids that age."

"Tell me about that," she said quietly.

He scoffed. "Get real."

"No," she said, "tell me what you've seen and done."

"Sophie, you can't even handle a worm."

And that wall went back up so hard and so high she wondered if she'd been mistaken in thinking it had come down at all during the golden moments they had shared over the last week.

He shook off her arm, but she felt there was only one way to break the wall down. And she felt as if she *had* to, as if her life depended on reaching him and bringing him back here.

It wasn't like when she had kissed him in her office, launching herself at him, something to prove, an attempt to manipulate his impressions of her.

No, this was different.

It was a way of letting him know she could see him. She was coming for him, whether he liked it or not. He could jump off all the cliffs he liked, she was still coming, still going to find what was real about him.

She stood on tiptoes and touched her lips to his, tasted the sweet sting of the pure river water, the Razzle Dazzle Raspberry cooler he had sipped earlier and the sweeter flavor of who he really was. Strong. Courageous. True. Deep.

*Lonely.*

Could you really know those things from touching your lips to someone else's? Not always.

But this time, yes.

He pulled back from her, and she knew he had gotten the message because she could see the wariness in his eyes.

"What was that about?" he growled.

"Mrs. Fleckenspeck was watching."

He turned and surveyed the wide and very empty gravel shoulder where everyone who used Blue Rock parked. "I don't see Mrs. Fleckenspeck. And what happened to rule number six hundred, no public demonstrativeness?"

"There weren't six hundred rules!" she said indignantly.

"There might as well not be any if you're just going to break them." He sounded grouchy, not at all like the man who had delivered sweet peas to her office, not like the one who had risked his neck racing her down Sugar Maple Grove's sleepy streets, nor the one who had chased her with worms or jumped off cliffs trying to impress her. Oh, she was beginning to get it!

He liked it when *he* was the one breaking the rules, when *he* was the one upsetting the apple cart.

"Okay," he said, looking everywhere but at her, "I think our duty here is done. Let's go."

And she never let on for a moment how disappointing she found that, or the fact that he drove fast all the way home, as if he couldn't put enough distance between them and what had happened.

She had sensed something real in all this pretense. Had sensed if he confided in her about the burdens he carried, it would get real in a brand-new way, a way neither of them would be able to step back from.

How long had it been since he had trusted someone with who he really was? Had he ever?

Good grief! It struck Sophie that there was a possibility that she was every bit as in love with Brand Sheridan as she had been at fifteen.

And that it was unlike loving Gregg. This kind of love could cost her everything.

*Again.*

Her whole world could be shattered all over again. Was she strong enough for that?

Brand could still taste the pure water of Blue Rock and the sweet invitation of Sophie's kiss when he crawled into bed that night.

Maybe *he* was going to have to write some rules. Like no more kissing, *ever.* But then she would know.

It awakened something in him. Something that burned. And yearned and ached. Something that was desperate for someplace soft and safe and blissful to rest his weary head. Sophie, just Sophie, never mind bikinis that melted in water, made him burn and yearn and ache.

He'd been back in sweet, sleepy Sugar Maple Grove for a week. And the astonishing truth was he had not been bored, not even once.

The knot of tension that had become a part of him had been slowly uncurling, relaxing. Until that kid at the swimming hole, a reflection of his younger self, no doubt a young man addicted to speed, reckless and restless, without a care in the world, and talking about throwing this world away. He wondered now why young men were so damned eager to leave all this behind them.

*Think of something else,* he ordered himself. So he did. He contemplated the fact that his father wasn't home.

*Bingo at the St. James Hall* tonight, Sophie had told him when they'd arrived back at the house to find his father's car missing.

"Dad's leading a pretty full life." More and more he felt content about his father's circumstances.

"Oh, yeah, well, good for him." But she'd looked away. Despite how he was managing to reassure himself, her reaction gave Brand the uneasy idea Sophie knew something about his father that she didn't want him to know. That had been evident when he'd asked her what she knew about the fire. Something had risen in her face—panic?

That was okay. He knew things he didn't want her to know, either.

*Tell me what you have seen and done,* she'd insisted, for the second time, and for the second time he had felt the terrible sway of temptation.

For a moment, temptation had made him see her, not as a child who needed his protection, but as a woman who could help him carry the burden.

He snorted to himself. He'd come back to Sophie against his desire to think of something—anything—else.

But since he was here, what kind of man asked a woman to help carry his burdens? Why was it he hadn't even known how heavy they were until she had asked him *what have you seen and done* and part of him had felt as if it would *die* if it didn't tell her.

Sinclair had had the right idea, he thought reaching for the letters that had been sent home to Sarah some sixty-five years ago.

Private Horsenell had now been overseas for months. His letters were becoming less frequent and far less revealing. The initial excitement and curiosity had given way to a faint overtone of cynicism. He was no longer in Ireland, but, in the early days of 1943, in the south of France.

My dearest Sarah, this one read,

Please do not hound me to tell you of the things I have done. Most of it is unpleasant. Truly, you do not want to know, and just as truly, I do not want to tell you.
I send my love,
Sinclair.

But the last line seemed to be written as an obligation.

It was evident Sinclair was manning up and keeping his secrets to himself, Brand thought, putting the letters away, not having the heart to look at any more of them tonight.

Still, even though he put them aside, Sinclair and Sarah haunted Brand over the decades that separated him from them. He thought of them even after he had turned out the light.

Sinclair was changing, whether he knew it or not. The man he had first been would have never written with such blunt impatience, "do not hound me." There was something hard in Sinclair that had not been there before, it had crept into the last four or five letters. Brand did not think it boded well for sweet little Sarah, sitting at home pining for a boy who no longer existed.

When Brand had raced Sophie on their bikes, felt the wind and the speed and the surprising challenge of beating her, he had been, for the first time in a long, long while, a boy he recognized from the past. That boy, some forgotten part of himself, was being coaxed more and more to the surface with every second he spent in Sugar Maple Grove, and every second he spent with Sophie.

And, just like Sarah, Sophie would be nothing but disappointed if she thought that boy could ever come back completely.

And so would he.

Maybe next time she asked *what have you seen and done,* he'd try out Sinclair's line. *Do not hound me.*

Through his open bedroom window, Brand heard a car pull up, doors slam. Voices. The voices, his father's and Hilde's, went into the backyard and, out of curiosity, Brand got up out of bed and went to the window.

His father and Sophie's grandmother were in the darkness of the yard, leaning into each other, holding hands.

Then they kissed. Not a little peck on the cheek kind of kiss, either.

He pulled away from the window, feeling guiltily like a Peeping Tom. Brand felt astounded by what he had just witnessed and amazed by how angry it made him.

His father thought he had dishonored his mother by not coming to the funeral? How about replacing her so quickly, moving on to someone else as if she had not mattered at all?

He remembered Sophie's expression when they had talked about his father, and thought, *she knows.*

A betrayal. A good thing to remember the next time he was feeling tempted to trust her with his secrets.

He felt bitterly disappointed. Why? He was cynical by nature. He knew people disappointed each other. He was the foolish one for feeling as if he could trust Sophie with his life. And his secrets. Thank God he had not given in to the temptation to tell her anything tonight, though the urge to do so had been momentarily almost overwhelming.

He felt a startling desire to escape from this situation, to run.

But he was not a man who had ever run away from things that weren't easy. He had invited them. He had taken up his fighter's stance and invited the world to give him its best shot. The military had taken his restlessness and his recklessness and turned him into a gladiator who entered the arena willingly.

Every arena, he realized, except this one.

He had never before entered the arena of the human heart. Sophie had been so right by that pool today.

He found safety in danger. Danger engaged him physically. It gave him the rush of feeling intensely alive without the risk of engaging his heart.

Now he was aware of standing on a precipice far more dangerous to him than the Widow Maker could ever be.

*He was falling in love with Sophie.*

Falling was an accident. Jumping was a choice. No wonder he was so guarded against love. It had happened without his permission and without his planning. There was an element of being powerless to it. And in his world, being powerless was a weakness.

Mentally, he stepped back from the precipice. Mentally, he took charge.

He would finish fixing his mother's rosebeds, he vowed. That's how he would honor her, even if his father was incapable of it. And then he would confront his father about the new relationship.

And then he would go. His unit kept temporary quarters in California. He had not lived in barracks since he was a young pup, but he could go there until other arrangements were made.

Brand took out the cell phone he had not used for an entire week and sent a text message to his sister. "Dad seems fine." He hesitated. Did he add, "He has a new friend"? No. That was his dad's business.

Then Brand sent a text to his boss. He

couldn't stay here for a month. It was no longer the safest place in the world.

It had become the most dangerous.

Something had happened. He had fallen. For his hometown. For Sophie.

But he doubted he could ever come back here, to this way of life, not anymore than Sinclair Horsenell could come back here. They had something in them now that these small towns could not handle. And that nothing in a small-town girl's experience prepared her for—a man who was cynical. Jaded.

Damaged in a way that could not be repaired. Not by all that charm, not by all that innocence.

Not by all the love in the world.

What about his commitment to help Sophie hold her head up high again? To make it look to the whole town as though he was romancing her? He had tossed her schedule beside his bed and now he looked at it.

There was only one more thing. The engagement party of her ex-fiancé. If he went and broke both Slick Harrison's legs it would be a nonissue.

The kind of man who had thoughts like that could never have a girl like Sophie.

Besides, if there was one thing he had

always counted on himself to be, it was a man of his word. His four-year undercover assignment had made him doubt that part of himself, now he felt it was imperative he get it back.

He had told Sophie he would help her out. Just because she was part of the conspiracy of silence around his father's romantic life, did that let him off the hook?

No. Brian Lancaster would never have done the honorable thing. And Brand knew, at some instinctual level, that getting himself back after four years of pretending to be someone else meant behaving with honor. And integrity.

Even when it hurt. But not when it hurt Sophie. Except it *was* going to hurt her, because he'd take her to the damn party, but until then, he was avoiding her completely.

Because he could keep on getting in deeper with her and hurt her a lot later, or start pulling back and hurt her a little now.

He was pulling back and it was for her own good.

# CHAPTER EIGHT

THE dress had been a last-ditch attempt to fix something that was broken. Sophie Holtzheim had never owned a dress like the one she was wearing. Not even that wedding gown she had donned, unbelievably, only two weeks ago, did what this dress did.

Iridescent green silk, the dress was the first time Sophie had ever splurged on a designer label.

Now, she could clearly see why people did.

The dress didn't just adore the female body, it worshipped it. The dress was ten times sexier than that bikini had been, which seemed impossible, given the differences in the amount of fabric, but, nonetheless, it was true.

This dress floated around her, a whisper of sensuality. It delicately hugged certain assets, celebrating the sensuous curves of her breasts and hips.

The color and the fabric made Sophie's skin look as smooth and flawless as a glass pitcher of heavy cream. The length, ending just above her knee, made her legs look slender and endless.

And the shimmering color brought out something spectacular in her eyes. Well, the dress, and an hour of makeup instruction at the local cosmetics counter!

Still, Sophie was aware that all the hopes she had invested in this dress, that it could fix something broken, were not justified. And the *something broken* was not her reputation in Sugar Maple Grove, either. She didn't care if Gregg Harrison fell in his own swimming pool because she looked so spectacular. That was no longer what she needed to fix—she didn't give a hoot about the town's perceptions of her.

It would not fix whatever had gone wrong between her and Brand.

She knew it the instant she went to the door and saw him standing on the stoop, breathtaking in a tux, the shirt the most pristine white, the bow tie perfectly knotted, because the look on his face when he saw her did not change from the look she had been putting up with on his face ever since they had been to Blue Rock nearly a week ago.

All week, he had been coolly distant. When

she had showed up at his rosebed, ready to work, he had announced it was really a project he wanted to do himself, to honor his mother. *It's personal.*

That was not something you could really argue with.

But she soon found out it was not just the rose garden. He didn't want to go fishing, either. Or to the movies. He didn't want to ride their bikes downtown for ice cream.

Point blank: he didn't want to be with her.

If she'd had an ounce of pride she would have canceled tonight, but dammit, from the start it had been all about tonight. This was the point: to make it public that she was so over Gregg.

And naturally, she had hoped the dress would sway Brand.

But she could see instantly that it had failed.

When her grandmother came to the door to see them off, she said, in German, "See if he can dance, Sophie. There is nothing like a man who can dance."

And he said to her grandmother, his German perfect, much better than Sophie's, "I'm afraid I am no dancer."

Her grandmother actually looked pleased that he spoke German, as if it troubled her not a bit that he had been eavesdropping on what they had assumed were private conversations since his arrival. Embarrassed, Sophie reviewed some of the things her grandmother had said, tried to remember her responses.

But maybe it wasn't the details that mattered so much as the deliberateness of his deception. Sophie felt something shiver along her spine, and, looking at his carefully schooled features, she thought maybe she didn't know him at all.

They walked down the walk and he held open the car door for her—he'd borrowed his father's vehicle for tonight—and closed it quietly after her, with all the polite remoteness of a paid escort.

Which, in a way, he was. Just a guy doing a gal a favor. She was the one who had let the boundaries blur, she was the one who'd begun to bring expectations, she was the one who had read way too much into stolen kisses, shared laughter, physical awareness, a daring leap from a rock.

"We need to discuss the breakup," he said as he took the driver's seat, pulled away from the curb smoothly.

Since she felt what they needed to discuss was the fact he spoke German and had never once admitted it, she was not prepared for that.

Even though she knew the dress had not worked, even though all week she had felt something slipping away from her, even though she had an unsettling sense of not knowing who he was *at all,* Sophie felt unprepared for that. Completely.

"Excuse me?"

"The breakup," he repeated. "If I just leave and never come back it's just going to look like you've been ditched again. That was hardly the point of this whole exercise."

"Are you leaving?"

"Yes."

"I thought you were staying for a month."

"You can't count on a guy in my line of work, Sophie." This was said harshly.

"You're never coming back?"

He glanced at her, then looked straight ahead. He didn't answer.

Which she took to mean he was never coming back. How could she feel so bereft? They were supposed to be playing. Pretending.

But she had caught a glimpse of the truth. She loved him as much as she had when she was fifteen.

And she was going to be just as devastated now as she was then. When he left Sugar Maple Grove.

She wanted to wail at him, *How could you never come back?*

Instead she thought, I only have a little while longer to convince him this is a place worth coming back to.

*That I am a girl worth coming back to.*

"We don't have to have a public breakup," she said, not looking at him, looking out the window. "I can pretend we're talking on the phone, e-mailing for a while And then just let it fizzle out after a few months."

"Make sure it looks like it's you who let it fizzle," he said. "Tell people my job was just too demanding. It *is* too demanding for a woman who wants the things that you want."

"What do you think I want?"

"It's written all over you what you want." His voice had an edge to it. "A little house like that one right there," he nodded at a house they were driving by, a play set in the yard, with a baby swing and a regular swing.

"Sandboxes and tricycles," he said in a low voice. "A husband who is home at night. Picnics and fried chicken on Sunday. The kind of life Sugar Maple Grove lends itself to."

"Are you saying that you won't ever settle down, Brand? That you don't eventually want those things out of life, too?"

"My job destroys relationships," he said grimly. "I've seen it happen a dozen times. It's not fair to ask anyone to share a life that is full of unpredictability and constant risk."

"That sounds so lonely."

"I'm not lonely," he snapped, and something about the way he said it made her look at him and think, *yes, he is.*

But she had already done her best to lure him in from his lonely world. For a while she had convinced herself she could. Now, glancing over at him, she saw the formidable will of the man. She saw that he had decided what he wanted, and that Sugar Maple Grove was not part of that. And neither was she. She wondered if she had ever known him at all.

But, for all the pain she felt, Sophie knew she had learned something real and something important. Two weeks in the company of Brand Sheridan had made Gregg seem like a cardboard cutout of a man that she had tucked in beside her to make her feel as if she was really experiencing a relationship, when, in fact, she had settled for a cheap imitation.

How was that for an irony? This relationship—the pretend one—felt real, whereas her real relationship had felt pretend.

At her instructions they left Sugar Maple

Grove behind them and traveled a twisty country road until they reached the impressive gate of the Harrison estate. A sign swung in a gentle breeze. Today it had lavender balloons on it, to match the ugly theme of the invitation, Sophie thought sourly.

"Pheasant Corpse Estate," he read the sign out loud, his voice heavy with cynicism.

"*Copse,* not *corpse!*"

"Whatever. Wow. Do they give themselves titles, too? The Duke and Duchess of Dead Pheasant Estate?"

"This is where I was going to live," Sophie said, reacting to his sarcasm, feeling defensive, as if he was criticizing *her,* her dreams.

She remembered how she used to feel as she drove up the long, winding, tree-lined drive. It curved through a little forest and past a stream, and then opened up into a grove where a grand house was located.

The house had once been a two-story farmhouse, but clever additions over the years gave it the fairy-tale look of the country estate written on the gate. The shingle siding had been recently stained in a lovely dove-gray, the white of the porches and shutters and trim gleamed with fresh paint.

She used to feel as if this was a safe place.

As if, finally, after the deaths of her parents, all was going to be well with her world again. She was going to be part of a family. She was going to have a place to call home in a way her house had never been since her parents had left it.

She realized it was the loss of that vision that she had mourned as much as the loss of her relationship with Gregg. Perhaps more so.

And then Sophie realized, shocked, that for her the danger was in choosing safety. This was the place designed to protect her heart after the deaths of her parents. In safety was the danger she would stagnate, never discover her true potential, never live fully.

Tonight the house was lit from within, every light on, spilling gold out huge paned-glass windows over the sweep of the front lawns.

"You can pull around to the back," she said with unconscious familiarity. He did, and, as she had guessed, cars were being parked between the house and the barn. Not that the barn housed animals. It had been turned into storage for vintage cars a long time ago.

As they drove past the back of the house, Sophie could see that the stone patio was already overflowing with guests, that gas lights winked off the turquoise water of the swimming pool.

"Let me get this straight. You were going to live with his parents?" he asked, finding a parking spot on the far side of the barn, a good distance for her to walk in the three-inch stiletto heels of the shoes that had set off the dress so perfectly.

"We weren't going to live with his parents. There's a suite."

Brand made a growling noise.

"His brother lived there until he got established, too." She recognized something even more defensive in her voice.

He cut the engine, and when she reached for the handle of her door, he gave her a dark look. She sat back, waited.

He came around to her door, opened it, offered her his arm.

"You were going to live with his parents," he said with disgust.

She would rather not have taken his arm, but the ground was uneven, and she was feeling a little wobbly on the shoes.

"I don't see anything wrong with that," she said stiffly.

"*You* wouldn't."

She could hear laughter, tinkling of glasses, voices as they approached the back lawn, the terraces. It occurred to her she did not feel one ounce of trepidation about seeing Gregg. Or his fiancée. Not one.

"What's wrong with it?" she demanded. "Living with his parents until we got established?"

But she already knew. It was *safe*. And she hated it that he could see that so clearly.

"What's wrong with it? What about running around naked? What about making love in the backyard under the stars? And on the kitchen table? What about passion taking you so hard you scream with it? Sob his name. Beg him to make you feel as if the universe is exploding?"

He wasn't even trying to keep his voice down.

The world he was painting—a world governed by passion instead of safety—filled her with a kind of agony. She fiercely longed to know the wild part of her that her need for safety had prevented her from ever discovering, ever knowing.

But she had never wanted to feel anything like that with Gregg. Or with any other man. She wanted to feel those things with him. With Brand.

Even as his words stirred something wild in her, a longing, she recognized that Brand, usually so controlled, sounded very angry, angrier that she had ever seen him.

And she realized she felt angry herself.

"Don't you miss any of that, Sophie?"

"But not with you, of course." Her voice snapped. It felt as though the anger exploded in her. How dare he bring her to the brink of all life could be and then abandon her there with her heart full of this terrible longing, her body nearly quivering with it?

For a moment he went very still. He stopped and took a deep breath. He looked at her, hard, and she could see he had seen the dress, and her. And that it had had exactly the effect she had wanted. With a man less determined, maybe it could have fixed whatever was broken between them. Maybe it could have taken them to that place of pure passion, where reason was given a rest.

But Brand looked away from her, shoved his hands in his pockets, rocked back on the heels of his shoes and studied the star-studded sky, gathering himself, gathering his strength.

And she knew why. He was about to tell her good-bye. He was doing his duty, escorting her to the party. But it was really good-bye and it had been for a week now.

"You always knew we were pretending," he said quietly. "That was our deal. You always knew it would never be me that chased you around the kitchen table until you were breathless."

She yanked her arm out of the crook of his. "So nothing about this time here has been true, Brand. Nothing?"

He hesitated, her heart flew up in hope, and then fell like a bird with an arrow through it when he said coldly, "Nothing."

"You," she spat out, "are the most dishonest man I have ever met."

"Don't even get me going about honesty," he said.

"Really? That's funny. I don't remember tricking *your* elderly grandmother."

"Your elderly grandmother who is out in my backyard kissing the daylights out of my newly widowed father?"

"You entertained yourself at our expense!"

"And you knew about my dad. You knew about my dad and your grandmother. And you never said a word."

"For your information," Sophie said, biting out each word, her enunciation perfect, for once not stumbling all over herself, "your Dad is twice the man you'll ever be. He's not afraid."

"Yeah, like I'm afraid."

"Your dad is not afraid of love."

He was silent for a moment, and then said, "Are you telling me he *loves* your grand-mother?"

"Ask *him*," she snapped, "and you know what? Forget the gentle breakup. Forget the e-mails and the slow fizzle. In fact, forget we were ever together."

She didn't care that her voice was rising, and that people close to the edge of the lawn had turned toward them. "Forget this whole shameful sham. Because you know what, Brand Sheridan? I don't need *you* so I can hold *my* head up high!"

And then she walked away from him.

It was disastrous, of course. A heel turned over on the uneven ground of the driveway.

When he walked toward her, looking like he was going to offer his big strong arm—rescue his clumsy little sweet pea one last time—she cast him a withering look, took the shoes off and walked in her stockings over the gravel toward the lights and noises of a party she didn't dread in the least.

Brand watched her go, her shoes in her hand, sashaying down that drive without a glance back at him.

It was a moment he had somehow lived for: to see finally that she didn't need him anymore. He had seen the truth in the furious light that had sparked in her eyes right now.

Sophie Holtzheim could make it on her own. She was like a tiny bird who had fallen from the nest, and he had picked her up, stroked her feathers until she was ready to fly.

And it seemed to him, seeing her in that dress tonight, he had never seen a woman more ready to fly.

He just hadn't expected to feel quite so sad to have to let her go.

He watched her for a moment longer, then, unable to resist, he made his way to the edge of the lawn, aware this might be the last time he ever saw her.

The patio was crowded, but he picked her out of the crowd instantly. It wasn't just the dress—that impossibly sexy, fantastic dress—that set her apart, though it did. It was the way she carried herself, like a queen.

The confidence, her sense of herself, was radiating from her. He could see in the way people looked at her that they noticed it.

He watched her until she got to the bar.

He was not sure how, over all that noise, he heard her. But he did.

"Whiskey on the rocks. Make it a double."

Even ten minutes ago he would have told

her to take it easy. Now, it was clear his days of telling her anything were over.

The way she looked tonight, gorgeous, glorious, *on fire,* it occurred to him that his first night back here, he really had seen a goddess in the garden. She just hadn't known it yet. And maybe she didn't see yet what he saw so clearly.

He stood there for a moment, in awe of the woman she would become. Soon, every guy in the place would be all over her. They would be bringing her drinks and asking her to dance, later they would probably get bolder and try to coax her into the shadows to steal kisses from her.

And from the look on her face, she wouldn't have one bit of trouble handling them.

And if she did, if she floundered with this new power she would have over men, it was not his problem. She was not a little girl anymore. He was not her protector.

She didn't need him.

As he thought of that, he felt a void open up in him that could never, ever be filled.

He stood at the edge of the crowd for a moment longer and then, before she could see him watching her, he turned and walked away.

Brand let himself back into his father's

house quietly, went under the sloped roof of his boyhood room, checked his messages.

Arrangements were in place: check the unit office when he got to California, he would be given temporary accommodations and a temporary assignment, teaching new recruits to FREES the techniques of very advanced rope rescues.

That was his life. If for a while, here in Sugar Maple Grove, he'd forgotten that, it didn't really matter. So, he'd fallen.

You picked yourself up, you dusted yourself off and you got on with it. You didn't look back, either.

He packed his bag, hoping to slip out unnoticed, not ready to confront his father, but of course, this was the one night his father was home.

"I thought you took Sophie to that party."

"I did. She didn't need me to stay. Dad, I have to go back to work."

"Tonight?"

"It's sudden, I know."

"You fought with Sophie," his father said, watching him.

"It wasn't a fight."

"You promised her you'd help her hold her head up high."

"In the end she figured out no one can help you with that."

"You didn't hurt her, did you?"

"Less now than I might have later."

"Ah." His father watched him, sighed. "You know. About me and Hilde."

"The path worn out between the two houses gave you away."

"There's nothing to give away. I'm not ashamed."

"Really? Then why didn't you just tell me?"

"I didn't expect *you* to understand. I knew you'd be angry, and you are."

Brand said a word he'd never said in front of his father before, watched the doctor flinch from it.

"There's no need to be vulgar," his father said.

"I'm a rough man in a rough profession," Brand said. "You never let me forget that. That I let you down by choosing my own life. I've been a constant disappointment to you. The funeral just cemented how you felt anyway."

His father looked stunned. "Brand, that's not—

Brand held up his hand. "You couldn't or wouldn't forgive me because I couldn't come home for her funeral, as if I'd betrayed the thing that mattered most to me. And all that time, while you were judging me, you couldn't even wait a decent amount of time before you replaced my mother? Yeah, I guess you could say I'm angry."

"Sophie told me about the work you were doing, that other people might have been hurt or killed if you came home."

"Sophie shouldn't have needed to tell you that," he said stiffly. "It might have been nice if you just believed the best of me."

"I'm sorry."

Brand was not sure he had ever heard his father say those words. Certainly not to him.

"Dad, how long after Mom died before this started?"

"Stop. Don't make it cheap and tawdry, and most of all don't make it disrespectful of your mother."

"How can I make it anything else?"

"This is what you don't get," his father said, softly, something broken in his voice. "Life is short, Brand. When it offers you something good, you don't always get a second chance at it.

"I loved your mother. Maybe you can live without love in your life. It seems you can. You're still at that age where you regard time as endless, something that never runs out. If you pass on something, well, heck, there's lots of time to get back to it later. But I saw time run out with your mother, how quickly it can happen, without an ounce of warning."

"I've seen time run out, too." Brand said.

His father looked at him, seemed to see him maybe for the first time in many, many years. His expression was concerned. "I guess you have, Brandon. I guess you've seen some terrible things. A father wants to protect his children from those things, but I couldn't protect you. You were always so headstrong, always moved away from what I wanted for you.

"All I'm trying to say is that if things follow the natural order, I don't have as much time left as you. I don't want to waste a minute of what I have left mourning things gone so intensely that I toss the gift God is trying to give me, now, back in His face.

"I don't know if you can understand that or not."

But the thing was, Brand could understand it. He even envied the fact his father could make the choice he himself was incapable of making.

"I have to go."

"Are you going back to do something dangerous?" his father asked, and Brand could see so clearly what love did. It made people afraid for the ones they loved. It confirmed the wisdom of his walking away from his dad, from Sugar Maple Grove, from Sophie.

Was he going back to do something dangerous? *Probably.* If not sooner, later. But he didn't say that. He said, "Nah. I think they're sticking me in training for a while."

And the relief on his father's face made that final act of protecting him worth the lie.

And after only three days instructing, Brand was sent on an assignment. He didn't even have time to unpack his bags. It was a military mission that used all his physical and linguistic skills. Sophie had been so right. In this sense of urgency and danger and mission, Brand felt safest.

An operative was caught in a foreign jail; their mission was to free him at whatever cost. The operation required training, discipline, precision and timing. It was physically highly dangerous, it was fast. It was the perfect antidote to the soft mission he'd spent four years on.

But it wasn't the perfect antidote for his loneliness. Danger and adrenaline did not give him the escape he had come to expect. They did not fill the spaces. They felt, oddly, like cheap imitations of what real feeling felt like.

He'd known a different kind of rush now.

He'd known the rush of racing bikes down Main Street in Sugar Maple Grove. He'd known the pure delight of bailing out a leaky boat with Sophie. He'd had the rush of that out-of-control feeling of *falling*.

Falling for Sophie.

And now, he practiced the discipline of a man who wanted to taste more but forced himself to walk away. For her. For her own good.

Now he had to put away those days of perfect summer. He needed to set up his life again. A place of his own, close to base but off base. He needed to fill his minutes with busy work so that he would not even think of her, not give in to the temptation to call her just to hear the sound of her voice.

*Couldn't I? Couldn't I just call? Just once? To see how she is?*

As he was unpacking the few things he owned, he came to the duffel bag that he had taken to Sugar Maple Grove.

At the very bottom of it were the letters from Sinclair Horsenell. He realized as he thumbed through them that he had read all of them.

Except one.

He opened it now. It was dated the beginning of May 1944. Private Horsenell did not know that D-day and the end of the war loomed large, but Brand did.

Dear Sarah,

I am writing you with the most unhappy of intentions. It is my wish to discontinue our engagement. Please do not think it is about you, for it is not.

It is about me. I am not the boy who left you. I have become a man I do not know, whom you would not recognize. I have seen and done things of such a horrible nature they are written on my soul.

How can I come back to the world I remember but can no longer belong in? How can I come back to you?

I urge you to find a man who did not come to this place, who was too young to give himself to this violent struggle, or who was an only son who stayed home and farmed his land. I urge you to find a man who has retained a gentle and considerate manner that is worthy of you.

I urge you to find a man who does not wake in the night screaming, who has not

had the blood of his fellow man splash
into his face, who will not carry the stench
and the cries of the dying to his grave.
With my gravest best wishes for you,
always,
Sinclair Horsenell.

And Brand knew, after he put that letter
away, that he would not phone Sophie. That the
very choice to be a warrior had excluded him
from what he had vowed to spend his life protecting.

His choices had changed him. Made him a
man who could not accept love because of the
price others would have to pay in order to love
him. He had seen that in the relief in his father's
face when he had lied to him, telling him there
was no danger in what he would do next.

Sophie would be better off, just as Sinclair
had said to Sarah, to find a man who was not
haunted by the things he'd done, a man who
knew no other realities beyond the one of
Sugar Maple Grove.

Brand had scorned Gregg Hamilton, but
what if that was exactly the kind of man
Sophie needed?

"Maybe one not content to live with his
parents," he muttered out loud.

And yet, when he thought of those things he had said to her that last night, he hated it that it would not be him. Hated it.

He knew he would make himself crazy if he did not leave the sweet summer madness that had struck him in his hometown behind him. For good. No looking back. No "what ifs," no regrets. No asking about her when he talked to his father. No surfing the Internet to follow threads with her name in them.

But for all that he was resolute, it seemed that, like Sinclair, Brand wanted Sophie to know it wasn't about her. Sinclair had said it eloquently. So, he would have one last contact. Not in person. Not even by phone.

But just so she knew it was not about her.

These letters did not belong to him, anyway. They belonged to the history of a small town. And when she read them, she would understand. He was a warrior who could not go home.

But in the end, he could not resist the temptation to send her not one thing, but two. He sent her that packet of letters, and he phoned the art gallery on Main Street in Sugar Maple Grove and arranged to have a painting sent to her, a painting of an old red boat tied to the end of a dock....

When he sent those letters he didn't feel,

not like a warrior, he felt like a weakling. And like the loneliest man on the planet.

Then it hit him like a bolt of lightening.

*He loved her.*

He loved Sophie Holtzheim.

Enough to protect her from the worst thing that could happen in that nice safe cozy world she had made for herself. Loving him back.

Hours later his phone rang. There had been a hostage taken by a terrorist cell in a faraway land. The hostages were being held on the thirty-first floor of what had once been a posh hotel.

It was, of course, getting international press coverage, so his boss was concerned about sending him. Because of Chop-Looey, they didn't want him photographed. On the other hand, they needed their best climber, one with the skill to get in and out of a hotel window thirty-one stories off the ground.

Brand didn't give a hoot about the press being there. He had to do that job. And he had to be realistic. Some of the hostages might not survive the rescue. He might not. And that was the type of thing that he never, ever, wanted to bring home to someone like Sophie.

# CHAPTER NINE

IN the days after Brand left Sugar Maple Grove, Sophie discovered that anger had an energy to it that was far preferable to self-pity, even the righteous self-pity of a heartbreak.

She had never been an angry person, but in those days after Brand departed, Sophie made up for lost time. Every time she thought of him, and that was with unfortunate frequency, she found she felt so much better if she wrecked something.

She had a pile of snapped pencils at her desk, shredded papers, two coffee cups with no handles, a shattered plate and a heap of twisted-beyond-repair paper clips.

She had punched the numbers on her calculator so hard she'd had to junk it, jammed her printer trying to force the ink and wrecked her stapler purposely trying to pound staples through too many papers as she spat out his name.

She felt furious with him: for leaving, for making her love him, for ruining her last-ditch effort to put together her shattered dreams, a task she now recognized to be as futile as trying to put together Humpty Dumpty after his tumble from the wall.

By week two, it had stopped being fun breaking things, but her anger was unabated.

Only now, Sophie didn't direct it at Brand.

She directed it where it belonged. At herself.

She'd been the one who had believed she needed someone else in order to hold her head up high.

That was what had gotten her into trouble with Gregg in the first place.

And her anger at herself drove her forward; she wasn't being that girl who waited for a man to protect and rescue her anymore. She was not going to be the girl she had been with Gregg—waiting helplessly and hopelessly for him to change his mind.

She was not waiting. She had wasted quite enough of her life moping. No, she was learning to protect and rescue herself. Sophie signed up for self-defense classes three evenings a week at Sebring's Gym in the neighboring town. In the same gym, they had a rock wall, and they offered climbing instruction, so she signed up for that, too.

It was time to find her own strength!

The third week after Brand had left, it hit her that he really wasn't coming back. And he wasn't phoning, or sending any e-mails, either. There was no sense rushing home to check the blinks on her answering machine, there was no sense rushing to work to check her e-mails.

As the longest, hottest summer in the history of Sugar Maple Grove drew to a close, she bought a new bathing suit. Not some ridiculous piece of film and fluff that melted in the water, either!

No, a one-piece, plain black, with a sturdy racer back. She celebrated who she intended to become by going to Blue Rock by herself. She dropped her towel and swam across the inky-green water of the pool.

She ignored the temptation to relive something that was done, to remember being here with him, to remember his words that she had been the most beautiful of them all, and she began to climb.

She stopped at Blue Rock.

*This is good enough,* she told herself, *high enough, a great enough demonstration of courage and independence.* But it wasn't. She turned her back on Blue Rock and began the treacherous climb to the Widow Maker.

Her limbs were trembling from exertion

when she finally pulled herself onto that last outcrop of rock.

Her nerve was gone completely, but the horrible truth was that she was more afraid to try and pick her way back down the rocks than to jump.

She stood at the edge. Her heart beat in her throat. Her hands were slick with the sweat of pure panic. What if she didn't jump out far enough and caught a rock on the way down? What if she slipped while she was trying to launch, and fell instead of jumping? What if she twisted in the air, and landed wrong and really, really hurt herself?

"I do have a gift for things going wrong," she reminded herself.

Now people gathered at the pool had started to notice she was up here. She saw several shielding their eyes against the sun that was bright on her back.

*Jump,* she ordered herself. All her muscles coiled, but fear held her back. She did that half a dozen more times. Now everyone down below was watching her. The sun was sinking at her back.

If she didn't do something soon, she was going to be up here all night. A laughingstock, *again.* A rescue crew might have to be called.

What if word got back to him? That she was a chicken?

No! How was she going to live with herself if she was a chicken.

*Jump,* she told herself. Only this time it was different.

She heard a voice whisper, *Sophie, I know who you really are.*

Who was it? Brand? Her father? Her mother? His mother?

Whoever it was, the fear evaporated, and she whispered, "Honor."

And then she stepped off the end of the earth with absolute faith in who she really was.

The tumble through the air was remarkably brief. The water, when she hit it, felt like concrete. She plummeted through it, her feet actually touched the bottom of the deep, deep water of the canyon of Blue Rock.

She shoved off it, broke the surface.

The people who had watched her were clapping and cheering. And she was laughing.

Because it had been so much easier than she had expected. What she had suspected about Brand Sheridan was all too true. The kind of courage it took to fling yourself off a rock into the pool below was nothing in com-

parison to the kind of courage it took to leave
your heart vulnerable in a cruel world.

On week four she bought a motorcycle.

And squeezed in lessons to learn to ride it
between rock-climbing and self-defense. Her
self-defense instructor asked her out. So did a
man she met at the climbing wall. She said no,
but she was pleased nonetheless.

Just when she told herself she was completely over him, over Brand Sheridan, forever
and for always, the painting arrived.

She didn't like it the way she once had. It no
longer seemed like an invitation to spend a quiet
perfect summer day with a fishing pole in the
company of someone you cherished. It seemed
a lonely picture, a choice *not* made. A life lived
elsewhere, while the boat and the pond waited
for people who never came. She put the painting
in a closet where she didn't have to look at it.

She told herself that was how completely
she was over him. Even his gifts could not
cause a flood of sentimental longing in her.

But then the letters arrived. The painting
didn't even have a note, the letters a brief one.

Sorry, I seem to have packed these by
accident. They belong to you.

Just as with the painting, she wanted to dismiss the longing his being in touch created in her. She almost turned the letters over to Bitsy.

But something stopped her.

He had said the letters belonged not to the historical society but to *her.*

She put them in her bag, and that night, in the sanctuary of her own bed, she began to read. The letters read like a novel, and it was deep in the night before she got to the last one.

She didn't want to read it. She didn't want to know. But she had to read it. She had to know.

When she finished the last letter, she was sobbing.

Surely Sinclair had come back and married Sarah? Surely this last letter had not really been the end?

One thing Sophie was good at was researching history. By the closing of her office the next day, she knew the entire horrible truth.

On old microfiche from the *Sugar Maple Grove Gazette,* she found the banns that had been posted on January 1947 between Sarah Sorlington and Michael Smith. Then she found the write-up for the wedding of Sarah and

Michael, not of Sarah and Sinclair, dated June of the same year.

Sophie could barely read it through her tears. "The bride wore ivory silk and carried forget-me-nots."

Forget-me-nots? Because they matched her eyes, or because she could not forget him, even as she married someone else?

Sophie cried even harder when she found the obituary for Sinclair Horsenell. She cried for a man who had died years before she was born, died alone in an old-soldiers' home. He had never married. He was survived by brothers and sisters and nieces and nephews, but no wife. No children.

Up until then she had thought she was over her angry phase. But after she read about Sinclair dying alone, she went to the second-hand store next door to the Historical Society and bought a whole box of dishes.

That night, in the Historical Society's concrete bunker of a basement she threw every one of those dishes against the wall. Even when she had broken every dish in that box, her fury had not abated. She was furious at Sinclair for being so stupid and stubborn, but she was way more furious at Sarah.

What kind of selfish, weak-minded girl

could not read between the lines of that last letter and see the lonely desperation of a young soldier who had lost himself?

That poor man had lost faith in himself, and he had lost his way back to all the things he had once taken for granted. Where had Sarah been? Why hadn't she gone to him and brought him the map that would lead them home?

And then, sitting there in the rubble of the broken dishes, she knew, suddenly, with quiet certainty, why Brand had sent these letters back to her.

And it wasn't because they were the property of the Historical Society.

It was because he was a man who lived with the loneliness of having seen and done things that set him apart from the people he loved.

Like Sinclair Horsenell, he did not trust that anyone had kept the memory of who he really was alive and strong. Like Sinclair, he did not logically see how he could find his way home.

Suddenly she knew that's what it had all been about: the self-defense class, the rock-climbing, the leap from the Widow Maker, the purchase of the motorbike.

It had all been about being the woman who wasn't afraid to go get him, even if that meant following him into hell to bring him back.

It was about believing that love, not logic, would provide the map that would show both of them the way home.

She heard that voice again, the one she had heard on the rock. The one that had said, *Sophie, I know who you really are.*

And she recognized who spoke those words. Not Brand. Not her father. Not her mother. Not his mother.

It was the voice of her deepest self, her soul.

And it knew exactly who she was, and exactly what she needed to do.

Brand was exhausted. And heart-sore. It had already been too late for two of the hostages by the time FREES got on scene.

He walked up the stairs toward his apartment and went still. The lights in his suite were on. Had he left in such a hurry he'd left the lights on? Possible, though not likely. The press had been ordered not to show his face, but who knew?

As he drew closer he heard music.

The hair on the back of his neck rose, then settled. No bad guy—some remnant of Looey's operation who had spotted him because of the press coverage of the hotel hostage rescue—was sitting in there waiting for him with the lights on and the music blaring.

Still, he went up the steps quietly, reached for his key above the door molding. It was gone. The door was ajar. He stood to one side of the door, tilted his head, looked in.

He had a direct line of sight through the whole tiny apartment, except for the bedroom. There was a suitcase just inside the door.

And then he saw Sophie Holtzheim in his kitchen. The rush he felt was way different than the one he had felt being lowered off the hotel roof down to the thirty-first floor.

She looked amazing in a white tailored shirt, snug jeans, sandals. Her hair looked as if it had been cut, not short, but styled. It looked glossy and glorious, it begged for the touch of a man's fingers.

If he wasn't mistaken, the smell of chocolate-chip cookies was wafting out the open door. As if the sight of her wasn't enough to make him feel weak with longing!

He had never felt so happy to see someone in his whole life, as if a box inside him he had deliberately closed was bursting open. And it contained the sun. His whole life seemed to go from dark to light. The part of him that he had tried to keep cold, for his own protection and for hers, was melting faster than spring ice off Glover's Pond.

How was he going to keep her from seeing that?

He slipped inside his apartment, and she turned and glanced at him.

She was wearing makeup. Just a hint of it that made her cheekbones look high, her mouth sensual, her eyes astounding.

Was it seeing her here, in his space, instead of against the familiar backdrop of Sugar Maple Grove, that made him see her so clearly?

Or was it the fact she had become, completely, that woman he had glimpsed striding away from him the night he had last seen her? Sophie looked as if she had come into herself totally, was completely comfortable with her power.

Her smile rose up to meet the sun, and the brilliance of it meeting that lid-off-the-sun feeling inside him created a sensation akin to that of trying to ride fireworks.

"What the hell?" He kept his voice gruff, he folded his arms over his chest.

"Hello, Brand. Nice to see you, too."

He frowned at her. "How did you get in here?"

"Your dad told me you probably kept the key above the door."

"My dad knows you're here?"

"He thinks I'm the best thing that could ever happen to you."

*That's not the point. Of course she's the best thing that could ever happen to me. The point is, I'm not the best thing that could ever happen to her. Hadn't she read the letters? Didn't she get it?*

"This is California, not Sugar Maple Grove," he said, skirting the issue of best things. "You can't just be in here baking up cookies with the doors unlocked."

She held up a hand. "Stop. No more. If I need protection, I'll buy a rottweiler."

"You don't need protection in Sugar Maple Grove. Which is where you belong."

"Not up to *you* to decide where *I* belong."

Well, he'd been right about her coming into her power. "Have you been messing with my kitchen?"

"If I'm going to be staying for a while, I thought I might as well put a few things away. Buy you a cookie sheet. What's a kitchen without a cookie sheet?"

"It's called a bachelor pad. And what do you mean, if you're going to be staying? Here? In my house, *here?* No, you're not."

"Yes, I am. Until you come to your senses."

"Sophie, there is nothing sensible about you coming across the country to be here, and then thinking you are staying here."

"Oh," she said, "luckily, I'm not the one who has to come to my senses. And I'm all done being sensible. I figured out playing it safe is the most dangerous thing I could do. Stagnating. That's a dangerous thing."

Brand could tell she had not been stagnating. It was in everything about her: the confident curl of her lips, the sashay of her hips, the light in her eyes that was both playful and unsettlingly powerful.

"You're not staying here," he said, curtly.

"You look exhausted," Sophie said soothingly. "Come have some cookies, right out of the oven. Your mom's recipe."

He knew the smart thing to do would be to back out that door and hightail it for safe ground. But he was in the grip of something larger than himself, and he could not break its hold.

Brand moved into his apartment, reluctantly sat at the kitchen table. He could smell her.

Clean and tangy, pure and promising. Promising a respite from what he had just come from.

"Have a cookie," she coaxed.

He knew he shouldn't touch those cookies,

but the battle was short. He took one, took a bite, closed his eyes in pleasure.

"Do you want milk?"

"I don't have milk," he said crankily, opening his eyes, staring at her, thinking, *This is a dream, and I'm going to wake up alone. When did I start hating being alone so much?*

*Chase her away. Let her have the truth. Make her go back out that door.* "It goes sour when I have to leave. That's what I do. I leave. For long periods of time. I can't always say when I'm coming back."

He hesitated. "I can't always say *if* I'm coming back."

He found a glass of milk in front of him. *Don't drink it,* he ordered himself. It was probably like some secret nectar. Once he drank it, he'd be lost.

He took a sip.

And was lost. He'd been living on his own for eight years. And this was the first time he had ever felt as if he'd come home.

The cookies, the milk, Sophie watching him, the exhaustion, the people he couldn't save.

He put his head in his hands and drew a deep and shuddering breath.

And felt her hand on his shoulder.

"It's okay," she said softly. "I have your back."

"You don't even know what that means," he snapped. "I just took fourteen people out of a hotel where they'd been taken hostage. Only twelve of them were alive."

She was behind him. Her arms curled around his neck, and he found his head pillowed in unbelievable softness.

"Aww, Brand," she whispered.

And that was all. How could it possibly be enough? How could that possibly lighten the weight he carried inside of him?

He was aware that this feeling could become addictive. Before he knew it, he wasn't going to be able to let her go, even if he wanted to.

"I could have died," he said. "What kind of life is that to offer someone? It isn't. You're going to have to leave."

"No."

"Yes."

"No." Every bit as strong as his *yes,* possibly stronger.

"You can't stay here without me inviting you."

"Kick me out, then."

But he couldn't. Already there was something about her being here that he wanted to sink into and hang on to. Forever.

The one word he could not have in his vocabulary!

He grabbed at a straw. "It won't be good for your reputation in Sugar Maple Grove if you stay here with me," he warned her.

She actually laughed at that. "I'm not worried about my reputation."

"I am," he sputtered. "You can't stay here. It's not decent."

"I'm staying. I'll leave it up to you how decent or indecent it becomes. For a while, anyway."

"I don't think your grandmother would approve of this."

"That just shows you don't know the first thing about my grandmother. You should know more, since she was letting her secret self out when she spoke German around you."

"My dad's going to kill me if I let you stay here." The straws he was reaching for were becoming weaker and weaker and they both knew it.

"No. He encouraged me to come. He said that time was too short."

"Oh, hell, the time-is-short lecture."

"It's true, Brand. Let's not waste any more

of it. You just told me you could have died on the mission you were on. Do you know how I would have felt if that had happened? I would have felt as if I had wasted the most important moments of my life. Moments that I should have been with you and weren't. Brand, I—"

He knew what she was going to say. He knew it. "Don't. Don't say it." It would be worse than the cookies and the milk. It would swamp him. It would make him weak when he wanted to be strong.

But she wasn't a woman who was going to rein herself in. She said it anyway.

"I'm here because I love you. I don't want to waste another minute."

What could a guy say to that? He could say he loved her back, but that seemed as if it was giving in without even making an effort to keep her safe from loving him.

"I'm here to court you, Brand Sheridan."

"This won't end the way you want it to," he said miserably.

"Ah," she said, not the least perturbed or concerned. "I don't think either of us can know that until the courtship is over."

*I love you.*

He was right. Her words swamped him, stole

his resolve to be strong, stole his sense of knowing right from wrong.

"What about your job?" he asked, a last desperate reach for a straw. "You can't leave your job. You can't burn your bridges for something that isn't going to work."

"Oh, I brought all my research with me. The Historical Society's board of directors all thought it was a wonderful idea for me to get away for a while to put together the draft of the book on Sugar Maple Grove during the Second World War. I can work on it while you're on a mission."

"I only have one bedroom," he pointed out.

"It's okay. I'll sleep on the couch."

"The hell you will. I'll sleep on the couch."

She smiled at him. "If you insist."

And somehow he realized he had been *tricked* into agreeing she would stay here. But that didn't mean she'd win. She could stay here if she wanted. He could ignore her.

Except he couldn't. Because that night, after he'd gorged himself on cookies that already had some kind of love nectar baked into them, she talked him into a game of Scrabble and trounced him with thorough enjoyment. And after Scrabble, she went into his bedroom and came out in a little pair of pure-white baby-doll pajamas that made his mouth go dry and his heart beat in double time.

"We need a few rules around the courtship," he said. "Don't expect a kiss good-night. These quarters are too close. There's no telling where that could lead."

*Especially with her in baby dolls!*

She'd looked at him with wide-eyed innocence, and said, "You're absolutely right. I should have thought of that myself." And then she'd blown him a kiss, and gone into the bedroom and shut the door behind her.

Naturally, he wasn't safe, and she'd known it! When he went to use his bathroom, a red bra was hanging over his shower rod. Sophie in a red bra. No, not just any red bra, that one. That one that looked as if it was constructed from raw silk threads and fog.

Less true words than *I'll sleep on the couch* had never been spoken. It was soon evident to him his days of sleeping were over.

Because he had milk he could have cereal for breakfast. He tried to read the box and not notice her sitting across from him in her baby dolls, reading the paper that was his, sipping her coffee, her naked legs folded under her. No candy-floss pink on the nails anymore.

Fire-engine red. To match her bra.

"Look, we need a few more rules," he said hoarsely, "For the courtship."

"I'm listening."

"No red bra in the bathroom. And you can't wear those around the house."

She pretended she was thinking about it. "How about a trade?"

"A trade?" he asked warily.

"I don't leave my underwear around. You take me bike-riding after work. Along the boardwalk. Maybe we can stop and have hot dogs for supper."

He considered. "Okay."

And that's how the courtship of Brand Sheridan started: with bike rides and hot dogs. Then, in exchange for the removal of the black bra from his shower rod, she wanted to try in-line skating. By the time she wanted to go to a live theater presentation he knew it was no use bargaining over where she left her skimpy, sexy little undergarments.

Having her underwear out of the bathroom wasn't helping him sleep at night. The moratorium on the baby dolls was a farce. Her pink pajamas, with long sleeves, full legs and the cartoon monkeys doing yoga on them were as sexy as the baby dolls, though logically he knew that wasn't possible.

She liked having cocoa before bed, and they would stay up way too late talking, laughing, sometimes playing Scrabble.

He was now so sleep-deprived, he was getting in trouble at work. He was making stupid, novice mistakes. His concentration was shot. He was late for roll call because he phoned her at lunchtime to make sure she had locked the damn door. He didn't respond to a direct command because he was mulling over the fact she had *laughed* when he told her to lock the door, to go make sure it was locked.

"Is your job always so exhausting?" she asked him soothingly when he dragged himself in that night. "This will help. I made you a treat." It was roast beef. And Yorkshire pudding. He already knew. His mother's recipe.

"This isn't a courtship," he told her, three days in. "It's a hijacking. It's a hostage-taking. I hope you get tired of this soon!"

Before he fell in any more deeply.

But she didn't and he did.

There was something about not being in Sugar Maple Grove that set them free. The familiar backdrop was gone. Nobody was watching. She wasn't the girl next door; he wasn't the boy next door.

They were getting to know each other on a different level—as adults, as equals. She wasn't his sweet pea anymore.

She was a woman. Fascinating. Multifaceted. Sensual. Fun. Smart. Curious. She had an unexpected taste for adventure.

At her insistence, they found a climbing wall, and she showed him what she had learned.

Brand had been climbing all his adult life, but it had never been quite the experience it was going up the wall behind her, her harness doing things to her butt that made it more sexy than the baby dolls!

Sophie loved trying new things, was so *ready* to leap out of the comfort zone of a small-town girl with limited experiences available to her.

She thought it was fun to take public transit! She couldn't get enough of the ocean and bought her own snorkel and fins. She planned picnics on the beach so they could watch the whales go by and the sun sink down.

And he, reluctantly at first and then with more and more enthusiasm, loved finding new things for her to try.

She especially liked ethnic food. He even found a Middle Eastern restaurant that had rose-petal ice cream.

And for all that she embraced everything new, she was still the old Sophie, too, a woman content to work on her collection of stories for the Historical Society, and to try out cookie recipes on him.

As he grew more exhausted by her courtship, lying awake on that couch at night imagining her sleeping in his bed, imagining what it would be like to give in totally, go to her, taste her, hold her, have her, she grew more invigorated.

The exhaustion was taking a toll. His walls were coming down. He was telling her things she had no business knowing. They just slipped out of him in these intimate little moments she had a way of creating.

Who knew intimacy could have so little to do with red underwear?

He told her things he couldn't expect her to handle. He told her about burying his best friend three days after they'd been deployed overseas. He told her about playing the role of Brian Sinclair and betraying every single person who had come to like and trust him.

He told her about the hotel rescue and the face of a blonde woman he hadn't been able to save who haunted his dreams.

But the thing was, she was handling his

secrets just fine. And every day that he trusted her with a little more of himself, something eased in him.

Something that had been held way too tight for way too long began to relax.

She'd been there two weeks when he got it. It wasn't a flash of light. He was just worn right out.

"You win," he told her, when he came in after an extra-hard day of trying to train in his sleep-deprived state. She'd made strawberry lemonade. "You win, Sophie. I surrender."

He hoped she knew that words more foreign to a warrior had never been spoken.

Nor had they ever been spoken with such heartfelt relief.

"No," he said, staring at her, feeling the blessed relief of surrendering, allowing himself to contemplate for the first time exactly what *that* meant. "Wait. You don't win. I win. Because even though I don't deserve you, and even though I don't want to inflict this lifestyle on you, you're still here. And I have a feeling you're just not going to go away."

"You're right, I'm not."

He went to her. He allowed himself to touch her. She was so soft. Her skin was so beautiful and so flawless. His fingers felt as if they had waited all his life for this moment of absolute surrender when they could worship her with their tips.

He took the plump temptation of her lips in his and allowed himself to feel it and not fight it.

Her lips opening to his, inviting him deeper, calling him to know all of her—that was exciting! Every single thing that had ever passed itself off as excitement before that had been a lie.

"I love you," he whispered. "I want to marry you. I feel as if I will die if I don't have you to come home to, you to look forward to for the rest of my life. I feel as if I was dying of loneliness and didn't even know until you came, Sophie. You didn't court me. You rescued me."

There was something bigger than both of them in the air when her eyes met his, and she teased his lips with her tongue, and slipped her hand inside his shirt.

He had a sense of the adventure that had been his life not ending, but beginning in a brand-new way.

A way that required more of him than had ever been required before.

All of life would be a courtship, a dance, a celebration.

"Sophie, will you marry me?"

One word. His whole heart stood still, his whole life stood in the balance while he waited to hear that one word.

And when he heard it, it was as if her soul had spoken to him. It was not so much a word as an affirmation of the power of love to win.

To bring a lost warrior home. And to heal him once he got there.

"Yes."

# EPILOGUE

THE Internet was an amazing thing, Brand thought, but even he was sometimes newly amazed by it.

For instance, if you typed in the phrase *What Makes a Small Town Tick,* imagine that you could be transported back over time to a grainy video of a small-town girl about to win a big-time speech competition.

Funny, she wasn't as geeky as he remembered her being at twelve, right around the age she'd been when she had first moved in next door to him.

She was cute as a button, tiny on that big stage, brave somehow.

Her voice had a little quaver to it as she started talking about all the charms of small-town living, but it grew stronger as she warmed up. She talked about funny things like the time the rumor had gone through town like wildfire that the President was coming to Sugar Maple Grove. She talked about picnics and Blue Rock and ice cream on hot nights. She talked about front porches and unlocked doors.

And then she talked about a little boy who had gotten cancer and how the whole town circled that family and raised money for him. She talked about the Francis house burning to the ground and the old-fashioned barn-building that had raised it back up.

Finally, she looked directly into a camera she probably had not known was there, and she said in a voice that wasn't quivering at all anymore, in a voice that was strong and soft with conviction, "What makes a small town tick? Love does."

He froze it right there, on a little carrot-topped girl with braces and freckles. He could see in that ancient video a hint of the woman she was going to be. He could see the beginning of the bravery that had gotten her through some terrible things.

He could see the beginning of a woman brave enough to come after him. Brave enough to know he *needed* her to love him, he *needed* to love her.

All those years ago, when she had said it was love that made a small town tick, she had missed a bigger truth.

Love was what made her tick.

Watching Sophie's younger self, he allowed himself to think, if it's a little girl will she look like that? Be like that?

They had been married three years. He had left FREES and returned to what he had always liked most about his work. Brand and Sophie had started a school here in the shadow of the Green Mountains, thirty miles from where he was born.

The school, called Higher Ground, was for vertical-rescue specialists, and his reputation was now cemented.

He did what he loved every single day, working the ropes, teaching others: lowering, highlines, Stokes baskets, technical, rappelling. Sophie ran the office, using all those considerable organizational skills she'd used at the Historical Society and putting together her book.

They worked together, they lived together, the love just seemed to grow deeper and better every day. Love. That was the real higher ground.

It was as perfect a life as any man could ask for.

"Brand, what are you doing?"

Her voice was so soft behind him. She came

and leaned on his shoulder, he felt the gentle brush of a taut belly, the little life inside there kicked at him.

"I couldn't sleep."

She looked over his shoulder at the computer screen and laughed. "Good grief, Brand, this is not what most men are looking at on the Internet in the middle of the night when they can't sleep."

"What do you know about most men, Mrs. Sheridan?"

"That they aren't anything like you." She wrapped her arms around his neck, played with the diamond stud in his ear.

The hole where it had been pierced refused to grow over. She had gotten him the diamond stud instead of a wedding band, knowing he didn't want to wear a band that could get caught when he worked with ropes.

He didn't consider himself an earring kind of guy, but she thought it was sexy as hell, and he loved it when she got *that* look on her face just from looking at it.

Once, his younger self had chased excitement and danger, had been fooled by those false highs. Brand had a growing sense of having *needed* to be that younger man, he felt as tolerant of his younger self as he did of hers.

He had needed to be who he was to be able to recognize truth when it found him.

There was nothing more exciting than this. Loving another human being. Creating another human being.

Now he was a man who knew it didn't get much better than Sophie's delicate fingers toying with the diamond stud in his ear as she looked over his shoulder at the computer screen.

Considering how big her belly was, it was probably some kind of sin how her fingers on his ear were making him feel.

"I was kind of cute back then," she decided.

"You still are kind of cute."

"I know."

They both laughed. He loved the confidence in her, the radiant beauty, the sassiness of a woman who was loved above all things and knew it.

"I was a nerd," she decided. "But a cute nerd."

"She's going to be just like you," he decided. "It's a good thing she'll have me. She'll need me to protect her."

"We don't even know if it's a girl."

"I do," he said stubbornly. "I know it's a girl. I've kind of missed having someone who needs me. I was born for it."

"To protect?"

"To be a daddy."

"Yes," Sophie whispered, "you were. And Brand? The daddy thing?"

"Uh-huh?"

"It's going to be sooner rather than later, because I'm having this funny little pain. Right here."

She guided his hand to her belly.

Brand was a man who had looked into the face of death and never flinched from it. He was a man who made his living scrambling up and down incredible, stomach-dropping heights. He was a man who, for his entire life, had pushed himself to heroism, who had welcomed risk and made friends with danger.

He swallowed hard. She was the one person who knew he was only a man, after all. She was the one person in all the world around whom he could let down his guard.

But not tonight. Tonight he would be as strong as a man could ever hope to be. Because she was going to have to be as strong as a woman could ever hope to be. He could match that. He had to.

This was what he'd been born to do.

"Don't you worry, Sophie Sheridan," he said. "I've got your back."

Sophie laughed. "You're terrified."

She was the one person in the world who could see right through him.

"Your dad and my grandma are on their way," she told him gently. "Just in case I get a little too preoccupied to have *your* back."

Once, in the arrogance and restlessness of youth, Brand Sheridan had walked away from all a family meant and all that it offered. He had thought he needed other things more: excitement, thrills, adventures.

But it was the nature of love how thoroughly it forgave a man who realized his errors, who came to know there was only one *real* adventure.

Brand got to his feet and took Sophie's hand. He looked at her long and hard and deep.

And the word that came to his lips and his mind and his heart was not a battle cry at all, but an affirmation.

"Honor," he said softly, his voice strong and sure.

And then he scooped up his wife as if she weighed nothing at all, and with her arms around her neck and her sweet breath stirring against his chest, Brand Sheridan moved effortlessly, fearlessly, toward the future.

# ROMANCE 2-in-1

## Coming next month

### CATTLE BARON NEEDS A BRIDE
#### by Margaret Way

Zara Rylance was Garrick's friend, his lover – but that was five years ago, before she flew to the city and out of his life. Now she's back and Garrick won't let her run again!

### SPARKS FLY WITH MR MAYOR
#### by Teresa Carpenter

When Dani's nominated to be mayor, the busy single mum says 'no'. But when she meets her gorgeous, arrogant opponent Cole, she finds herself saying 'yes'…to more than just the challenge?

### PASSIONATE CHEF, ICE QUEEN BOSS
#### by Jennie Adams

Ever wondered what happens when ice meets fire in the kitchen? Find out when passionate Lorenzo, Rosa restaurant's head chef, discovers his buttoned-up new manager is his old flame, Scarlett!

### RESCUED IN A WEDDING DRESS
#### by Cara Colter

Charity worker Molly has a crisis moments before meeting her new boss! Luckily, self-made entrepreneur Houston can't ignore a damsel in distress, or in this case, a wedding dress!

## On sale 3rd September 2010

Available at WHSmith, Tesco, ASDA, Eason and all good bookshops.
For full Mills & Boon range including eBooks visit
**www.millsandboon.co.uk**

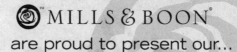

## MILLS & BOON

### are proud to present our...

# Book of the Month

## The Baby Gift
### A beautiful linked duet
### by Alison Roberts from
### Mills & Boon® Medical™

### WISHING FOR A MIRACLE

Mac MacCulloch and Julia Bennett make the perfect team. But Julia knows she must protect her heart – especially as she can't have children. She's stopped wishing for a miracle, but Mac's wish is standing right in front of him – Julia…and whatever the future may hold.

### THE MARRY-ME WISH

Paediatric surgeon Anne Bennett is carrying her sister's twins for her when she bumps into ex-love Dr David Earnshaw! When the babies are born, learning to live without them is harder than Anne ever expected – and she discovers that she needs David more than ever…

Mills & Boon® Medical™
Available 6th August

Something to say about our
Book of the Month?
Tell us what you think!
millsandboon.co.uk/community

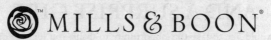

# 2 FREE BOOKS
## AND A SURPRISE GIFT

We would like to take this opportunity to thank you for reading this
Mills & Boon® book by offering you the chance to take TWO more
specially selected books from the Romance series absolutely FREE!
We're also making this offer to introduce you to the benefits of the
Mills & Boon® Book Club™—

- **FREE home delivery**
- **FREE gifts and competitions**
- **FREE monthly Newsletter**
- **Exclusive Mills & Boon Book Club offers**
- **Books available before they're in the shops**

Accepting these FREE books and gift places you under no obligation to buy, you may cancel at any time, even after receiving your free
shipment. Simply complete your details below and return the entire
page to the address below. You don't even need a stamp!

**YES** Please send me 2 free Romance books and a surprise gift. I
understand that unless you hear from me, I will receive 5 superb new
stories every month including two 2-in-1 books priced at £4.99
each and a single book priced at £3.19, postage and packing free. I
am under no obligation to purchase any books and may cancel my
subscription at any time. The free books and gift will be mine to keep
in any case.

Ms/Mrs/Miss/Mr _____ Initials _____

Surname _____

Address _____

_____

_____ Postcode _____

E-mail _____

Send this whole page to: Mills & Boon Book Club, Free Book Offer,
FREEPOST NAT 10298, Richmond, TW9 1BR.